MW01039179

ALSO BY WILL WIGHT

**The Last Horizon**

*The Captain*

*The Engineer*

**The Traveler's Gate Trilogy**

*House of Blades*

*The Crimson Vault*

*City of Light*

*The Traveler's Gate Chronicles*

**The Elder Empire**

*Of Sea & Shadow*

*Of Dawn & Darkness*

*Of Kings & Killers*

*Of Shadow & Sea*

*Of Darkness & Dawn*

*Of Killers & Kings*

*For the most up-to-date bibliography, please visit* ***WillWight.com***

# CRADLE

---

**I**

UNSOULED

**II**

SOULSMITH

**III**

BLACKFLAME

**IV**

SKYSWORN

**V**

GHOSTWATER

**VI**

UNDERLORD

**VII**

UNCROWNED

**VIII**

WINTERSTEEL

**IX**

BLOODLINE

**X**

REAPER

**XI**

DREADGOD

**XII**

WAYBOUND

---

# UNCROWNED

CRADLE : VOLUME SEVEN

WILL WIGHT

Uncrowned



*Book and cover design by Patrick Foster*
*Illustrations by Teigan Mudle*
*Limited Edition Hardcover cover illustration by Teigan Mudle*



*www.WillWight.com*

1 2 3 4 5 6 7

Limited Edition Hardcover: 978-1-959001-39-3

Hardcover: 978-1-959001-40-9

Trade Paperback: 978-1-959001-41-6

PUBLISHED BY

PRINTED IN CHINA

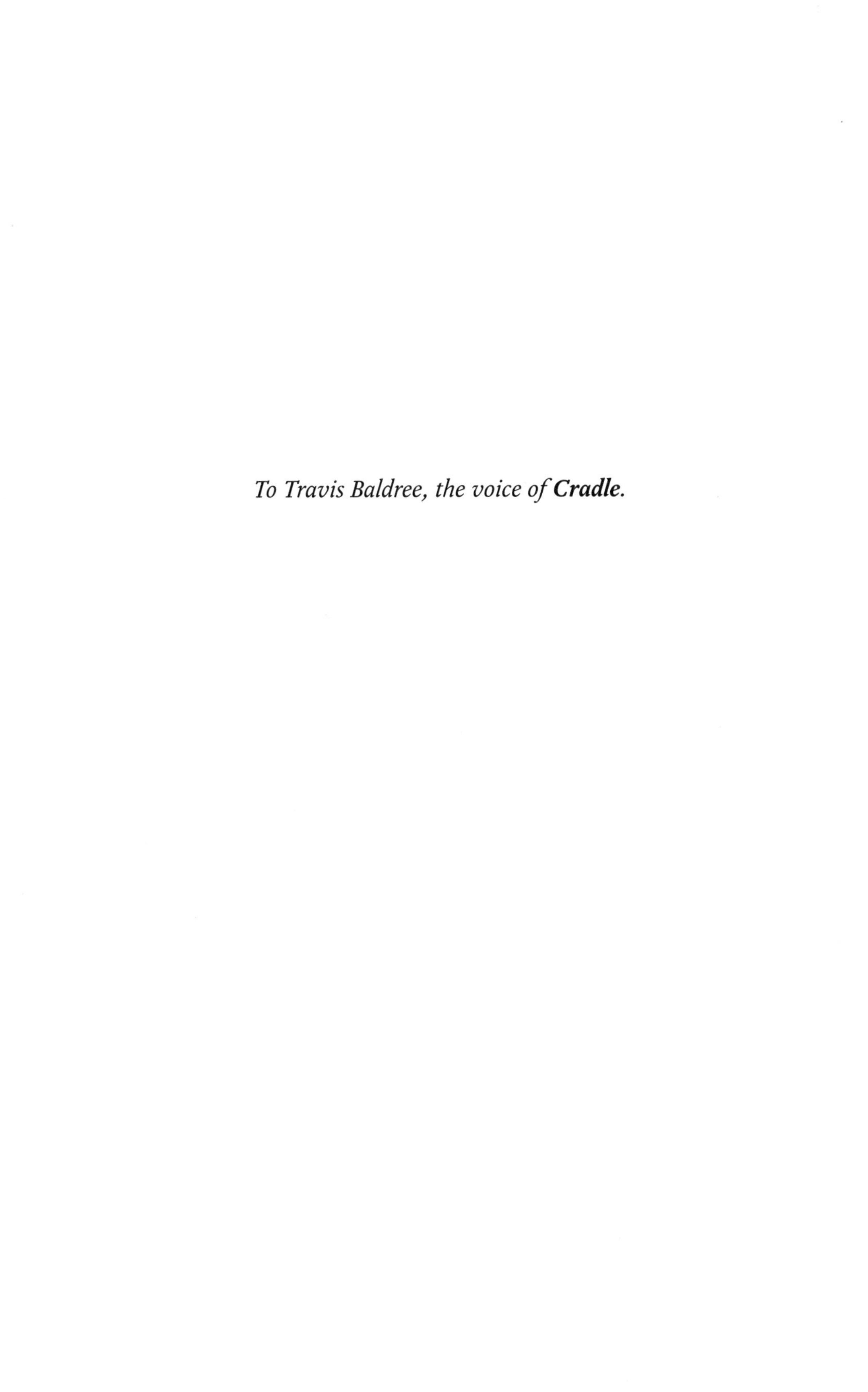

*To Travis Baldree, the voice of* ***Cradle****.*

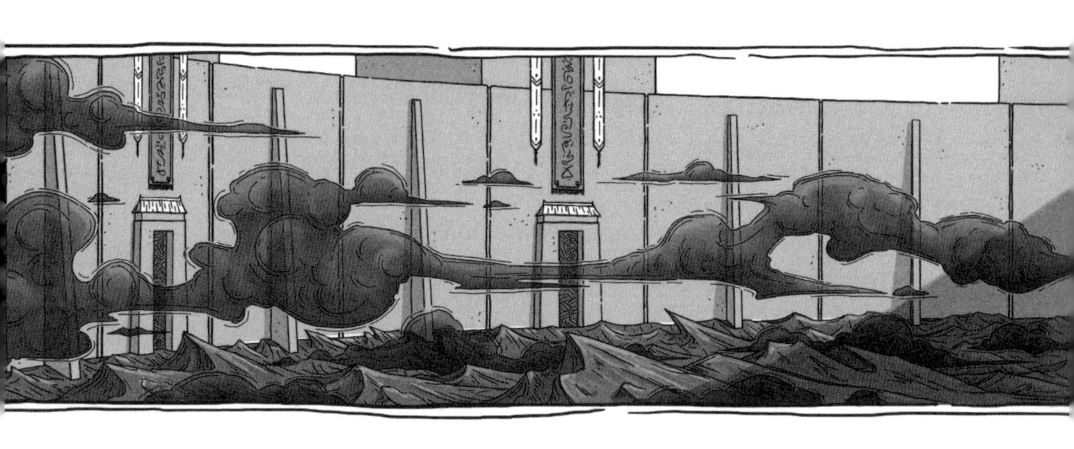

# PROLOGUE

"Something is wrong with your home," Orthos rumbled.

"It's not my home," Kelsa said.

As the sun rose over Sacred Valley, Samara's ring faded away to a dusty arc of white around the eastern mountain's peak. A bag of fruit over her shoulder, Kelsa led Orthos to the base of a different mountain. She had found a hidden grove tucked away between hills, surrounded by wilderness and far from the nearest road.

It was there that she'd hidden her father.

"I don't mean this...hatchling's cave." The sacred turtle snorted smoke. "I mean your whole valley. My power has leaked away day by day since I arrived, and now I am no higher than a Jade."

They crested a hill, looking down onto thickly clustered trees and a creek trickling from a nearby spring. Tents, huts, and lean-tos surrounded many of the trees, and perhaps half a dozen people looked up as she approached. Other exiles.

Kelsa reached out to a nearby boulder, letting her madra activate a security script etched into the stone. It shone briefly purple, the color of her White Fox madra, disabling the boundary field that would send out alarms if the wrong sacred artist entered.

She gestured Orthos forward, but his words had caught her attention. "You were stronger before?" When she thought back to how he had destroyed that detachment of Fallen Leaf artists only hours earlier, she couldn't hold back her excitement. "How much stronger?"

The turtle lifted his black, leathery head in pride, his eyes shining circles of crimson. "I was a Truegold before your grandparents were born."

"Gold?" Kelsa exclaimed.

Orthos' chuckle shook the ground as he lumbered forward. "You should see your brother."

They descended the hill into camp together, but Kelsa still hadn't contained her shock. She had known her brother was dead. She was certain of it. Or she had been yesterday.

Kelsa caught the sentry, a Kazan clan man she knew who stared at Orthos with eyes wide as fists. She explained that Orthos was an ally.

Though she didn't explain why she was leaving the turtle with him. Just because he had fought the Fallen Leaf School didn't mean she could trust her father's safety to him.

When the sentry finally understood, she turned back to Orthos and lowered her voice. "Stay here. I have an errand to run, but I'll have more questions about Lindon when I return."

Orthos examined her with black-and-red eyes, smoke drifting from his shell, but eventually he nodded.

She left in the wrong direction, and when she had put enough trees and tents between her and the turtle, she looped back around to go see her father.

Wei Shi Jaran was right where she had left him, as expected. He crouched on a stool beneath a roof of oiled canvas stretched between two pale branches of an orus tree. Their belongings were organized into boxes around him—Kelsa liked to be neat, and her father tolerated that—and his cane leaned up against the tree trunk. A large boulder blocked the wind from one side.

He had a gameboard spread out on a makeshift table in front of him, running his fingers over the pieces so he could tell one from the other. Occasionally he reached up to scratch at the wrappings around his ruined eyes.

At first, every glimpse she caught of her twice-crippled father had filled her with pain and righteous rage. Now, after almost three years, the wrath had faded, leaving hollow sadness.

She let none of that into her voice as she spoke—loudly, in case he had missed her footsteps. "Sixteen orus fruits!" she declared. "One of them lit up the detector. I think it's on the verge of becoming a spirit-fruit."

Jaran moved one piece forward then reached out to the other side, feeling the opponent's piece as he played both sides of the board. "Trouble?" His voice was rusty with disuse; he probably hadn't spoken with anyone all day. He liked to share stories with some other old men in the camp, but they didn't gather until evening.

"Fallen Leaf artists," she admitted. She didn't want him to worry, but her fight could jeopardize the safety of the entire camp. "I'll spread the word tonight."

He straightened, and now his voice sounded more like the father she'd grown up with. "Did you kill them?"

"Not me, Father. I found an ally."

Something heavy slapped the ground behind her, and she whirled around.

Orthos stood behind her, examining Jaran with scarlet eyes. "I am your ally," he said. "I will not harm you."

"How did you find me?" she demanded.

"No one in this camp is even Jade. You might as well all be blind." He examined Jaran. "At least he has an excuse."

Jaran rocked back as though slapped, and the breath froze in Kelsa's chest. The despair could catch her father like a flood, and if this was the stone that finally dragged him under...

Her father began to laugh. It was a weak chuckle, but that was the most she'd heard out of him in months. "This one is Wei Shi Jaran." He gave a slight seated bow. "It sounds as though you saved my daughter's life."

"You are her father?" When Jaran nodded, Orthos hesitated, and Kelsa begged the heavens that he wouldn't mention Lindon's name. At least not before Kelsa got the truth out of him.

Finally, the turtle said, "I am Orthos."

"You have quite the voice, Orthos. Forgiveness, but are you not human?"

Orthos straightened. "I am a majestic turtle and a descendant of the black dragons of the Blackflame Empire."

Jaran bowed more deeply than before. "Gratitude, Orthos. I am ashamed that I can't see you myself. I would love to hear the story of how you came to save Kelsa."

"I will tell you," the turtle said gravely. "But first I believe I should speak with your daughter alone. She has questions that I must answer."

Jaran was visibly confused, but he nodded, and Orthos began to walk away without any further discussion. Kelsa dropped her bag of orus fruits near her father and hurried after the sacred beast, reaching out to grab his leathery skin and pull him forward.

He was hot. She snatched her fingers away and shook them out. It seemed the smoke rising from his shell wasn't just for show.

"Lindon never mentioned that his father was blind," Orthos muttered, too softly for his words to carry.

That stirred up too many emotions in Kelsa for her to sort through. She was impatient for him to tell her more about her brother, angry on her father's behalf, and adrift in half a dozen other emotions she couldn't name. But she decided to answer the implicit question.

"He wasn't," she said bitterly. "The Heaven's Glory School came to the Wei clan looking for a girl. 'The disciple of the Sword Sage,' they called her, said she had killed a bunch of them. They said Lindon had taken her home."

She relaxed her hands, which had tightened into fists. "Obviously it wasn't true. You can blame whatever you want on an Unsouled."

Orthos grunted as he walked, tilting his head to watch her out of the corner of one eye.

"The clan elders immediately gave us up to Heaven's Glory," she whispered. "They didn't even hesitate. All three of us were taken for questioning, and I went along. I thought they would let us go once they knew we had nothing to do with it. I didn't realize my parents had resisted. The School blinded my father as a punishment, but my mother is a Soulsmith. She was taken."

She spoke through a tight throat. "When I got an opportunity, I ran with my father. They didn't leave much of a watch on us, but they suddenly cared about us once we ran. They've been looking for us ever since…and I haven't seen my mother in years."

Kelsa had intended to trade that story for Orthos' story about her brother, but she didn't trust her voice anymore. While she took deep breaths, cycling er madra and getting control of herself, Orthos spoke.

"He isn't Unsouled," the turtle said.

Kelsa's heart was still in turmoil, but somehow hearing that Lindon wasn't Unsouled was stranger than hearing he might be alive.

She had already accepted his death. She and her father had dreamed of other possibilities, but they both knew it was true. As soon as the Heaven's Glory School had decided he was an enemy, he was dead.

It relieved her to hear that he was alive, of course, but if that were true, then why hadn't he come home? Did he really rebel against Heaven's Glory and escape? Or did he give in to them to save himself?

"He made it to Copper?" she asked quietly. That would help explain how he had survived.

Orthos reached out and uprooted a small, dry bush with his mouth. He began to chew, speaking around a mouthful of splinters. "He was Iron when I met him."

"Iron?" That was difficult to believe. "How did he make it so high?"

The turtle stopped chewing and gave her a strange look. "Outside of this...death-trap...Iron is nothing. If he had stopped at Iron, I would not be here."

She wanted to hear the full story, but this was such an absurd claim that she had to hear the end of it. "You're saying he's Jade?"

"Jade...If Lindon returned today and saw what I've seen, he would leave every Jade in the Heaven's Glory School as a pile of ashes."

Kelsa's hopes receded. She had somewhat believed him at first, but this was too ridiculous. To begin with, his claim contradicted itself. "You said that entering the Valley made your spirit weaker. If that's true, he couldn't be any stronger than a Jade."

Red-and-black eyes met hers. "I said what I said."

He was a confident liar, she had to give him that. But he had known her name. She settled onto the ground, leaning her back against a nearby tree. "All right, Orthos. I think you owe me a story."

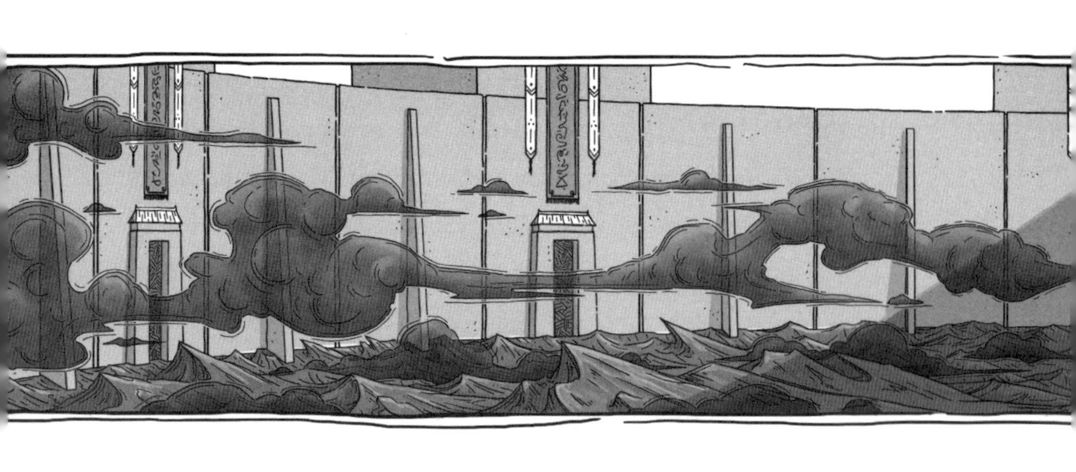

## Outpost 01: Oversight

Makiel, the Hound, stood at the center of creation and watched the past. He had finally caught his prey.

He drifted in the arctic air, surrounded by the home he had carved in the north pole of the planet he'd created. Every atom and idea in this place was focused on enhancing his sight, like a great telescope at the heart of existence.

There were only a few criminals in all existence that could steal from him. He knew exactly who to look for. He just hadn't known where.

Until this morning, when Suriel reported a world missing.

That was the thread he followed backward in Fate. Back, to find where he'd failed.

He reached out, tapping into the Way Between Worlds, and opened a celestial lens. It formed into a rectangular screen of purple-tinted light only a few feet from him, but the image was fuzzy and indistinct. Her wards, veils, and shields, protecting her from detection. The same ones that had stopped him from seeing her in the future.

They had done their job. She had slipped by unnoticed.

But no one could defy the Hound once he caught their scent.

Her wards crumbled, and the image snapped into focus. He could watch the image play out with nothing more than his eyes, but he needed as much information as possible. His attention sunk into the lens, and he became the criminal.

**[Target Found: the Angler of the Crystal Halls. Location: Iteration 002 Haven, approximately one standard year ago. Synchronize?]**

**[Synchronization set at 99%]**

**[Beginning synchronization...]**

Iri was robbing the Abidan.

She stayed focused on her excitement to distract her from the fact that she was packed inside a box buried beneath one of the most secure Abidan facilities in their vault-world of Haven. The box was ten meters by ten—hardly a coffin—but it was so packed with shining amplification crystals, gold rune-boards, tubes of fluid, and matter condensers that she had almost no room to move.

Not that she needed much room. She had always been small and skinny, and ascending out of her original world hadn't changed that about her. It had turned her hair a bright, electric blue—not the most subtle color—and marked each of her eyes with a shining blue triangle inside her irises. It was the stamp of the Endless Pyramid, the artifact that had made her who she was.

The last thing she'd stolen as a mortal.

Iri's bare feet stuck out from the end of frayed pants. She braced one foot against the cold metal, hauling on a lever in the ceiling with her whole body weight. She could have drawn it down easily with her will, but she was trying not to draw attention. That meant acting physically as much as possible. Lines of runes and symbols flared all over the ceiling, and a hologram bloomed in the center of the room.

It was a map of the Way. It started as a single blue light in the middle, shining like the core of a galaxy. Rivers of sapphire light snaked out from it, forming branches, until it was a tangled nest of blue with little white spots hanging on it like berries. The Iterations.

She waved her hand through the light on the outer edge of the orb of branching lines. A cluster of lights shone...and two of the Iterations darkened from white to a swirling gray. Corruption in Sector Seventy-two, and both worlds were still there. The Reaper hadn't come for them.

Iri cackled to herself and swept the map away. As she'd suspected, Ozriel was gone. The Abidan were spread too thin.

Her operation was a go.

She reached out and grabbed Ziomachus, an obsidian wheel packed with the energy system of a long-dead world. It was with this artifact that she had earned her name and built her worlds-famous collection.

She held her hands apart and the black wheel hovered between them. Gold symbols shone on both sides as it responded to her will, filling the room with another shade of light.

Invisible, a strand of her authority slipped up through the soil. It slithered undetected past the detection-wards and patrolling energy constructs that protected against incursion from below.

The line of power slid easily through the foundation, composed of an ore intended to disperse such power. It oozed up, past the Abidan Hounds and Spiders and Ghosts, guided by the force of Iri's intentions.

The vault was a seamless cube of mirrored steel bigger than the box in which Iri waited. Suspended in the center of a sealed room, it floated in midair, guarded by such workings of the Way that even Iri and Ziomachus could never penetrate it.

If the Abidan fell and the guards plundered the rest of the Iteration and returned home, Iri could spend a millennium trying and find no purchase. It was the perfect defense.

So the Angler sat with her power extended like a fishing-line, dangling outside the impenetrable vault. Waiting.

She knew what was locked in the vault, and she knew that with Ozriel dead or missing, the Hound would send for its contents. He would never come himself—that would leave too much of a trail—but this vault would soon open. She only had to be patient.

For nine months, she waited.

Finally, a lesser Hound arrived at the facility. She sat up, the triangles in her eyes burning. Through hundreds of meters of rock, she could see the authority of Makiel on this messenger.

She summoned Ziomachus to her hands, sat down, and kept a tight rein on her excitement.

The messenger passed through layer after layer of security, taking most of the day. Before sunset, he was allowed into the room with the vault. He waved a hand, and his Presence provided the key.

The mirrored cube unfolded like a paper box spreading itself flat one facet at a time. As it unraveled itself, it drifted down until the polished metal sat on the floor, presenting its contents: a rack of weapons.

Each was black and sleek and curved—bladed tools from a simpler age. To the mortal eye, there was nothing special about them. They would be neither effective weapons nor farming tools, these dozen scythes.

The Angler flexed her will, and the obsidian wheel floating between her palms began to spin. Faster and faster it spun, filling her room with a shrill whine and casting off brighter golden light.

She struck with the fullness of her power, and every alarm in the world of Haven went off at once.

Doors snapped shut, sirens screamed, sentries snapped their heads in her direction, constructs took aim at the box buried beneath the ground that they had overlooked for months.

The assistant of Makiel reacted appropriately for a man of his standing and skill. He projected a shell of Way-power around the scythes, lunging for the nearest weapon with his hand and with his mind.

But the invisible line of Ziomachus had already touched them.

With the authority of the Angler and the ancient artifact combined, they rewrote one property of the weapons: their position in space.

The scythes were not, in fact, in a rack within a secure facility. They were inside a locker that Iri had prepared exactly for this purpose.

In no time at all, it was so. The locker, empty a moment ago, was filled with twelve black scythes.

Just before the Abidan security measures reduced her to a fond memory, Iri mentally slammed her emergency retreat.

Then she and her room vanished.

She drifted in the bright, endless blue of the Way, safe for the moment. Her Presence took over navigation of her vessel, scrambling her direction and taking her to random Iterations one at a time to disrupt the search. When the Spiders were thoroughly confused, she would slip out of their web and back to her fortress at the Crystal Halls. Where these scythes would be the crown jewels of her collection.

Except...they didn't work, did they?

The Scythe of Ozriel was unique, and these were only pale imitations. It would take the greatest craftsman in all the worlds to cobble them together into something resembling the original. Something worthy of display in her Halls.

Iri cracked her knuckles and got to work.

**[Synchronization interrupted. Target lost. Continue search?]**

**[Searching...]**

Makiel's Presence guided his own power without need for his conscious intervention. He let it work, hunting down the Angler.

Meanwhile, he closed his eyes. He had never augmented his body the same way the others had—ascension had preserved his physical form, made it so that he never had to worry about the burdens of mortality, but he had never altered the human body that had brought him that far. He had seen no need to.

His skin was dark and wrinkled, his hands calloused, his hair winged with silver. He had often been told that he looked like an old soldier, but he was as timeless as any of the other Judges.

Moments like this made him *feel* old. Weight settled into his bones, his joints, and his eyes cried out for sleep he no longer needed. It was not a true physical sensation, he knew. Merely a feeling. But it weighed him down nonetheless.

Those scythes were no creations of Ozriel. They were his. Reproductions of the real thing. The true Scythe of the Reaper could erase a world with no waste or corrupted residue, but such power should never rest in the hands of one man. Makiel had done his own research into duplicating the weapon, and he had stored his twelve most promising failures in Haven, where no one could find them or steal them.

No one but the Angler.

He had even looked into fate to see if she could break in, but it had been such a remote possibility that he had discounted it. As soon as the theft was reported, he had begun hunting her down. But this was not the only pressing concern that required his attention, and his experimental scythes were not the greatest threat in the cosmos.

At least, they hadn't been. Until the Phoenix had found a dead world.

Now, they were all on borrowed time.

Lindon sat on a chair in the center of a dungeon. Contraptions that looked like torture devices lined the walls: a copper lobster claw that crackled with lightning, a black coffin standing upright, a spool of wire with blood-spirits coiling around it, and a host of others. It was hard to see the walls through all the tools that covered the stone.

Though both Akura Charity and Mercy had assured him that he would be safe here, he still worried. If he tried to fight his way free of the Akura clan headquarters, he wouldn't make it ten steps down the hall.

He had seen their guards on the way in.

The lone door opened, and an old man entered. He was bald, with a long, wispy beard and immaculate black-and-white sacred artist's robes. He had the same Goldsign that Mercy did, with hands dipped in tar-like madra up to the elbows. In those gloved hands he carried a book-sized slate.

Lindon rose and pressed his fists together in respect, but the old man did not acknowledge him.

"I am Akura Justice. I am told that the Sage of the Silver Heart has selected you to represent our family in the Uncrowned King tournament."

Purple eyes looked up from the slate, and Justice released his veil. Suddenly, the pressure of an Archlord's spirit filled the room.

Though there was no attack, Lindon felt his eyes water and his breath constrict.

"This is subject to my approval," Justice said, his voice hard. "I am the First Gatekeeper of the Akura clan, and it is my job to inspect any goods from the outside that are to be in the presence of the head family. I would never contradict the orders of the Sage, but should I find that you are not up to the clan's standards, I will recommend that you be replaced in the tournament and imprisoned for wasting the family's time."

He slapped the tablet against one black-gloved palm, and the smack echoed throughout the room. "Am I understood?"

If Lindon had felt any hostility in the man's spirit, he would have flinched at the sound of the slap. He felt only ice-cold resolve.

Lindon was certain that Justice meant every word he said. "I understand perfectly, honored Archlord. I thank the Akura clan for their hospitality and the Sage for her high estimation of me, but I too believe that I am unworthy. If I were permitted to return home—"

He cut off as the Archlord's spirit tightened, and this time Lindon sensed anger.

"Your voice should be used only to answer questions. If the Sage and I say you are a prince among men, it is so. If we say you are a worm groveling in the dirt, it is so."

Fear and frustration warred in Lindon's chest. He was afraid of stepping on the Archlord's temper again and frustrated by his forced induction onto the Akura tournament team. All he wanted was to leave.

But what would he do if he returned? Mercy lived here, and Yerin and Eithan were competing in the Uncrowned King tournament.

If he left, he would not. The Blackflame Empire competitors had already been chosen.

"Sit," Justice commanded, withdrawing his spirit back into a veil.

Lindon obeyed. This inspection would determine his fate, one way or another. He couldn't hold back in the tests—an Archlord would know—but still, he hoped to fail. At least then he could return home and rejoin Yerin.

Unless Akura Justice made good on his threat and tossed Lindon in prison.

The Archlord reached out, and a long spike with jagged glass on the top floated over to him. "Hold out your left hand," Justice said, and Lindon reluctantly did so.

He only had one real hand left.

"This device measures your lifeline." The spike was over a foot long, but Justice pushed the sharp end into Lindon's wrist only enough to break the skin. It was only a minor sting, easily ignored. The top end of the jagged glass began to glow green.

"If you are not really under thirty-five, you should tell me now," he said sternly. The green brightened. "The color of the light indicates your age, and it cannot be fooled. If it turns yellow, you will fail, and be charged with wasting family time."

The green color stayed bright. In fact, it grew stronger.

"It seems you are eligible." Justice gave no sign of any reaction. But he also did not withdraw the spike. "Now, the brightness of the light will illustrate how strong the lifeline itself is, and thus how resilient your life-force. I couldn't tell you how many young sacred artists have ruined their lifelines with elixirs or ill-advised bargains, sacrificing their future for short-term...gain..."

The light had only grown brighter and brighter.

Now it was blinding.

Justice finally jerked the spike out of Lindon's skin, and the light died away. One side of the Archlord's face twitched. He threw the glass-capped spike carelessly aside, but an invisible force caught it, and it drifted back over to its place on the wall. A deft manipulation of aura using soulfire, or so Lindon assumed. His spiritual perception was restricted, and even if it were not, using it in front of Justice might seem rude.

"Lifeline is...uh, adequate." Justice scribbled something down on his tablet. "But your spirit is the most important." The copper lobster claw floated over to him. "Your hand once again."

This time, Lindon was even more reluctant to hand over his arm. Justice slid the metal around his flesh, and sparks tingled on Lindon's skin, but fortunately the claw did not snap shut.

"Two cores? Hmph." Characters of blue light floated over the instrument, and Justice read them with a displeased look. "You aren't the first to try it, but they're always shallower than one alone. This tool will measure the capacity of your cores, and we'll see if your spirit is—*Heavens above!*"

He looked at the device. Swept his spiritual perception through it. Checked it again.

"Did I pass?" Lindon had confidence in the depth of his cores, thanks to the Heaven and Earth Purification Wheel, but he was nervous that the Archlord's outburst meant he had discovered Lindon's Jade cycling technique. Eithan had warned him to keep it a secret.

"...you pass." Justice made another note on his tablet. "So far." He didn't reprimand Lindon for speaking.

The next six tests passed in silence. Justice had tools for gauging madra density, recovery rate, and stability, which all registered within acceptable limits.

Lindon had to step into the upright coffin, which crushed him with pressure from every angle, testing his physical strength. His blood was taken and examined for blood essence. A thorn-covered cap that pricked his scalp assessed his spiritual perception.

In those three tests, he scored above average. Justice praised him grudgingly, but nothing caused him to react like he had in the first two. He seemed to have recovered his equilibrium.

"Your basic capability has reached the standards of the tournament, which is no surprise, given that you attracted the Sage's eye." He had seemed surprised enough a few minutes before, but Lindon said nothing. "However, potential alone is not enough. You must be able to draw out your abilities to their fullest extent. What good is an army of strong soldiers without a skilled general to lead it?"

He summoned a bucket-like tool from the wall nearby. Rings of script on the outside began to glow purple, and only when he reached up did Lindon recognize it as a helmet.

"Now we come to the mental tests," the Archlord continued. "Reaction speed, memory, force of will, and resistance to incursion. These tests have disqualified many would-be geniuses, so I hope you are prepared."

Within Lindon's mind and spirit, a voice spoke up.

[Oh, those sound like games!] Dross said. [I love games!]

That night, Akura Charity entered Justice's office to find him slumped over his desk, drinking.

When he did not rise to greet her and show proper respect to a Sage, she knew he was truly disturbed.

"Have you laid your concerns to rest?" she asked.

The old man stared deep into the wall, bottle dangling from one hand. "He's a monster."

"I take it you approve."

"Until today, I wondered why you did not recruit Eithan Arelius. When I met him, I suspected him of surprising depth. I understand now, but..."

Justice took a long drink from his bottle. The spirits spilling from his lips burned his beard. Smoke actually rose from the white hair. "Fate can be so...fickle. How many children like him have we ever seen, even in our clan? If I had such talent at his age..."

He didn't finish the sentence, but his expression grew melancholy.

Charity needed to cut off this line of thinking. Justice, a distant cousin of hers, had reached Archlord before she was born and been stuck there ever since.

"The heavens care nothing for our plans," she said. "When they grant their gifts, we can only try to use them to our advantage. What did you think of his results?"

"He has cores like deep lakes and a lifeline like a thousand-year ancestral tree. Were those his only gifts, I would call him merely talented. Certainly nothing to rival young Mercy. But his mental tests...perfect scores in all categories. I've never seen anything like it. If he has the skill to bring out his full potential—"

"He doesn't. But he will."

Yerin steeled her nerves as she faced her opponent. Her fingers did not shake, but she trembled on the inside. She was an Underlady now, but instinct told her this was a fight she still couldn't win.

Eithan, her opponent, stood on the opposite side of the Skysworn practice arena, running a comb through his long yellow hair.

The practice arena was a broad oval a hundred yards long and about fifty wide in the middle. Banded plates of scripted metal covered the walls, scratched and pitted from years of collateral damage. An enormous cloud with a flame at its heart adorned the floor—the Skysworn emblem.

Railings around the outside held Skysworn both in and out of armor. Many had gathered to watch a match between Underlords, especially two who were infamous.

Neither Yerin nor Eithan wore their green armor. She had found a black sacred artist's robe like the ones her master had worn, and Eithan wore an intricate many-layered ensemble of red with patterns of gold stars.

Eithan pocketed the comb and faced her with his perpetual smile, blue eyes sparkling. "To surrender, rather than first blood, I imagine?"

Yerin steadied her breathing, slowly drawing her master's sword. The pale blade caught the harsh light of the scripts overhead. "I'm aiming to push myself to the edge and over. Leaning on you to do the same."

"Of course! It is the duty of the master to train his disciples directly."

Six gleaming sword-arms stretched out behind Yerin, and she released the control on her spirit. The edges of her robe, and her hair—longer than she was used to—fluttered in the wake of her released power. Some of the Skysworn Golds took a step or two back from the railing.

"I'd contend you should take this seriously." Silver sword-aura crackled around Yerin's limbs. "Because I will." She calmed her heart, focusing on Eithan. Something deep in her spirit still told her this was a hopeless fight...but that was all the more reason to take it.

In a flash, she kicked off.

Using the soulfire she'd gathered, she pushed behind her, a simple shove against the wind aura that propelled her forward. At the same time, she fed madra into her Steelborn Iron body. It filled her with unstoppable strength.

Her movements would be a blur even to Underlord eyes, her sword an arc of blinding white as she swung for Eithan's throat.

Casually, he leaned backward. The cold blade passed over his nose.

She had already expected that. The three sword-arms on her right side shone brightly with her Enforcer technique: the Flowing Sword. They gathered madra and aura within them, becoming sharper and more powerful as long as she held the technique.

While she was still turning into the heavy swing of her sword, her Goldsigns swept at him like claws.

He slid to the ground, pushing against the floor with his right palm, which launched him past her blades. Only by an inch. The sword-arms caught edges of his hair.

But she didn't stop her turn. She leaned into it, spinning around, filling the other three sword-arms with the Flowing Sword as well. They extended as she spun, sweeping at him backhand.

She had always known that the first, heaviest attack wouldn't touch him. She had prepared three, each following the other with virtually no lag between them.

Yerin didn't see how he evaded the third attack, only that he did. Her spiritual perception was locked on him, and he ended up on his back foot.

She leaped into the air, flipping around to see him beneath her. Her feet met the ceiling and she kicked off, shooting downward, her Goldsigns still filled with the Flowing Sword. Her master's sword rang like a bell.

The sword-aura detonated into the Endless Sword, a storm of invisible blades exploding away from her. She had even poured soulfire into the technique, magnifying it far beyond what she could manage on her own, so the storm shook the entire arena. Scripts lit up all around the walls, protecting the bystanders from the wild, deadly aura.

She slammed into the ground blade-first, her Goldsigns spearing into the stone floor. The chamber rumbled with the impact, air screaming as her Ruler technique sliced through it.

She ended up on one knee, sword and six arms driven into the stone. She pulled them out, releasing the Flowing Sword. Silver light drifted into the air, flashing and crackling over the edges of her seven blades.

Eithan stood nearby, unharmed. He whistled.

"If I didn't know better, I'd think you had some unresolved aggression against me. Would you like to talk?"

Yerin ground her teeth. This wasn't enough.

The Akura clan would be preparing Lindon and Mercy for the Uncrowned King tournament in nine months. If she wanted to keep up with them, she had to break through her limits.

She dug into her spirit and touched her Blood Shadow.

Instantly, the parasite bloomed beside her, a copy of her in shades of red. It had grown in detail ever since she had started practicing the Sage of Red Faith's techniques for raising it; it looked just like her, if her eyes and hair and robes were all red, and her skin had a pink tinge to it.

It had been torn apart by the Seishen Underlady Meira only a week before, but Yerin had reluctantly given it the food it needed to recover. Her advancement to Underlord had affected it too, so now the Shadow was not only whole, but stronger than ever.

She still hated using it. Even touching its spirit with hers disgusted her.

But only a fool tossed aside a weapon.

The Blood Shadow often failed to follow her orders, but this time, it focused totally on Eithan. Its expression was serious, its perception locked on Eithan's. Six gleaming crimson sword-arms emerged from its back, and liquid red madra oozed from its palm and formed into a copy of the Sword Sage's weapon.

Eithan opened his mouth to say something, but neither Yerin nor her clone were in the mood to listen.

The arena echoed with cracks of thunder once again as Yerin and her Blood Shadow unleashed everything they had.

The Shadow came in, low and savage, and Yerin jumped over it. Eithan had to go high to avoid the parasite, and he found Yerin already airborne, plunging her blade at his chest.

Now that they were both Underlords, Yerin's Steelborn Iron body gave her the overwhelming advantage in strength. Even if Eithan used a weapon to block, the impact from her strike would launch him into the stone wall.

Without hesitation, or even losing his grin, Eithan smashed his fist into the flat of her sword.

Not only did it deflect her sword off-course, but he had shoved against the weapon, pushing him to the side. Adjusting his trajectory in midair.

Before he could land, her Shadow slashed upward with all of its blades and a host of Striker techniques. The razor-sharp crescents of blood madra caught him in a wave.

For an instant, Yerin thought she'd gotten him.

She wasn't worried about his safety. She couldn't be. If she held back against him, she'd never be able to push him to his breaking point. And she had to, if she wanted to ever catch up to him. Her master would have beaten him, even as an Underlord. She was sure of it.

Eithan shoved one palm forward, and pure madra blasted out of his hand in a wave. It was almost colorless, with the bare tinge of blue-white to it, and it wiped the Striker techniques from existence before engulfing the Blood Shadow itself.

The spirit gave a silent scream as it resisted, its form wavering and melting like wax before a campfire.

Eithan released his technique as he fell, landing easily next to the Shadow, which lay in a quivering half-melted lump.

Yerin had already released a Rippling Sword at him, a wave of deadly sword madra.

He wiped it away with a casual backhand, then began to clap.

"Well done! I was trying not to use any techniques, but you backed me into a corner. I have a few pointers for you, as well as perhaps a few insights into your training going forward—"

He cut off as Yerin marched forward and seized him by the collar. Her anger burned hot.

"Serious, Eithan! Be serious!" She shook him as her Blood Shadow re-formed behind her. The spirit's anger boiled against hers, feeding her fury. "I don't have a Dross! I don't have a Sage left to light my way! All I've got left to help me is you, so I need you to *stop holding back!"*

Eithan's smile was calm. "As you wish."

Yerin released him, taking a step back and steadying her breaths. "That's more than nothing, then." Her Blood Shadow felt like it wanted to tear Eithan apart with its teeth. Focusing her spirit, Yerin raised her master's sword.

Before she could make a move, every protective script in the arena lit up at once.

To her spiritual senses, the atmosphere grew painfully heavy, as if the air had suddenly turned to water. Her spirit screamed a warning, and she threw the Endless Sword up like a barrier, surrounding herself in sword-aura.

Her Blood Shadow exploded. Blood madra splattered all over the walls in a spray as though it had been struck by the hand of a Monarch.

Yerin had seen nothing. She had felt only a brief spike of pure madra.

Where was Eithan?

She cast her perception out for him, but she sensed nothing. She spun in place, hunting for him.

He was right behind her.

His smile was gone, his eyes twin needles of ice. His hostility was so thick she could taste it. A fist squeezed her spirit, and it was all she could do to keep her madra circulating. She gathered a Rippling Sword at the edge of her blade, whipping a quick Striker technique at him.

Eithan did nothing to stop it. The madra cracked against invisible armor that coated every inch of his skin.

He pointed his finger up, and only then did Yerin realize there was something above her.

She leaped back, but the seething cluster of blue-white stars against the ceiling followed her. She raised her sword, filling it with madra.

A cascade of blue-white light speared down, powerful enough to drive right through her spirit.

It lanced into the ground in front of her. When the light faded, the floor was completely unharmed.

Her muscles shuddered in relief, and she lowered her pale sword. Her Goldsigns sagged, and she stared in disbelief at the spot where his technique had landed.

Eithan slid over to her, grin returned, his overbearing malice withdrawn. The protective scripts around the arena faded. The bystanders had gone silent.

Yerin stared at the untouched floor. “What are you?” she asked quietly.

“An Underlord,” he answered. “People always think that the way to improve your power is to push for advancement, but that’s not always true. A child and a veteran swordsman, given the same weapon, are vastly different opponents. With enough skill, there's no reason you couldn't do what I just did. In your own way, of course."

Yerin looked over at the puddle of blood madra pulling itself together. "Teach me."

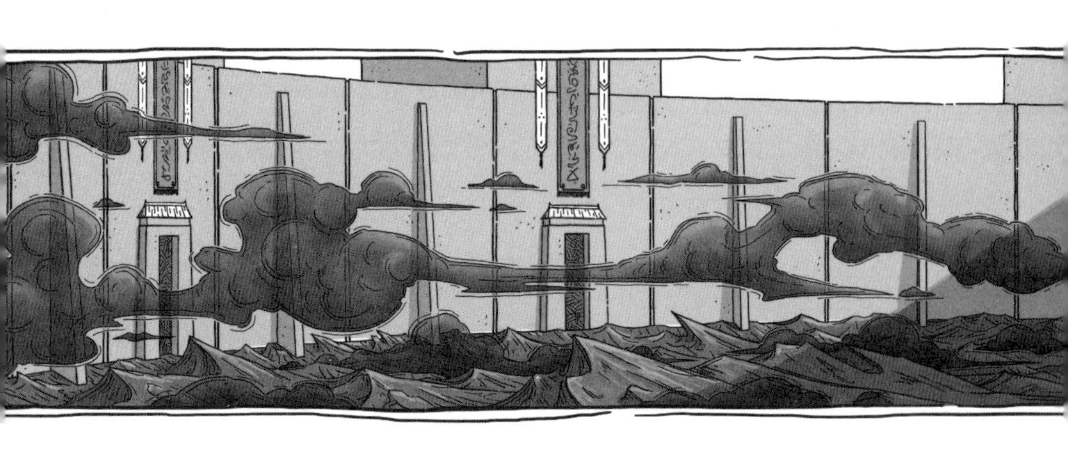

A week had passed since the Sage's transportation had brought Lindon to the city of Moongrave.

From the outside, the Akura capital had looked less like a city and more like a fortress for evil giants. Remnants out of a nightmare guarded its black and spiked walls. Their physical manifestations were so detailed and solid that he almost mistook them for twisted sacred beasts. He hadn't been able to see the end of the city's walls, which stretched all the way into the horizon.

Dark towers rose from behind the walls, and the cloudy sky crackled with purple lightning. The spiritual weight reminded him of the Night Wheel Valley, as though if he opened his perception too wide he would be blinded.

From the inside, Moongrave gave off a different impression.

It seemed as though everything inside had been designed by an artist, like a dark paradise. Carefully cultivated rows of glowing blue, white, and pink flowers flanked gardens of black trees that sheltered flickering, shadowy shapes. Remnants and sacred birds flew through the sky, often carrying passengers or pulling floating carriages.

Lindon had spent most of his time here isolated, but the crowds he glimpsed always walked at a relaxed pace, gentle and civilized, as though they had all the time in the world.

When he looked out over the city, it stretched before him like an ocean. He could scarcely imagine an end to it.

Now, Lindon followed Mercy through a pair of iridescent doors that swung open before them, revealing a broad hall that seemed to be woven from liquid black branches and glowing stained glass in shades of blue, purple, and violet. A long walkway stretched out to the back of the room, with rows of benches on either side.

The benches held a crowd of three dozen young, purple-eyed Underlords.

Mercy strode between them, waving excitedly to some she recognized. These shuddered back or looked away, pretending not to see her. Only a few waved back halfheartedly, though they looked pained as they did so.

Rather than focusing on Mercy, they all seemed to prefer watching Lindon. Like a pack of proud wolves watching a scrawny dog that had dared to wander among them.

[They don't look happy to see you. Maybe if you smiled a little more.]

Charity appeared at the end of the walkway, on a raised dais beneath a stained-glass depiction of a giant female figure covered in purple armor.

The Sage of the Silver Heart looked over her relatives with no expression. She looked no older than they, no older than Lindon, but she had the poise of a judge.

She was a slight woman, but one in complete possession of herself, as though every movement of her body were deliberate. She wore the same fine, layered black-and-white robes as the rest of her family, but her outfit had been designed to suit her. The others seemed only imitators.

The Akura Underlords all rose to their feet, dipping their heads to Charity. "Greetings to the Sage," they shouted in unison, and the force of their voices shook the room.

Lindon stopped walking when the Sage appeared in front of him, but Mercy grabbed him by the wrist and pulled him forward to stand next to her.

A number of eyes focused on that black-gloved hand on his arm, and already-cold gazes grew frigid. Delicately, he slid his hand back.

"Young Lords and Ladies, you have fought hard to serve the clan in the Uncrowned King tournament," the Sage said. Her voice was placid and cool. "To have made it this far, you are the best of your generation. However, only one of you will earn the ultimate honor, and that one will fight as part of a team with these two. I thought it fair that I introduce them."

Soft violet light rose around Mercy, outlining her for the room. "You all know Mercy. The daughter of the Monarch, she bears Eclipse, Ancient Bow of the Soulseeker, and the Book of Eternal Night. To fight alongside her, you must prove yourself her equal."

Lindon expected the crowd of ambitious young Underlords to look eager for the opportunity, but it was the exact opposite. They seemed to lose all their spine when their eyes fell on Mercy, shifting in place, staring into the ceiling, clearing their throats, or fidgeting uncomfortably.

Lindon glanced at her out of the corner of his eye. Was she so amazing, or were these Akura Underlords not as impressive as he'd imagined?

For her part, Mercy didn't seem to care what the crowd thought of her. She was craning her neck, looking over the heads of the first few rows, as though searching for a particular face among them.

Light began to rise around Lindon, who straightened himself to try to project dignity, but Mercy interrupted before the Sage could speak. "Pride? Where are you?"

The spotlight highlighting Mercy dimmed back into shadows. "Akura Pride," Charity commanded, "step forward."

From the back of the room, behind a taller Underlord, a man moved into the walkway.

He looked to be about Lindon's age, but almost two feet shorter. He had the same black hair, pale skin, and purple eyes of his family, but swirling tattoos flowed down from his ears and chin, down the sides of his neck, disappearing into his clothes. They looked like trails of ink, but they seethed as though alive, so Lindon assumed they were his Goldsign.

He stood straight, straining for every inch of height, and he glared at Lindon as he emerged.

Mercy brightened at the sight of him. "Pride!" She scurried forward, stopping as the short Underlord held out a firm hand.

"Control yourself," he said angrily. "This is not the place."

Mercy's shoulders slumped, and she shuffled back to Lindon.

"Who is that?" Lindon whispered.

"My little brother." She let out a long, heavy breath.

It was always awkward to step into another family's affair, and this time Lindon was all the more aware that he was the only outsider in the room. Some of the faces he saw had eye colors other than purple, but they still had the look of the Akura clan.

A feeling in his spirit drew his attention back to Pride.

The short Underlord stared at Lindon with murderous hatred. Lindon could sense it like a stench on the air.

Dross gave a whistle. [He doesn't like you, does he? Do you think he knows you left his cousin to die?]

Lindon hurriedly averted his eyes as violet light rose up from beneath his feet.

"The stranger is Wei Shi Lindon Arelius," Charity announced. "He rose up from nothing in the Blackflame territory, developing a pure madra Path with the guidance of an Arelius clan Underlord, and inheriting a fire and destruction Path from the former Imperial family. He now practices them both. He distinguished himself during the local selections, and he owes our clan a debt. I have called him here in order to repay that debt with service."

*There* were the hungry looks Lindon had expected earlier. Every Lord and Lady in the room eyed Lindon like they couldn't wait for Charity to leave so that they could tear him to pieces. His spirit shivered more than once as they scanned him.

Pride had never looked away from Lindon. "You have chosen

him over us, Aunt Charity? ...and Mercy?" His voice smoldered with barely-contained anger.

Mercy seemed surprised that he had included her.

"I have," the Sage said smoothly. "I believe he can bring glory to the Akura clan, and if two-thirds of our team consists of family members, that will be enough."

"Then Mother's nomination goes to Mercy, and yours to the outsider. Only Uncle Fury's nomination remains for us. What if there are two of us more qualified than this Blackflame?"

Charity leaned forward as though about to take a step. The first row of Underlords shifted back.

"Have you advanced to Archlord while I went north, Pride?" she asked.

Pride shivered. "I apologize, Aunt Charity," he said, the boldness in his voice fading. "My concern is for the honor of our family. I will treat him as an *adopted* member of the clan."

Lindon didn't know exactly what that meant, but several of the wolf-eyed Lords suppressed sudden smiles. He felt like he had been threatened.

"An adopted clan member *and* a protected guest," Charity added. "That will be acceptable."

Mercy gave him a consoling pat on the shoulder, and Pride bared his teeth as though he almost couldn't keep from throwing himself at Lindon.

The Sage let a whisper of her spirit move over the room, which quieted all speech. "I trust none of you will waste too much of Lindon's time. Or Mercy's. Over the next nine months, we will be training them even harder than we train the rest of you. At the end of that time, my father will hold a competition to select the final competitor of the Uncrowned King tournament. I suggest that you all try your hardest to distinguish yourselves."

With that, Charity turned to Lindon and Mercy, speaking in a lower voice. "I will now leave you to get to know your peers. I believe it could benefit everyone. Mercy, can you handle it?"

Mercy, still looking at her brother, nodded.

"Good. Father will be along to train you any moment. I hope. In the meantime, please keep Lindon safe."

"What?" Lindon said. "I mean, ah, forgiveness, but...couldn't I come with you?"

"Think of this as an opportunity for training," Charity said. Then, a breath later, she faded into the shadows.

Leaving Lindon standing on the dais next to Mercy.

Half of the Akura Underlords surged forward at once, but Mercy stepped in front of Lindon. "I'm back, everyone!" she called. "I've missed you! Hey, I've got an idea: why don't we have a little competition to celebrate my return?"

The crowd wilted back.

"Are they afraid of you?" Lindon whispered to her.

"In a way they're afraid," Mercy said, but she didn't keep her voice down at all. "We compete for standing and favor a lot, and I've beaten...yeah, I think everyone here at least once." Some faces flushed, or fists tightened in embarrassment, but no one said anything to dispute her.

"I hoped they would be glad to have me back," Mercy said sadly, her gaze drifting back to her brother.

Pride pushed his way through the others. He looked from his

sister to Lindon, standing right behind her, and his face twisted with the hate that Lindon had sensed earlier. Was he so offended that Charity had chosen Lindon?

"We've all seen what Mercy can do. Now that she's an Underlady, I'm sure she's even more...impressive."

Mercy walked toward him. "Come on, Pride, let's go home first. I missed you."

He held up his hand again, just as he had before, but he didn't look at her. He was fixed on Lindon.

"None of us have seen what you can do, Arelius," he said. "How about you show us?"

[I can think of many ways this could go wrong,] Dross said. [So many ways. In fact, I'm having trouble imagining a way in which this goes *right*.]

Lindon was in perfect agreement. "I apologize, brother Pride, but I must save my strength for training."

Pride's spirit exploded out of its restraint. Benches pushed back, the shadows darkened, and black tattoos crawled on his skin.

*"Brother?"* the Akura Underlord choked out, his skin red with rage.

[Is that an insult here?] Dross asked, but Lindon was just as baffled.

Pride disappeared in a puff of shadow.

He reappeared in front of Lindon in the same instant. Black lines coiled over his skin, spiraling up each of his fingers and his arms, even across his face. He struck with thunderous force, punching at Lindon's chest.

Thanks to Dross' enhancement of Lindon's mind, he reacted in time. The Soul Cloak sprung up around him, a blue-white haze of energy, and pure madra carried power through Lindon's body. The back of Lindon's fist knocked Pride's away, but rather than following up with another attack, Lindon hesitated.

This was his chance.

Pride's left hand took Lindon in the chest, and a burst of black madra exploded from it. An ice-cold detonation launched Lindon backward, into the purple stained glass.

His back smacked into it, but the glass didn't crack even a hair. Instead, Lindon slammed against it as though into stone.

But the pain in his body was nothing to the pain in his soul.

Whatever technique that punch had contained, it had struck at the madra channels in his chest, searing his spirit. The shock blanked Lindon's mind for an instant.

He came back to himself as he lay crumpled at the bottom of the wall, but Pride had not given up. Mercy had barred his path with her staff of slick, twisted black madra, and was trying to talk to her brother.

Lindon extended his perception to try and get a sense of Pride, but it was hard to read him. It was as though Lindon's spiritual senses slid away.

[A property of shadow madra, I'm sure,] Dross said.

That would make it harder to react to anything Pride did, and more difficult to read his techniques. *Pay close attention,* Lindon said to Dross.

He could drop it here. Let Mercy take care of her brother.

But this was his opportunity to leave. If he could show Charity that he wasn't the right choice for the competition, she would send him home. Mercy would make sure nothing terrible happened to him.

If he played this correctly, he might be able to learn something too.

He would have to make the fight convincing, so he pulled Blackflame madra from his core. With the Path of Black Flame filling him, holding back became twice as hard. He didn't want to take a loss. He wanted to teach Pride a lesson.

The Burning Cloak sprung up around Lindon, a flame of black and red surrounding his body, and the dragon advanced.

Lindon rushed forward, slamming his white Remnant fist over Mercy's staff and into Pride. The short Underlord caught the blow on his forearm, but the force still launched him down the entire hall and out the open doors.

He landed on his feet, but Lindon had followed him with another punch.

Shadow burst like smoke where Pride had stood, and he disappeared again, Lindon's fist passing through immaterial darkness. He turned, expecting Pride behind him, but something slammed into his ankles. Pride had gone low, sweeping Lindon's legs out from under him, and Lindon pitched onto his back.

As he hit the ground, the air rushing from his lungs, Lindon hurled a dragon's breath upward. Pride would have followed up with a new attack, ready to hit him while he was down.

Sure enough, Pride had followed him, and a beam of black-and-red madra caught him full in the chest.

Lindon cut off the technique immediately, for fear of drilling a hole in Mercy's brother, but Pride was unharmed. Gray haze covered his skin, and the Blackflame madra had simply washed over him.

He drove his fist down onto Lindon, and an orb of shadow madra exploded from the hit, this time into Lindon's stomach.

Lindon's spirit screamed in pain, and so did he.

His consciousness blurred away for longer than it had before. This time, when he came to, he found Pride glaring contemptuously at him from fifteen feet away.

Mercy stood over him, veil lifted, her staff in the form of a bow.

"...test yourself against *me*," Mercy was saying, with more anger in her voice than Lindon had ever heard. "If you're too much of a coward for that, then go cry to Mother."

Pride looked to the side, past his sister. "Uncle Fury, do you want *this* representing the Akura family?"

A man walked into Lindon's view, laughing sheepishly, as though he felt guilty about something and was trying to laugh it off. He wore a loose black sacred artist's robe, but only one layer, with a bare chest revealed beneath. He looked to be perhaps thirty-five or forty, with hair made of living shadow. It rose and drifted and shifted like sea-grass in the currents. Unlike the others present, his eyes were bright red.

"Hmmm, I don't know." Fury's voice was bright, reminding Lindon more of Mercy than of anyone else he'd met in the family. "He looked pretty weak, but you *did* attack him before he was ready."

"Talk to Aunt Charity," Pride insisted. "He doesn't deserve her nomination."

Lindon's hope rose as his Blackflame madra faded away. Akura Fury evidently had the power to decide the competitors for the Uncrowned King team. He could send Lindon home.

"Eeehhhh...I taught Charity myself, when she was a girl. She's always had good eyes."

Lindon pushed himself to his feet. The ache in his body was dull, but the pain in his spirit was sharp.

With effort, he pushed his fists together to salute the man he suspected was a Herald.

"Forgiveness, but I was not raised with the training of the Akura clan. I do not see how I could be worthy to compete beside Mercy or Pride."

Pride's head jerked back as though Lindon had struck him, but Mercy sighed. She knew what he was doing.

Akura Fury turned red eyes to him and gave him a pitying look, hands in his pockets. "I don't see much in him either, but Charity knows him better than I do. But hey, there's still a slot left! I'll have my selection fights in a few months, and then you can show me what you've got."

Pride gestured angrily to Lindon. "Haven't I already?"

"I'm afraid I'm not his opponent," Lindon said, as though it were a painful admission.

[Orthos would have ruined your ruse by now,] Dross said. ['Grr, a dragon doesn't pretend to be weak. Throw fire at him!' It's a good thing I'm here to help.]

Fury let out another embarrassed laugh, but spread his hands. "Sorry, boys! It's not up to me."

Pride glared again, mostly at Lindon, but sparing some for Mercy as well. Finally, he bowed to Fury and stomped away.

Lindon searched his mind for a new line of attack. The rest of the young Lords and Ladies were still watching, and if he presented himself as *too* weak, they might really try to kill him.

Fury scratched the back of his head. "He's pretty mad. Even more than usual."

Mercy's bow shifted back to a staff, and she leaned on it. "It's my fault. I'll go talk to him."

"Nah. It's training time!"

Mercy ran to hide behind Lindon, which put him in the awkward position of standing between a Herald and his niece. "Sorry, Uncle Fury, but I have to get Lindon settled in. And I really should speak with Pride. Just give me a few minutes, and then I'll be ready."

"Or better yet," Lindon said hastily, "you could send me home! Wouldn't that solve everything?"

Red eyes moved to the rest of the crowd, and Fury jabbed a finger at Lindon. "Someone take care of him, okay?" Then he grabbed Mercy around the waist, picking her up with one arm. "Now, training!"

Mercy protested, but Fury had already leaped.

Through the clouds.

Lindon and the others stared up to where they had vanished, but they never came down.

Leaving Lindon weak and lost, surrounded by hostile strangers.

His hopes of leaving came crashing down around him, but he might have won another small consolation. *Did you get it?* he asked silently.

[That's a lot of pressure when you put it that way, you know that? If Pride's Path is the same as Mercy's, he should only have four techniques available, and he used four. So I have a *reasonable* model, but not what I'd call a perfect one.]

Lindon looked through the hole in the crowd where Pride had left. *That's good enough to start.*

One of the young Underladies finally agreed to lead Lindon to a guest room where he could recover from his wounds. She said nothing as they leaped over black ponds filled with glowing white fish, trees that scraped at the sky, trying to grab them, and statues with amethysts for eyes. They jumped from one tall, black building to another, and she showed no consideration for his wounds.

Lindon had fought for his life while in worse condition than this, though even the Soul Cloak felt painful running through his strained madra channels. As a Truegold, he would have had to exhaust himself to keep up with her and may have injured his madra channels doing so. But his Underlord body picked up the slack, and he followed her to their destination.

She looked him up and down as they landed as though surprised that he was still on his feet, but she said nothing. In fact, his Bloodforged Iron body had already begun repairing his physical injuries, straining his spirit even further while doing so.

They stood before a three-story home with black tiles on the roof and a smooth gray wall surrounding the property. Trees and bushes poked over the top of the wall, so he assumed a garden surrounded the house. Upon close inspection, Lindon took it for an inn. The Akura clan would have plenty of traffic from the outside; he only had to hope that they would pay for his stay.

A servant in black-and-white layered robes and a cap stood next to the plated iron gates, bowing when she saw the Akura Underlady.

"He's a guest," the Underlady said, speaking for the first time. "Get him registered."

"I will see to it at once, Underlady," the servant said into the ground.

Without another word, the young Akura woman took off again, leaping away.

The servant bowed to him. "Greetings, Underlord. Please allow me to provide you with a key and, if this residence is suitable for you, I will enter your name into the clan registry as a guest at this location."

She held both her palms out flat, a black card resting on them. A script gleamed in its center like moonlight.

"Gratitude," Lindon said, taking the card that he assumed was the key. "If you don't mind, would you show me the way to my room?"

He tried to find the place he could touch the card that would cause the gate to open, but as soon as he ran his pure madra through the script, the iron plates rose soundlessly up. They hung overhead, suspended on wind aura, waiting for him to pass beneath.

The servant woman spoke hesitantly. "I apologize for correcting the Underlord, but I was obviously unclear. The house is yours."

The statement sent equal parts excitement and alarm rushing through him. He didn't want a house here; he wanted to leave. On the other hand, it was a *house.*

The Wei clan had spoiled him for space, but all the houses of the Shi family added together would have made up only one story of this building. And there were three stories.

From the inside of the wall, he realized the yard was much bigger than he had imagined; it stretched all the way around the house, and he couldn't see the far end. It was covered by bushes that flowered a glowing blue, and trees with fruits like red glass. The aura was as thick here as anywhere in Moongrave, and somehow the house gave off a calming feel.

"I am...grateful," Lindon said, "so pardon me for my ignorance. This house is mine? No other guests will stay here?"

The servant looked offended. "No, sir! My staff and I will maintain the house and grounds and provide meals upon request, unless you require isolation for your training. There is a soundproof, spiritually contained basement for meditation, and the garden is at your disposal. If you require anything for your training or daily needs at any time, please let me or any of the servants know."

Seeing that he was still skeptical, she continued. "For as long as you are a guest of the Akura family, you will be considered the owner of this house, whether you leave tonight or stay here the rest of your life." Her voice echoed with pride, as though she took personal responsibility for the quality of her service.

Lindon couldn't help admiring the Akura clan. They hadn't made the best impression on him, but they certainly weren't cheap.

While he was here, he would squeeze out all the benefits he could.

"In that case, could I trouble you for some clothes?" He had been transported here without warning, and he only kept one change of clothes in his void key. "And please let me know if this is too much, but I could use some mental enhancement elixirs, madra restoration pills, and—if you can spare one—a parasite ring."

He searched her face for reluctance as he tested the boundaries of the family's generosity. She didn't bat an eye, giving a precise bow. "Of course, Underlord. Will there be anything else?"

Lindon didn't hold back. "Yes, as long as it isn't a problem. I'd like as many high-quality pure madra scales as you can find, some firewood, a hot meal whenever is convenient for you, sealed water jugs, preserved travel rations..."

She listened attentively, bowing when he was finished. "Your requirements will be fulfilled in haste, Underlord."

Not only did the servant not balk at any of his requests, but everything was delivered within the hour.

Most of it he set aside for his training or daily use, but some items went into his void key—the restoration pills, some firewood, three water jugs, ten travel rations, a steel knife, and a sturdy travel blanket. Now, no matter when they sent him home, he had already made a profit.

The thought cheered him immensely.

When he finished his preparations, he locked himself into the basement: a vast, bare room the size of the entire floor above. He inspected the scripts himself, checking that he was truly isolated, and then released Dross and Little Blue.

The Sylvan Riverseed couldn't wait to scurry out of his void key, chattering her frustrations at him like an irritated mouse. She was upset that he had left her alone in there for so long, glaring at him with a face the color of the deep ocean, hair flowing behind her like waves. She slapped his shin with one blue hand, leaving a spark of cool energy.

[You're right to complain,] Dross said. [It's actually wonderful out here. Beautiful sights, fresh air...oh, it's amazing. And I can leave whenever I want to. Watch!]

Dross spun into Lindon's spirit and back out, projecting his body of pebbly purple flesh, with one eye taking up most of his body. His mouth moved as he spoke, revealing sharp teeth, and he waved his two stubby tentacle-arms in the air as though demonstrating his freedom.

Little Blue folded her arms, sulking.

"Dross, do you think you're helping?"

[Not helping *you*.]

Lindon tried scooping up Little Blue in his hand of flesh, but she scurried away from him. He had to chase after her, begging her to stop while Dross egged her on.

After ten minutes of running after her all over the basement—and trying not to step on her by accident—he finally caught her. She stopped in place, allowing him to get a hand around her, and he gently lifted her into the air.

She refused to look at him.

Lindon held up one of the pure scales that the Akura servant had brought. It was high-grade, roughly what would be produced by a Truegold. Since no one reached Truegold without harvesting aura, the Akura must have purified other aspects of madra to get this scale.

"I'm sorry. Peace?"

Little Blue turned up her nose at the blue-white coin.

"I have more, if this isn't enough."

She squeaked. Sometimes he had to ask Dross to translate for her, but this time he thought he caught her meaning.

"Mine? You want me to make one?"

She nodded.

"We get these for free. As many as we want. I'll make them for you myself when we get home, but while we're here..."

He trailed off as she squirmed in his hand, turning her back on him.

Finally, he sighed and gave in, beginning the process of gathering his madra together to produce a scale. It didn't take long, but the quality and stability required to Forge a perfect scale put a strain on his madra channels. Which, in his condition, caused him real pain.

When he finished, holding a perfect translucent blue scale between his fingers, she turned back around. The scale was bigger than her head, but her mouth enlarged in an instant, and she gulped it down.

She flashed sapphire, giving a whistling breath of satisfaction and patting her stomach.

"I do apologize," he repeated. "Friends?"

She chirped brightly and dashed up his arm, coming to rest on his shoulder opposite Dross.

[Good for you, holding strong in your negotiations while his spirit is wounded. You can't let him pressure you into helping.]

Two cold spots pressed against him as Little Blue suddenly grabbed the side of his neck. He felt an odd tickling as she sent her awareness into his spirit.

Since when had she been able to do that?

When she discovered the injury to his madra channels, she gave a high-pitched wail, flooding his spirit with her cleansing power.

Her madra helped, but it was a bit like throwing a bucket of cold water on a sunburn. He hissed and gritted his teeth, his spine straightening. Spiritual pain wasn't necessarily any *worse* than physical pain, but it was much harder to ignore.

The sharp spike of discomfort began to ebb almost immediately, and he could feel his spirit recovering already. Little Blue burbled apologies, leaning against the side of his face.

"I'm perfectly fine, see?" He turned to smile at her.

On his other shoulder, Dross gasped. [What *is* that? Do you feel that?]

Lindon hadn't before Dross pointed it out, but when he focused on his perception, he felt a dark hole in the center of the basement that he swore hadn't been there before. The basement was well-lit by scripts drawing their power from a madra furnace upstairs, but he could feel a black spot in the middle. Now that he noticed, he was starting to see it, like a puddle of smoke gathering on the floor.

Dross drifted closer, peering with his giant eye. [I don't ever... oh, it's her!]

Lindon recognized the madra shortly after Dross did, but by then it was too late. Akura Charity materialized from darkness in the center of the basement. Lindon immediately pulled Dross back into his madra channels.

Or he tried. His madra channels were blocked. He focused his spirit, pulling at Dross. The spirit remained where he was, peering curiously into the Heart Sage's eyes.

"Well," Charity said, "this explains a few things."

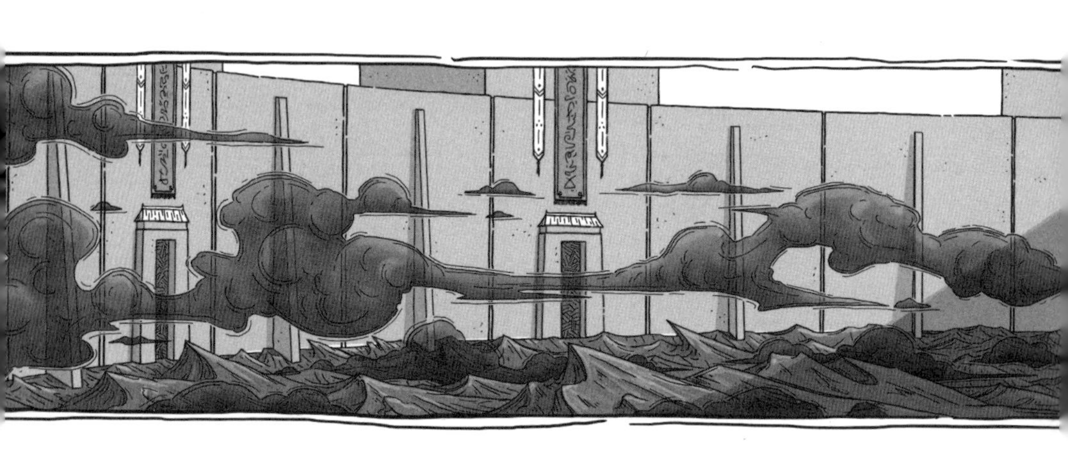

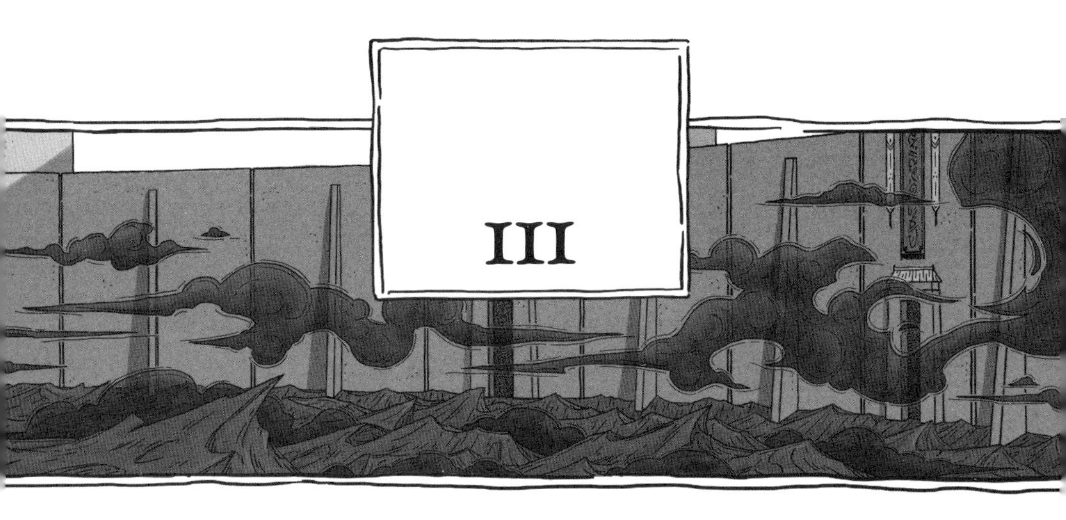


LINDON STOOD STILL, QUIET PANIC GROWING IN HIS MIND, AS Akura Charity examined Dross. The spirit was the creation of Northstrider's Ghostwater, and as far as Lindon knew, was completely unique. Lindon could easily imagine someone as strong as a Sage murdering him in order to pry Dross from his Remnant.

But Eithan had sensed Dross' presence without understanding his nature. Lindon had to hope that others wouldn't be able to tell how valuable he was either.

[You're the Sage of the Silver Heart!] Dross exclaimed. [I didn't know much about you before the last few months, but when you blanked those minds, just *bam!* and they're out, I was impressed. And jealous. I mean, not jealous! Well, yes, I was...I *was* a bit jealous.]

"You bonded with a mind-spirit," Charity said, still examining

Dross. "And a surprisingly advanced one, considering how stable its manifestation is. Now I understand how you did so well on your mental tests."

[Not to take credit, but that was entirely me.]

"And you have taken a drop of ghostwater as well," she went on. "Between the two, it's no wonder that you have such an impressive mental foundation."

That wasn't totally accurate, but Lindon took the way out that she'd offered. "I could never hide anything from a Sage. I was blessed to stumble on good fortune inside the Ghostwater facility."

"Not just there," Charity focused on Little Blue, who ducked shyly behind a lock of Lindon's hair. "It would seem that you have been blessed by the heavens on more than just one occasion."

Lindon thought of the glass ball burning quietly in his pocket. "I humbly agree."

"And yet you were beaten today."

Lindon usually thought of the Sage as cold or impassive, but this time he detected the anger behind her mask. He chose his words very carefully, feeling his breath come more quickly.

"I am honored by your estimation of me. But, if you'll allow me an observation, I am also lacking in basic knowledge and skills. Your Underlords are not. If Pride were my enemy, I might find some way to stop or defeat him, but within the confines of a judged duel, I'm afraid I am truly not his match."

He had long been aware of his weaknesses. He had worked hard and learned much in the past two years, but in many areas, he still hadn't caught up to those sacred artists who'd received the best training their entire lives. He'd made it as far as he had through relentless determination, reliable companions, and leaning hard on his areas of strength.

As Charity remained quiet and studied him, her expression grew more and more distant, as though she were contemplating some abstract problem.

Sweat beaded on his skin. He had been honest with her, hoping she would respect his humility, but maybe he had misjudged her.

He pulled Little Blue down from his shoulder, cradling her in his hands to comfort her.

"You don't know what we're fighting for, do you?" Charity said at last.

"For the pride of the Akura clan, and I'm not certain that I am worthy to carry such a great burden."

She slowly nodded, like she had come to some conclusion. "And you don't feel such pride, so you do not value it."

Dross looked between them, his wide eye staring into Lindon from an inch away. Lindon began to sweat in earnest. "I do not dare to underestimate the pride and honor of a Monarch's family, which is why I feel that I may be unsuited for this task. If the reputation of the Akura clan affects the survival of nations, I don't—"

"It does," she interrupted. "It affects *your* nation."

Lindon stopped.

"The dragons have been pressing in on us for longer than you can imagine, but we have managed an unsteady balance. Now, with the uncertainty of the Dreadgods added in, all has been called into question. Every major house and family is pushing their boundaries to gain as much as they can.

"The Uncrowned King tournament is an exhibition of our future military power. If the Dragon King believes we are weak, he will take what he wants from us. If the *other* great families believe we are weak, they will not help us. There is no sense investing in a loser."

She pressed her fingertips together, and though she was over a foot shorter than Lindon, it was as though she towered over him. "They want the Blackflame Empire."

Dross gasped.

Lindon didn't want to believe her. He wanted to think she was lying to him in order to motivate him to fight. But she didn't need to lie, she could simply order him to do as she wished, and he would have no choice but to comply.

And it made sense. The Empire had once been ruled by dragons, and now the dragons wanted it back.

He followed her line of reasoning, but he still held out hope. "How far do we have to make it?"

"Farther than the gold dragons," she answered. "But there is far more at stake in the tournament than this. If at least one of you does not reach the top eight and become one of the Uncrowned, preferably Mercy, then we may find ourselves in great danger."

That brought him to one final question, the one that had loomed larger than any other ever since Charity had kidnapped him.

"Then why me?" he asked. "If it's so important, why bet on a stranger?"

Charity glanced down at Little Blue, who had scrambled down his body to hide behind his ankle. "I have many reasons. Let it be enough for you that I think you can win." Purple eyes returned to his. "So will you stop this charade, or will you allow others to decide what happens to your home?"

[We don't know for certain that the gold dragons wouldn't rule better than the Akura clan,] Dross pointed out. [And there's no reason it has to be *you*. This Pride or one of the others will still fight even if you're not here.]

Lindon stood up straighter, looking down on the Sage. "I will fight."

He had never been willing to leave the fate of his home in someone else's hands. He wasn't about to change his mind now.

[That's good, because I was lying before. The royal gold family of dragons is notoriously vicious and cruel, especially to humans. I just didn't want to worry you.]

Charity brushed her hands clean like a woman done with a mundane task. "Now, however, you have a problem. You have given the other Akura Underlords a reason to think you are weak. They taste blood, and they will not allow you to rest."

Lindon thought back to the fight with Pride. The other Underlords had watched him with disdain...and jealousy. They would be coming for him.

He felt more pressure from that than he had before. Only minutes ago, he would have been satisfied with disqualification.

"Pardon, but I will need help addressing my weaknesses. I do not have the formal training in combat that your relatives do."

Charity nodded. "If you are to fight under my family's name in the tournament, this lack of knowledge must be remedied. You will be facing sacred artists of varied and unknown abilities. You must be able to determine their capabilities quickly and respond appropriately under any circumstances. This is not a training regimen that should be attempted in only nine months, and yet you must complete it."

She addressed Dross. “If he hopes to meet the deadline, he will rely on your help.”

The purple spirit puffed himself out, closing his eye and folding his arms across his body. [Leave it to me! I’ll drag him through, no problem!] He opened his eye a crack and added, [...on second thought, actually, it sure would be easier with a little bit of your madra to help me. Just a taste?]

Charity stared at him, impassive as always.

[No? That’s, ah, that’s all right then.] He forced a chuckle. [I was joking! That’s a little mind-spirit humor for you.]

There was a subtle flicker of power from the Sage, and she held up a silver-and-purple scale. Its madra drew Lindon’s eyes to it almost hypnotically, and the room seemed to darken in its presence.

[Oh, you...you’re doing it! See, I told you she would help instead of wiping us from existence.]

She flipped it to him, and Dross swooped in to snap it up like a bat taking an insect. As soon as the madra entered him, he shuddered at the flood of energy.

“It’s gentle and stable,” she said, “but it is still an Archlord’s power. Be careful.”

Without a word of acknowledgement, Dross faded back into Lindon’s spirit. He could feel Dross processing the scale: it felt tiny but unbelievably powerful, like a thunderstorm the size of a fingertip.

Lindon bowed. “Gratitude. Will he be all right?”

“A spirit of that density should be fine. It should absorb the scale’s essence over a week or two, during which it will not be conscious or able to serve you. After that time, you should find its efficiency greatly increased.”

[Ah, now *this* is the good stuff,] Dross said into Lindon's head.

*Stay quiet,* Lindon urged him. *Don't let her know you're awake.*

[I'm sure the Sage would appreciate the master's grand work more than you do.]

*Please. I don't want to be killed and have my Remnant dissected.*

[I'm not rushing off to be dissected myself, but we can trust Charity. I have a good feeling about her.]

Charity handed Lindon a multi-faceted ball that fit in her palm, like a dark red jewel. It sat in his hand, warm and heavier than he'd expected.

"This is a training program we use to train our Coppers in close combat. It will contain information and training programs about all five basic categories of Enforcer techniques and how to react to them. When you have achieved a perfect score, tell your house servants, and they will deliver a message to me."

"Forgiveness," Lindon said, "but it's a Copper test?"

"It is a test of knowledge and skill, not of power. Superior advancement will not help you, though your experience will." She folded her hands in front of herself. "As a Copper, Mercy earned a perfect score within three days. Just so you have a...benchmark."

Her shadow began to crawl up her feet, but she looked up as though staring through the ceiling. "You have a visitor," she informed him. "Another young Underlord dissatisfied with my decision. They cannot reach me, so they take out their frustrations on you, hoping I will change my mind."

Lindon took a deep breath, bracing himself, thinking of the pain in his spirit that Little Blue had just relieved. His flesh was still tender.

She noticed. "Would you like me to stop them?"

He would, and Little Blue urged him to with a whistle in his ear. Even Dross made an appreciative noise in his mind.

"If I didn't have your protection, would they be allowed to challenge me?"

She inclined her head. "You are a worthy guest. They would be permitted to duel you openly, so long as no one was injured too badly."

"Then let them, if you would. I'll consider it training."

If his problem was a lack of battle experience, then there was no better solution than to face a gauntlet of opponents at his own level. It would help build up Dross' knowledge too, to help him predict fights in the future.

And when Lindon grew skilled enough, he could make a powerful demonstration in front of all the other clan Underlords. One that would prove beyond a doubt that he deserved to be on the team.

But he didn't look forward to the beatings he was about to take.

Charity gave an expression that might have been an approving smile or just a quirk of her lips. "Don't let it become a distraction." Then shadow swallowed her, and she vanished.

Then Lindon went upstairs to let in the Underlord who hated him.

The young Akura challenged him to a duel, fought in Lindon's own basement, with a construct to project the fight as witness.

He controlled a fan of a half-dozen flying swords, using pulses of shadow and force madra to keep Lindon at a distance as Lindon dealt with the weapons. Lindon made the mistake of focusing on the swords, knocking them away with his hands and allowing his opponent to overwhelm him at a distance.

He should have ignored the swords, taking the hits with his Bloodforged Iron body, and broken the Akura's concentration by outmatching him in Striker techniques.

Lindon came to this conclusion while he lay on the floor of his basement, aching, waiting for his Iron body to repair the holes in his skin.

If it had been a real fight, Lindon could have won. He consoled himself with that fact.

He had explosive constructs stored in his void key that he had prepared for his fight with Kiro but never gotten a chance to use, not to mention his Skysworn armor, which would have held up against the swords for long enough to close the distance. And Lindon had to hold his techniques back; he could hardly use dragon's breath to its full potential when it wasn't a fight to the death.

But Lindon had faced plenty of life-or-death situations. He wasn't preparing for a deadly showdown; he was training for a series of matches with rules and limitations. These elite Akura Lords were far better suited for fights like those. He was playing their game, and he had to learn how.

He would learn by losing.

When his body had recovered enough and Little Blue had soothed his spirit, he rose to his feet. His stance was unsteady. Pain shot through his joints, and he wanted nothing more than to lie down and wait for his aches to fade. No one would blame him if he slept. Dross would encourage him.

But sleeping wouldn't move him forward.

"Dross, could you show me my opponent?"

Lindon's vision blurred for a moment, and then the young

Underlord appeared opposite him, six scripted blades floating behind his head.

[Did you *see* how fast that was?] Dross said. [And look at all that crisp detail! I already want more Sage madra, and I haven't even finished digesting it yet. Will she give me some more when I'm done, do you think?]

Lindon resolved to find out. He was afraid that revealing Dross' appetite would make Charity suspicious about his nature, or that making too many requests would anger the Sage, but he could push a little.

Improving Dross might be just as important as training himself.

Dross simulated the battle, and Lindon attempted his strategy. If he ignored the swords and fought with only Striker techniques, he could indeed pierce through the opponent's techniques and kill him before Lindon himself died, but that resulted in a dead opponent and a few severe gashes on Lindon. There had to be a way to win without murdering the other person or taking wounds himself.

Lindon tried again.

When Dross grew tired, Lindon switched over to the Enforcer training. The device left by Charity projected images into his mind, so it felt much like practicing with Dross. But this one transported him to entirely new scenarios.

First, he stood on an icy mountain as the wind whipped snow by him. Flocks of ice-feathered birds flew past, slicing the air with their wings.

A bald old man, wearing only a wrap around his waist, blazed with golden light. He slipped away from one diving bird, crushed another with a fist, and spun into a kick that knocked a third from the sky. As he fought the flock, his movements blurred until Lindon could barely follow them.

Charity's voice echoed everywhere. "The full-body Enforcer technique. It is common and flexible, and its properties depend on the madra, but it does not excel in any area as a more specialized technique might. Full-body Enforcement often radiates light or has external markings, but even when it does not, it can be easily sensed by anyone Jade or higher."

The scene changed, and suddenly Lindon found himself deep within the earth. Shining green sap dripped from the ceiling like a very slow rainstorm. A woman walked through the sap, wearing a very broad, flat cap that kept her dry. Beneath her hat, she wore a long cloak with a high collar, so Lindon could see almost nothing of her.

"Attack techniques are also very common," Charity's voice said, as the woman cocked her fist back.

The fist began to shine with white madra, which shaped into a tiger's head and roared as the sacred artist plunged her fist into a nearby stalagmite. The impact shook the entire chamber, the force blowing her cloak back. She had to hold onto her hat with one hand. The stalagmite cracked.

"These are, just as they sound, individual attacks that carry the power of a technique behind them. They are considered Enforcer techniques because they primarily enhance the effect of a single motion, even though they may project power outward as Striker techniques do."

The stalagmite, cracked by the woman's fist, exploded as a tree-sized worm burst from within it. The worm screamed, revealing a round mouth filled with teeth on all sides, and the sacred artist gathered madra into both hands.

"Indeed, many such techniques have characteristics of both Striker and Enforcer techniques, and could be developed in either direction depending on the needs of the Path. Enforcer attack techniques carry more power than full-body techniques, but as a result they can be clumsier. They tend to leave the user open for counterattack."

The scene changed again, and Charity took Lindon through examples of movement techniques, weapon techniques, and defensive techniques.

*How am I supposed to get a perfect score?* Lindon asked Dross. *Will there be a quiz?*

[Oh, this is more than just a dream tablet. It is interactive. I'm sure...ah, you see? Here it is.]

Now Lindon stood in a blank white room, but the man in the loincloth stood in front of him.

"This man will randomly use Enforcer techniques ten times in a row. You must accurately identify the type of technique within one second."

It was harder than Lindon had expected because he couldn't use his spiritual perception. The illusory man was a void to Lindon's senses, so he had to rely on visual clues alone.

Dross, of course, identified every one instantly. When the man adopted a defensive posture, so Lindon was sure it would be a defense technique, Dross correctly called it as a full-body technique.

"How did you know?" Lindon asked.

[His breathing, his arms, his calves, his posture, and the way his eyes moved.]

"...oh."

If Lindon simply had Dross hand him the answers, he would have passed immediately. But he had to learn on his own.

After two hours, when he had finally recognized every detail about the man's techniques, he thought he'd finished. Then the woman in the hat and cloak appeared.

"This woman will randomly use Enforcer techniques ten times in a row. You must accurately identify the type of technique within one second."

Her madra was completely different from the man's, and she showed different physical cues. It was harder to see her at all, shrouded as her body was.

[If you're going to finish this in three days without my help, I hope you have some Dream Well water left. You're going to have to go without sleep.]

Lindon did have some, but not much. He was down to one jar and two small bottles. He had used it sparingly, primarily to nourish Dross, and he didn't want to use it up here.

But he did use just enough to stay sharp.

Especially because, the next day, no less than five different Akura Underlords challenged him to duels.

Between fighting, recovery, and the analysis afterward, it took him two days and a night to complete the Enforcer training.

He handed the dark red jewel-device to his servant with a heavy heart, telling her to report to Charity. Even as an Underlord, he had beaten Mercy's accomplishment as a Copper by only a few hours.

Though the test had nothing to do with advancement, he was older and more experienced than Mercy had been as well. He had hoped to finish within a few hours.

Charity did not send him a comment in return. Instead, she sent him a new gem-construct. This one was dark blue, instead of dark red, and contained information on Forger techniques.

Lindon got to work.

**INFORMATION REQUESTED: SESHETHKUNAAZ, KING OF DRAGONS AND MONARCH OF THE EASTERN ASHWIND CONTINENT.**

**BEGINNING REPORT...**

**PATH: WASTELAND.** The Path of the Wasteland has aspects of earth and wind, and its techniques take the form of blowing golden sand. It is a versatile and adaptable Path, often used to call sandstorms, form complex shapes from sand at great distances, and scour flesh from bone.

Gold dragons have a natural affinity for fire and water aura, but Seshethkunaaz was born in the desert. An exile, he was left by the rest of his kind to die.

He was found by a group of human nomads, who saved the dying dragon and raised him as part of their family. He formed a contract with one of their children, providing him with enough pure madra to dilute his spirit. With time and great effort, he was able to change the nature of his madra and embark on the Path of the Wasteland.

He and his contractor were raised as brothers, and they advanced together at great speed. When he reached Underlord, he took on a human form like that of his contractor. His adoptive parents shortened his name to Sesh, introducing the two of them as twin brothers, and explaining Sesh's remaining draconic traits as part of his Goldsign.

For years, they remained content. Until Sesh's brother killed a child.

In a conflict between hot-tempered boys, Sesh's young contractor lost his temper. He struck a Lowgold, forgetting his strength as an Underlord. His victim perished instantly.

In many lands, an Underlord would not be held responsible for any actions against a Gold. But the laws of this nation prohibited the murder of anyone regardless of advancement, and the young victim was the descendant of a powerful clan.

Sesh's family fled in the night, but they were soon caught. Sesh's brother was executed for murder, reckless use of power, and fleeing justice.

To this day, the King of Dragons walks the desert in the form of a human boy, hair dark and skin tanned by the sun, wrapped in a cloak against the harsh wind. He admires humans, but hates human *civilization,* that collection of unnatural rules under which the weak are favored above the strong.

If power and survival were the only laws, he believes all would benefit. Even humans.

**SUGGESTED TOPIC: SESHETHKUNAAZ AND THE DREAD WAR. CONTINUE?**

**Denied, report complete.**

Naru Saeya, sister of the Blackflame Emperor, hovered above Yerin. Emerald wings from the Path of Grasping Sky barely flapped as wind aura held her motionless in the air. Even when they both stood flat on the ground, Saeya loomed over Yerin, but that wasn't enough. She just had to fly too.

She wore sacred artist robes in a color that matched her wings, and the cloth was as fresh as if it had been sewn this morning. Her hair had been tied back into a tail, all the better to fight, but a fan of peacock feathers still stuck up over her ear.

Yerin glared at those feathers, clutching an iron bar in her hands. This was a handicap she had given herself; blunt instruments gathered no sword aura. She had to beat her opponent with combat skills, not with her madra techniques.

It was more irritating than she'd expected.

"You expecting us to get much practice done when you're hanging from the ceiling?" Yerin asked.

The ceiling in this wing of the imperial palace was over a hundred feet tall, and Saeya wasn't even close to it. If she had been, maybe Yerin could have dashed up the wall or tried something else.

The Emperor's sister looked as irritated as Yerin was, holding her own iron bar. She had refused to take any weapon advantage over her training partner.

"It will only go the same as before," Saeya said.

Yerin sharpened her senses, letting madra flow through her Steelborn Iron body. Strength flooded her Underlord body, and she felt invincible as she never had as a Truegold.

"One more try," Yerin said through gritted teeth.

Saeya didn't say anything, but wind madra gathered up inside her, and then she vanished in a blur of green. Yerin swung her bar with all her strength, whipping up a whirlwind in the training room, but she hit nothing.

A sharp pain cracked against her back.

"If I slow down enough to let you hit me," Saeya said from behind her, "you'd break me in half."

The Naru woman walked around to Yerin's front, letting her practice weapon drop. "We're a bad match. I have virtually no defense against your Path, so if you had a real sword, I'd have to keep my distance. When you don't, either I'm too fast or you're too strong."

Saeya hurled her iron bar so hard to one side that it struck against the wall like a bell and sent a chip of stone flying.

Yerin felt like doing the same thing. The iron bar felt odd in her hand, and she looked down to see that she had squeezed fingerprints into the metal.

"You want to go into the tournament betting that you'll only face good matches?" Yerin challenged. In truth, she felt the same way. Neither of them were getting good practice out of this.

Naru Saeya took deep breaths, clearly fighting down her frustration. "We need to be familiar with each other if we're going to fight side-by-side. Maybe we should spar together against another pair of Underlords."

"Cheers and celebration, you've struck gold. I'll sit here and polish my sword while you find another pair of Underlords who can match us."

The Blackflame Empire had doubled its number of Underlords during the competition in the Night Wheel Valley, but over the last few weeks, Yerin had found out firsthand that most of the newly advanced Lords and Ladies weren't much to her. If she held back everything from her Path, they weren't her match in swordsmanship. The gap only widened with madra.

The only young Underlords worth anything to Yerin had been stolen by Akura Charity.

The older Underlords would be a real challenge, but they had one and all left the capital to deal with their own responsibilities. They had been gone for too long during the qualification fights, and now they had to make up for lost time.

As far as Yerin knew, only two people left in the city could challenge her or Naru Saeya. One was the Emperor, who was busy signing laws and looking stern. The other was Eithan, and only the heavens knew where he had vanished to.

Naru Gwei had dumped Yerin and Eithan out of Stormrock at the first possible opportunity and had suggested that he wouldn't come close to Eithan ever again without an Imperial command.

"We fight for the honor of the Empire," Saeya said, "but we can't sacrifice the stability of the Empire for the honor of the Empire. This is our problem to solve." She didn't sound happy about it. She stared out the window overlooking Blackflame City, glaring at the buildings below as though they were holding her back.

"Then let's stop fighting like Coppers." Yerin tossed her iron bar aside, too. She walked over to the corner, where she had propped her master's sheathed blade. "We gather up every Underlord and Truegold we can get our hands on and face them all at once. Pile on enough straws, and eventually we'll feel the weight."

Saeya let out a long breath. "You're right, we should. It's important that we get you more experience against different opponents."

"If you had so much more experience than me, you'd be too old for the tournament."

"There's a big difference between thirty-five and...what are you, twenty?" The tall woman eyed Yerin.

Yerin herself wasn't sure how old she was, but twenty had to be about right. "Thought you had to be *under* thirty-five."

"As long as you haven't begun your thirty-sixth year by the time the tournament begins, you're eligible," Saeya said. "I qualify by less than a month. That's the human standard, of course. Some sacred beasts can be almost—"

Saeya stopped. She turned from the window in a way that Yerin recognized: she had sensed something.

Yerin extended her own senses, feeling a growing shadow in the next room. It was cold and dark, like the air of the Night Wheel Valley leaking into Blackflame City.

"Akura clan likes to take their time," Yerin muttered. They had been promised training support from the Akura Sage, and this must be it.

She strode forward, joined by Naru Saeya, throwing open the doors to the hallway outside their training room. An ornate chest of black wood sat on the crimson rug, emanating darkness. Its lid shone with the moon-pale image of a mountain range topped by three stars—the symbol of the Akura family.

A shiver passed through Yerin's spirit as a construct in the box scanned first her, then Naru Saeya.

Confirming their presence, the box opened, its lid slithering apart.

The sense of spiritual power within blinded Yerin's eyes and her perception at once, but it instantly improved her mood. The Akura clan lived up to their reputation if they were sending gifts that felt like *this*.

Saeya's expression had softened into something that looked like awe. "We'll have to track Eithan down to give him his share," she said absently.

"I'd bet a sackful of gems against two hairs that he's standing around a corner waiting to pop out." Yerin knelt to pick up the box.

When Yerin straightened, Saeya had turned all the way around to stare into the training room they had just come from. "No...he's climbing up the side of the tower to slip in through the window."

"Counts as a corner," Yerin said, carrying the chest back through the door.

As Naru Saeya went to the window to look down, Yerin settled on her knees in the center of the room, rummaging through the box. It was divided neatly in three, and from the feel of each section alone, she could tell which section belonged to each of them.

Small, narrow tubes leaked sword-madra, certainly containing scales intended for Yerin. A series of stones next to them would be dream tablets, and that was it for her. Scales and dream tablets, though the tablets looked a little strange, polished and cut like gemstones. Maybe that was how the Akura family preferred them.

The partition next to hers contained Saeya's share: more scales and dream tablets, as well as a small scroll with a wing on it. Eithan's section had no tablets, only scales of pure madra and a pile of books and letters.

Naru Saeya had clearly lost patience waiting for Eithan to climb up. With wind madra, she reached over the side. Eithan came drifting up, bundled in green-tinged air, hanging like a doll in invisible hands. His long blond hair dangled, and he was breathing heavily, but his smile didn't suffer.

"Good evening, ladies!" he said. "I was trying to surprise you, but I'm afraid climbing up a smooth wall using only my fingertips was more tiring than I assumed. You know, this tower is very tall."

Saeya dumped him onto his feet, heading toward the box, but she kept her eyes on him. "You're not hurt, are you?"

"Only my pride." Eithan stretched and knuckled his back. "And also the skin of my fingers."

Naru Saeya brightened when she reached the box. "Top-grade scales! Before the Night Wheel Valley, those alone would have been worth more than everything I owned."

With both hands, she picked up a jeweled dream tablet, her eyes glazing over as she sunk into it. Eagerly, Yerin started to do the same.

Eithan extended a hand, stopping her. "Don't be too eager. One of those is a sound transmission construct, perhaps for Akura Charity to contact you. The rest are training courses, sent under the assumption that we wouldn't have any worthy opponents to train against here in the Empire."

"We don't," Yerin said. Despite Eithan's words, her excitement for the tablets had just gone up.

"Don't we? What did you learn by training against Saeya?"

Yerin's fingers were still itching to pick up one of the tablets, but

Eithan had a purpose for asking questions like this. Usually. And he hadn't touched his own pile of books.

She noticed they hadn't sent *him* any training courses.

"I need a better answer to fast feet and good eyes," Yerin said. "Same thing as when I'm fighting you. If I can trap them in with the Endless Sword and stop them from running around like a newborn rabbit, I'll win. If they slip past me and land a hit, I'm dead."

"And how would you solve that problem, if the heavens granted you one almighty wish?"

She nodded to him. "I'd take your ability. Eyes of my own give me a better chance to move. Or I'd ask the heavens to make me faster than any sacred artist living. But since that's nothing but dreams and shadows, I can double up the Endless Sword with the Shadow." She still grimaced and felt a pang of revulsion whenever she mentioned using the Blood Shadow. "Cover more ground, give them less space to run."

Eithan stroked his chin. "Would you like my help?"

That was typical of Eithan, leaving her with a fake choice. Of course the only correct answer was yes; how could she turn down training before a tournament in front of the entire world? Her master never would have.

"I sense that my reputation is under attack, so let me defend myself," Eithan continued. "You are already on the right path. With or without my help, you will close off your weaknesses. If you feel that you would benefit more from figuring this out on your own, I will respect that."

She sensed unusual sincerity from him. Cautiously, she asked, "What would you suggest?"

From within his outer robe, he withdrew a long stretch of bright blue silk, probably meant to tie a different set of his robes closed. He held it up for her inspection.

"One answer to superior awareness is improving your own," he said. "As you fight, tie this around your eyes and rely on your spiritual perception instead."

She almost laughed at him. "I'm not an Arelius. I can't see without my eyes, I can only feel. And only if there's madra."

If she closed her eyes and focused on Eithan, he felt only like a mass of pure madra. When he attacked, she would feel a spike of danger, but that told her almost nothing about where the attack was coming from. Relying on her spiritual perception to fight was like trying to find her way through a maze by smell.

"Sometimes," Eithan said, "I do forget what it is like not to see all around me." He let his eyes drift closed. "I spent my childhood learning how *not* to see, how to deafen myself to my opponent's heartbeat, their rasping breath, their gurgling stomach. But my actual spiritual perception was no better than yours."

His eyes opened again. "You will have noticed upon reaching Underlord that your senses can be cast wider and farther than ever before. I suggest you challenge yourself in an area that most Lords and Ladies ignore until they are a higher stage: to make your perception *sharper* and *deeper*. I myself took on this training, when I first realized how long the journey to Overlord would be. It's a small advantage over your fellow Underlords, but it can turn the tide."

He held out the blindfold with one finger.

"Maybe one of the others will be some kind of challenge with this on," Yerin said, stuffing the blindfold away. "You're not going to tell me that there are six more levels of this training, are you?"

He shook his head. "This is entirely up to you. The more you restrict your physical senses, the more you will get out of this training. You might reap a greater reward than I did; blindfolds are only so effective for me, you see."

Naru Saeya still sat in a cycling position, eyes distant.

Yerin returned her attention to the Akura clan box. "That's enough about me. What did they pack for you?"

He still hadn't leaned over to look through the chest. "Combat records and manuals from the main House Arelius on the Rosegold continent. I mastered most of these as a child. Still, it can be nice to see something from one's ancestral home."

"Thought you grew up here." Yerin snatched a dream tablet from the box.

"I was born there, raised here, and then returned there as an adult for a number of years. Most of those I knew on the other side are gone, but I have a message I'd like to deliver to the others."

In spite of herself, Yerin was curious. "What message?"

"I will tell them to hold on," Eithan said softly. "Help is coming." Something in the box caught his attention, and he reached down, brushing aside his manuals to find a letter. "Ah, and look, a letter from the Sage herself. She hopes that we will find these simulated opponents useful...some other things, I'm not entirely interested... and intends to retrieve us in approximately eight months after the Rising Earth and Frozen Blade teams." He tossed the letter down. "Well, at least we have a time limit."

He had to have noticed when Yerin's spine stiffened and her hand froze on the dream tablet, but he didn't ask what was wrong. He merely watched her, his expression somewhat curious.

"...the Frozen Blade school?" Yerin's eyes flicked to the Sage's sword against the wall. "They're going to be there?"

"They're one of the larger vassal factions under the Akura clan, so I imagine they will be."

"So the Winter Sage will be too, then."

He peered into her eyes and for some reason grew more excited. "You know the Sage of the Frozen Blade, don't you?"

"Like an arrow that missed my neck," Yerin muttered. "My master almost married her."

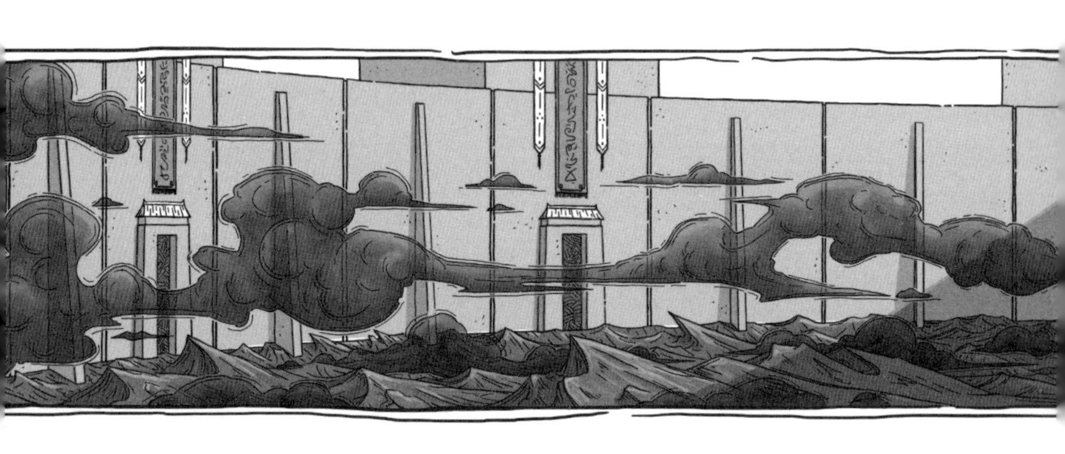

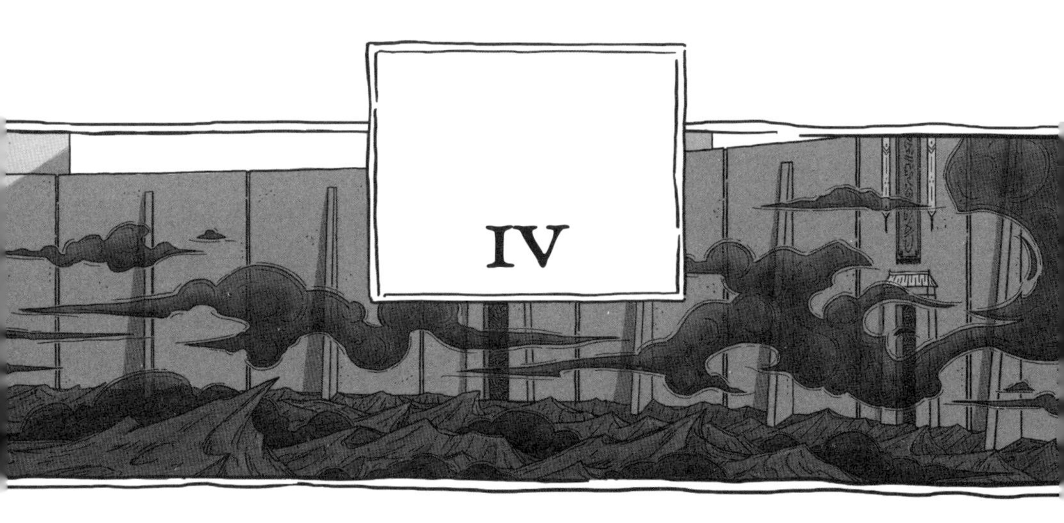

# IV

THROUGH THE EYES OF HER LIVING FORGER TECHNIQUE, A SILVER-and-purple owl, Charity watched Lindon.

The owls were made of her own madra, a blend of shadow and dream aspects, so they could be difficult to detect. Though Lindon was alone in the bare basement of his guest house, he gave no sign of noticing the owl in the corner.

She checked on him every few days to ensure he was following her training program and that none of the Akura Underlords had beaten him too badly. So far, he had exceeded her expectations. Not only was he finishing her training courses faster than she'd planned, his actions demonstrated obvious determination. He rose early and worked late. Even while eating, he took notes.

The pen she had provided him looked tiny in his hands, and he hunched broad shoulders over the desk. Unkempt hair fell around his face, and he wrote at a feverish pace. He was a large young man, built like her father, and that appearance could be used as a weapon.

But he was not taking care of himself. His eyes had rings under them, ugly welts and fresh scars remained in spite of his Iron body, his hair was unwashed and his skin pale. Whenever he glanced up, his eyes were dull but determined, as though he'd pushed himself to stay up all night every night.

Sometime soon, she would have to force him to take a break. She wanted him pushed to the very limit he could handle, but no further, and she had seen too many gifted young sacred artists ruin their minds, bodies, or spirits by over-training.

She removed her consciousness from her owl and drew a book from the pocket of her outer robe. She made a quick note to find a task for Lindon that might help him relax.

When she looked up from her note, her father stood in front of her desk.

Akura Fury held up a hand in greeting. "Hey, Charity! Who are you watching?"

With his wild, shadowy hair, his bright red eyes, and his huge frame, Fury should have been a terrifying figure. Many of the family's enemies found him so.

But for those who knew him, his personality undercut all possibility of intimidation. He acted on his own whim, and it was almost impossible to get him to do anything he didn't enjoy.

He looked forward to fights most of all, so advancing to Herald had been one of the great regrets of his life. Now it was so hard to find a worthy opponent. Fury spent most of his time veiled and restricted, trying to wheedle Lords into duels.

Charity let her madra flow into an orb at the corner of her desk, and the owl's viewpoint was projected into the air. Now her father could see what she'd seen: Lindon in his basement, slamming his empty palm into a scripted tower the height of his chest.

The scripts on the tower lit up, but Lindon shook his head, frustrated. His Sylvan Riverseed, playing at his feet, ran over to pat him on the ankle.

"Oh, it's Mercy's friend. How is he?" His tone was only mildly interested, and Charity knew that if Fury wasn't intrigued, he might wander away at any second.

There would be little danger of that once he heard what she had to say. The trick would be keeping him interested without having him challenge Lindon to a duel.

"His most frightening aspect is comprehension speed," she said. "His mind-spirit should still be asleep, but he has completed all the training I prepared for the first six months."

Fury rubbed his hands together. "Really really really...How long has he been here?"

"Three weeks."

"Hmmm, I see, I see." A dangerous interest gleamed in Fury's red eyes.

"But his techniques are poorly developed," she added hastily. "I'm having him do self-guided technique training. With a little more effort—"

She looked to see how he was taking it, but he had already vanished. Seconds later, he showed up in her projection.

Lindon turned around, surprised by the sound of a casual "Hey!"

He had been prepared for the possibility of someone showing up out of nowhere as soon as Dross had pointed out the Sage's owl in the corner, but this wasn't Charity's voice.

Had one of the young Underlords come straight into his house? He hadn't sensed anything...

[Try not to panic, but you are now sharing a sealed basement with a man who could destroy this whole city. I recommend deep breaths.]

Lindon fell to his knees when he saw the intruder: tall, robes open to bare a muscular chest, red eyes, shadowy hair, broad grin that reminded him of Mercy.

The Herald, Akura Fury.

He and Dross had done a bit of research in the few weeks since arriving at Moongrave. Fury was Malice's child from before she was a Monarch, and he was the Sage Charity's father. He was the only direct descendant of Malice to have ever made it to Herald, and was Malice's favored child.

He was known for waging war singlehandedly. His techniques toppled cities and blighted forests. He had killed a dragon Herald, the Eight-Man Empire had a bounty on his head, and some cultures included him in their mythology as an omen of war. He was Malice's sharp sword, a legendary one-man force of devastation.

Fury dropped down into a squat and twisted his head almost upside-down so he could look Lindon in the eyes. "It's going to be hard to talk like this."

Lindon rose to his feet, staring into the wall, but Fury bobbed and weaved so that his face was always in front of Lindon's. Finally, Lindon gave in and met his eyes.

"Saw you were practicing a palm strike. It just so happens that I...who's this? Hey there!"

To Lindon's horror, Little Blue had scurried up to the Herald's feet, staring up at him from the ground. Lindon darted forward to grab her, but Fury had already squatted down again.

He gave a broad, open smile, holding one hand out to Little Blue.

With a cheery ring, Little Blue reached up to grab Fury's fingers, hauling herself up onto his palm. She immediately ran up his arm to his shoulder, staring at his face from an inch away.

Lindon was afraid to move. This looked friendly enough, but he was terrified that the Herald would grow suddenly offended and crush the Riverseed from existence.

"What's your name?" Fury asked gently, and Little Blue gave a series of chimes in response.

"That does make sense. Are you having fun here? No problems? ...yeah, training can be lonely. You'll be back with your friends before you know it. Speaking of friends..." He turned to look at Lindon, and so did Little Blue. "What do you think of him?"

Lindon had never before been so worried about Little Blue's opinion.

She made a long, complicated whistle. It carried more meaning than Lindon could untangle.

Fury's drifting, shadowy hair rose to a point. "*Really?* Well, I look forward to that day."

Little Blue squeaked and hopped off his shoulder, sliding down his robes like a child down a hill. Then she scurried back over to her toys: a pile of miniature junk that Lindon had arranged for her to play with.

Lindon tried to smile. "Apologies. I'm sure she intended no disrespect."

Fury gave a blank look, as though he didn't understand what Lindon meant. "Oh, okay. Anyway, she seems to think that you'll pose a threat to me one day soon."

Lindon felt as though every pore in his body had started to squeeze out sweat. "She didn't mean it! Certainly, I wouldn't oppose the Akura clan. Did she really say that?"

"You should give yourself more credit. Sylvans with a state of existence this complete are good judges of character. And I hear the leader of the gold dragon team is out for your blood."

Lindon winced—he could imagine why the gold dragons might be after them. But Fury beamed at him.

"If you can't threaten me in a few years, I'll be disappointed!" He gave a broad, hearty laugh as though he expected Lindon to share it.

Lindon forced a few chuckles.

Fury ran a finger under his eye as though to wipe a tear away. "Ahhh, that's enough business." He clapped his hands together. "Charity says she has you doing focused technique training. Let me see that palm strike again."

Again? So it hadn't been just a Sage watching Lindon train, but a Sage *and* a Herald?

He pictured an entire room full of people crowding around to watch him lose fights and practice his self-taught techniques, and he suddenly felt very self-conscious.

[Don't worry about that,] Dross said. [You already have me watching you all the time. What's a few more?]

Feeling Fury's eyes on him, Lindon hesitantly stepped up to the post that Charity had delivered to him.

The script on the center was three concentric rings. He was trying to control the output of the Empty Palm so that he could light up either all three or just the one in the center. The ultimate goal was to improve the effect of the Empty Palm so that he could use it for more than just disabling the enemy's core.

Lindon drove the Empty Palm into the script, trying to spread his madra out as much as possible. Two rings lit up.

He shook his head and prepared to try again, aware of Fury's attention on him, but a hand on his shoulder stopped him.

"Okay, that's enough." The Herald pulled him away from the pole. Fury put his chin in one hand, thinking, as his black hair drifted away behind him. Finally, he snapped his fingers. "Seems to me you've got a few options. You could go with a standard Enforcer attack technique, like this."

Lindon felt the madra moving in the Herald's body, sure that the man had exaggerated the spiritual movement for illustration. Fury gently slapped the pole, there was a surge of black madra, and all three rings lit purple.

"If you keep developing it in this direction, you could make it so that a direct hit on their core blocked out their powers for a little while, or even crippled them for life. A hit anywhere else could deal some real damage to their madra channels, which is about the same thing."

He took a few steps away from the pole, then slowly drew his hand back, pulling madra into it with the motion. His spiritual movements were overstated again.

When he thrust the hand forward, a black lance of madra speared through the circle from five feet away. All three circles lit up.

"You are projecting madra, so you could develop it into a Striker technique. It's a little slower and weaker, and you'd be giving up the ability to lock down their entire spirit for a while, but you could still disrupt their madra channels. In most fights, that will be just as good."

Fury laced his fingers together and cracked his knuckles, walking past the post. "Or you can try for the best of both worlds. It'll take a little more work, but I like the flexibility."

He cycled his madra obviously once again, this time in a more complicated pattern. He was facing the metal-plated wall, in between the bands of script that ran along the ceiling and the floor.

When his hand crackled with black madra, he gently pushed it against the wall. A palm strike at one-thousandth the speed.

When it touched the wall, a dozen black hands, Forged from madra, struck at the same time. The room thundered as though he'd cracked the wall in two.

Every hand left a ragged handprint blasted into the metal.

Lindon stared in awe. It was as though he'd struck with thirteen palm strikes at once.

Fury turned, grinning and shaking out his hand. "This is the Crushing Black Palm. It's a Forger echo technique and an Enforcer attack technique all together. Not that you need to do exactly what I did, but you should be able to learn something from it, yeah?"

Lindon was staring at the wall, his mind churning. *Dross, did you get that?*

[I mean, I *remember* it, but I don't know if I can help *you* do it. He's using shadow madra, and he's just...you know, a lot better at this than you are.]

Dross ran him through a quick simulation in his mind. Lindon moved slowly on the outside, cycling his madra, trying to create the feeling that the Herald had just produced.

The first models that Dross fashioned didn't work well. It was a hard feeling to grasp; Fury had been using shadow madra, and Lindon was trying to make use of the same principles with an entirely different aspect. Not to mention that he'd never tried Forging something so quick and rough. It was more like a Striker technique than like Forging a scale.

He ran through the motions, both spiritually and physically, at reduced speed as Dross worked to process new possibilities and present them to him.

After a few false starts, Lindon made an attempt. It was like localizing the Soul Cloak just to his arm while executing the Empty Palm as he always had, and at the same time projecting a second copy of the technique off to the side. It took all of his concentration, aided by Dross, and it still felt as though he'd cobbled the technique together.

When he struck the post, he lit up all three rings of script. And there was a blue-white blur in the air above and to the right.

"Wrong," he muttered.

[On the right track, though!] Dross encouraged him. [Who knows? By the time the tournament starts, you might be able to slap all the spectators at once.]

Lindon snapped out of his concentrated trance to find Fury

looming behind him, red eyes blazing, shadowy hair writhing in excitement. He wore a crazed Eithan-like grin.

"Now *that* is what I like to see," the Herald said. "Let me run you through a few more possibilities."

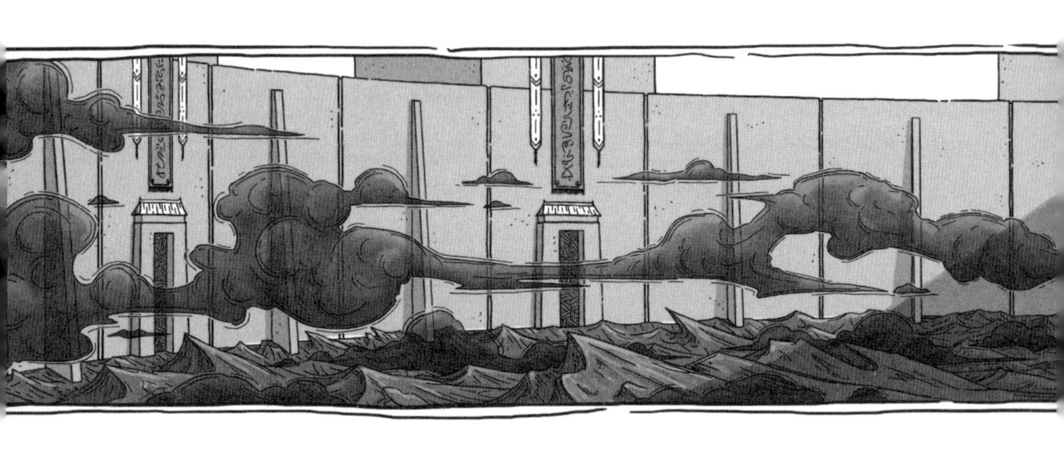

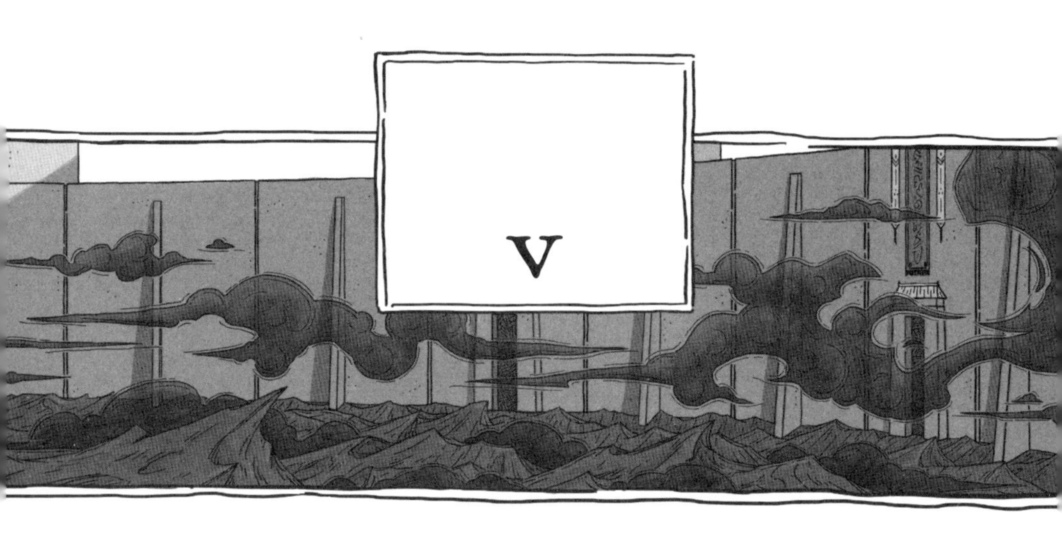


LINDON SLID ON HIS BACK ACROSS THE SMOOTH FLOOR OF HIS BASE-ment. As he came to a stop, he spat out a mouthful of blood from a gash in his lip.

A short girl with long pigtails and a massive hammer stood over him. She snorted as she turned away, saying something he couldn't hear over the ringing in his ears. No doubt it was cutting.

*That's her third time, isn't it?* Lindon asked silently. These conversations with Dross gave him something to focus on besides how much he wanted to stop taking beatings.

[My model of her was at about ninety percent before, but now it's a nice and clean one hundred. If you had asked me for a combat report, you would have toyed with her. Why *didn't* you do that?]

Lindon dabbed the flesh around his eye, now tender and swollen. *I almost had her on my own.*

This time, he had gotten close with the Burning Cloak and landed a solid hit with his right hand. He could have activated the hunger binding in his arm and drained her madra or unleashed dragon's breath that would have torn her apart.

But he was trying to beat her using his pure madra alone. With only two combat techniques, it was a rough trail to walk.

Lindon rose unsteadily to his feet as the Bloodforged Iron body drew on his madra, but he stopped as he realized the girl with the hammer hadn't left. She stood with her arms crossed as her friend took over.

When they came to beat him, they almost never came alone.

A tall, lanky Underlord had been shifting from foot to foot in the corner, waiting for the first fight to be over. Now that it was his turn, he stepped forward eagerly, conjured lightning around his fists.

The observation construct intended to witness the fight drifted in the air around them, and Charity's silver-and-purple owl lurked in the corner.

"Wei Shi Lindon Arelius, I challenge you," the young man said.

Lindon wanted to give up.

But this was the path he'd chosen.

"I accept," Lindon said, though his voice wavered.

That was all the Akura Underlord needed before he cast a dome of crackling lightning over them both. A Ruler boundary field.

Lindon had fought him twice already. The boundary field was weak, only enough to give Lindon the occasional twitch or twinge of pain, but his opponent used it as a distraction to keep Lindon from concentrating on any larger techniques. In the meanwhile, he whittled Lindon down with thin whips of lightning.

Not every Akura clan member followed a shadow Path. He had learned that lesson early on. It was better for his training this way, because no doubt he would face opponents of all different aspects in the Uncrowned King tournament, but that meant the torments were new with each defeat.

This time, Lindon *really* didn't want to lose again.

He'd practiced against this young man's model a dozen times. With full use of his abilities, Lindon could win easily. It was all about keeping the fight short. With only his pure madra...

Lindon kindled the Soul Cloak as a lightning whip came flashing at him. He dodged, closing the gap, ignoring the sting of the boundary field.

The Akura triggered a binding in his bracer, and a pulse of force madra flooded out, pushing Lindon away.

But Lindon had already been reaching for it. As soon as the construct was activated, Lindon's right arm was ready. He drained the madra as it came out, so it didn't even slow him down.

The force madra rushed through his Remnant arm in gray veins, but he grabbed it and cycled it through his hunger binding. He had to use it up or vent it, or it would pollute his arm or his own madra.

His control over force madra was lacking, but it was enough for a very simple attack technique. Lindon's punch to the Akura's chest flashed gray as it struck, smashing the enemy backward.

He flew into the wall, cracking his head against the metal plates, and Lindon dashed after him. He gathered madra into his Empty Palm, and the young man looked up with fear in his purple eyes.

Lindon hesitated.

His instinct, born from the last two years of bloody competition, told him to finish off the enemy immediately. If Lindon hit the Akura too hard, he might kill him.

It was only a moment of indecision, but it was enough. The lanky young man reached out to the boundary field, gathering it into one larger bolt of lightning.

It struck in a flash of light, and Lindon passed out again.

He woke up on the floor, aching and groaning, with Little Blue injecting soothing madra into him. She patted his forehead.

He glanced up to find that his visitors still hadn't left. Instead, another Underlord had joined them.

Akura Pride, short and glaring, folded his arms and glared down at Lindon. He stood apart from the other members of his family, and from the looks they shot Pride, Lindon gathered that Mercy's brother still wasn't the most popular.

"Give up," Pride said abruptly.

Lindon pushed himself to his knees. When he straightened his back, he could look Pride in the eyes. "They were just giving me some pointers on my techniques. Nothing to be upset about."

The girl with the pigtails snorted.

"Go home," Pride continued. "Leave my sister alone. Give up on the tournament. You won't even make it past the first round."

Lindon was sick of kneeling before Mercy's brother. He rose to his feet, where he towered over Pride.

"That's why I'm grateful to your cousins for their help in my training." Lindon smiled, tasting the blood on his teeth.

He had trained against Dross' model of Pride many times.

Though Dross couldn't swear to its accuracy, Lindon only won three out of every ten simulated matches. Even with his full power.

In a real fight, he'd have to cheat.

Pride stepped so close that his chin almost touched Lindon's chest. He stared up, eyes full of rage. "Uncle Fury's selection is in ten days. I want you to be there. And when I win, I will challenge you in front of everyone. I will beat you into the ground every day until you give up or you can't fight anymore."

"...apologies, but at some point I would just decline the duel," Lindon said.

"Even better. Someone who will not face a fight against a strong opponent is unfit for the tournament."

Lindon shrugged. "That's up to the Sage, isn't it?"

Pride glared at him for a moment longer, then took a step back. "Wei Shi Lindon Arelius, I challenge you."

It had only been a minute since he had fought the boy with the lightning Path. And a few moments before that, he'd been beaten by the girl with the huge hammer. Despite his Iron body's work, he was bruised and battered all over. He throbbed with pain just standing there.

Nonetheless, Lindon clenched his jaw and said, "I accept."

It ended no better than the last time.

He used his full set of abilities, but he was hardly in his best condition. Pride and the others left him conscious but reeling, staring up at the ceiling.

[My Pride model has been significantly improved,] Dross said. [Believe it or not, you pulled out more of his skills during this shameful beating than the last one.]

Lindon pulled himself up. He could barely stand.

"Show me," he said.

In preparing for the tournament, Charity didn't have enough time in the day. There were always more people who needed her commands, enemies who needed her deterrence, projects that needed her personal supervision.

As an Archlady, she needed very little sleep. Most nights, she could go without. But she tried to keep a regular pattern of rest anyway. A rested mind, she'd found, was a sharp mind.

Before bed, she checked in on Lindon. She had yet to find him resting.

Only a few days after her father had given him some pointers, she took another look at him. He sat diligently cycling, but even through her owl, she could see that he was out of balance.

His eyes were half-open and blank, his hair was matted and unwashed, his clothes were rumpled and stained with blood, and he hadn't shaved in days. His Sylvan Riverseed lay curled up in his lap, sleeping, and he looked as though he would pitch over at any second.

She had intended to let him go a few more days before intervening, but everyone had a limit. This was his.

Charity glanced down at herself. She perched on the edge of her bed, hair undone, wearing only a thin single-layer robe. She wasn't suitable for greeting a stranger. So instead of ripping open a human-sized tear in space, she made one about the size of her hand.

And she slid a construct through. It looked like a dream tablet made from a purple gemstone, but it was instead a rare and valuable transmission construct. She doubted he would recognize how valuable.

The instant the small portal appeared, Lindon's eyes snapped open, and he reached out his pale right hand and caught the falling construct.

Charity spoke through the spatial connection before it closed. "A mind needs more than training to keep it active. Do not wear yourself out before the tournament begins. That construct will be active for one hour after sunset every other day. Do not waste the time. Instructions are contained within."

She let the portal close, but continued watching through one of her hidden owls.

At first, Lindon examined the gem suspiciously. He swept his spiritual sense through it, examined it from several angles, and then finally activated it. She could see on his face when he realized that it was a transmission construct, because his suspicion deepened.

She smiled.

A moment later, Yerin Arelius' voice came through, speaking loudly through the stone in Lindon's hand. "...who is this? Am I supposed to talk into this? Is it going to carry a message, or what?"

The change in Lindon was like the sun coming out from behind the clouds. He looked like he'd gained a full night's sleep in an instant, and he began speaking eagerly into the construct at once.

Charity let her owl dissipate, cutting off the vision, and settled in to sleep.

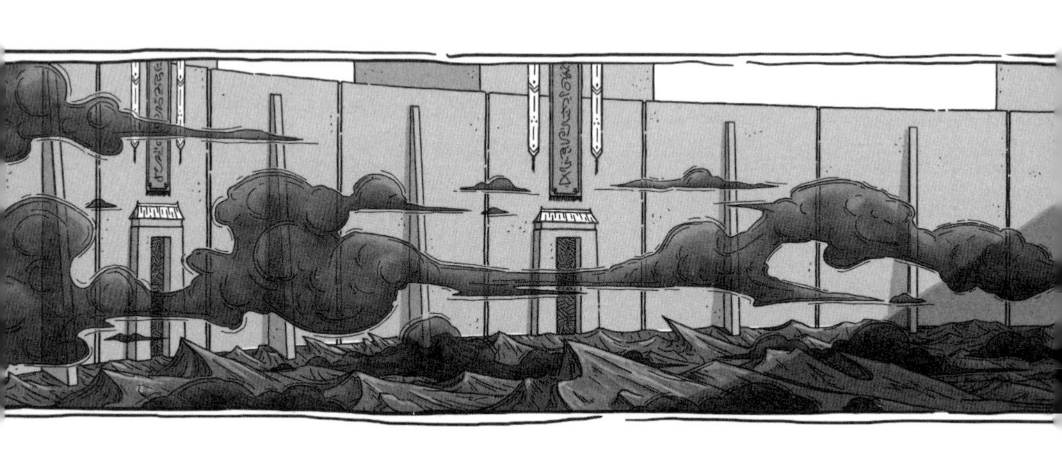

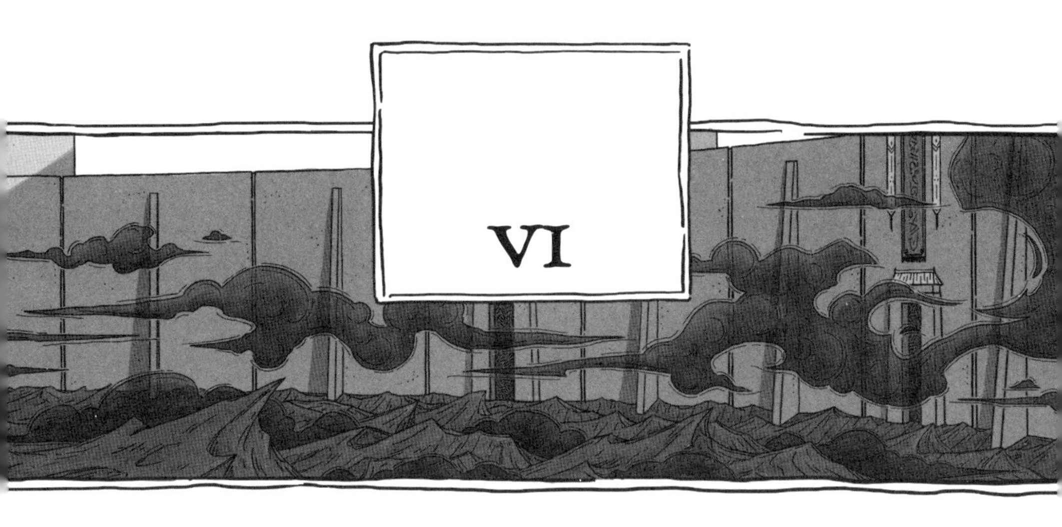

# VI

Lindon sat on the roof of his house in Moongrave, watching the skies as he spoke with Yerin. Lines of cloudships followed each other in even lanes, passing over dark towers and black-leafed trees, and Yerin's voice came from the jewel-construct sitting on the tiles next to him.

"...and I can beat Saeya so long as she keeps that sword locked away. If I had a weapon with a binding I could use, you can bet I'd be whipping her like a stubborn mule."

The shadow aura hung so thick in the air that it tinged all the stars with a slight purple haze. He settled onto his back as he responded.

"Forgiveness, but I'm glad you don't. I might have to fight you."

A short laugh came from Yerin's side of the construct. "I'd need *something* to knock you off track. Don't have any surprises you haven't seen."

"I'm the one who needs a surprise." Lindon's early attempts to fight a model of Yerin made by Dross had not gone well. When she didn't respond, he continued. "I've actually been working on something that might catch you off-guard, but I can't tell you too much." That should have caught her curiosity, but she still didn't respond. "Yerin?"

He glanced at the horizon. Darkness had completely swallowed the sun, leaving the stars, the buildings in the city, and the vehicles passing overhead as the only lights.

Dross made a sound like he was clearing his throat. [Well, *I've* been working on something. I'm just using your brain.]

Lindon ignored him, sitting up and cradling the transmission construct. Sure enough, only a glimmer of light remained in its depths. It was deactivating on the time limit the Sage had left.

He let pure madra flood into the construct, along with a wisp of gray soulfire. He had learned early on that providing it with more madra would boost its performance for a short time.

Indistinctly, Yerin's voice drifted through the air. "... there? Lindon?"

Lindon brought the construct close to his mouth. "We're out of time. I'll talk to you the day after tomorrow." The weight of that time settled on him. *Two days* before he could have a break like this again. He added, "I wish you were here."

The construct went dark.

Lindon tucked the jewel of Forged madra away, laying back down against the tile. Two phoenixes of violet flame circled each other in the sky, and he watched them as they ducked into clouds and reemerged.

Part of him wished Charity hadn't given him the construct. Being able to talk to Yerin five times in the last week had made the time between unbearable. He'd never realized how short an hour was.

[You know,] Dross said, [I can't tell if these talks make you feel better or if they highlight just how alone you really are. Anyway, I'm sure the best thing to do is not think about it. Just stuff those feelings *way* down deep where they can never hurt anybody.]

The phoenixes vanished, and Lindon realized he was lying on his own roof for no reason. He stood, stretching his arms. "I'm going to sleep early. You should, too. We have a big day tomorrow."

[We're still going with your plan, then? Oh, good. Good. I was worried you had changed your mind to something reasonable. No, don't worry. Just go to sleep and dream of success. Maybe that will help somehow.]

The next day, Charity sat next to Fury in a viewing tower overlooking one of their fighting stages.

"I know this is to choose your representative," Charity said, "but I didn't think you'd show up."

Sixteen young Underlords—the last remaining candidates for the main Akura team—were lined up on the arena beneath them. Several dozen possibilities had already been eliminated, whittled down to this elite group.

An Overlord barked instructions at them—he was Fury's great-grandson, Charity's grand-nephew. The Underlords bowed to him and then to the tower where the Sage and the Herald waited.

The stage itself was a polished black square a hundred yards to a side, and the Akura family emblem glowed at the center. One large star and two small stars, all over three mountains. The stars and the mountains glowed purple.

The star on the left represented Charity. Fury was the star on the right, and Malice the largest star in the center. The one that rose over them all.

He tilted his head back, swallowing a bowl of soup bigger than his head. When he finished, he let out a long, satisfied breath, then picked up a loaf of bread. "Intuition," he said between bites. "I feel like something interesting is going to happen."

Two Underladies stepped up, saluting one another. One of them, Akura Grace, had a real shot at winning. She looked more like Malice than most of the Akura descendants, full-figured and beautiful, with long raven hair. While she had failed to bond with any of the Books of Seven Pages, she had developed considerable mastery of her sword and shadow Path and carried a long, curved saber on her back.

Grace's opponent was sadly unremarkable. She had made it this far by sheer luck.

At the end of the fight, the two bowed to one another, Grace unharmed and her challenger bleeding from the arm. There had been no tension there.

"And here comes something interesting now." Fury tossed the uneaten half of his bread over his shoulder.

At first, Charity assumed he was talking about Grace's match, and she wondered if her father was feeling all right. Then she paid more attention to her spiritual sense.

Another young Underlord had removed his veil and walked toward the stage. He was tall and strapping, with a stern expression and a build that reminded her of Fury. He wore the black-and-white robes that the Akura family used for many of their disciples, with a glittering halfsilver hammer badge hanging from a ribbon around his neck.

When he stepped onto the stage, he pressed the fist of his white Remnant arm against his human left, bowing toward their viewing tower.

The Overlord demanded to know what he was doing there, but Charity sent a quick pulse of her madra, signaling him to stop. Pride and several of the others shouted angrily for him to stop, and a few other young Underlords began to climb onto the stage, ready to attack him.

Lindon straightened from his bow, ignoring the others and looking up at Fury and Charity. "Pardon the interruption," he said, his voice echoing throughout the arena. "Since the winner here is going to be my teammate, I thought I would check their abilities for myself. One last time."

Audacious of him to try something like this. He was leaning too hard on Charity's favor. She was inclined to remind him of his disrespect...but only if she had been supervising this contest alone.

She knew what her father was going to say.

"Granted!" Fury shouted happily. "The winner fights Lindon!"

"Apologies, but I had something else in mind." For the first time, he turned to look at his peers around him.

Charity detected disdain in him, along with more confidence than she had ever seen in him before. Suddenly, even she was intrigued.

"I challenge every Underlord here."

They all reacted. Some shouted out of wounded pride, some prepared techniques, others laughed or called insults.

Fury turned to Charity eagerly, his red eyes flashing with excitement. "Where's Mercy?"

"The sixth island."

"She'll want to see this." He rose from his chair and started cycling his madra, but she stopped him.

"I'll get her." Fury would fly over there faster than sound, snatch up Mercy, and leap away with no warning. Charity's way was faster. With a moment of concentration, she stretched her spiritual awareness all the way out to the sixth of the thirteen Phantom Islands.

Mercy was tempering her concentration, pulling her four techniques from the Book of Eternal Night while nightmare beasts assaulted her mind. Charity seized her in the middle of her trial, pulling her through a fold in the Way.

Teleporting so quickly and precisely was the limit of Charity's ability, and she had always been skilled with spatial transport. Mercy tumbled onto the platform, her training outfit muddied and gray, her hair tangled and messy. She shoved herself up using Eclipse as support, and the sacred bow hissed.

Mercy looked around in a panic, disoriented. "Ah! What? Where am I? What? ...what?"

Charity used one pulse of her madra to soothe Mercy's thoughts, and another to command the Underlords below not to form into an angry mob and beat Lindon to death. "Your friend has just done something interesting. We thought you might want to watch."

Mercy perked up. She leaned her weapon up against the wall and peered over the edge of the platform at the other Underlords below.

"What did he do? Wow, Pride does not look happy." She pulled her hair back into a rough tail, tying it in place with a string of Forged madra.

"He challenged everyone to a duel," Fury said, moving up to stand next to her. "I was just about to let it happen."

By their relative ages, Fury should have been Mercy's ancestor many generations removed. Instead, they were half-siblings separated by centuries.

Such was the reality of life in a Monarch's family.

Mercy waved down to Lindon, who looked surprised to see her. "Does he know how strong they are?"

"Everyone down there has fought him at least once," Charity responded. "Most of them multiple times. They did not enjoy seeing him placed above them, so they took out their frustrations on him."

Without looking, Mercy extended a String of Shadow and pulled up a chair. "As long as he knows what he's getting into, then we're about to see a show."

Fury slapped the railing in excitement. His red eyes gleamed, and his voice boomed out over the field. "First fight: Akura Shiria! Wei Shi Lindon! Let's see it!"

The others cleared off the stage, leaving Lindon and the girl with the hammer and pigtails. Shiria was a distant enough descendant that she had a normal name, and her force Path had been selected for her by her outsider father. But she still had the black hair and purple eyes.

Lindon had fought her five times in total, losing every time.

In his head, he'd trained against her two hundred and sixteen times.

As soon as the stage cleared, she loosened her hammer from its strap on her back, cycling force madra. Her Goldsign, a silver ring around her neck, began to hum. A pair of golden anklets started to activate, drawing a movement technique to her feet.

She couldn't use the Akura bloodline armor, but she hit hard and was surprisingly adaptable.

"Begin," called the Overlord in charge of the stage.

Lindon slammed an Empty Palm into the air on his left. Rather than many echoes, like Akura Fury had created, he Forged one huge echo at the moment of impact and superimposed it over an Enforced palm strike.

As a result, when Akura Shiria finished her movement technique and appeared suddenly to Lindon's left, an Empty Palm the size of her entire torso caught her in the chest. The blue-white hand that struck her was ten times bigger than Lindon's and disappeared immediately.

Pure madra rushed through her core and her entire madra system, sending her spirit into chaos. The construct in her boots failed, her Goldsign dimmed, and her cycling jammed to a sudden halt.

The physical strike hit her with full force, driving all the air from her lungs, and her eyes bugged out. Without her spirit Enforcing her body, she lost her grip on the hammer, which tumbled from her limp hands.

She fell to her knees, wheezing for a breath.

"You favor attacking from the left side," Lindon said, "and your movements are too wide when you use your boots." She also tended to cycle her madra too far in advance of her attack, so it was simple to follow her with his spiritual perception.

"Victory: Wei Shi Lindon Arelius." The Overlord glanced up at the viewing tower.

Akura Fury nodded and stroked his chin, and Charity looked as impassive as ever. Mercy cheered.

"Second fight," Fury called. "Akura Courage."

Courage, it turned out, was the young Underlord with the six flying swords and the Striker techniques. He strode up full of confidence, fanning his swords out behind him.

Lindon had only fought him once and hadn't caught his name. He might have other secrets up his sleeve, because Dross' model of him was not as precise as some of the others.

But Lindon had trained against it ninety-one times.

His eyes burned black.

"Begin," the Overseer called, and Lindon fired a finger-thin bar of dragon's breath over his opponent's shoulder. It burned a line across the top of his outer robe, and smoke drifted up from singed cloth. His flying swords still hadn't reached Lindon yet.

The blades froze in midair. Courage's purple eyes had gone wide with shock. Clearly, Lindon could have put that Striker technique through his throat.

"You're too slow to start up," Lindon said simply.

"Victory to Lindon." The Overlord sounded angry this time, so Lindon wondered if Courage was a close relative.

Fury stood and laughed again, preparing to call out the next match when Lindon interrupted.

Dross heaved a deep breath. [And now the foolishness begins.]

"Forgiveness, honored Herald," Lindon said, "but I had a different plan in mind."

He looked to the remaining Underlords, more than half of whom looked angry enough to storm the stage at any second. The Path of Black Flame continued burning through his spirit.

"I challenged *all* the Underlords here," Lindon said.

Of the remaining fourteen Akura Underlords, twelve of them looked instantly to Akura Fury, waiting for his permission. Only two continued watching Lindon: Pride and his distant cousin, Grace. Pride looked ready to commit murder, but Grace watched him with distant confusion in her purple eyes, as though she were trying to figure out his angle of approach.

Fury's wild laughter preceded the words, "Go wild, kids!"

Twelve people leaped onto the stage, and Lindon sharpened his attention as Dross slowed the world down.

Seven young men and five women in Akura colors sprinted for him, drawing weapons and kindling techniques. Sword madra flashed in a silver wave, Forged needles of venom flicked for his neck, and a spear sailed through the air.

Thanks to Dross, Lindon had time to consider his response.

Dragon's breath seared into a girl's leg as Lindon snatched the spear out of the air with the explosive movement of the Burning

Cloak then hurled it back. Dross projected their movements onto his sight, like ghostly outlines of the future. Lindon fell in line with the projections as though following a dance he had long memorized.

He ducked a fan of sword madra while rolling to avoid a spray of poisoned needles and drilling a finger-thin bar of dragon's flame through a boy's shield. As he'd hoped, Charity or Fury called out whenever they considered someone eliminated, so he didn't have to hurt anyone too badly.

As they grew closer, he poured soulfire into the Burning Cloak. It propelled his every movement with such force that it became hard to control, each step a leap and each punch launched like a cannon-shot. Without weeks of practice, he would have tumbled straight out of the arena's bounds.

By the time they reached him with their weapons, there were seven remaining.

So quickly that it sent pain lancing through his spirit, Lindon emptied himself of Blackflame madra and switched to the Path of Twin Stars.

That transition was the most dangerous time, and in his predictions, this was where he failed most often. Without Dross' calculations, he would have been ground into paste between a Forged fist, a body covered in the amethyst Akura bloodline armor, and a blast of forcc madra.

In the fraction of a second when the Burning Cloak dropped and the Spirit Cloak rose up around him, he slipped each attack by a hair's breadth.

When the pure madra Enforcer technique filled him, the fight ended.

He broke two legs and three arms, cracked a set of ribs, and drove an Empty Palm into an armored chest. A glowing blue-white handprint five times bigger than his own struck at the same time, quickly Forged out of his Twin Stars madra and shoved into his opponent's spirit.

Her spirit trembled, the armor shrank away, and she collapsed to her knees. Lindon stood, breathing heavily and focusing on his spirit to keep his madra under control. He was the only one standing.

Fury now sat on the railing at the edge of his viewing platform, legs dangling, leaning forward so that it looked like he could fall off at any second. But the tower was only about thirty feet tall; a fall from that height would threaten him no more than a stiff breeze.

Charity still showed no expression, but Mercy saw Lindon looking and clapped her black-gloved hands together eagerly.

Lindon never had to use more than three techniques against any single opponent. His madra channels were a little strained, having to use so many techniques in a row with no breaks, but he had plenty of power left. He had taken one shallow cut, a few impacts that would bruise if not for his Bloodforged Iron body, and a spiritual attack to his core that he had drowned with pure madra.

Nothing worth complaining about after an overwhelming victory.

[Don't let me interrupt you with *reality,* but we're not done.]

Dross was right. There were two rivals left.

"Next opponent," the Overlord said wearily, "Akura Grace."

Most of the young Akura Underlords would be considered attractive; they were physically trained and had delicate features, with the resources of the Akura family to take care of them. Even their battle clothes were finely made, and they all had bodies remade in soulfire.

Akura Grace was on another level. Her every movement was beautiful, her skin smooth, her long hair thick and dark. As she walked onto the stage, she met his eyes with a clear gaze, carrying a lightly curved saber in both hands. She drew the weapon in one elegant motion and set the sheath aside.

Lindon had fought her only once. She had challenged him and won without injuring him. He got the impression that she was really evaluating him, not taking out a grudge on him as the others had, and she had gone away disappointed.

Now she looked interested again, like her ancestor, Fury. She readied her sword.

She had no other constructs on her besides the blade, her sacred instrument, though of course she could have something stored in her soulspace or a void key. But he suspected she wouldn't. Like him, she was pushing to train herself, not to seek a lonely victory.

[My model for her doesn't have a lot of testing,] Dross said. [Should we think about this a minute? That's a good idea, let's think about it.]

"Begin!" the Overlord called.

Grace's sword was already at his neck.

Lindon had back-stepped immediately, expecting the rush. She used a full-body Enforcer technique that shrouded her in shadow, and she moved with a grace that proved her worthy of her name. Her advantage in this fight was her weapon. Lindon had completed some basic Iron-level weapons-training courses provided by Charity, but he'd never found a weapon that he felt suited him.

Though that was a problem now. She channeled an Enforcer technique into her weapon, and a shadowy black edge expanded its length and width a few inches. It moved faster now, a dark blur, and its movements were harder to track.

Lindon used the Soul Cloak. With the control it gave him over his movements, his Underlord body, and Dross' enhancement of his mind, he danced out of the way. She grew faster and faster, but he stayed inches away, even when she began to mix Striker techniques into her attack patterns. Sharp black crescents of madra flashed out at him, slicing the air, but he evaded them all.

Finally, she grew frustrated, stopping her sword for a moment to pour soulfire in it. Colorless flame flickered up and down the blade's length in an instant, and the pressure coming off of the weapon doubled.

But it provided the opening Lindon had been waiting for.

As soon as she stopped, Lindon gathered a gray flame of his own from the quiet bonfire burning in his spirit. He funneled it into a twist of spirit behind his cores, a binding in the making. The location of his Soul Cloak technique.

The smooth blue-white aura around him turned almost tangible, like a waterfall flowing in reverse up his body.

Before she swung, Grace realized what he'd done. She poured soulfire into her own full-body Enforcer technique, but it was too late.

In one motion, he closed the gap between them and jabbed two fingers into her wrist along with a pulse of pure madra. It disrupted her strength, loosening her grip, and he took the weapon from her.

But he didn't turn it to point the blade at her. He released the Soul Cloak, holding her sword out to her hilt-first.

Her purple eyes were wide with astonishment, her lips slightly parted. She took the weapon back absently.

"Lindon's victory." The Overlord sighed. He was almost inaudible over Mercy cheering and Fury clapping.

Grace scooped up her sheath, slipping the weapon inside. Then she turned back to him and pressed both fists together.

"Thank you for the match," she said quietly.

Lindon returned the salute.

Then Pride strode onto the stage. Shadow madra pulsed around him, and Lindon could make out a phantom image in the air behind him: a red book made of madra, its cover sealed with silver chains.

Rather than announcing the sixteenth fight, Fury remained quiet. Pride glowered at Lindon, his spirit unrestrained.

In a way, Lindon was more confident against Pride than against Grace. He had fought Pride twice and seen more of his Path both times. Dross was confident that his model of the young man was at least eighty percent accurate.

But of the four hundred and fifteen simulated matches Lindon had held against Pride, Lindon had won only two hundred.

Pride used exclusively Enforcer techniques. If he managed to move in close, he won. Lindon won only when he kept his distance and peppered Pride with dragon's breath.

They stood facing each other in silence as the defeated Akura members stared at them.

Pride drew himself up to his full height, his eyes moving to the viewing arena. His madra spun quickly, and Lindon started cycling for the Burning Cloak.

"Enough." Charity's quiet voice swallowed up all else.

Akura Fury looked to her in childish disappointment, but both Pride and Lindon drew up short.

"Wei Shi Lindon Arelius, step back," she continued. "Your point is made. Let all see that I have made my selection, and it is final."

Pride bowed, and then turned away, his every step heavy with obvious frustration.

Lindon looked up to the tower, uncertain. He had expected to fight Pride last of all, so this sudden change wrong-footed him.

Charity stood up, surveying them all. "I suppose now we should have the actual selection tournament."

"Eh, I'm going to pick Grace or Pride," Fury said. He hopped down from the thirty-foot tower, landing easily on the ground below, and then began to walk away. "Fight it out between the two of you. Best two of three matches, return to good condition in between each match, Charity's the judge."

His figure blurred as he shot away.

[What an abrupt man,] Dross said.

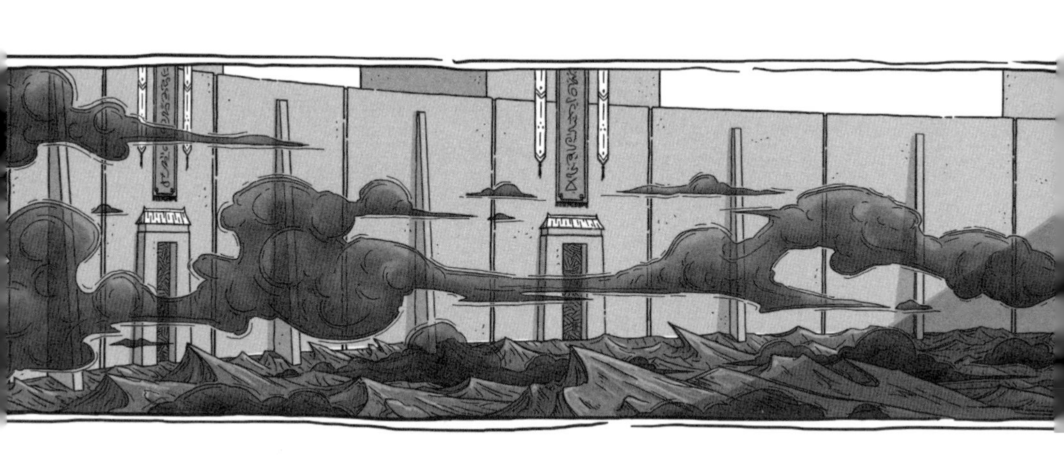

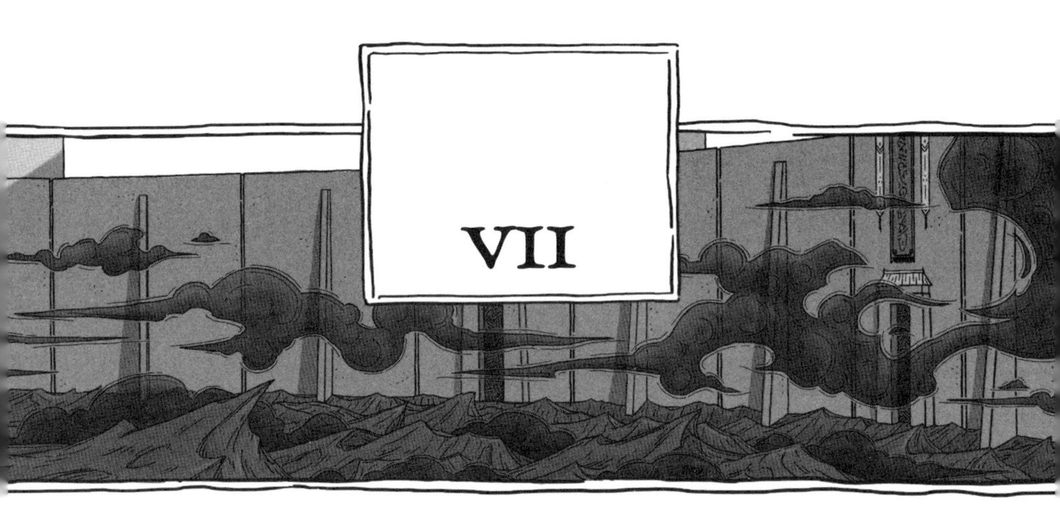

# VII

Lindon hadn’t seen Mercy much since arriving in Moongrave, but after the Akura clan acknowledged him as a qualified participant in the Uncrowned tournament, the situation changed. Now Charity required him to appear in public with members of the Monarch’s family to reinforce his new status. Since Charity and Fury were far too busy, that meant Mercy or Pride.

He had immediately chosen Mercy.

Delighted, she had taken the opportunity to bring him to a show. They now sat side-by-side in a theater box reserved for the Akura head family, looking down on the rest of the audience and on a broad stage. Onstage, sacred artists performed what they called ‘drake-dancing’; they rode serpentine lesser dragons through the air in complex acrobatics, narrowly dodging each other and a barrage of dangerous techniques.

The spectacle focused on the stunts, but the story engaged Lindon the most. The rider on the black drake was a fallen prince trying to regain his kingdom, but every step he took brought him further away from his true love.

An hour in, the director called an intermission, and the drakes landed. They carried their riders backstage to the sound of applause, and the audience's murmurs rose to a dull roar.

Lindon immediately began cycling the Heaven and Earth Purification Wheel.

Mercy cried out when she saw his eyes shut, and she clapped her hands in front of his face, startling him out of the cycling trance. "You really don't take any breaks, do you?" Her purple eyes shone with amusement.

"Apologies, but I don't have time for breaks." The truth was, he was embarrassed at how easily he had been swallowed up by the show. For a few minutes, he had almost forgotten to improve himself.

Mercy turned her body in her seat, folding black-gloved hands on the arm of her chair. "I've *never* seen you voluntarily take a break. Even in the Skysworn, you were cycling or practicing until you collapsed. Do you not have any hobbies?"

Lindon thought of training as his hobby, but he searched for a more appropriate answer. "I used to work in a library."

From Mercy's face, that was clearly not what she wanted to hear. "What do you *like* doing?"

That felt like the wrong question, but it took him a moment to find the words to explain why. "It's not about what I like. I'm *years* behind you and Yerin. I have to work harder to catch up."

"Lindon, this isn't a test. What do you enjoy?"

"I like Soulsmithing," he responded. He was answering from the gut, but that was the most honest answer he could think of. "It's satisfying to come up with something that works, because Remnant pieces never combine like you expect."

Mercy leaned even closer to him, eagerly awaiting more.

"I enjoy research. Searching through volumes of information and pulling out just the pieces you need, then putting them together." He shrugged, self-conscious. "It doesn't *sound* fun when I say it like that, but that's what came to mind."

Mercy's tone became overly casual. "What about your talks with Yerin?"

"Of course." This time, Lindon didn't need to consider his answer. "She's always excited to train, and that makes me enjoy it more. Having to advance on my own these last few months has made me realize..."

He trailed off as the music started up beneath them. The director emerged back onstage and began to announce the second part of the drake-dancing show.

Without turning from Lindon, Mercy raised her hand, palm-out.

The director corrected himself mid-sentence. "Ah, it seems that the show will resume in just a few more minutes."

The musicians lowered their volume. A few members of the audience glanced up at their box, but most people kept their eyes low.

Lindon stared at Mercy. It seemed there were more perks to being a Monarch's daughter than he realized.

She lowered her voice to barely above a whisper. "So I've never asked, but now that we've got this chance to talk...what exactly *are* you and Yerin? Are you..." She twined her fingers together.

Lindon felt like every light in the theater had turned onto him.

"First I thought you were together," Mercy went on, "and then after watching you and finding out you had both been adopted into the Arelius family, I figured you might have thought of yourselves as brother and sister. But the more I watch you...there's something there, right?"

Excitement painted every inch of her face. The music stayed low, the crowd murmured, and the show wouldn't start until Mercy allowed it to.

Lindon's face burned, and he dug for an excuse to get himself out of the conversation.

[Just move your mouth and make words come out,] Dross said. [Your thoughts are a mess, so talking isn't going to make it any worse.]

"She...makes me want to work harder," Lindon began. "When I'm not with her, I feel like something's wrong. But everything is based on advancing together. That's all we do."

He looked down at the stage so he wouldn't have to look into Mercy's purple eyes anymore. "If we tried to do more...what would that look like? Would we have to give up advancement? Would we have anything in common?"

"And you're okay with that?" She sounded confused.

He responded honestly. "I don't know."

Mercy settled back into her seat. After a few seconds, she waved her hand. The music swelled again as the show resumed.

"Well," she said with a sigh, "there's one easy answer: make it to Monarch. Then you can spend all the time you want on romance and no one can say anything. Just ask my mother."

On the day Lindon was to leave for the tournament, the entire Akura family turned out in force.

In an open courtyard so vast that Lindon could not see the end, an uncountable number of people had gathered. They organized themselves into squares, some more precisely than others, representing the families and sects and clans within Akura territory.

It was an ocean of humanity. The noise they generated shook the ground.

Black towers rose evenly between the squares, and a grasshopper-like Remnant of white smoke wavered on top of each of those towers. The spirits played haunting music that drifted over the scene, weaving in and out of the crowd's titanic murmurs.

Lindon watched from above, on a platform supported by a violet Thousand-Mile Cloud. He stood to Mercy's left, while Pride stood to her right. Charity rose above them all, floating on a platform of her own.

They were on display. Two minutes after they rose into the air, the noise of the crowd heightened into cheers, and the music peaked in triumph.

Lindon stood stiffly, his mind choking on the sheer scale. In any direction he looked, he saw more people than he had ever imagined existed.

Constructs in each of the towers projected an illusory image of the three Underlords into the air so everyone in the endless crowd could see. Lindon could now see himself as a forty-foot-tall figure of madra, as flawless as anything a master of the Path of the White Fox could have produced. Every time another construct farther away sprang to life, showing Mercy and Pride and Lindon, a further burst of cheers erupted from the crowd around it.

This was a staggering display of the Akura clan's wealth. The weight sunk in as it never had before: he was representing them, a power that dwarfed the Blackflame Empire. Whether he liked it or not, he was one of the clan's faces now. He had to please them. The force of their displeasure would crush him.

Charity spread her hands, and a gentle ripple of madra drifted out over the crowd. Lindon was certain that even she couldn't reach the end of the gathered people, but when those in the center quieted, a wave of silence spread out over everyone.

The Sage began with a speech designed to reinforce the power and dignity of the Akura clan, and how their family was synonymous with the stability of humanity. Lindon listened intently until he realized he would learn nothing of value. This was only to impress everyone with the importance of what they were doing.

Instead, he examined his illusory image.

He had always been tall, but next to Mercy and Pride, that was even more apparent. With Mercy in the center, it looked as though they were arranged in descending order of height. Mercy came up to his chin, and Pride only his shoulder.

His expression had always looked like he was spoiling for a fight, but since ascending to Underlord, he had changed in a dozen tiny ways. Now he looked stern. *Too* stern, or so he thought as he examined the giant projection of his face. His discomfort made him look like a judge ready to order an execution. He tried to relax, but the situation was too tense.

He was dressed, as were Mercy and Pride, in the best the Akura clan had to offer. He wore a stiff outer coat with a high collar that flared behind him like a cape and plum-colored inner garments, tailored tightly.

The outside of the coat was black, but the inside was a bright violet that looked like it was on the verge of starting to glow. There was a line of script ringing the lowest hem of his coat that actually *did* glow bright violet, and after examining it thoroughly, he had been disappointed to find it was only decorative.

The one concession the Akura family had allowed him was his badge. Halfsilver now, representing his rise to Lord, the badge hung over his chest. It sparkled with bright points like stars in a gray sky, and its presence near his chest made him slightly uncomfortable, like a spiritual itch.

Halfsilver interfered with the orderly control of madra, and while it wouldn't hurt his sacred arts unless he tried to channel madra through it or kept it pressed against his skin, he still wished it were made of ordinary silver instead.

Pride wore an outfit much like his, without the badge, and Lindon was somewhat relieved to know that he had found the one person with a less friendly face than his own. Pride stood as though he were looking down his nose at the world, but his perpetual glare made him look like he needed a good punch.

Mercy looked just as at home as her aunt. Her outfit was sleeker and smaller than her male counterparts, and her hair had been tied up into intricate waves laced through by silver strings and dotted with amethysts.

She stood perfectly at ease, her black-gloved hands resting in front of her, the hint of a smile on her lips. The clan had given her powders and paints for her face, so her skin was flawless, her lips a shade more red, her eyes deeper.

The biggest difference between the three of them was their eyes. Lindon's were black—not Blackflame oceans of darkness, just ordinary dark human eyes—while the other two were the deep purple of the Akura head family. The same purple shared by the closest square of people, the ones arranged on a dais at the front of all the rest. Instead of standing on the courtyard, these each had a cushioned chair, their ranks rising up in tiered rows. The Akura head family.

These weren't just the elite Underlords who had been eligible to potentially compete in the tournament, though he spotted some of them too. Akura Grace leaned back in her chair with her eyes closed, so that Lindon thought she might be cycling. Or sleeping.

But she was one among hundreds of all ages, from white-haired old men and women at the top row to squirming children of six or seven at the bottom. Not all of them had the purple eyes—maybe about half, as far as Lindon could see.

As a group, they stared at him just like everyone else.

When Charity had finished speaking, and the overwhelming cheers from the audience settled down, an old man from the Akura family spoke up. He described the troubles the Akura clan at large faced—incursions along their northern border, famine in the south, a loss of territory to nature, and so on.

As Lindon was beginning to wonder what his point was, he then moved on to how distinguished performance in the Uncrowned King tournament would solve all those problems.

Respect of their fighters would cause the wicked Dragon King to stop his raids to the north. Rewards taken from the other factions would make them rich enough to settle the famine, and new trade deals would open with other Monarch nations. Soon they would see an unprecedented golden age, with their youth leading the way as they pushed into the north and drove the dragons out, conquering the continent for humanity.

Thunderous applause followed, so much that Lindon couldn't hear Mercy commenting into his ear. The cheers continued for five minutes.

Another weight settled on him. Whether victory in the Uncrowned King tournament would really make all those changes for the common citizen of Akura territory, he didn't know. This all may have been a show designed to draw support from the people for the competition.

But at the very least, they *thought* it mattered to them. This human tide would be listening for news of his performance, deciding whether Lindon had done them proud or let them down.

The Blackflame Empire's fate would be controlled by this tournament, but so would the lives of millions of other people he would never meet. His performance, the people he defeated, would matter more widely than he'd ever imagined. The knowledge settled into him.

He had to be worthy of it.

When the cheers began to fade, a sleek black cloudship slipped in from overhead. Its design made it look small, though it dwarfed even the Blackflame Emperor's ship. It looked almost like a slice of Stormrock, the floating Skysworn city. Lindon's stomach lurched as his platform began to drift upward, toward the ship.

Mercy and Pride raised their hands and waved to the crowd, Mercy eagerly and Pride reluctantly. Lindon did so as well, having been instructed to mirror anything the other two did. Once again, the crowd roared.

The platform dropped the three of them onto the deck of the airship, and Lindon let out a breath. "Are we finished now? Is it over?"

"Learn patience," Pride ordered him, and Mercy rolled her eyes at her brother.

"We're going to fly off to make it look like we're leaving," she explained. "Cheers. Well-wishes. Promises of victory. Everyone's happy. Then we're going to loop around and pick up everyone else. The whole family's coming."

Except for the servants, Lindon would be the only one aboard the massive cloudship whose name wasn't Akura. That thought was no comfort.

"How long do we have to travel?" he asked carefully.

"It usually takes eight months to reach the center of the Ninecloud continent," Mercy said, "though the journey is risky. There's never a guarantee of success. But the tournament is in two months, so the Ninecloud Court has sent us superior propulsion constructs and a navigational construct to ensure we reach our destination in six weeks."

[A navigational construct, you say? That sounds like it might be full of delicious, delicious secrets.]

A different part of the statement had intrigued Lindon. "Ninecloud?"

Pride sneered at him. "The tournament is hosted by the Ninecloud Court. I suppose you've never heard of them."

With Suriel at his side, Lindon had stood among the Court itself, watching Sha Miara's coronation. He hadn't known at the time, but he now suspected she was a Monarch.

Lindon gave Pride a smile that made the shorter man ball up his fists. "It so happens that I have."

With her blindfold tight, Yerin sent her perception around the cloudship. The heavy scripts manipulated wind and cloud madra, keeping them in the air. Sealed in a construct below, powerful rainbow madra provided by the Ninecloud Court fueled the ship and gave them the speed necessary to reach the tournament in time.

The crew of the ship were mostly on Paths of cloud or wind, which allowed them to do their jobs, but Yerin sensed at least one on a fire Path and one that used force techniques.

Naru Saeya was a brighter spot than any of them, a concentration of wind madra, but Eithan proved more difficult to spot. Pure madra was easy to overlook. Yerin strained her perception not to reach further, but to drill deeper.

Her Blood Shadow stirred, hungrily reaching out, which gave Yerin another thing to distract her. She pushed the Shadow down, still scanning the deck, gripping her sword tightly. If she had to wrestle with the spiritual parasite for long, she would never find Eithan.

She heard nothing, but she felt him for an instant, a faint whisper of danger in her spirit. Her sword came up, ringing with her

Ruler technique, and the air was sliced apart by dozens of invisible blades. Many of the crew stopped in their tracks, and Naru Saeya's spirit quivered in surprise, but Yerin ignored them and tore off her blindfold.

Eithan stood before her, frozen in mid-lunge, eyes wide. His one outstretched hand held a silver comb, which he had been using to attack. Its top half fell off, cut by the Endless Sword, and plinked to the deck. The edges of his ornate pink-and-gold outer robe were shredded, and a few strands of his hair drifted down.

He wasn't cut, but Yerin had never felt so victorious in all her life.

She raised her sword into the air and gave a triumphant shout as though she had just captured an enemy's fortress. Naru Saeya cheered along with her, applauding furiously, and several of the crew joined in.

After a moment, Eithan's shocked expression melted into an appreciative smile, and he added a few claps of his own. "If I had thought you'd pick it up so quickly, I'd have tied my hair back."

Yerin drew in a deep, satisfied breath, looking up at Eithan. "Next time, I'm drawing blood."

"You sound so eager."

She reached into her outer robe and pulled out the purple crystalline construct that had been delivered to her months ago. It wasn't the time for her to speak with Lindon yet, so he might not be able to answer, but it was at least the right day.

Yerin held it out to Eithan, who provided pure madra to activate it. Sword madra would work, but it would wear the construct down faster. It was already on its last legs.

But she wouldn't need it for much longer. In only seven more days, they would reach the Ninecloud Court. Lindon might be there already.

The construct shot sprays of madra essence in brightly colored sparks, and the light within it flickered. Dream and shadow madra twisted around each other into a whirlpool, and Yerin caught the faint impression that it was drilling into something...deeper.

But the impression was gone in a moment, and Lindon's voice came through, distant and weak. "Yerin, can you...may not...much longer."

The cloudship shuddered as the crew prepared them for landing; they would touch down soon to allow their scripts to draw on aura and refuel. The wind picked up as they descended, which didn't make it easier to hear.

"Lindon," Yerin shouted into the construct. "I cut Eithan!"

"That's not strictly true," Eithan pointed out, but she waved him to silence.

"...apologies...what did you...Eithan?"

"I cut him! I finally sensed him coming!" She had shared her progress in this training exercise with Lindon, and while she had sensed Eithan before, it was never quickly enough to interrupt his attack. He strengthened his veil every few days, and she'd begun to worry that she would never catch up.

Lindon's distant voice grew excited. "Really? That's...how did...even him."

The construct's light flickered again, and the sound died out. Yerin lowered it, trying to shake off her disappointment. Eithan could power the device again, but it was reaching the end of its life. Besides, she would be able to talk to Lindon directly in another week. Their cloudships were both supposed to arrive at about the same time; two weeks before the start of the tournament.

She pushed out a smile for Eithan and tucked the construct away. "You'll have to watch yourself from here on. Won't be able to sneak around like a rat."

"I wouldn't be so sure; I have many other rat-like qualities that will serve me well."

Naru Saeya stepped up, multi-colored sword in her hand. "My turn to cut Eithan."

"While Yerin is making excellent progress, she did not cut me. I want that to be clear."

"Draw your comb."

Yerin stepped back while Naru Saeya and Eithan exchanged blows. They both had Iron bodies suited for speed, which had recently made it hard for her to follow their matches.

Now, by extending her perception over the both of them, she could sense the changes in their spirit much more clearly and quickly than before. Those small shifts gave her a sense of what would happen a moment in advance.

She continued thinking about it as their cloudship touched down. It felt similar to how her spirit sometimes warned her in moments of danger, as she sensed signs of approaching hostility that her conscious mind was not yet aware of. That was the ability she was training.

But there was another layer to it, one she was just beginning to touch. Sometimes her spirit warned her of danger before she could have sensed anything. What was it feeling?

Her mind returned to the construct that allowed her to speak with Lindon regardless of the distance. She could track the shadow and dream madra as they twisted into one another, but they were held in place by...something else. There should be a third element there, but she felt nothing.

It was a vague concept, and as she wondered about it, she extended her perception around her. Beyond Eithan and Saeya's fight, she stretched it into the trees that now rose over their cloudship.

The aura was rich here, and she felt the power of the wind as it played through the leaves. A storm gathered overhead, but fire aura had gathered within it, so it was going to be a bad aura-storm.

Those happened sometimes, especially in lands with strong vital aura. She and her master had been forced to travel through rains of fire or winds of scorching poison, though of course she'd had a Sage's protection at the time.

She found herself sensing for gaps in the aura, still chewing on the vague feeling she'd gotten from the construct.

Instead of an answer, she felt danger.

Saeya and Eithan jumped away from her at the same time Yerin's spirit screamed a warning, and all three of them shouted to the crew at the same time. Far overhead, a winged golden form split through the clouds, diving down toward them.

A gold dragon. It must have hidden in the overwhelming fire aura gathered overhead, disguising itself even from Eithan.

It had a serpentine body, four clawed limbs, gleaming fangs, and shining eyes. Its scales glittered even in the dim light of the overcast day, and it descended on them like a golden spear.

Yerin's sword leaped into her hand, and her six sword-arms flashed behind her. She gathered up the sword aura, shaping it to her will, focusing the Endless Sword on the tip of her master's white blade.

Saeya stood upright, her emerald wings spread behind her, peacock feathers standing up straight behind one ear. She made a fist, and wind aura snagged the dragon's wings in mid-flight.

The creature shuddered as though stumbling in midair, losing a bit of speed, but broke the Ruler technique after a moment of concentration.

Eithan looked up at the sky, yellow hair streaming behind him and hands in his pockets. Behind him, blue-white stars of Forged madra began to appear.

"Too late," he said.

At the same time, the gold dragon cracked open its jaws. It spewed bright orange liquid flame in a thick stream, like a burning river, down on their ship. Gold dragon's breath. The Path of the Flowing Flame.

Yerin unleashed the Endless Sword which, as expected, only scraped a shallow line across the gold dragon's scales. She hadn't intended it to be a lethal blow, she only wanted to throw off the dragon's aim.

It didn't work. The dragon's head jerked, and the line of Flowing Flame madra scorched the ground to one side of the ship, but only an instant later the sacred beast pulled its head back. Fire madra blasted through the bottom of the ship with a sickening crunch that Yerin could feel through her feet.

The dragon caught itself in the middle of its dive, flapping its wings to hover in midair. Yerin could feel the force of the wind and the pressure of its spirit; it had the power of an Underlord.

Yerin pooled madra in her sword, gathering up the Rippling Sword technique, and slashed at the air. A wave of razor-sharp energy swept at the dragon, but a round plate of bronze emerged from behind the creature, sweeping around and catching the Striker technique. Yerin's madra burst apart on the shield.

The dragon reached out to the aura around it, resonating with its soulfire. It was far too weak to be an attack—Yerin could feel that immediately—but it was still a complex aura manipulation technique that Yerin wasn't sure she could match.

Words, half in her ears and half in her head, soon formed from aura of wind and dreams. "Where is the Blackflame?" the dragon demanded in a feminine voice. A voice Yerin had heard before.

She hadn't heard it in many months, and she had never seen this form before, but a female gold dragon with a grudge against Lindon...there was only one she knew of.

"He's dead," Yerin said to Sopharanatoth. "Choked on his soup."

A spiritual scan passed over the whole cloudship, sending a shiver passing through her soul. Yerin didn't expect the dragon to retreat just because she found out Lindon wasn't around, and besides, Yerin wasn't the same weak Highgold that she had been when she'd first met Sophara. She had no problem challenging an Underlady now.

Yerin slid up to Naru Saeya, keeping her sword out. Voice low, Yerin asked, "Can you gct me up there?"

"That would be a bad idea," Saeya responded. Sweat rolled down the sides of her face, and she licked her lips.

Yerin looked to Eithan for confirmation, and he nodded.

He didn't seem as worried as Saeya did, but he hadn't banished the stars gathering in the air behind him either. "Feel for yourself."

Yerin reached out toward the dragon with her perception...and suddenly Sophara loomed a hundred times larger in her vision. Yerin's spirit quivered like a kicked puppy.

This was not someone she had any chance of defeating. Not on her own.

But she wasn't on her own.

Sophara showed no intention of attacking. She gave an angry roar, her wings beating the air, and turned to fly away.

A Rippling Sword caught her in the flank the same time as a lance of light from Eithan's star. A fist of green wind madra grabbed at her tail. Yerin's technique actually drew blood, Eithan's crashed onto the bronze shield floating around her, and Saeya's drew her up short.

"I have not allowed you to leave," Naru Saeya declared, rising up on wings of her own.

Yerin felt a burst of pride that all three of them had come to the same conclusion. None of them were a match for Sophara, but she wasn't invincible, and she'd been foolish enough to come here on her own.

This was exactly the time to attack.

The cloudship's crew had leaped over the side at the first sign of Underlords clashing, and the ship itself still listed to one side, having a chunk burned out of it by gold dragon's breath.

Sophara only flinched at the damage from their techniques. Blood rolled down her scales, but she still faced them with slowly flapping wings. "I don't need to waste time with you," her aura-born voice said. "You are already done."

Once again, she turned. Another volley of techniques reached her, but they were either dodged, deflected by the floating shield, or crushed by her own madra.

Yerin and Saeya tried twice more, but Eithan gave up almost immediately, letting his Forged stars dissipate back into aura. He sighed. "This will be inconvenient."

Naru Saeya turned sharply, staring down at the deck beneath her feet. "Is it gone?"

"All but a spoonful."

Yerin extended her own perception down to the cloudship. She couldn't sense the damage to the hull—she could only sense spiritual powers, nothing physical—but that scarcely mattered. It was the network of scripts and constructs running the ship that actually got them places.

Many of them were still intact. She figured the crew could have them in the air again inside a day.

But the containment around the Ninecloud madra was broken. The fuel given to them had mostly faded into useless essence.

She pushed back a spike of fear. "We're not walking there, that's certain. If you had to place a bet, how long would you say it's going to take us?"

"Another month," Naru Saeya said sadly. "At best."

The tournament's opening was in three weeks.

Yerin walked over to the side, looking down to stare at the smoking hole in the ship. "Well...here's hoping they come looking for us before then."

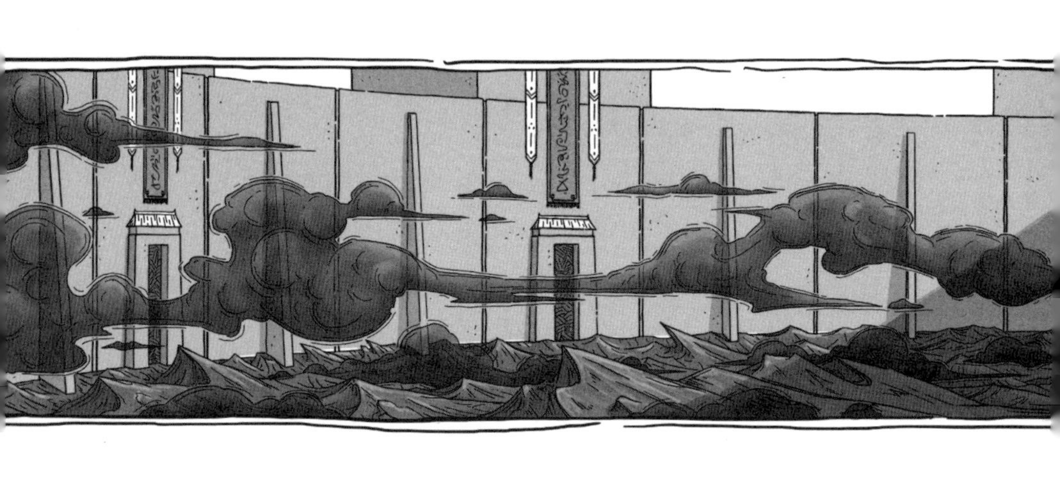

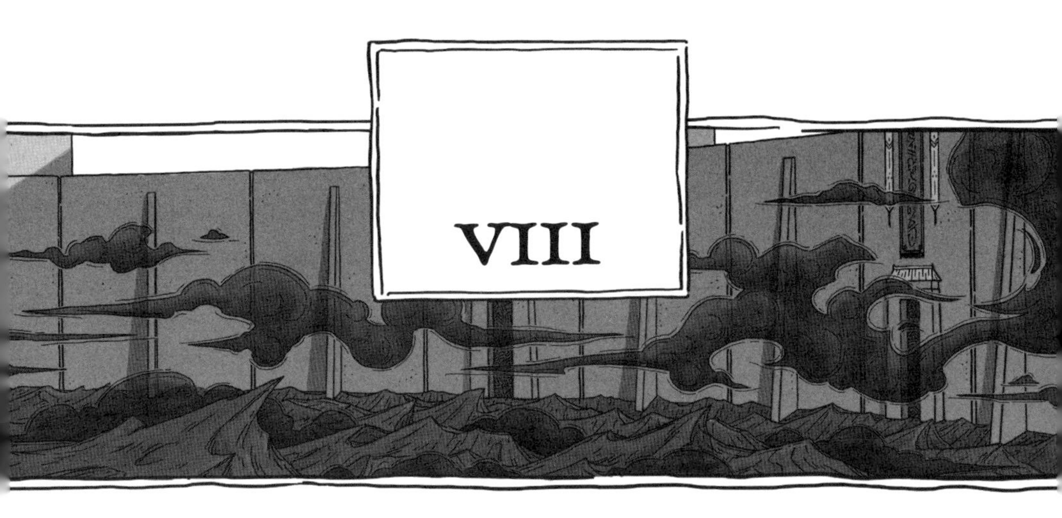


The Ninecloud Court looked as though it had been ripped from a dream.

Rather than a city, it looked like a jeweled palace so vast that Lindon couldn't see the end. Shimmering glass bridges connected one ruby tower to another, and shining castles floated on white clouds that sparkled every color. Blue birds with wingspans that looked a mile wide trailed rain from their tails, leaving rainbows falling behind them.

The iridescent structures built on one another, leading up to one tower in particular: a rose-tinted diamond spire encircled by a solid rainbow that reminded Lindon of Samara's Ring back home.

Lindon reached into his pocket, clenching Suriel's marble. Somewhere in that complex—maybe at the top of that tower—was where heaven's messenger had taken him to see Luminous Queen Sha Miara. Years ago, Suriel had assured him that he couldn't make it with the power he had at the time.

And now here he was.

Without warning, rainbow light shimmered around the cloudship. Lindon began cycling Blackflame, but none of the Akura Lords or Ladies looked concerned. A moment later, a woman's gentle voice poured in from everywhere.

"Good morning, honored guests! I am the Ninecloud Soul, voice of the Court, and we welcome you to the eighteenth Uncrowned King tournament! The first round will begin in two weeks. In the meantime, we will guide you to your rooms."

He couldn't see the source of the voice. The rainbow light hovered around their ship, which began to drift toward a nearby amethyst tower.

[It's interesting how humans decide whether or not to panic by watching others,] Dross noted. [What if all of you are wrong together?]

*Charity and Fury are aboard. If they're wrong about what's safe, then I guess we're all going to die.*

Other cloudships were being pulled into other neighboring towers at the same time. In fact, the air might have been more crowded than the streets. Maybe the Blackflame Empire team was somewhere among them.

He sent a thread of pure madra into the voice transmission construct he held in his hand.

[That poor construct. Worked to death. You're a cruel man.]

Yerin's voice came through in a whisper, and Lindon pressed the device to his ear. But he couldn't make anything out; her words split and cracked like dry leaves. He poured more pure madra into it, but finally the faceted surface of the construct cracked as well. He felt the binding inside warp, deforming past usefulness.

He lowered it, sighing. It had been wonderful being able to speak with Yerin even every other day, but he had pushed the construct past its original lifespan. It wasn't meant to last half a year, he was sure.

[There are sects that would have considered that a legendary treasure, handing it down to their descendants to call for help in times of dire need,] Dross said. [I just thought you ought to feel guiltier.]

*The Sage can afford it,* Lindon responded, but he was disappointed that the construct had finally broken. Now he wouldn't know when to expect Yerin. Maybe she was finally here. Would he be allowed to see her before the tournament?

As the ship drifted closer to the shimmering jeweled tower, another cloudship joined them, pulled by the same rainbow madra toward a dock next to theirs. This ship was made of pale wood and drifted on a white cloud, but it was much smaller than the Akura clan's. On the deck were a scattered handful of blue-robed sacred artists.

Their ship had clearly suffered some damage. Scorch marks dotted the hull, and sprays of cloud madra hissed from the bottom.

One woman onboard spotted them and walked over to the edge. Just when Lindon thought she would leap over, she vanished midstep, appearing on the deck of the Akura cloudship. She dragged a gust of icy air with her.

The new arrival looked young, perhaps midway through her

twenties, with sun-browned skin and long, flowing white hair. She wore sky-blue sacred artist's robes decorated with snowflakes like white flowers. Along the outside of her forearms ran a frozen line of ice down her skin. A straight-bladed sword hung in a blue sheath on her back.

Charity did not appear surprised to see her, instead giving a shallow bow. "Min Shuei. It seems you ran into some trouble on the way."

Lindon, watching intently, startled when Mercy rushed up behind him and grabbed his arm in excitement.

"That's the Winter Sage! I haven't seen her since I was a girl!" She leaned forward, staring at the newcomer. "She's taller than I remembered."

The Winter Sage's expression crumpled as she stared at Charity, as though she were about to cry. "Charity! Where *were* you?"

"I was not aware you were in trouble," the Heart Sage said stiffly. "Why did you not contact us? I would have sent my father to your side in a moment."

"It was Xorrus," the white-haired woman said, and now her speech was tinged with hatred. "By the time I sensed her strike, she was already flying away. She drew the blood she wanted."

Akura Charity was still cold as usual. "Your team?"

"She killed one of my boys," Min Shuei said, full of sorrow. "He was only twenty-six, and so full of talent. His mother hasn't eaten in weeks. His father swore to mount a dragon's head on his wall for every year of his son's life."

"But only one?" Charity clarified. "You still have two competitors left?"

The tanned woman turned horrified eyes to the Sage of the Silver Heart. "*Hundreds* died, among them one of the most talented students I've ever had. He cannot simply be replaced!"

"And yet he must be," Charity said. "I am not insensitive to your grief, but this competition is our best chance to strike back. Have you selected a replacement yet?"

The Winter Sage bristled with rage, and icy madra spread to every corner of the ship.

Lindon shivered, his skin prickling as sword-aura stung him in response to this woman's anger.

Charity did not muster her madra in response, but nor did she seem moved by the other Sage's hostility. They faced one another in silence as the other Akura members scurried away, evacuating the deck.

Then a door slammed open, breaking the quiet. Akura Fury strode out, his black hair rippling like a flame and his chest bare as always. For the first time that Lindon had seen, his expression was totally serious.

"I smell Xorrus," the Herald said.

The Winter Sage gestured back to her cloudship, which by that time had settled at the end of a dock sticking out of the emerald tower. The Akura cloudship shuddered as it, too, was drawn into a dock.

Servants in rainbow robes waited for them, bowing, but no one left the ships yet.

Fury drifted up on a cushion of wind aura, using his soulfire to float. He moved as naturally as if he were on a wind Path, effortlessly flying over to the white cloudship, hovering next to the burn-scarred hull.

"Amazing," Lindon said.

"That's a Herald for you." Mercy chewed on one of her black-gloved thumbs for a moment before saying, "...you should know that there's been a feud between my family and the gold dragons for generations. Uncle Fury especially. He's considered just behind Northstrider and the Beast King as a great enemy of dragon-kind."

[Third place isn't bad,] Dross said.

Fury ran his hand along the scorched wood of the Frozen Blade cloudship. "This can't have been more than a week ago. She was alone?"

The Sage of the Frozen Blade closed her eyes and took a deep breath, bringing her madra under control. "A wing of lesser dragons burned down an ancestral grove as we traveled. I stopped to deal with them, but they were only bait so that Xorrus could strike against my Underlords."

Fury's red eyes burned. "You were lucky not to lose everyone. But now we have greater concerns." He turned to Charity. "Xorrus is only the Dragon King's left hand."

Before he'd even finished speaking, the Heart Sage's voice echoed throughout the cloudship. "Be on alert. We have two remaining vassal teams that have not yet arrived: the Temple of Rising Earth and the Blackflame Empire. We have every reason to believe that one or both have suffered an attack."

A shiver passed down Lindon's spine.

"I will approach the Ninecloud Court for assistance," she continued. "In the meantime, use any methods available to contact our teams. If we can determine their location, we can send protection."

Lindon fumbled in his outer robe for the broken communication construct. He poured madra into it, flooding it in an instant and creating a shrill shriek of sound. The binding only dissolved faster, but he flooded it with even more power. Even an instant of connection would reassure him that she was still alive.

Mercy squeezed his arm with one black hand. "Nothing to worry about. We have much better lines of communication with the Empire than with the Frozen Blade school. If something had happened, we would have known."

That would be reassuring except for the concern in her own voice.

Dross didn't help.

[That's right, don't worry,] he said. [I can see why you *might* be worried. The Blackflame Empire *is* closer to the dragons and even weaker than the Frozen Blade school, so you might expect them to be in much greater danger. But you can't ignore the possibility of good luck!]

The construct in Lindon's hand exploded, sending fizzing chunks of madra flying in all directions.

Mercy patted him again. "Someone onboard will have a way to communicate with the Naru clan. I'll find out where they are."

Lindon tried to thank her, but he was focused on the damaged cloudship. The gold dragons had done that to weaken the Akura clan in the tournament. They were the ones who would get the Blackflame Empire.

He remembered Ekeri, the Truegold who had suspected him of carrying around a treasure from Ghostwater. She had hounded him relentlessly until he had barely managed to kill her.

If the Akura team didn't perform well enough—if *he* didn't—her family would take over the Empire. Including his homeland.

Maybe they had already...

Before his thoughts could make it too far, his spiritual perception screamed at him. He collapsed to his knees as the two Sages and the Heralds dropped their veils at once. They all looked west, across the jeweled city, but through his watering eyes he couldn't see what had drawn their attention.

Most of the other Akura clan members on the deck had crumpled just like him, but he noticed that the Ninecloud servants on the dock only flinched in their multi-colored robes. They did not shrink back.

The rainbow light returned to surround the cloudship, and the pleasant female voice that had greeted them drifted through the air again. "Welcome, guests. Please enter your rooms."

"We have reason to worry for the safety of our teams," Charity said. "Can you confirm that the Rising Earth and Blackflame Empire teams are still en route?"

"The Rising Earth team missed their arrival date last week," the invisible Ninecloud representative admitted. "Enter your tower, and we will be happy to give you a full accounting of their absence."

"We will have our own accounting," the Winter Sage said, her voice furious. Still staring into the west, she drew her sword. Lindon wanted to see what she was watching for, but she raised her weapon into the air.

It looked the same as Yerin's.

Hers couldn't be the only white-bladed sword in the world, but Lindon recognized it immediately. He had been with Yerin when she'd pulled it from the Sword Sage's body. This was exactly the same as the one Yerin carried, from the shape of the hilt to the length of the blade.

He wasn't sure what to make of that. Had Yerin's master carried a sword from the Frozen Blade school?

A winged silhouette flew from one of the distant towers to the west, growing larger and larger, clutching something huge in its talons. The shadow resolved into a dragon, golden and serpentine, with a cloud of sand rolling around it like smoke.

Its wings were each big enough to strike their cloudship from the air, and it bared its gleaming fangs. Golden dragon eyes, with their vertically slitted pupils, glared at the ship.

The power of its spirit enveloped the city, driving air traffic away. Cloudships and winged horses fled at the dragon's approach. This gold dragon's power rivaled Akura Fury's.

A Herald.

[Xorrus,] Dross said, [left hand of the Dragon Monarch. She is called Desert-bringer, the Breath of Destruction, the Eternal Sandstorm.]

Lindon could barely breathe, but he tensed further. *How do you know?*

[Just like your new friend Fury, she was one of the Heralds who formed the original pact of Ghostwater. I found a record of her *personally* ignoring me.]

From this distance, it was clear that the dragon Herald was carrying a massive chunk of stone. Perhaps the top of a tower or a segment of castle wall.

He strained against the spiritual pressure to keep his eyes clear and open; a fight here could kill him and everyone else on the cloudship. Surely the Sages would know that better than he. They would hold back.

The dragon's mouth opened, and her mocking laughter shook the ship. Xorrus said, "A gift from my father to the Queen of Shadows."

She darted upward, deceptively swift, and dangled the stone over their ship. Its shadow covered Lindon entirely.

Then she dropped it.

The masonry was big enough to crush the ship, but Lindon didn't even have time to flinch before Fury caught it. Hovering two dozen feet over the deck, he held up the massive rock with one hand, staring upward. He didn't seem to strain in the slightest.

But from this angle, Lindon could see an emblem carved into the stone, larger than Fury's body: a series of rising stalagmites.

"Oh, you wiped out the Rising Earth sect?" Fury's tone was light, even conversational. "I see, I see."

The rainbow light around their ship intensified. Now the voice from the Ninecloud Court sounded nervous. "Honored guests, we humbly ask that you please settle your grievances in the arena. The collateral damage from a clash between you—"

Fury hurled the boulder.

It shot toward Xorrus with such an explosion of force that the wind pushed back everyone on the deck. A deafening roar tore through Lindon's ears, and he could no longer keep his eyes open.

When he opened them again, the gold dragon was laughing. The cloud of sand around her had grown. Had she dissolved the boulder into sand?

Akura Fury laughed with her.

Together, the Heralds laughed and laughed, but every second Lindon grew more nervous. *Dross, if they start fighting, how much trouble are we in?*

[I wouldn't say we're *safe*, but it's nothing to be worried about. Heralds never come to blows. And besides, look how friendly they are!]

Charity had dropped her veil, her spirit unleashed, though she looked as calm as ever. And Min Shuei, the Winter Sage, still bared her sword. Small blades of frost, barely visible, played in the air around her in a constant snowstorm. Her expression twitched and her hand shook as she fought to keep herself under control.

Fury's laughter died down first, and he sighed as he wiped a tear from his eye. "It's funny, isn't it? Life is funny. I brought you a gift too!"

Charity's voice resounded in Lindon's mind. *Get down!* The mental command was so strong that everyone on the cloudship threw themselves to the deck at once.

Then Akura Fury struck.

A dozen black palms, each bigger than the ship, slammed into the gold dragon at once. The handprints of shadow madra dissolved the cloud of sand, but they didn't crack scales. They seemed to sink into the dragon's spirit. She roared in pain and gathered up golden fire in her mouth.

Cords of multi-colored light looped around both Heralds, locking their bodies and spirits in place. Xorrus' dragon breath dissipated, but she didn't struggle against her rainbow bonds.

Her pained growls turned into laughter once again. "A cheap price for the Temple of Rising Earth."

The Ninecloud Court voice echoed over them all, this time sounding stern. "By the power of Luminous Queen Sha Leiala, we have restrained you. You are still our guests, but do not take our Court lightly."

*Sha Leiala?* Lindon thought.

[Monarch of the Ninecloud Court,] Dross explained. [Do you not understand how to pick up on context clues?]

*What about Sha Miara?* Lindon asked. Suriel had taken him to her coronation two years before.

[Never heard of her.]

Xorrus bared her fangs in a smile as the light of the Ninecloud Court dragged her backward. "I hope your sister will give my granddaughter some competition."

Fury turned back to his ship, letting the light pull him away as well. "I don't think it matters. What do you think, Charity?"

Charity, cool as ever, inclined her head toward Xorrus. "I'm sure she will do your family proud," the Sage said, "before the tournament ends and I kill her myself."

Xorrus struggled against the light, snapping her teeth, but she was still pulled inexorably away.

As the dragon vanished, and Fury and the Sages withdrew their spirits, Lindon finally drew a deep breath and stumbled to his feet. He was still digesting everything he'd heard, but there was one encouraging fact among them: Xorrus had never mentioned the Blackflame team.

[That's good news!] Dross said. [Maybe she didn't think they were worth her time to kill! Unless she *did* kill them and just didn't think it was worth mentioning.]

Mercy returned, propping herself up on the staff of twisted black madra she called Suu. She panted as she spoke. "Sorry! I got stuck under the pressure. Did you hear what they said?"

"Sopharanatoth," Lindon repeated. "Isn't that..."

Mercy nodded. "Yerin and I fought her after you killed her younger sister in Ghostwater. I couldn't tell for myself, because I was too weak at the time, but rumor says she's supposed to be strong." She caught her breath for a moment and then added, "She might be favored to win."

A Herald's granddaughter had a personal grudge against him, and she was one of the strongest in the tournament.

[I wish I could say I was surprised,] Dross said. [Oh, wait, I could lie.]

*We'll have to watch her fights,* Lindon thought.

[How will that help us when we're avoiding her and letting someone else beat her?]

*We want to beat her early.* If he could beat her, he could weaken her influence and make it harder for her to get revenge *and* keep the Blackflame Empire out of dragon hands.

The rainbow light around Fury faded, and the Ninecloud servants in rainbow robes streamed out from the dock to usher the Akura clan inside. Lindon noticed they did their best to keep even their eyes from landing on Fury.

The Ninecloud voice echoed once more, "Now please have a pleasant stay in the Ninecloud Court. If there is any convenience you wish, allow us to serve you. Enjoy our hospitality within your tower for the next fourteen days, and then the tournament begins!"

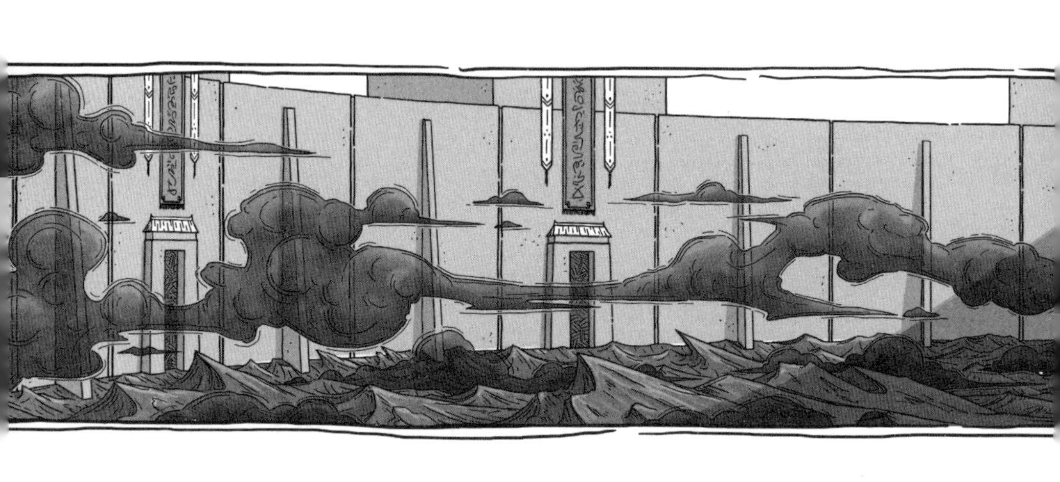

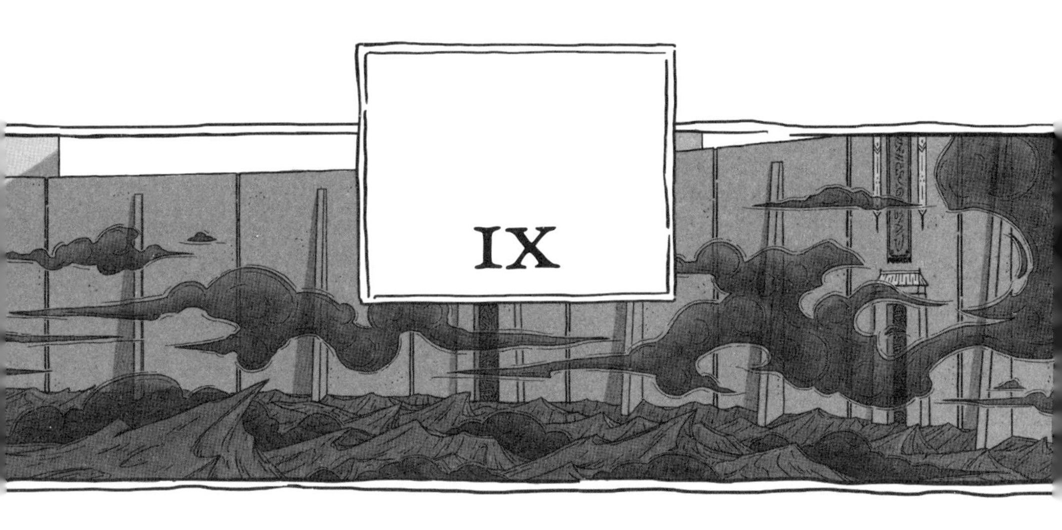

# IX

YERIN'S MASTER HAD OWNED SEVERAL PAINTINGS. HE DIDN'T PUT them up anywhere, he just pulled them out every once in a while to admire them. Passing over the Ninecloud countryside was like flying through one of those paintings.

The trees had pale white bark and the leaves were of every bright color. Thousand-Mile Clouds were born naturally here, so they floated all around, some as big as islands. Vines and bushes spilled over their edges, or clusters of houses, and winged horses and tiny cloudships filled the skies.

The capital city shone in the distance, glittering like a handful of jewels that spread across the entire horizon.

"Ninecloud City," Eithan said, "one of the largest cities in the world. Capital of the Ninecloud country, home to the Ninecloud

Court. In the distant past, they were named by the same culture that named the Blackflame Empire. Among their virtues was a certain philosophy: why use many names when you can recycle the same one?"

Their half-repaired cloudship crawled across the sky to the point that Yerin wished she could get out and push. The jeweled city looked as distant as the sun that rose behind it. "Will we be making it by noon?"

"Noon in three days, maybe," Eithan responded. "If we hope to make it to the opening of the first round in a matter of hours, we have no choice but to trust in the mercy of a greater power."

Naru Saeya chewed at her bottom lip. "I could fly ahead. Unlikely I'd make it by noon, but I could perhaps make it to the city borders by nightfall."

"No point to that," Yerin said bitterly. "Might as well keep limping along. The closer we get, the better our odds that some Herald takes mercy on us and scoops us up."

Still, as the sun rose, Yerin stood at the bow of the ship and stared into the distance. She hoped, she wished, she prayed to the heavens, and she kept her perception wide open. They were competitors in the Uncrowned King Tournament, one of the biggest events in the world. Somebody would come for them.

When the sun burned straight overhead, she knew the heavens were deaf.

One of the crew walked up to Naru Saeya, telling her they needed to set down so that their scripts could restore their cloud. Here, it would be dozens of times faster than back home, but that would make no difference. They might as well take a whole day.

Yerin dropped to the deck, leaning her back against the railing, finally letting her spirits sink to the depths. Here she had lost her chance to measure herself against her master, to compete with Lindon, to see how she rated against the best in the world. And it was all because she couldn't get there in time.

She consoled herself with the knowledge that the tournament stretched over months. At least she would be able to *watch* the matches.

Somehow that made things worse.

She had tucked her head between her knees and shut off her spiritual perception when someone nudged her shoulder. She stretched out a sword-arm and jabbed it at him, sure it was Eithan. But he caught the limb and said her name in a low voice.

"Yerin. I think you ought to look up."

Annoyed, she glanced up. A shape flew toward their ship, a blur of hazy white madra. She stretched out her senses and felt a blend of ice and sword madra. The feeling of a wintersteel blade.

Yerin shot to her feet, brushed herself off, threw her hair back from her face, and nervously adjusted the sword on her belt.

"If I'm not mistaken, that's your friend," Eithan said.

The shape had now resolved itself into the form of a woman with long white hair, flying through the air after them with no cloud to support her, but Yerin didn't need to see to recognize the madra.

"Is that the Sage of the Frozen Blade?" Saeya asked excitedly.

"Cheers and celebration for us." Yerin inhaled deeply, evening out her breathing.

The last time she had seen the Winter Sage, Yerin's master had delayed their engagement indefinitely in order to take Yerin north-west. On a quest to train her and potentially learn to keep her Blood Shadow under control.

Min Shuei had...not taken it well. Yerin didn't think she'd ever met anyone who wore their emotions as openly as the Sage of the Frozen Blade. Yerin had once seen her cry because a rainstorm was too beautiful.

She would have known immediately that the Sword Sage was dead, so Yerin had felt no pressure to carry the news herself. In fact, she had hoped that she wouldn't see the Sage again for as long as possible. From the first moment that the Sword Sage had taken Yerin back to the Frozen Blade sect, the Winter Sage had never approved of her.

Yerin did not expect that to change.

The Winter Sage flew in at blinding speed, using nothing more than the control over aura given to her by her Archlord-level soulfire. She was not a wind artist, so it was a masterful display of control as she swooped in and lightly landed on the deck.

Her skin was tanned, her hair long and white, though she had the appearance of a young woman. A sword identical to Yerin's rested at her hip; it was the sister to the weapon she had gifted Yerin's master, long ago. Two swords, crafted by the Sage herself.

She landed, and Naru Saeya bowed immediately, but Min Shuei's focus fixed on Yerin. Her eyes burned with fury, and her lips quivered, but she said only, "Yerin."

Yerin nodded her head. "Winter Sage."

The Sage's face transformed into a mask of grief, and she sounded as though she were about to cry. "Why didn't you come back home?"

Yerin's stomach tightened, and she was forcibly reminded why she had never gotten along with the Sage. "I stayed with your sect for a whisker more than half a year. That's a long jump away from a home."

"You could have at least told me what happened *yourself*."

"I'd bet my soul against a rat's tail that you knew as soon as I did," Yerin said. "Didn't get up from your chair to avenge him, did you?"

The Sage staggered as though Yerin had struck her in the heart with an arrow. Yerin's master had always argued that Sages should go out and use their powers for the good of as many people as possible, but it would take an act of the heavens to dislodge the Sage of the Frozen Blade from her sect.

"If you knew..." The Sage's voice shook. "If I traveled *there* to avenge him, I would be as vulnerable as he was. Vengeance is a poor reason to allow myself to be killed by ignorant barbarians. And what good would it do? Would slaughtering Jades and Irons bring him back?"

A sudden surge of guilt caught Yerin off-guard. She shouldn't have used vengeance to provoke the Sage. Not only was it not fair, but it wasn't as though Yerin had gone out of *her* way to get revenge. She could have returned to Sacred Valley and carved through the Heaven's Glory school at any time, but she knew herself that it would accomplish nothing.

But something the Sage said caught her interest. Was it Sacred Valley itself that had opened the Sword Sage to the attacks of mere Jades? Yerin had always assumed it was the poison. But if there was something about the place...

Seeing that Yerin had not responded, the Winter Sage drew in a sharp breath, looking to Eithan and Saeya. "I'm here to bring you back, but the introduction has already begun. If you don't want to be disqualified, we should hurry."

Yerin shook herself as Naru Saeya thanked the sage for her assistance. The Winter Sage's appearance had knocked Yerin off balance, but this wasn't time to get lost in her own head. She had fights to win.

Wind aura, guided by the Sage, swept up both Eithan and Saeya. The Naru clanswoman spread her wings and reveled in the sensation, while Eithan stood, smiling gently as though he stood on solid ground.

Yerin bowed at the waist. "Apologies," she said to the Sage. She sounded too much like Lindon for her taste, but she pushed on. "I pushed too hard. Please bring me along so that I can bring honor to my master's memory."

A single tear ran down the woman's tan cheek. She whispered, "I hope you can."

*I hope so too,* Yerin thought.

**INFORMATION REQUESTED: LUMINOUS QUEEN SHA MIARA, MONARCH OF THE NINECLOUD COURT**

**BEGINNING REPORT...**

**PATH: CELESTIAL RADIANCE.** Uses royal madra to disrupt, control, and manipulate the madra of others. Has no effect on vital aura, and therefore no Ruler techniques, so a Celestial Radiance artist's ability to influence the physical world is largely limited to their ability with soulfire.

Royal madra, the rainbow-colored signature of the Ninecloud Court, is in fact a spiritual mutation of pure madra that occurred long ago in the Sha bloodline. From childhood, they can control the spirits of others, and over the centuries they have refined this power into a set of techniques and polished these techniques to perfection. Using their innately powerful madra, they solidified control over their nation and their continent, naming both after their sigil: a nine-colored cloud.

One of their most closely guarded techniques is known as Heaven's Wish. Once only, a practitioner can pass on their spirit to another. Far more thorough than the adoption of a Remnant, this technique allows for the near-total transfer of power and skill to an heir, though some knowledge is still lost.

Miara's mother, Sha Leiala, ruled over the Ninecloud people for two hundred years. Only three years prior to the eighteenth Uncrowned King tournament, she did battle with a host of powerful plague-spirits born beneath a disaster area in her country. Though she was victorious, her lifeline was damaged, and she was forced to pass on her inheritance years earlier than she planned.

Thus did Sha Miara, a girl of only twelve, inherit a Monarch's power.

The queen's death was a secret known only to a few, but still that secret leaked to rebellious elements within the Ninecloud Court. They sent a fleet of cloudships to the capital city, intending a coup. When they were struck down by the full might of a Monarch, they determined that Leiala's death had been nothing more than a false rumor.

The Sha family encouraged that belief, and the illusion of Sha Leiala still makes regular appearances all over the nation. As far as the citizens know, their queen is healthy and strong.

By royal decree, Sha Miara's name and her true identity as the Luminous Queen are known only to the Sha family, their direct servants, and the other Monarchs. She remains isolated in her palace, surrounded by the same faces every day.

But she is still only fifteen years old, and isolation is boring.

**Suggested topic: The destiny of Sha Miara. Continue?**

**Denied, report complete.**

Lindon's room in the Ninecloud Court gave him the taste of a Monarch's hospitality. Trays of fruits lined the walls, complex constructs attended to his every need, and the bed hypnotically lulled him to sleep. A flock of birds lived in the rafters, filling his day with their sweet song. There was even a bubbling spring in the center of the room.

He hated it.

For two weeks, he'd been unable to leave. All of his questions about the Blackflame team were answered with "They have not yet arrived." His room was connected to Mercy's and Pride's, but they knew no more than he did.

When the day of the tournament arrived, a team of servants spent an hour adjusting Lindon's Akura uniform, making sure that the script on the hem glowed bright violet, brushing the black cloth, straightening the high collar. He had never worn clothes so fine in his life.

Only once he and Pride and Mercy were all prepared did the floating constructs of the Ninecloud Court—which looked something like glistening red crabs floating around on rainbow clouds—instruct them to gather behind the door in Mercy's room. They would be picked up shortly.

When the door finally slid open, revealing Charity standing there in sacred arts robes not unlike their own, Lindon spoke first.

"Pardon, but has there been any news of the Blackflame team?"

He had expected to be cut off, or for Charity to brush his concern away. Instead, she let a look of sympathy cross her face.

"I'm sorry," she said, and his heart froze. "We've heard nothing. They have not yet crossed the border into Ninecloud. The Queen has not yet arrived, so we cannot petition her to find them, but the gold dragons have not claimed responsibility. We must assume that they have been delayed and will not arrive on time."

*Delayed,* Lindon thought numbly.

[Delayed isn't bad!] Dross encouraged him. [Delayed could mean anything. Maybe they're lost!]

"Please," he begged the Sage. "You brought me here. Can't you find them?"

Charity sighed. "I have limits to my skill and my power. When

I set up the gates to the Night Wheel Valley for your Empire, I had my grandmother's assistance. A Monarch could find them and bring them here easily, and perhaps another Sage. As for me...I have owls out searching. I am sorry."

Clutching Suu in one hand, Mercy asked a few more questions. She looked as panicked as Lindon was.

But he didn't hear the answers. When Charity walked away down the hall, Pride striding after her, Lindon followed like a puppet.

His Remnant arm began to twitch with the disorder in his spirit. He wanted to *do* something, to start looking for them. Or to avenge them.

After only a few minutes of walking, Charity ushered them into a plain gray room with tables, benches, shelves, and cabinets lining the walls.

"This is your team preparation room," Charity said. "It is located inside the grand arena itself. Here you will make yourself ready for each round and leave behind any weapons that are not permitted in the round. No one can access this place except our team or authorized representatives, so they will remain safe."

Pride pulled a void key from around his neck and began unloading his belongings into a cabinet. Lindon stood there, running over questions in his mind, and Mercy watched him.

Charity met his eyes then reached up with two fingers. Madra of shadow and dreams played around her fingers, and Lindon jerked his head back. Dross, however, said [Oooh, I wonder what *this* is,] and put up no defense whatsoever.

The Sage's fingers tapped Lindon's temples.

His doubts, fears, and worries washed away as though he'd been cleansed. He took a deep breath, like a weight had been lifted from his chest.

What was he worried about? His worry couldn't make things any better. He had a task to do, and there was no point distracting himself before he had concrete information. Any number of things could have happened to the Blackflame team, so why speculate?

Lindon gave a shallow bow to the Sage. "Gratitude."

"Don't thank me," Charity said. "It's only a temporary mental block. No matter what happens, I need you to give this round your full attention. But when the Monarch finds them...I will allow you to react however you need to."

Lindon nodded. That seemed fair. Following the lead of the others, he took off his void key and his halfsilver badge and placed them into a cabinet. Shame about the void key; it contained enough weapons to make any fight much easier.

Charity turned to Mercy. "There will be no sacred instruments allowed in this round."

Mercy was still watching Lindon. "Aunt Charity, that can't be..."

"It's necessary. Now prepare yourself."

Slowly, Mercy leaned Suu against a wall, but Lindon had already moved to stand next to Pride at the end of the room. A scripted section of stone would obviously slide up when their preparations had been completed.

Briefly, he wished he was standing side-by-side with Yerin and Eithan instead of the Akura team. But wishes weren't productive, so he merely acknowledged the desire and refocused.

"If you don't even make it past the first round," Pride said, "you will answer to me."

Lindon was relieved. "Really? Thank you. I was afraid I'd have to answer to your mother."

Pride glared at him.

[Whatever Charity did to you, I'm going to have to learn that trick. I like you much better like this.]

The script on the door shone as Mercy joined them, and Charity took a step back.

"I will be watching your progress on the Akura viewing platform. Do our family proud."

Pride loudly promised that he would, and Mercy nodded, but Lindon remained focused on the door ahead of him. When each of the runes in the script-circle lit, a rumbling of stone sounded, and the section of wall began to slide open.

Letting in a wave of noise.

Deafening cheers crashed over them as the door slid upward, giving Lindon his first view of the arena. The floor was dark gray and smooth, and it seemed very slick—if it was stone, then it was highly polished.

Mercy left first, followed by Pride, and Lindon behind, as he'd been instructed.

As they left the room, bright light and noise overwhelmed him.

His Underlord body adjusted almost immediately, and he took in his surroundings. They walked onto the floor of a massive arena, so large that it looked like it had been designed to host the clash of armies rather than individuals.

Above them, an illusion of light and dreams projected them into midair at a thousand times the height. A giant projection of Mercy waved to the crowds around her, flawlessly reproduced by madra.

Her name unfurled on a banner behind her, and the Ninecloud Soul's voice spoke from all around them: "Representing the Monarch Akura Malice, the Akura prime team presents Akura Mercy, the favored daughter of the Monarch herself."

The noise redoubled. All around the arena stood eight towers, each built to illustrate the glory of a Monarch faction. The structure had been explained to Lindon already: the Monarchs would watch from a floating platform above each tower as their families and followers watched from within.

As the Ninecloud Soul announced Pride, Lindon glanced back at the Akura tower. It towered over their waiting room, at least eight stories high, all made of wood such a dark purple that it might as well have been black. Unlike many of the other viewing towers, the stands in each level were hidden, covered by shadow madra. He could see nothing from within, though he could still hear the cheers.

Above the tower floated a shrunken mountain growing from shadowy clouds. Dark-leaved trees dotted the mountain, along with a few luxurious-looking houses, but Lindon couldn't make out the details.

Charity and Fury would watch from up there, as would Malice whenever she arrived. The Akura had certainly embraced the image of looming threat.

"The final member of the Akura prime team is an adopted member of an Arelius branch family and a member of the Blackflame Empire vassal state. By the mercy of the Heart Sage, he was raised up to represent the Akura clan: Wei Shi Lindon Arelius!"

The cheers were no less loud for Lindon than for the other two, but he detected a distinct note of confusion, as though many in the crowd could not figure out why he was there.

[I sympathize,] Dross said.

Lindon and the other two walked across to the center of the arena, kneeling in circles that had already been arranged for them on the ground. They knelt next to twelve other young Underlords and Underladies: the Ninecloud Court teams.

They had been introduced before the Akura clan, so Lindon had missed their introduction. But over the last fourteen days he had asked for information on the other teams, so the announcement wouldn't have included anything he didn't already know.

...or so he had thought before he glanced over to get a look for himself. His gaze froze at the young woman in the front of the wedge, the closest position to the center. The same position that Mercy occupied for the Akura.

She looked to be a few years younger than Lindon, maybe fourteen or fifteen, with pale skin and long, blood-red hair. While the others from her faction all stared curiously at the Akura team, she knelt with her back straight and her eyes closed, hands folded on her knees, as though she couldn't care less what happened around her.

Lindon's nerves pushed at the restraints of the madra Charity had placed around him. *Dross, what was the name of the Ninecloud team leader?*

[Sha Dellian. You think that's him?]

*No, I don't.*

Even if Dellian looked more feminine than his description suggested, he had orange hair, not red. Lindon's memories of his time with Suriel were still very clear, and if he added a few years onto Sha Miara, she might look exactly like the Underlady sitting there.

But there was no way Suriel would have shown him a vision of someone stuck at Underlord. She had placed Sha Miara, as a little girl, on the same level as Northstrider or the Eight-Man Empire.

[Maybe this is her sister,] Dross reasoned. [Or a copy of her grown in a vat and compelled to destroy her enemies.]

Lindon resolved to look up her name after the ceremony.

After the prime Akura team, the Ninecloud Soul announced the Akura backup team. Led by Akura Grace, they had been added to fill the gap left by the destroyed Rising Earth team.

Those three sat in the row behind Lindon and Pride, who were themselves seated behind Mercy.

Once again, the cheers took on a strange tone. Lindon thought he heard some jeers mixed in from the other stands. It was considered embarrassing to bring two teams from your primary faction, implying that you weren't confident enough in your vassal factions. It made the Akura clan look weak, like they didn't have enough reliable underlings and had to make up the difference.

Two of the Underlords behind him whispered to one another, but Grace cut them off. When Lindon glanced behind him, she nodded to him.

After them came the Frozen Blade team. Two of them were Underladies older than Lindon, wearing sky-blue robes and with icy blades extending from their forearms. Their black hair was streaked with white, and they carried blue-sheathed swords.

The third was a young Underlord who stumbled after them in a poor imitation of their poise, his own sword cradled in both arms. It was clear which of them was the last-minute replacement.

Then came the moment he was waiting for...and the announcement from the Ninecloud Soul that he'd dreaded.

"The final vassal team of the Akura clan, the Blackflame Empire, has not arrived," the pleasant female voice said. "Therefore, at this time, the Akura clan is permitted to form a backup team from any remaining qualified individuals."

This time, the buzz from among the stands was as loud as the cheering had been earlier. Most of the other towers were not shrouded like the Akura clan's, so Lindon could see the stares aimed their way.

His restraint, reinforced as it had been by Charity, continued to crack. What had happened to Yerin? It was difficult to imagine anything surprising Eithan, but he wasn't the biggest fish in the pond anymore. If a Herald had shown up...

The rainbow light turned its focus to the tower next to the Akura's, which was the plainest of all. It looked like a normal wooden tower separated into eight floors, each of them filled with raised tiers of seats and bustling with humanity of all descriptions, as well as dozens of sacred beasts. One figure stood out on each level: a man or woman in gleaming gold armor.

"I present to you the representatives of the Eight-Man Empire and the Ghost-Blade warband, the squires of...one moment. Apologies to the Ghost-Blades, but it seems we have a late arrival."

When the stone door behind him began to grind open, Lindon spun all the way around.

Yerin led the way, hair streaming behind her like a banner and wind whipping at her black robes. He had heard her voice every other day for the last seven or eight months, but now the sight of her crashed over him like a wave.

She was *real.*

He wasn't used to seeing her without her scars, but when her eyes met his, she visibly brightened, and a half-smile tugged at one corner of her mouth.

The relief was so sudden and overwhelming that Charity's restrictions on his emotions collapsed. He struggled to sit straight and to keep his breathing ordered.

Eithan strode to catch up with Yerin, holding her back for a moment as Naru Saeya took the lead. No doubt that was supposed to have been their marching order all along.

The Emperor's sister was tall and resplendent, emerald wings spread, and she accepted the cheers at her introduction with visible grace. The crowd was noticeably less enthusiastic about the vassal teams, but she made her walk and settled into her place behind the Frozen Blade team with poise.

Eithan, after her, waved cheerily to everyone. His long golden hair was flawlessly combed, and he wore a dark blue outer robe wrapped in white and black. Lindon was sure the Arelius family symbol would be sewn into the back. In other words, he looked the same as ever, and winked at Lindon as he settled into his own seat.

Lindon exchanged looks with Yerin again, reassuring himself that she was really there. When she caught his gaze, she jerked her head back toward their waiting room.

He craned further, twisting almost all the way around, and saw the door closing on the Winter Sage. She must have been the one to bring them back. Before the stone passed in front of her, he noticed her complicated expression.

Once the Blackflame Empire team had been settled and Lindon's heart had calmed down, he realized the Ninecloud Soul was introducing the Eight-Man Empire teams. Each of their four teams came from a different warband: Ghost-Blade, Flame-Gift, Blood-Chorus, and Nine-Hands. Based on his research at the Akura clan, the names were usually related to the primary Path practiced by each band.

Next to the plain wooden tower stood a structure of steel and glass that shone brightly in the sun. Before reaching Underlord, Lindon wouldn't have been able to stare at it directly without hurting his eyes. The Monarch platform overhead was a huge globe of dark water, suspended in midair, with a half-seen creature circling in its depths.

Northstrider's platform. Lindon repressed a shudder, reminded of Ghostwater.

"The unaffiliated sects and independent sacred artists gather in the name of Northstrider, the great Monarch who lost his life only a short time ago in battle against the Weeping Dragon," the Ninecloud Soul said. "May we all die with such honor and courage."

[He's *not* dead, right?] Dross asked nervously.

*We know he isn't. I've seen him since then.*

[Are you *sure* you can trust this Suriel? Maybe she showed you an illusion or a recording! ...oh no. That's it, isn't it? It was a recording. Oh, he's dead. He's definitely dead.]

*You've seen the memory,* Lindon thought. *You tell me. And he must have been the one to stop Charity from saving Harmony in Ghostwater.* Over the last few months, he had asked some careful questions about what had happened back in Ghostwater and had pieced together his own answers.

[Right, right, of course. This is all part of a plan. A *secret* plan. Do you think he'll show up?]

*Hopefully not,* Lindon responded.

[I won't say anything. But think how happy he'd be to see me!]

Only one participant of Northstrider's caught Lindon's eye: a young-looking but haggard man in a tattered gray cloak. His green horns glistened in the sunlight. Ziel.

*He's eligible?* Lindon asked Dross, surprised. *The last time we saw him, he was considered a Truegold.*

With the damage to his spirit, it was a surprise that Ziel could use the sacred arts at all. Lindon strongly suspected that he had once been at least an Overlord, maybe an Archlord, but someone had twisted and tormented his spirit until even producing the power of a Gold was a stretch. Maybe he was regaining his former powers.

[I assumed he was about a thousand years old,] Dross said. [He talks like he was born old.]

Lindon tried to get Ziel's attention without moving around too much, but the horned man kept his eyes on the ground. He settled into the middle of the pack, in between the two other members of the Beast King's faction team, and collapsed into his assigned circle as though trying to melt into the floor.

Massive blocks of pale stone held up by fluted columns made up the next viewing tower. The people inside were draped in white and by and large had bright yellow hair, though Lindon noticed there were fewer people in these stands than in any of the others.

Above their tower, a cloud flashed constantly with bright blue lightning. It was an impressive display, but it emitted none of the spiritual pressure that came from the other Monarch platforms. Lindon doubted there was anyone up there.

The Arelius Monarch, after all, had been killed.

As the Ninecloud Soul announced the team from House Arelius, each of whom might have been Eithan's cousin, Lindon noticed that they got even weaker applause than most of the vassal teams. And all three members stared at Eithan before sitting down.

Lindon turned to see Eithan's reaction, but he greeted his relatives with a bright grin and a wave. Was Eithan hiding his real feelings, or was his reaction to seeing his relatives for the first time in years really so uncomplicated?

The next tower was one of the most eye-catching. It looked to be made of copper clockworks with gaps filled in with glowing Remnant parts of every size and description. Dark-skinned people filled the stands, each of them accompanied by at least one puppet construct. They whirred through the air, marched up the stairs, hung on chairs, or dangled from the ceiling.

Instead of a Monarch platform, a tree covered the roof of the tower, so large that it doubled the structure's height. It was made of blue-green light, like a Remnant, but with a layer of density and detail that Lindon had never seen. He could see grooves in the bark, veins in the leaves...and Lindon's soulfire-refined eyes picked out eyes in the center of each leaf.

This was Emriss Silentborn, Queen of the Everwood Continent and Monarch of Titan's Grove. The Remnant Monarch. While most of the other Monarchs exuded an overwhelming spiritual pressure even while veiled, Emriss gave off a soothing, reassuring presence. Almost a familiar one, though Lindon was sure they had never met before.

[Emriss is the most public of the Monarchs,] Dross said, [and it's rare to see her stay in the same place long. It's thanks to her that you humans can all speak to each other; she spends her life traveling around and gifting people with language.] He thought for a moment. [We should try meeting her. I bet she has a real fondness for mind-spirits.]

Directly across from the Akura clan stood a tower made from massive logs like undressed trees. They had no tiered seats like most of the other stands, only big open platforms where dragons—some in human form, some not—jockeyed for position. Those on the lowest platform were almost all in the form of dragons, but the higher tiers had more and more in the guise of humans. Silken veils shrouded the top layer of the tower.

The Monarch platform was by far the smallest. It was only a single covered throne, floating on a cloud of sand over the tower. A boy sat in the chair, wearing nothing but a worn wrap.

Lindon focused on him, catching a glimpse of sandy hair, golden eyes, and pale skin, but very quickly removed his eyes. His spirit screamed danger even from just *glancing* at the King of Dragons, as though staring for more than a second would draw his wrath.

He only *looked* like a twelve-year-old boy, Lindon knew. He was a Monarch, and perhaps the oldest of them.

Far beneath him, his descendant led the march out of the waiting room.

As the Ninecloud Soul announced Sopharanatoth, leader of the gold dragon team, her golden eyes focused on Lindon. Her human form was mostly complete, but patches of gold scales dotted the pale skin of her cheeks and the backs of her hands. Her nails resembled claws, and her thin golden tail whipped the air behind her.

Her face was sculpted into a fine image of human beauty, and her clothes were ornate layers of red and purple, but she stared into Lindon with such fury that he could feel it in his spirit. She spared some for Pride, and settled on Mercy as she sank to her knees only a few feet across from the Akura team.

Lindon couldn't see how Mercy responded, but he kept his eyes on Sophara. She radiated hate, glaring at their whole team.

[I don't know about you, but I'm relieved. Someone truly dangerous would keep their emotions in check.]

Lindon hoped that was true. The earlier he could get a lead on the gold dragons, the more he could relax.

He'd thought of the dragon team as the last, but in fact there was one more. A tower that he hadn't paid much attention to until now... but when he did, it sent a spike of alarm through him.

The Monarch platform at the top was a palace that floated unsupported by clouds. It had open sides with no walls, only pillars supporting the roof containing a garden that looked like a paradise. Carefully cultivated trees and bushes spilled from the sides along with a shining waterfall that trickled down to the ground, and Lindon was certain he heard distant music within. That was the most ordinary part.

Beneath it, the tower was divided into four floors...with each floor representing a Dreadgod.

Lindon had done some research into the Dreadgods after the Bleeding Phoenix's attack on the Blackflame Empire, and a little more during his time in the Akura family. Much of the common knowledge about them came from rumor, hearsay, or legend. But he had put together a basic picture.

The top floor of the viewing tower contained blue seats, and was carved with the image of a dragon surrounded by crackling lightning. The Weeping Dragon. Its cult, the Stormcallers, filled the seats. Their Goldsigns—sparking rings of lightning around each arm—lit the inside of the floor.

The next floor down was all white, topped by the image of a crowned tiger and filled with sacred artists with cloths tied around their mouths. The Silent Servants, cult of the Silent King.

Lindon was already too familiar with the inhabitants of the red floor, who called themselves Redmoon Hall. Other than wearing red and black, they had very little in common—some were followed openly by their Blood Shadows, but others did not keep theirs visible. Their floor was covered by a carving of the Bleeding Phoenix, a crimson bird with wings spread.

The leader of their team caught his eye: Yan Shoumei, the girl he'd met in Ghostwater. Her hair hung over her eyes like a hood, and her Blood Shadow slithered formlessly around her.

He hoped she didn't remember him.

Finally, on the ground floor, the members of Abyssal Palace wore hoods and stone masks. Their seats were black, and they gathered beneath the image of the Wandering Titan, a turtle-shelled armored warrior.

No Monarch controlled the Dreadgods. No Monarch could, as far as Lindon understood the world. But someone had gathered the four separate cults together under one banner, and by process of elimination, Lindon could guess who it was even before the Ninecloud Soul named him: Reigan Shen, Emperor of Lions and Monarch of the Rosegold continent.

Lindon watched the Dreadgod teams emerge from the waiting

room with disgust, and he wasn't the only one. *No one* cheered for them, not even their own tower. The Stormcallers and Redmoon Hall emerged to uneasy silence.

Even Sophara the gold dragon stopped glaring at the Akura team to spare some hostility for the Dreadgods. The Ninecloud Soul's voice had the slightest hint of a condescending tone to it as she announced each cult, though of course she did not openly disparage anyone. The Ninecloud Court would not offend Reigan Shen.

When Abyssal Palace took their seats, the focus shifted back to the eight wedges of twelve sacred artists seated in the center of the arena.

Music swelled, celebrating the completion of the announcement. Nine-colored fireworks burst overhead, and the Ninecloud Soul began a speech about the power of the sacred arts and the glory of the upcoming competition.

Finally, as the fireworks and the music reached a crescendo, the illusion in the center of the arena turned to a column of rainbow light.

"Sacred artists," the Ninecloud Soul announced, "glorious Monarchs, the time has come! Let the first round of the eighteenth Uncrowned King tournament finally...begin!"

Between each tower, a list appeared written in the air, each bearing ninety-six names: all the fighters, ready to be ranked. Applause and cheers shook the ground, and Lindon tensed his body and spirit.

"The contents of this first round are a mystery to the participants," the voice continued. "We will give each young person a chance to demonstrate the full range of their skills and specialties, and their performance will be judged by a panel of independent judges gathered from all throughout the world."

Rainbow light indicated another hovering platform, much more humble than the rest, enclosed so that Lindon could not see anyone inside.

"The Monarchs have agreed to abide by the judgment of these experts, so the results of this tournament should never—"

**"Hold."**

A deep voice echoed throughout the arena, and everyone stopped. A wisp of Mercy's hair, which had been blowing in the wind, froze in place. The wind itself stopped blowing, and some of the fireworks froze mid-explosion. Lindon's breath locked in his chest. Even his thoughts seemed to slow.

A ragged, blue-edged hole opened in midair, and Northstrider stepped out.

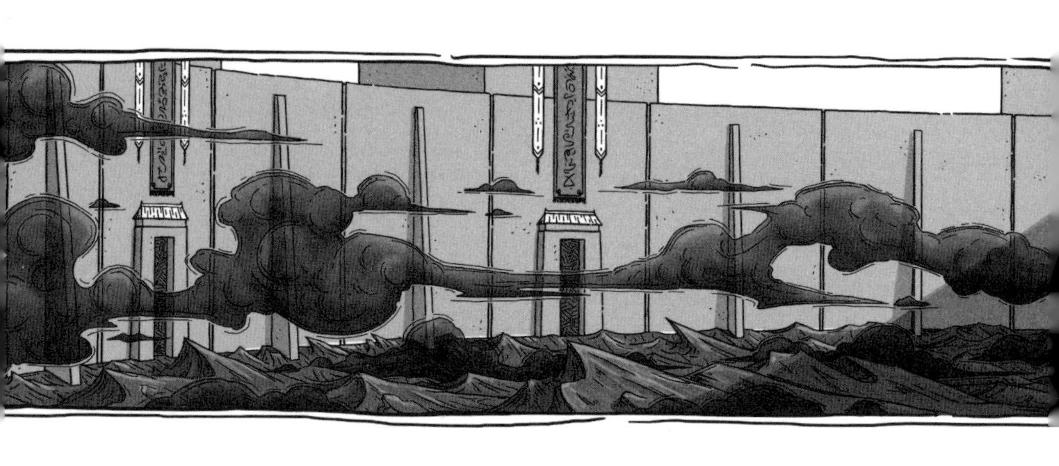

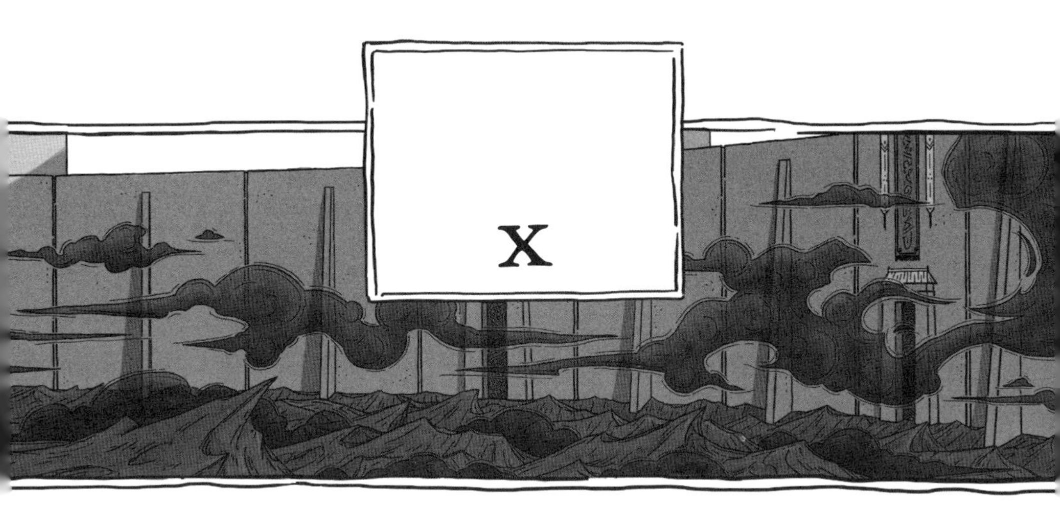


SURIEL HAD SHOWN LINDON A VISION OF NORTHSTRIDER, AND he had seen an image of the Monarch projected by a construct in Ghostwater. Seeing him in person was a guttural shock, like catching a glimpse of a mythical beast.

Northstrider was tall and powerfully built, with broad shoulders and defined muscles. His long, wild hair and unshaven face suggested he'd been wandering in the wild, and his skin was browned by long exposure to the sun. His eyes were golden and vertically slitted, like those of the gold dragons, and black scales covered his hands up to his elbows.

He wore rough, shapeless, dirty clothes that looked as if he'd scavenged them from different places and replaced each piece as it wore out. His shoes didn't match, an armored leather sleeve had replaced one leg of his pants, his belt was a thick rope, and his "shirt" was a series of cloths wrapped over and around his chest. He looked like he'd dressed himself by robbing beggars.

But his will held the entire arena in thrall, and even with his spirit veiled, the sense of his power was overwhelming. His gaze carried behind it the weight of an emperor.

Northstrider looked up to the flying paradise with its crystalline waterfall spilling over the edge.

A second later, another figure stepped out of nowhere. He was shorter than Northstrider, but just as broad, with chiseled and handsome features that looked as though they belonged on the statue of an ancient king.

Lindon had heard that the Monarch of the House of Shen was a sacred lion, and indeed this man's gold-tinged white hair and beard blended into one majestic white-gold mane. He was dressed like the Arelius family in a white linen skirt that fell to his feet and a white wrap across his chest.

In contrast to Northstrider, the newcomer's simple clothing looked like intentional fashion. The cloth was pristine, his belt was made of shimmering goldsteel links, and jeweled rings glinted on every finger. He held a golden goblet in one hand, and he gestured with it toward the column of rainbow light, which had frozen along with everything else in the world.

The light streamed down once again, and Lindon heard the Ninecloud Soul draw in a breath. However, she never lost her professional tone as she announced, "Guests from all over the world, history has been overturned! We are joined by the legendary Monarch Northstrider himself! We ourselves believed he fell in battle years ago, but no rumors can constrain him!"

Deathly silence met her. Everyone else was still frozen. Lindon was starting to suffer for the lack of air.

"Wise Monarch of the Hungry Deep," the voice said gently, "would you release your hold on the audience so that they may celebrate your presence?"

Northstrider still faced his opposite, and made no reaction that Lindon could see, but his restriction released. The wind blew, the fireworks drifted down from the sky, and Lindon heaved in a breath as the crowd took in a collective gasp.

The other man, who Lindon assumed to be the Monarch Reigan Shen, clicked his tongue impatiently.

Rainbow light flowed around him as the voice of the Ninecloud Court spoke. "It is our honor to present the Emperor of the Rosegold continent, who needs no introduction! Sacred artists, prostrate yourselves in humility before the greatest of lions, the creator of the Path of the King's Key, Monarch Reigan Shen!"

Thunderous applause. Lindon and most of the other competitors joined in; no one wanted to have their breath stopped again.

The Arelius teams, he noticed, did not clap. They stared at the Monarch as though daring him to strike them down.

Reigan Shen spoke without quieting the audience, but his languid voice filled the arena nonetheless. "Northstrider! We are pleased to see you here. We knew you would never have fallen to a mere serpent."

Shen might as well have been talking about the weather for all Northstrider reacted.

"I judge this tournament now," Northstrider announced to the entire arena, and his tone left no room for debate. "The contestants will fight under my protection and according to my will."

Reigan Shen shook with silent laughter, waving his goblet through the air. "That hardly seems fair, does it?" he asked, voice amused. "Who is to stop you from declaring your own team the victor? Or exiling our team to the void? Not that we would accuse you of such...petty conduct."

He sipped from his goblet, watching Northstrider over the rim.

Lindon didn't know what he expected to see. Northstrider's face might as well have been carved from stone.

Finally, Shen waved a hand in irritation. "Fine. If none of our peers has an objection, then we have none. You are certainly...overly qualified to supervise the squabbling of children."

If Shen was attempting to get a visible reaction out of Northstrider, he failed. The Monarch of the Hungry Deep walked away, and the Ninecloud Soul sounded shocked as she made her declaration.

"On behalf of the Ninecloud Court and in the name of Monarch Sha Leiala, I announce a...sudden...alteration to the rules," the voice said. "Rather than our distinguished panel of judges and experts from all across the world, the competition will now be judged by a Monarch directly! This is an unprecedented honor to the contestants, and a mark of glory for what will surely be the greatest tournament ever held!"

The audience gave some confused cheers after that, though Lindon stayed focused on Northstrider.

The Monarch paid no attention to the lesser sacred artists around him. His eyes moved from one Monarch platform to the next, as though watching for something that Lindon couldn't see.

He was looking for the reactions of his equals...or perhaps challenging them.

Reigan Shen stepped into nothing and disappeared, and no other Monarchs objected. When he had finished turning to each of the other seven towers, Northstrider folded his arms and closed his eyes, waiting for the Ninecloud Soul to continue her speech.

Obviously, in his mind, the matter was settled.

[He's going to watch us *directly!*] Dross said breathlessly. [...what if he doesn't like how I look? What if he thinks I have too many arms? Or *not enough?*]

As if Lindon didn't have enough to worry about, this brought a new source of panic. Now Northstrider would be watching their fights closely...and if he looked closely enough at Lindon, he would find Dross.

Would he consider Lindon a thief?

When the Ninecloud Soul paused in her speech, Northstrider spoke again without opening his eyes, and his voice reverberated throughout the arena. "As all participants are under my protection, they should fight freely. None may die unless I allow it, and they will be restored to perfect condition when necessary. So it shall be."

The pillar of rainbow light shone brighter. "The Ninecloud Court thanks the Monarch for his support! Now, with all surprises settled and no further changes, we come to the beginning of the opening round! Monarch, we begin at your will."

Lindon drew himself inward, breathing steadily, cycling his madra. He could feel Dross doing something similar, focusing his attention.

"Begin," Northstrider said.

In a flash of blue light, everyone vanished.

When Lindon found himself in a dark cave, he immediately extended his spiritual perception and realized he was alone. There were powerful constructs buried beneath the ground and many scripts in operation, but no other living souls.

*Why divide us into teams just to separate us?* he wondered.

[False hope,] Dross said confidently. [Lift up your spirits and then just smash them to pieces.]

Lindon stood in a cavern of dark, jagged rock a few dozen feet wide and the same distance high. Lights speckled the ceiling like tiny stars. The cavern was much longer than it was wide, perhaps three hundred yards distant, and he could see no entrance or exit.

Before he could adjust to his new surroundings, the ground shook. A white dome split the rock beneath his feet, rising under him. He tried to leap off, but an invisible barrier prevented him, keeping him standing on the dome.

Dross screamed. [The earth is attacking! Kill it! Kill it!]

The dome rose up to the height of a house, giving him a look to the far end of the cavern. Against the distant wall, a black dome rose in exact parallel to the white dome on which he stood.

In front of his white dome, soldiers made of matching white rose up from the stone. The size and rough shape of men, the soldiers rose in three rows, each with about two dozen figures standing shoulder-to-shoulder. The edges of their line scraped the walls.

The ones in front carried shields and spears, the second row carried bows, and the final row were all individual sacred artists with their own Paths. Some of those had claws, some conjured flame, and some had haloes of light around their head.

The army of black figures looked exactly the same. It was like a game board, each side precisely matching the other.

In the air before Lindon, characters appeared in golden flame: "Defeat the Army."

Then the front ranks of the armies rushed at each other.

The invisible wall containing Lindon vanished, but he didn't move away from the dome. When the golden words had appeared, a scroll had also fallen out of nowhere into his hand. He unraveled the scroll and read it.

The armies, it said, were perfectly matched. He could see as much just from observing the way the white and black soldiers would pierce each other at the same time. They replaced themselves endlessly—Lindon watched that happen too. After a pair of front-line soldiers fell, two more rose from the stone in the back, then hustled to return to the front.

However, the situation would not remain in a stalemate forever. The black soldiers would replace themselves faster and faster until eventually the white side was overwhelmed.

Lindon's objective was to lead the white army to victory by either eliminating all the black soldiers or destroying the dome representing the black base. Competitors would be ranked based on how thoroughly and how quickly they completed their tasks.

This was only the first of fifteen trials making up the first round of the competition. After that, the scroll contained no new information.

[Easy enough,] Dross said. [Just fire at the base. Give it a quick lick of dragon's breath, and we'll be on our way.]

Lindon doubted that would work, and he was too far away to hit the black dome anyway, but he needed more information.

He hopped down from the dome, dashing forward without using an Enforcer technique.

*I'd like to avoid showing too much,* Lindon said silently to Dross. *The audience is watching us, and we want to give our opponents as little information as possible.*

[Ah, I get it. A stealth mission. That's what I was born for: stealth. I'm so sneaky I hardly exist.]

Lindon ran through the back line of white soldiers—they parted to let him pass, but there was no empty space to the side for him to skirt around. He could feel now that each of these constructs had the power of an Underlord. He didn't know if they were created by powerful experts or ancient artifacts, but they would not be simple to defeat.

The battle raged around him, crushing his spiritual sense and shaking his body. Shield-bearing warriors slammed against each other, rattling Lindon's teeth, as Striker techniques scorched the air above him.

Black stone soldiers loomed over him, and though he was still a little far for his dragon's breath to be effective, he tried shooting a bar of black-and-red madra at the enemy dome.

As he'd expected, a globe of water rose from the sacred artists in the back row, swallowing up his technique. They would counter any attack he made on the enemy base.

Lindon retreated, sharing a quick discussion with Dross.

[They're using the same techniques and tactics over and over, so I could probably build a model of any one. But it'll take a little longer to hold the whole battlefield. I think the simplest solution is to eliminate one or to tilt things in our favor.]

Lindon agreed, but he'd have to show off his Blackflame Path to do so. He was feeling the pressure of time—as far as he knew, the other Underlords had all completed their task by now—but he suspected the hazards of rushing were greater than taking his time.

*The purpose of the first round is to give everyone a chance to display their full power, even if they won't make it any further in the competition,* Lindon said. *Real victory will be if we can pass without showing all the cards in our hand.*

[Oh, that's a good plan! As long as you don't fail. You don't think you'll fail, do you? That would be embarrassing, round one. Right out of the gate.]

Lindon backed up toward his dome. Two white soldiers climbed out of the stone, nodded to him, and then hurried to the battle. The gray stone of the plain healed as soon as they left.

He knelt and pressed his left hand to the rock, extending his spiritual perception. *How does this work?* he asked Dross.

[Hmmm...there are three different bindings down here making the soldiers, and then there are scripts that contain and control all the little fiddly pieces that make everything work.]

*Could we disrupt it?*

[Yes, but actually no. You feel that shield around the bindings? Right there, feel that? The second you try and send any madra down there, that's going to get in the way. It would take you longer to blast your way down there and destroy the bindings than it would to just kill some soldiers. Which is the plan I would recommend, by the way.]

Lindon flexed the fingers of his right hand. *But the shield is a madra construct? Not a script?*

[Oh, *I* see where you're heading with this. Yeah, that might work. It's all made of Lord-level madra, not like it was made by a Sage or a Monarch, so it's possible. Give it a try. The only thing to lose is the entire competition.]

Pressing his white Remnant arm to the ground, Lindon activated the binding. Hunger madra reached out, sticky threads of greed running down the stone toward the construct that produced the soldiers. The shield sprung to life, a spiritual dome surrounding the constructs, but the tendrils of hunger madra latched on. And began to feed.

Gray madra flooded into Lindon's arm, and he had to break off contact to vent it into the air in an explosive spray of force. Two more tries, and he'd drained the shield completely. The script surrounding it was dark and un-powered, the construct vulnerable.

Lindon stood, shaking out his aching right hand. *All right, now the trick will be getting through the soldiers to the other two constructs.*

[Eh, well, you don't want to show *all* your cards. You still have to show a few.]

Lindon ignited the Soul Cloak.

From the comfort of her mansion on the Akura floating mountain, Charity looked down onto the arena through a viewing-mirror.

The audience down below watched a handful of images at a time, each projected in crisp detail by light and dream madra into the center of the arena. The Ninecloud Court tournament staff would select the most interesting visions and share them with the audience.

The gold-scaled Sopharanatoth burned a hole straight through the black soldiers, running through the gap for their base in seconds. She tore through all attempts to slow her down.

Her image transformed into Yerin, whose sword-aura radiated out, blasting chunks from every black soldier at once. Her Path was perfect for annihilating large ranks of weaker enemies, and only a minute or two passed before she had reduced her opponents to gravel. Though the black soldiers would re-form faster than the white, it wouldn't be enough to overcome such a disadvantage.

One of the Weeping Dragon's acolytes in the Stormcallers was up next, calling living blue lightning from clear skies to destroy his opponents. Then the image became a boy from the Wastelands in a gray cloak, running on green circles of force over the opposing lines and smashing the enemy base with a fist enhanced by Forged script. One after the other, shocking and impressive scenes played themselves before the audience.

But Charity was not shackled to that presentation. Though she wasn't in the same room as her grandmother, all of the private Monarch platforms had access to their own viewing constructs.

Charity reached out to a script-circle at the side, etched into a diamond tablet the size of her two hands put together. It was a treasure worth cities, but the Ninecloud Court had provided several to each Monarch.

With a flicker of spirit, Charity watched her niece and nephew. The tablet grew clear, and in its depths she could watch whichever trial she wished without alteration.

Mercy fired Forged arrow after arrow, and even though she didn't have a bow, her Striker techniques were powerful enough to destroy or seal the enemy sacred artists in the back row. She wiped the most dangerous foes from the battlefield, and as soon as they regenerated from their constructs, a hail of shadowy arrows met them again. It wasn't long before the white army overwhelmed the black.

Mercy passed in six minutes, twenty-seven seconds. That put her in fourth place...for this first trial of the round. There were fourteen trials to go.

Not a bad start. The top sixty-four by the end of the round would pass; there was little chance that either of Malice's children would come close to failing.

Pride fought alongside his soldiers, tearing a spear from his enemy and putting it through the head of another. When he'd torn a gap in the front line, he was released into the archers. A wolf among sheep. Each of his fists shattered stone, and his movements were a blur compared to the Forged soldiers.

The sacred artists had to band together to lock him in place, but that drew their attention away from the rest of the line, creating weaknesses. Soon after Mercy's, his soldiers mopped up the enemies.

Eight minutes, eight seconds. Twelfth place. A respectable beginning.

Then she turned her attention to the third member of her team.

At two minutes, Lindon had returned to his dome and pressed his hand against the ground. She could sense a little of the spirit involved, enough to know he was manipulating the madra of his hunger arm, but not specifically to see what he was doing with it. She thought he may have been drawing on the constructs for power until he vented the force madra into the air.

Another minute passed. Then he activated his pure madra Enforcer technique, madra rippling around him in a blue-white flame, and dashed into the soldiers.

His movements were quick and fluid, though not as quick or as coordinated as she knew he was capable of. That was good—he at least recognized the value of holding back.

When he finally broke through the third line of sacred artists, she expected him to attack the dome. So did the soldiers; three of the sacred artists in black used barrier techniques, surrounding their base in protection as archers fired on the intruder.

Lindon fell to his knees, sliding past the arrows, and dug his right hand into the ground. Hunger madra activated again.

He was attacking the constructs that produced more soldiers. Charity resisted the urge to put her head in her hands. He thought he was being clever, but it wasn't as though the soldiers would leave him unharmed.

As expected, they didn't. He had to break off his technique when a sacred artist swept a line of sword-madra at him, but he fell back down and continued draining the shield.

An archer fired an arrow at him, and he slipped under it, letting the projectile pass over his shoulder. Then he vented a bolt of stolen force madra into the chest of an approaching soldier, forcing him back.

And returned to devouring the construct.

Finally, as one of the destroyed archers rose from the stone behind him, he succeeded. The archer crumbled to dust half-formed, the construct creating it destroyed, and Lindon ran from his pursuers.

That was twelve minutes. Two minutes later, at fourteen minutes, forty-two seconds, his soldiers cleaned up the enemy.

Down in the arena, each of the shining lists displayed his current rank. Sixty-sixth. More than just speed was taken into account, and Lindon's victory had been messy. If he had cleanly destroyed the enemy base, he would have placed perhaps fiftieth.

Charity sat, tapping her fingers together, thinking. He had used only three techniques—his hunger arm, his dragon's breath, and the Soul Cloak. It would not be clear to many what exactly he'd done with his arm, and he had used neither of the other techniques to their full capacity.

He was keeping his weapons concealed. That could be an advantage. So far, he hadn't stood out; the display in the arena hadn't shown him once. Any opponent who did not do their thorough research would overlook him.

But if he wanted to win, he'd have to stand out eventually.

The second trial found Lindon in a much smaller room, about the size of the meeting rooms the Skysworn used back in Starsweep Tower. There was one table, two chairs on either side, and a metal box the size of his hand sitting on the surface.

"Open the Box," the glowing golden letters said.

A man made of Forged gray madra sat in the seat opposite

Lindon. He was much more detailed than the soldiers had been, with stone clothes and a fully developed face that registered boredom. He looked ordinary, like a shopkeeper tired of dealing with customers all day.

Once again, a scroll fell into Lindon's hand.

In the second trial, the box must be opened. As before, participants would be graded on both speed and skill. The man in the chair had the key to the box in his soulspace, and they could treat him as they would a living human being.

The box itself could be opened without the key, but only if the puzzle locking it was solved.

That was the end of the scroll.

Lindon put it down and looked to the man. "Apologies for my rudeness, but would you mind giving me the key to this box?"

The man snorted, looking away from Lindon.

[I wonder if you could bribe him,] Dross said, but Lindon had already picked up the box. There were sliding panels all over the box, and it looked as though if he slid them apart in the right sequence, the box would open. But every panel he moved affected all the others in an intricate, interlocking cascade.

*Dross, make a model,* Lindon said, holding up the box.

[Keep your perception on it, please. Hm, yes, yes, I see. Turn it slowly. Slower. Faster than that. All right. Slide some of the panels aside. Just play with it for a minute. Hm, interesting, interesting.]

*What are you doing?* Lindon finally asked.

[Oh, nothing, I was just thinking about what a nice vessel this would be for a memory construct. I've got the model.]

*And the solution?*

[I think so. Fiddle with it a little bit.]

"You'll never figure it out," the statue of the man said with a sneer, "but I could take pity on you and give you a hint. What has three legs—"

The box snapped open.

Yerin landed in the next room. Words appeared in front of her, but she couldn't read them. She didn't waste her time glancing at the scroll.

"Rules?" she asked impatiently. When she hadn't read the text in the first trial, the voice from the Ninecloud court had explained things to her.

"Open the box," the disembodied woman explained. "The man in the chair has the key in his soulspace, or you can solve the puzzle keeping the box shut. You will be graded on speed and skill, but you may use any methods you like."

Instantly, Yerin drove her hand—surrounded by sword madra—at the man's Forged gray throat.

He slipped aside, as fast as she was, and his eyes shone with a bright platinum light. "Thief!" he roared. A pair of axes appeared in his hands, and he revealed his spirit: Underlord.

He swung his weapons at her, but that was his mistake. The sword-aura around them rang like a bell, and sparks flew as the Endless Sword blocked both blows. His weapons flew to either side, and Yerin drove her hand through his chest.

He broke apart immediately, but the key didn't just fall to the ground, as she had hoped. A fake Remnant rose from his body, a towering shrimp-like creature with claws poised.

Yerin leaped into the air.

The instant the words "Open the Box" appeared, Sha Miara gave a delicate laugh. She placed her fingertips on the box, filling its every nook with her royal madra, the power that commanded all.

The puzzle solved itself.

As it popped open, she let a ripple of rainbow madra flow from her into the Forged man in the chair.

"Congratulate me," she commanded, and he fell to press his forehead against the stone.

Sophara held the box in her hand, drowning it in Flowing Flame madra. Golden power surged around it, heating it, breaking it down.

"That box is protected by the power of an Overlord," the man said, holding his chin in one hand.

The Underlady slipped some soulfire into her technique, pouring forth more madra. The box rose into the air at the center of a golden globe, blazing bright.

After less than a minute, molten metal poured out.

Eithan tapped the edge of the table with the scroll. "You look bored."

"I have to look after you," the construct-man answered, rolling his eyes.

"Ah, but that is your good fortune! For I am the most delightful conversationalist the world has ever seen."

"...I'm not going to tell you how to open the box."

Eithan folded his hands into his elaborately ornamented sleeves and leaned forward, smiling eagerly.

"I'm sure, I'm sure, but I need to wait a good minute or two before I leave. So tell me, as we pass the time, what's it like being you? Are you being controlled by an outside force, are you a copy of the one who created you, or do you only have your own rudimentary awareness?"

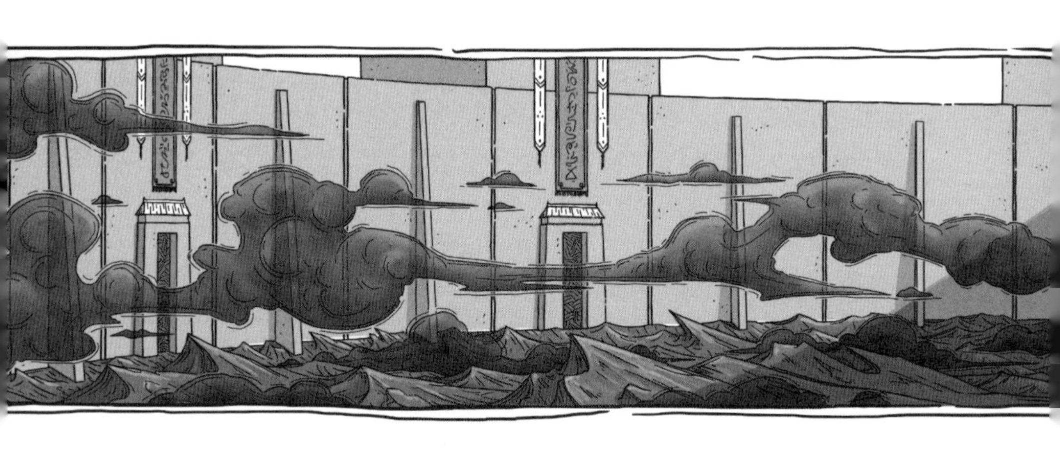

LINDON PASSED THE THIRD AND FOURTH TRIALS WITHOUT USING any new techniques. He was afraid that he might be exposing a few too many of Dross' capabilities, but who could tell what was going on inside Lindon's head?

[Northstrider,] Dross answered, as the darkness faded away to reveal the fifth trial. [Northstrider could. He's smart enough on his own, and who knows what version of me he's cooked up since Ghostwater? Maybe he'll pull me out of your brain *without* hurting you!]

Lindon resolved to use Dross as little as possible, but the fifth trial tested his determination immediately.

In a cramped room with a high ceiling, a nightmarish creature loomed over him. It was a giant shaped like a man, and its leathery gray skin bulged with muscle.

It hunched over him, dressed in ragged scraps of hide, its arms hanging so low that his knuckles scraped against the floor. It wore a hideous bone mask that grew over its face, a long red tongue lolling out of its mouth, and it carried a rough metal cleaver the size of Lindon's body.

At a glance, he suspected there was exactly enough room for the creature to swing the weapon.

Golden, fiery letters appeared in front of him: "Kill the Enemy."

There was no scroll this time. Instead, a monstrous gray hand swept a jagged blade at him.

With a hasty Soul Cloak and the reaction speed that Dross provided, Lindon slipped aside...but the impact of the cleaver against the ground shook the room, ruining his footing.

Lindon dashed forward, pushing through the creature's powerful stench. Another palm rushed at him, and Lindon had no choice but to catch the attack in his own hands.

He caught the strike, but the giant's strength shoved his body backward against the ground.

[I bet you wish you had a weapon,] Dross observed.

*Remind me to get one,* Lindon responded, calling Blackflame into his palms. The giant roared and lashed backward, and Lindon conjured dragon's breath.

Charity watched Lindon on the display in the arena for the first time. He shoved the giant's hand aside, drilled a hole in its arm with black dragon's breath as it tried to swing the cleaver at him, and then burned through its skull.

A round of cheering sounded in the crowd—mostly from the Akura section—but nothing particularly enthusiastic. The view soon returned to more exciting fights. Many of the failures were more interesting than Lindon. Some of them got cut in half by the giant, only to re-form seconds later and start the fight from the beginning while still trembling in fear.

She watched the closest ranking board as Lindon's name moved up to thirty-first.

He began the sixth trial only a few minutes behind the top competitors.

In the eighth trial, Lindon had to run through a hazy yellow fog that burned his lungs with every breath. Biting snakes and stinging flies lunged at him from within the fog, and the entire place was filthy with venom aura.

He managed to dodge the snakes, but there was no avoiding the flies. They and the fog filled his veins with poison.

Which his Bloodforged Iron body broke down almost immediately.

Lindon jogged forward without obstruction. His madra had been restored at the end of each test, so he fueled his Iron body without worry.

[You're probably falling behind,] Dross said. [You don't want to be in first, but you don't want to be in *last* either. Why don't you make up some time here?]

After giving it some more thought, Lindon activated the Soul Cloak and ran all-out.

On the board, Lindon's name ticked up to twentieth.

"Stay on the Bridge," the fiery letters told Lindon.

A bridge stretched out before him over an endless chasm. As he watched, it split into five bridges, each stretching in a different direction. The bridges began to undulate like swimming snakes, and then each bridge splintered into five more.

[Illusions, blech,] Dross said.

And Lindon saw one bridge stretching in front of him, perfectly straight. Ghostly illusions moved to either side, but they no longer fooled him.

Just like in the previous test, he ran steadily forward. The bridge was broken in places, but nothing he couldn't jump.

When he reached the end, he was a little disappointed. *Is that all?*

[Stay on your guard,] Dross said grimly. [Next is test number ten. The fifth trial was a mandatory fight, so if I'm right...]

The world darkened and brightened again, revealing a wide arena-like room filled with blowing wild grass. Another creature waited for him, a bone mask growing from its face, but its resemblance to the fifth-trial guardian ended there.

It was small, flat, and hunched, with grass growing from its back like fur. It clutched a staff topped with a human skull, and pale light pouring upward from the skull's eye sockets. The monster's forked black tongue flickered out of its mask, tasting the air.

"Kill the Enemy."

As soon as the letters faded, the creature raised its staff...and split into three. Its duplicates raised their staves, and all three faded away until they were halfway transparent. They ran around him, trailing green fog that drifted closer to him.

[Uh, they were supposed to turn invisible there. Pretend you can't see them.]

It was painfully obvious which of the three was real. The others looked like flat drawings, and he was the only one with depth. The two illusions ran around, rustling grass and pretending to release clouds of green fog, while the real one actually generated poisonous gas and crouched, motionless and supposedly invisible, amidst the grass.

Poison and illusions.

At the center of the poison gas, Lindon sighed. Then he speared the creature through the mask with a lance of dragon's breath.

Dross coughed. [Well, that one was free.]

Charity watched Lindon finish the tenth test in eighteen seconds.

He was first in the trial by a wide margin. This enemy toyed with the competitors using venom and dreams, immobilizing and entrancing them into wasting time. Even Sopharanatoth, first place overall, was trapped for six minutes in the fight before she managed to shake loose.

Lindon's place flipped up to tenth.

Now he had finally gathered attention. Behind Charity, some of the other members of her family highly ranked enough to join her on the Monarch's platform began to mutter, and she caught Lindon's name from more than one voice.

The Ninecloud Soul brought up Lindon's image five times. She had even speculated for the entire arena to hear about how Lindon had done so well in trial ten; did he have eyes that could pierce illusions? A spiritual sense developed far beyond his peers? Perhaps he had brought a Divine Treasure that could reveal the truth to him?

That was the closest to the truth, Charity knew. His mind-spirit must have held off the illusion for long enough that Lindon could destroy the real body.

Anyone with enough knowledge could make a similar guess, so that made four things he had now revealed. His Soul Cloak, his dragon's breath, his hunger binding, and his mind-spirit.

In her estimation, her niece and nephew were performing much better.

Mercy mixed her techniques together into her arrows, so they were hard to analyze, and had yet to reveal her Dream of Darkness technique or her bloodline armor. The Akura armor was common knowledge, but her command of it would not be. Their enemies would have to test her limits for themselves. The only ability Mercy had fully revealed was her proficiency with Striker techniques, which couldn't be helped.

Currently, she was placed seventh. Very respectable; her mother was likely proud. Malice was watching now, Charity knew; the Monarch had slipped in just as Northstrider arrived and now observed from the top of her floating mountain, though Charity had not been invited to join her.

Pride had used part of his armor but had revealed only two of his four Enforcer techniques. As a result, he'd taken a little too long and fallen to twenty-second place, but someone who specialized only in Enforcer techniques would have problems with such flexible scenarios as these. He would redeem himself in the duels.

Sophara was the real problem.

The champion of the gold dragons maintained a strong lead. If Charity hadn't known better, she would have suspected the woman had actually reached Overlord. Her madra was so dense and powerful that, combined with her strong dragon's body, she simply tore through most tests.

She held onto first place with an iron grip, which was inconvenient for Charity. If she actually won the tournament, Sophara's name would become commonplace all around the world, which would make it difficult to assassinate her.

In second place was Sha Miara. She publicly claimed to be an Underlady from a distant branch of the royal family, but Charity doubted that. Based on her level of command over royal madra, she suspected the girl might be the Monarch's daughter.

The only other one Charity spent time contemplating was Yerin

Arelius from the Blackflame Empire team. The real House Arelius had caused a stir when Yerin and Lindon were revealed as adopted members of their clan, and she was sure they were watching intently.

No fewer than three members of their Blackflame branch were participating in the tournament. Even if two were only adopted disciples, the Arelius clan wasn't in a position to turn down any potential source of strength.

Yerin had cut her way to eleventh, coincidentally only one place behind Lindon. She flagged on the tests that required flexibility but excelled in anything that could be solved with combat. That boded well for future rounds.

In all, Charity was pleased with her faction competitors. The Frozen Blade students were ranked in the thirties, except for their one replacement, who was struggling to maintain eightieth place. He wouldn't make it into the second round.

Their second Akura team was, on average, doing well enough. Grace held on to thirty-second place while her teammates were fifty-third and fifty-eighth. For a team Charity had arranged at the last minute, they were doing her proud.

All in all, she was satisfied.

If only the dragons hadn't been performing so well.

Only two of the twelve total dragon competitors were even in danger of elimination. The gold dragons were all in the top sixteen, and led by Sophara...they would be a deadly force in the second round.

That would be the real test. The first time when her humans would come to face their enemies.

She ran her eyes down the list, looking at the last person who was currently in a position to pass. Eithan Arelius.

Charity had thought his potential would be much greater than this. His command over his bloodline ability alone should have gotten him a higher position, but he was staying in sixty-fourth. He had been sixty-fourth in the ninth trial as well. And in the eighth...

Raising an eyebrow, Charity looked back over the results. In the eighth test, he'd been sixty-second. Seventh...sixty-third.

Eithan had bounced between sixty-fourth and sixtieth since the beginning of the round.

In the fifteenth and final trial, Lindon was forced to use the Void Dragon's Dance.

He fought five of the masked giants this time, in a wide-open arena that shot bursts of flames randomly from the ground. The air was full of fire aura, so it was easy to use his Ruler technique, but he had been determined not to.

After failing to clear all five enemies the first time and being painlessly sliced in half—a disorienting experience—he had decided he couldn't waste any more time. As far as he knew, he was ranked near thc bottom, and he had a clear method of winning. He only had to reveal one more of his abilities.

Reluctantly, Lindon gathered up the fire and destruction aura in the air, calling down a swirling vortex of flame. It consumed three of the giants, scorching the other two, leaving Lindon to slice them in half with dragon's breath.

As soon as they fell, a pair of golden characters appeared in the air.

"The End," they said.

Then the gold fire grew. It swallowed everything in an instant, erasing the world.

Lindon emerged, blinking, into the sunlight of the arena. He was seated on his knees, just where he had begun.

Less than a dozen people sat around him.

[Huh. I guess we didn't manage to avoid attention, did we?]

Lindon's heart fluttered with nerves. He had stood out. Now they were going to look him up. He'd have a harder time from here on out because he had misjudged his timing.

But then again...he had proven himself. Even if he failed in the next round, he had shown that he could compete with some of the best in the world.

It was a rush of emotion that Lindon had never felt before.

The crowd erupted into cheers, and the Ninecloud Soul shouted his name, but he was looking around at his competitors.

Sophara, the gold dragon, fixed him with the eyes of a serpent. She looked ready to blast him apart from there.

The red-haired girl from the Ninecloud section ignored him, cycling on the ground, but once again he had missed the announcement of her name. He turned to look at the list, to see the names of the people who had ranked ahead of him.

Then he heard a familiar shout from behind him, and he turned in place. From her knees, Yerin slapped her palm into the ground. "Bleed me! I was stone-certain I'd beaten you. How long have you been here?"

The arena rang with the sound of Yerin's name, and Lindon swelled with pride, but he answered modestly. "Only a few seconds. We practically finished together."

As Lindon looked to one of the glowing golden lists hanging in the air and saw his name in tenth place and Yerin's in eleventh, he had to remind himself that this was only the first round. It was meant to test their flexibility and to weed out those who were fundamentally unfit for the rest of the tournament. It didn't necessarily reflect those who would win the fights later.

[And look who beat you!] Dross said.

Lindon's eyes crawled up to eighth place, where Mercy's name rested. It was still bizarre to think that she was more capable than he was, as he had mostly known her as a Lowgold, but she was a Monarch's daughter. That was to be expected.

Seated in a cycling position on the ground, Mercy leaned over to exchange excited whispers with Yerin.

Lindon didn't see Pride's name, which made the day seem even brighter.

[I wasn't talking about Mercy,] Dross said, just as Lindon looked up to check the top of the list.

*Sopharanatoth, gold dragon team,* the board said. First position.

He looked down, and Sophara once again had her red-hot gaze on him.

Lindon's mood sunk, but not too far. His earlier reasoning came back to him: this was only the first round. Just because she'd ranked higher didn't mean that there was an impossible gap between them.

The thought comforted him until he noticed the second name.

*Sha Miara, Ninecloud Court team.*

He felt as though he'd been speared through the chest. He had already seen the red-haired girl seated calmly nearby, ignoring those around her, but he hadn't given her another thought yet.

His eyes moved involuntarily to the Ninecloud Court viewing tower, a crystalline structure of Forged madra and delicate stained glass. Their Monarch platform was a jeweled palace resting on top of a rainbow-colored cloud.

There was no way they could sneak their Monarch into this competition. It wasn't possible. The other Monarchs wouldn't be deceived, and surely she would gain nothing from pretending to be an Underlady.

[That's not even the worst part!] Dross said cheerfully. [She's only in *second* place.]

Lindon calmed himself. He hadn't even known what a Monarch was when Suriel first showed him Sha Miara. He had obviously misunderstood the situation.

He had to be wrong.

Back in the amethyst spire where the entire Akura faction stayed, Yerin and Lindon visited a tablet library. The second round wouldn't start for another week, and participants were encouraged to examine the records of their competition. The entire first round had been recorded, and they found dream tablet recordings of many opponents from before the tournament started.

Together, Yerin and Lindon sat on a couch and watched as

a sculpture of light showed them Sophara's performance. They watched all the way through the first round in silence, and when the illusion finally faded, they both remained quiet.

Finally, Dross spun out of Lindon's spirit and sat on his shoulder. [Good news! I can build a decent model of Sophara now. The bad news is that it will *absolutely* destroy you.]

Lindon wasn't surprised. If he hadn't sensed Sophara's spirit for himself, he would have assumed she was an Overlord.

She was physically stronger than Yerin, her dragon's breath came out faster than his, her techniques were smooth and precise, and she reacted so quickly that he wondered if her senses were as sharp as Eithan's. Watching her in the first round was almost hypnotic; she seemed to dance through each trial as though she'd known its contents in advance.

"At least you can train against a model," Yerin said bitterly. "Let's see how I stack up."

Lindon had explained Dross' models to Yerin months ago through the sound transmission construct. She'd been understandably jealous.

Yerin removed the dream tablet and replaced it in the projection construct with another they'd retrieved before: Yerin's own record of the first round.

Her weaknesses became apparent almost immediately.

"As long as it's not a fight, I'm as useless as feathers on a fish."

She'd torn through every combat, but had struggled to deal with anything else.

"Good thing the rest of the competition is a series of fights," Lindon said.

[As far as we know.]

Yerin sent out a sliver of madra and froze the image as a wave of sword aura devastated a line of Forged soldiers. "I wouldn't say no to a heavier weapon. I'm good enough against a batch of servants, but it'll take me a year and a day to cut through decent armor."

The illusion skipped ahead to her battle against one of the large gray-skinned warriors, and she had to dance around it until she eventually brought it down with enough cuts.

Lindon scribbled down some thoughts on a scroll that he'd brought for just this purpose. "I need something to defend myself." He blew on the ink. "Dross and I have been working on this. I brought the armor from the Skysworn and from the Seishen Kingdom, but armor is against the rules of the tournament."

[Also, the Akura Soulsmith library is virtually empty of any relevant information,] Dross said. [Each of them has their own suit of armor built in.]

"That too," Lindon admitted.

Yerin leaned forward to inspect Dross' round purple body. "You think you could run me through one of those models?"

[Maybe with some more of the Sage's madra. How about you ask her for more, Lindon?]

"She's already suspicious." Lindon had asked for as many scales from Charity as he dared, but it had eventually become clear that she thought he was spending the scales. She was sure that his mind-spirit couldn't be processing the power so fast.

Yerin brushed hair away from her face. "I've got some things I want to try. I know my Path is worth more than this; my master placed fifth in the first round."

She didn't sound too bothered, but Lindon could feel her disappointment. She'd let herself down in her own eyes.

His brush stopped, and he looked up at her. "If it was about where you started, I would never have caught up to you. The only thing that matters is where you end up." He returned to the scroll. "And our paths don't end with this tournament."

She didn't respond for so long that he stopped worrying about his notes and started worrying that he'd said something wrong. By the time he checked her expression, she'd sat down on the couch beside him again. Her hair hung down so that he couldn't see her face, but she sat closer to him than before.

[I think you've offended her,] Dross whispered into Lindon's mind. [Quick, throw yourself on the floor and beg forgiveness.]

Lindon swallowed. *I don't think so,* he responded, but before he could say anything to Yerin, rainbow light filled the room.

Both of them stood abruptly, staring into the ceiling from which the light streamed.

"Number ten, Wei Shi Lindon Arelius," the Ninecloud Soul said, her voice warm. "I have come to deliver your prize for the first round and information about the second round. Yerin Arelius, would you please leave the room for a moment?"

The viewing-rooms were essentially private booths, so it would be easy for her to step outside, but Lindon bowed to the Ninecloud Soul. "Pardon, but if it isn't too much trouble, would you allow her to stay?"

"No trouble at all. I needed to speak to her next, so this only saves me time." The rainbow light coalesced into an image floating in midair: a castle of blocks and mortar floating on a cloud. "As your reward for successfully passing the first round, our team of artisan Soulsmiths and architects will design for you a floating fortress according to your preferences."

The castle shifted into a more luxurious housing compound surrounding a courtyard, filled with trees and a shining pool.

"We can tailor the facilities to your style and needs, and even your Path." Now the house became a network of rocky hills and caves, with vents in the ground spewing jets of fire into the sky.

Lindon could practically feel the aura of fire and destruction even from the illusion.

He and Dross stared speechlessly at the image. Lindon felt a pang of regret that Orthos wasn't here to see this.

"Will we be able to use this prize in our next round?" Lindon asked when he had recovered himself. Dross was still staring, his mouth hanging slack.

"Regrettably, no. It will not be ready until the completion of the tournament, while the next round is in one week."

They had already been told that the second round would take place in a week; the rest of the city was in a non-stop festival until the end of the Uncrowned King tournament, but the participants were expected to spend their time training and preparing—which was what Lindon would have chosen to do anyway.

"And the nature of the next round?"

"A team elimination match between all teams at once," the Soul said serenely. "Those teams who survived the first round with all three of their members will therefore have an advantage."

"That's a lot less than a map," Yerin said. "Where are we fighting?"

"I cannot give you any more details until the day of the competition. However, I am permitted to say that you will be allowed to fill your soulspace, but can carry no other weapons or void keys. Any constructs you bring will be inspected to ensure that they fall within appropriate power parameters, which are contained within the tournament rules and can be reviewed at any time."

Lindon stored that away. He couldn't fit anything too powerful into his soulspace, but he and Dross should be able to make some preparations. "Gratitude. Now, the fortress...is that allowed weapons?"

"The fortress naturally includes a battery of defensive scripts and constructs, as it is intended to be a secure retreat. For the same reason, however, our intent is not to design you a weapon of war, but a safe place to live or travel."

Lindon asked further questions about the power source, guidance system, requirements for piloting, and maintenance. Most of them were standard systems, and the one consistent restriction on the fortress was size. The size of the Thousand-Mile Cloud construct remained constant for all participants. Dross fed a few questions through Lindon, rather than addressing the Ninecloud Soul directly, and Yerin piped up with a few as well.

"What do you plan to do with yours?" Lindon asked her. "Maybe they could complement—" He held out a hand, interrupting himself as an idea sparked in his mind. He spoke before he thought. "Wait! If you'll forgive another question, honored...Soul...could we combine our prizes? Would you allow us to have one fortress that's twice the size?"

"If number eleven agrees to it," the rainbow light said.

Yerin frowned at him. "Don't you think we'd be better off with two?"

"We're always traveling together anyway. We can make ours better than anyone else's."

She stared at him quietly for a long moment, which gave him enough time to realize what he'd said. He had essentially asked her if she wanted to build a home with him.

Heat rushed to his face, and she noticed, because her own cheeks flushed red and she hurriedly looked away. He almost apologized to the Ninecloud Soul and took back his words. He really hadn't been thinking. This could ruin his whole relationship with Yerin.

Mercy's voice echoed clearly in his mind. *"And you're okay with that?"*

Then his own: *"I don't know."*

[Look at that!] Dross said proudly. [I can play memories back for you! It's just like you're hearing it for the first time, isn't it?]

Lindon's heart pounded, and he looked back at the rainbow light so he didn't have to see Yerin's expression, but he didn't say anything. His proposal stayed on the table.

After the longest handful of seconds in Lindon's life, Yerin made a quiet noise that he thought might be approval.

But she hadn't *said* anything. Maybe she felt like he was pushing her into it. Suddenly his self-consciousness spilled over and out of his mouth. "Or not," he added, "if you don't feel comfortable with it. We can wait to decide."

The Ninecloud Soul twinkled. "Number eleven, no one can determine the nature of your prize but you. If you are afraid of reprisal outside the competition, you are entitled to the protection and enforcement of the Ninecloud Court."

Yerin coughed. "Who's telling you I'm afraid of anything? I agreed, I agree, I'm agreeing now."

"If you would perhaps let number ten leave, so that I can hear it from you without the possibility of coercion..."

"Did I say there was a need for that? Get it done."

Yerin looked away from Lindon, and the back of her neck was scarlet. He knew his face had to be even brighter than hers.

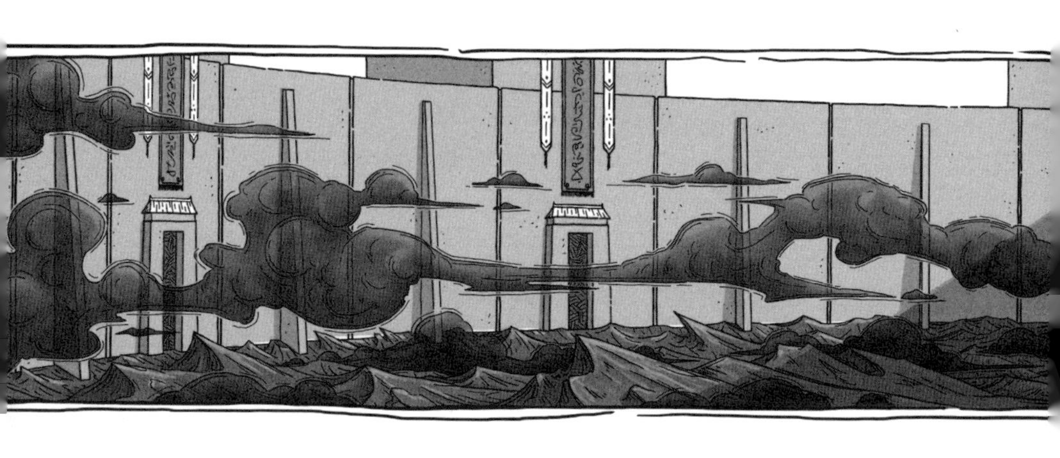

# XII

Eithan tapped his fingers together as the Ninecloud Soul produced another floating model of his flying fortress.

"Is this more of what you had in mind, number sixty-four?" The feminine voice from the cloud of rainbow madra was beginning to sound impatient. He couldn't blame the spirit. This was his eighty-first revision, and even artificially created spiritual networks could get testy.

"Perfection!" Eithan declared. His "fortress" was a broad square, stretched to the maximum dimensions, and filled with a series of gardens. It looked more like a plot of farmland.

"Now, are there any plants in particular that we can provide for you?" The Ninecloud Soul's exhaustion was beginning to strain its polite words. "Keep in mind, you are only permitted a limited total value."

"Nimblethorn root," Eithan said immediately.

The rainbow shimmered, confused, but one corner of the floating garden converted to a patch of thorny bushes. "Are you a refiner, number sixty-four?"

The Nimblethorn root was typically used as a medicinal herb to separate types of madra before spiritual surgery. It wasn't common, but it wasn't incredibly valuable either.

"Not much of one, I'm afraid. Now, how about some ancestral men'hla trees?"

Rumor said that Emriss Silentborn had been a men'hla tree before her ascension, and as such they were considered sacred in certain circles on the Everwood continent. It had a handful of uses for refiners, but it was especially valuable to Soulsmiths, as each of its leaves actually produced a separate Remnant. For many projects, one men'hla tree could be an endless source of dead matter.

The red in the Ninecloud Soul grew brighter. "I am afraid we can provide only one century-old men'hla tree."

Eithan affected disappointment, but the joke was on the Ninecloud Court. He didn't actually need this tree at all, he just wanted to extract the maximum value from his prize.

Of course, since they were willing to give him one, he would use it.

"Hammershell fruit," he recited. A prime source of force aura. "A hive of ivory bees. Cloudbell bush. A spring of Whispering Water. Starlotus pond."

His list contained nothing that the Ninecloud Court would balk at or flag as unusual. Some were more useful to Soulsmiths, others to refiners, and he mixed in some decoys with the ones he really needed.

When he stretched the process of designing his first-round prize to over two hours, the Ninecloud Soul said, “Allow me to remind you, number sixty-four, that there is no rush. You cannot bring this prize into the second round, so you can take your time planning.”

Eithan smiled into the rainbow light. “I assure you, I have taken my time. And not for the second round.”

“Seize the crown!” the Ninecloud Soul’s pleasant voice rang throughout the arena, and instantly a forty-foot image was projected in the center of the air.

It showed a sacred artist with a blank face approaching a golden crown, which hung suspended in a column of yellow light.

“There are thirty-two crowns scattered across a beautiful tropical island,” the voice continued. “The crowns can be easily identified, as they send up a beacon of golden light. When you place a crown on your head...”

The illusory image reached out, snatching the crown and placing it on his head. The beacon intensified, turning white.

“...then you must keep it on your head for a full minute! If you succeed, you will be instantly returned back here, qualified for the third round!”

The crowned sacred artist winked, then disappeared.

*Take notes,* Lindon ordered Dross.

[...all right, but are you *really* not going to remember this without my help?]

"Be certain you're ready when you put it on, because once you place the crown on your head, there's no going back! The crown is only removed if you are killed while wearing it!"

A weapon speared the sacred artist through the chest—no blood sprayed, but he fell over like a doll—and the crown rolled from his head. It glowed gold again.

"Not to worry; you are still under the infallible protection of a Monarch! If you die, you will be held for one hour, after which you will be returned to the island!"

The sacred artist appeared again, good as new.

Lindon could already see that the odds of moving on to the next round as a full team were low. They would have to gather three crowns before anyone wore one, and then channel them one at a time—but it would be obvious to everyone on the island what they were doing.

"In just a moment, the competitors will be transported to the island along with their teams! For those of you who lost your teammates in the first round, don't be discouraged: if you're alone, you only have to hold one crown!"

Though they would also have to defend themselves from all the other teams who would be out for their blood. Dying in the competition might not mean dying for real, but a one-hour delay for a lone sacred artist would virtually guarantee losing the round.

"Thirty-two crowns mean thirty-two spots for round three!" the Ninecloud Soul called. "Competitors, ready yourselves for glory! Prepare your plans, firm your resolve, and let your spirits—"

"Begin," Northstrider commanded.

The world faded away, and the rainbow light vanished.

Lindon found himself standing in the sand, a salty breeze ruffling his outer robe. Waves lapped behind him, reminding him of Ghostwater, and he hurriedly scanned up and down the coast.

Nothing but ocean, sand, and the thick trees of the island in front of him.

An instant later, Mercy popped into existence on his left, taking a deep breath and shaking out her hair. "I hate being launched through space without warning," she said. "It messes with my head."

Pride appeared on his right in a combat crouch. He clenched his fists, spinning around, looking for something to fight.

"Just as we planned." Lindon had hoped to bring his void key along, but that was against the rules. Any sacred instruments they brought had to be carried in a soulspace, which severely limited his room. But he could afford to carry around a handful of weak, small constructs.

He pulled a simple circular construct from among those in his soulspace. It was essentially a cluster of Remnant eyes, and he threw it straight up into the air, linking his spiritual perception to it.

The crude construct brought him far too much information, but Dross helped him sort it so that he could get a general glimpse of his surroundings. The island was vast and largely flat, with a few small hills, all covered in thick trees. He could see almost nothing of the ground beneath. He caught a glimpse of the ocean on the far side before the construct started to fall, but no other competitors.

...until a red diamond blasted from the trees, spearing through the construct.

His perception cut off, and he watched with his own eyes as a wave of Forged knives tore the cluster apart.

Chunks of madra dissolved all around him as he reported his findings to Mercy and Pride. "No crowns yet, but we're not alone."

Pride didn't respond, marching up to the trees. "Come on, Mercy. Let's go hunting."

Lindon pushed down his irritation. They had a plan: to stay put and call the other Akura faction teams to them. He was confident that the other factions would be trying to join forces as well; it was the obvious strategy.

"We don't know where the crowns will be placed," Lindon said without moving. "We should follow the plan."

Pride continued trudging through the sand. "They'll be put deep into the island, to encourage us moving toward one another. Try using your brain before you open your mouth."

One hour. If Lindon put a dragon's breath through Pride's back, he wouldn't have to deal with him for an entire hour.

Mercy let out a breath and jogged backward toward Pride, addressing Lindon as she did. "I know how he can be, but if we let him go alone, he's going to get torn in half by a Striker technique before the crowns show up at all. We should cover for him."

"I need *you* to cover for me," Pride said as he entered the trees. "Maybe we could use him for bait."

[His mother is definitely watching us,] Dross noted. [We'll have to be very sneaky when we stab him in the back.]

Lindon pulled out another simple construct, like a throbbing pink heart, and activated it. It began to flash brightly, each flash sending out a unique spiritual pulse. It wouldn't *do* anything, but the Frozen Blade and Akura backup teams had corresponding constructs that should be able to detect its signature from anywhere on the island.

He hadn't given the Blackflame team anything of the sort. Eithan and Naru Saeya would be able to find him regardless.

He was *supposed* to find a safe place and stay there while everyone in the Akura faction gathered together, but now they were walking into the jungle. Which increased the odds of enemies detecting them and made it harder for their allies to find them.

[I'm no strategy construct, but I wouldn't call this the best plan.]

The trees were thickly pressed together, the life aura almost choking in its strength. Without warning, a massive yellow-furred monkey came shrieking down from a tree, carrying wooden spears in both hands and emitting the spiritual pressure of an Underlord.

Mercy hurled arrows of black madra without hesitation, but the monkey slapped them aside, his weapons a blur. He was going to land straight on Pride, his feet extended like hands. He didn't have time to move, and Lindon held his technique. He wanted to see what Pride could do.

At the last instant, the short Underlord leaped and drove a punch into the monkey's gut.

Black and gray madra flashed from the point of impact, accompanied by a sound like a great flag snapping in the breeze. The monkey blasted backward, crashing into a tree hard enough that he left a crater that sent splinters flying.

By the time Pride landed, Lindon finally decided to release his Striker technique. Black-and-red madra struck the creature...

Several people locked their perception onto Lindon, and his spirit shivered. Their location construct was difficult to detect except by someone with the corresponding detection construct...but his dragon's breath was not so subtle.

"We have to move," he said, and even Pride didn't argue. The three of them darted into the underbrush.

The crocodile-creature had some hardy skin. It withstood Yerin's first strike.

Just not the next seven.

She left it in bloody pieces on the jungle floor. Naru Saeya lowered herself from the treetops, cradling a wounded left arm; she hadn't even cleared the trees, trying to get a look around, before a monkey had sliced her arm with a sharpened branch.

It hadn't penetrated the flesh far, but it was enough that the Emperor's sister had to use some healing salve. She winced as her flesh knitted together.

"Got to assume everything's out to kill you," Yerin said casually, wiping the crocodile's blood on the surrounding leaves. At least these monsters didn't leave Remnants, which meant they weren't sacred beasts. Not real ones, anyway. Maybe they were dreadbeasts.

Saeya ground her teeth against the pain as she flexed her arm. "My fault. I was careless."

Yerin had been expecting a nice verbal fight. Not getting one left her wrong-footed; it was like trying to insult Lindon and having him apologize. "...could happen to anyone. Just keep an eye up."

Saeya only nodded, taking no offense, extending her spiritual perception out into the distance.

"Liked her better when she had a temper," Yerin muttered. Saeya had a warrior's soul, and she had been placed in the sixties after the first round. Now, she was all business, determined to distinguish herself in the second round.

Eithan dropped from the branch where he had been hiding during the fight. Not a single speck of dirt or blood tarnished his fine white-and-gold robes. "She only has a temper to her enemies! To her allies, she is the gentlest—"

The tip of Saeya's rainbow sword found its way between his teeth.

Saeya wasn't even looking at him. The peacock-feather fan over her ear caught the air as she turned from one direction to the other, scanning the distance still holding her weapon in Eithan's mouth.

"Someone's using water madra nearby," she said. "I think the Tidewalker sect is in a battle. We have to pass through to make it to Lindon, so I say we pick off the winner on our way."

Saeya looked to Yerin, and the two traded nods. Saeya pulled her sword away from Eithan's lips and set off with Yerin.

Behind them, Eithan made a spitting noise. "Disgusting. It tastes like dust and flower petals."

They crept through the trees, getting closer until even Yerin could feel the water madra. Two water artists stood apart from three that used sword madra and...something else. Something strange. Dreams, she guessed, or shadow. Perhaps both.

She ducked and started to crawl forward, but two hands caught her by the sword-arms, holding her back.

Eithan looked uncharacteristically serious, which sobered her up in an instant. Saeya matched him, her eyes flicking into the distance as though she watched something Yerin couldn't see.

"Something's wrong," Saeya whispered. "They're not fighting. They're—"

She ducked in an emerald blur, and a serpentine dragon of water punched through the leaves behind her. A pulse of pure madra from Eithan dispersed the Ruler technique, leaving natural water to spray onto the ground.

In an instant, all three of them dropped veils and cycled their madra.

"It seems they were waiting," Eithan said at normal volume.

Through the jungle, the pair of water artists flanked them. From the glimpses Yerin caught, they had leathery blue-gray skin, gills working at the sides of their necks, and shark teeth; sacred beasts advanced enough to take on human form. Some kind of fish. If that wasn't the Tidewalker Sect, she'd eat her shoes.

The three others, two men and a woman, were the strange sword artists she'd already sensed. They wore gray robes and painted their faces with streaks of black. Each of them wore a crude one-handed saber strapped to their back and a greenish spirit that floated around their head. Their Goldsign.

"Tidewalkers and Ghost-Blades," Naru Saeya observed, hefting her colored glass sword. She showed no uncertainty, only determination and a little anger. Yerin liked her more with every passing second. "You're not even from the same corner of the world. What are you doing together?"

One of the fish-men hissed out a laugh. "Sink to the depths with your questions unanswered, little bird."

Eithan held a hand to his temple as though receiving a voice transmission. "They were...bribed to work against us. My mysterious, mystical senses tell me that...the gold dragons were responsible."

A ghostly sword bigger than a horse sheared through the trees around him. The Forger technique turned from gray to green as it passed through the plants, and each of them withered and died at its touch.

Naru Saeya dodged high, Yerin went low, and Eithan stood still. The technique moved over Yerin's head, below Saeya's feet, and shattered on the layer of pure madra coating Eithan's skin.

Eithan gave them all a friendly smile. "I'm afraid I've struck a nerve."

All five enemies attacked at once.

A brown-skinned man with short-cropped hair faced Lindon, holding an intricate orb that looked like it had been forged from copper. Brass, copper, and steel piping wrapped his chest, connecting to a metal tank on his back. It whistled loudly and gave off spiritual pressure like he had an entire Underlord Remnant trapped inside.

Lindon and Pride stood shoulder-to-shoulder, neither moving. Mercy was above and behind them somewhere, covering them, but they were not anxious to start a fight. Not only had none of the crowns appeared yet, but there were far more enemies than this one close by. A fight would draw them like flies.

[He's from Dreadnought City,] Dross said, for some reason whispering as though his mental voice might be enough to break the stalemate. [Everwood continent, fighting for Emriss Silentborn. They do strange things with Remnants over there.]

The man said something with an accent so heavy Lindon couldn't understand it. Though perhaps it was another language—he had heard *of* other languages, he had just never heard one spoken.

His brown eyes glanced from one of them to the other. Sweat ran down his face—he was as nervous as they were. When he saw no comprehension in their faces, he tried again, speaking slowly.

"Do not fight," he said in words Lindon could understand, just above a whisper. "Back away."

Lindon nodded, and together he and the man from Dreadnought City took slow steps back.

Pride darted forward.

The stranger's reactions befit an Underlord. A bright blue flame erupted from the tank on his back, and a hand bigger than his body reached out and caught Pride's approach. A Remnant hand.

There really *was* a Remnant in there.

The force of Pride's attack tore the hand apart, and Lindon felt the man's power shake, but then the orb in his hands flared to life. A bolt of blue light lanced from the center, spearing toward Pride's chest.

A gray light covered Pride, and the Striker technique glanced off, slicing branches from the canopy as it cut into the sky. His fist caught the Dreadnought citizen in the forehead, and with a black flash, the man's skull crunched.

Before he collapsed, the stranger dissolved to white light and vanished to wherever the dead waited for an hour.

He hadn't fully disappeared before a roar sounded from behind them.

[And there's his partner,] Dross said with a sigh.

A young woman with the same brown skin, eyes, and hair as the first Dreadnought City artist barreled through the jungle behind them. A silver Remnant's limbs surrounded her own; claws of madra covered her hands, paws her feet, and a snarling silver tiger head sat over hers. Both she and the spirit covering her had a look of fury in their eyes.

Lindon had no choice. The Soul Cloak sprung up around him, and he readied his Empty Palm.

The three of them took her on together.

Mercy fired an arrow at the woman's feet, and while she altered her stride to avoid the Striker techniques, Pride sent a devastating punch into her side. She twisted to catch the blow on her Remnant's arm, but Lindon was already driving an Empty Palm into her stomach. The blue-white madra covered her torso with a Forged handprint, and the energy cut through her madra channels and severed her connection to thc tank on her back.

The Remnant popped like a bubble and she tumbled to the ground, rolling through the grass. She shouted and slashed at Lindon, but no claws followed the motion.

An arrow split her heart a moment later, and she vanished.

Pride stood triumphantly over the spot where her body had disappeared, pointing at the empty space. "He was driving us back into an ambush!"

Lindon stepped close enough that he loomed over Pride, emphasizing the fact that Pride's head only came up to his collarbone. He was so furious he felt like he was channeling Blackflame.

"Did you not *know* she was there? I saw her on the way in!" Well, Dross had, but that was the same thing. "How is it an ambush when *we're* together and *they're* split up? They just wanted to meet up without attracting attention!"

Spirits vanished all around them as beasts and sacred artists alike veiled themselves to approach.

Pride's eyes were hard as purple stones. "You almost pushed us into a trap. I saved us."

"You turned us into *bait!* How are our teams supposed to get to us now?" They were already surrounded by enemies.

Mercy landed to the side, grabbing them both. "Let's have this conversation while running for our lives, what do you think?"

They ran together, Pride and Lindon keeping their speed down for Mercy, who couldn't fly without her bow.

Lindon swept his perception behind him, and his breath caught at what he felt. There were at least seven, maybe eight or nine enemies behind them. Their veils kept him from identifying their exact position, their Paths, or whether they were sacred artists or beasts. If some of them had veiled themselves more thoroughly than others, there could even be more.

The worst of it was, they weren't fighting amongst themselves. They were chasing the Akura team as though they'd been put on a scent.

[That's what we get for standing out!] Dross said in a panic. [They think you're extraordinary! Quick, let me talk to them and I'll let them know the truth.]

At that moment, Lindon's spiritual sense lit up as he felt a column of light descend from the sky. He jumped up as he ran, grabbing a branch and pulling himself high so he could push through the leathery leaves overhead and take a quick look.

Only a hundred yards in front of him, a column of golden radiance descended from the clouds. A dot in the center had to be the crown. And it wasn't alone; to its left and right, two more beams of light shone as a pair of crowns floated down.

Three crowns. Enough for a full team to advance to the next round.

Everyone would be headed for them, and he was caught between the prize and his pursuers. Trapped.

Yerin had fought against greater numbers more than once, but these weren't a handful of back-country sect disciples who'd managed to finally advance to Truegold. These were five of the deadliest Underlords of their generation.

When the fight started, it was brutal.

The three Ghost-Blades slashed out, Forging spectral swords the size of cattle as they swung, and clearly they had trained together. Their attacks came at subtly different angles only a whisper apart, so there would be no avoiding all three.

As they struck, Yerin felt the walking fish of the Tidewalker sect conjuring bubbles of dark liquid madra. They held back, waiting to react as she did.

Last year, Yerin would have dealt with the Ghost-Blades' attack and fallen for the Tidewalker follow-up. Maybe she could have survived the first volley, with the help of her Blood Shadow, but she would've lost in time. These opponents were too coordinated, too well-trained and too used to working together.

But she had a team of her own.

Yerin ignored the attacks and activated the Endless Sword. The three swords of the Ghost-Blades rang like bells, aura erupting from them like a storm and shredding their clothes and skin, drawing light wounds and knocking them around like hurricane winds. Even the Tidewalkers caught the edge of it, staggering back from the sting.

She attacked. Eithan defended.

He was in front of her before she saw him move, blowing the Forged madra apart with Striker techniques of his own. And from above, Naru Saeya launched a burst of green wind madra as the Ghost-Blades still reeled from Yerin's attack. From experience, Yerin knew it would snare them and drag them off-balance—easy prey for a blade.

The three of them had reacted together, months of training crystallizing in action for the first time.

But the enemy had training of their own, and greater numbers.

A defensive construct on one of the Ghost-Blades activated a yellow shield that blocked Saeya's Striker technique, so he stood strong as she dove in. The Tidewalkers refocused on her, Yerin whipped a horizontal Striker blade of her own at them to pull their attention back, and Eithan had to deal with further attacks from the other two Ghost-Blades.

They traded exchange after exchange in a quick second, Forger techniques blowing apart, Striker techniques tearing the leaves from trees, blades of aura grinding up earth. Stroke and counterstroke, attack and defense, from eight Underlords with no wasted time.

The air shook with continuous thunder. Yerin's spiritual sense strained to keep up, and her channels burned as she quickly switched from technique to technique. A chain of explosions blasted the forest around them in one long roar, and in seconds the jungle around them was a clearing of debris and churned soil.

Yerin moved as quickly as she ever had in her life, blasting away a Striker technique aimed at Saeya, ducking aside so Eithan could get a shot at an enemy behind her, driving her blade at one enemy and slashing her sword-blades behind her at another.

Even so, they were outnumbered.

Naru Saeya was the first to slip, a little too slow to block as she raised her sword with a wounded arm. She winced, instantly taking a Forged blade to the chest. A quick flood of green madra blocked it, but it sent her flying into a tree and then to the ground.

Yerin covered her with a surge of the Endless Sword, but therefore she couldn't cover Eithan, who had to focus on his own defense at redirecting a stream of water madra. Their formation collapsed, and then they were three individuals struggling to defend themselves.

Only a breath later, golden light streamed down from the sky. It poured through the leaves overhead; she couldn't see well enough to see how distant it was, but it couldn't be far.

Eithan reacted as though he'd known the crowns were coming,

taking advantage of the momentary flicker in his enemies' attention to let out a detonation of pure madra. His power swept over everyone, dense enough that it must have been reinforced with soulfire, and wiped away every active technique. Water madra fell apart, Forged blades vanished, Striker techniques died in midair, and Enforced punches fell limp on their targets.

The only one not affected was Eithan, who rushed toward one of the Tidewalkers to stab her with a sharpened stick, but the loss of madra had only disrupted her for an instant. She was already Enforced again, slapping him aside and stepping away so she and her partner could focus on them together.

Yerin could do nothing; it was all she could do to keep the Ghost-Blades from closing in on the wounded Saeya. The Naru helped as best she could, grabbing at them with her Ruler technique, but their enemies' soulfire-aided aura control was enough to keep them safe.

Yerin was on the verge of bringing out her Blood Shadow—an ability she hadn't yet revealed—when her spirit warned her, and she realized why Eithan had wasted so much madra on a split-second interruption.

It hadn't been an attack.

It was a signal.

Black dragon's breath lanced out from the trees. One of the Tidewalkers reacted in time to defend with a wide bubble of water madra, but the distraction allowed Eithan to land a blow on him. The fish-man's eyes bulged, and he flew back, tumbling through the bushes. His partner ran after him a moment later, and the two of them lost no time before scampering away.

Eithan let them run, turning to the Ghost-Blades. A hail of black arrows pulled them away from Yerin, and an instant later, a short man with shining purple eyes dashed among them.

They slashed at him, but crystalline amethyst armor materialized only for the instant it took him to block their blows. He slid through, a whirlwind, catching one enemy with his fist and another with a foot. They defended themselves, but the impact of flesh on flesh sounded like thunderclaps.

Instead of fighting his way through to the Akura team, Eithan had called the Akura team to them.

Yerin speared the closest enemy through the back as Lindon arrived, shoving dragon's breath point-blank into another Ghost-Blade's chest.

The two of them dematerialized at the same time, but the third—the farthest one from her—had managed to make his escape.

Panting heavily, Yerin slapped Lindon on his shoulder. Despite knowing that death couldn't touch them here, surviving still left her drunk with elation.

"Aren't you a welcome sight!" Yerin said, but Lindon never stopped moving. He grabbed her wrist and pulled her with him. Mercy and Eithan were seeing to Naru Saeya, who had made it back into the air, and Akura Pride had already run ahead. He wrecked his way through the undergrowth like a bull.

"Talk later!" Lindon shouted as he tugged her along, and she cast her perception behind her.

When she felt the now-unveiled presences hunting them, she sped up until *she* was dragging *him.*

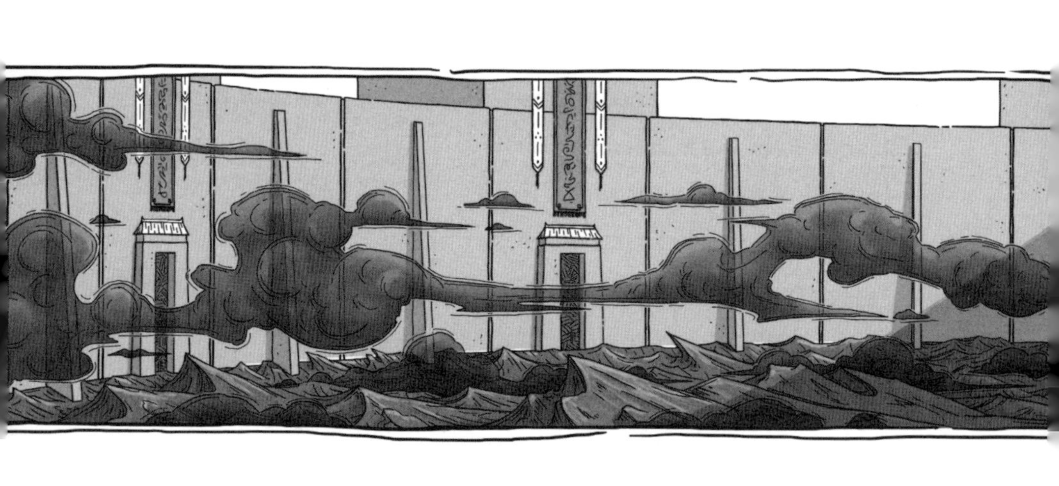

# XIII

It was a bloody fight around the crown. So to speak.

There was much less actual blood than in most of the fights Lindon had ever seen, as a lethal attack caused the victim to dissolve into light and rush away. Only lesser wounds left blood behind.

But it was chaos. They had reached the central crown, which had attracted the most competitors. And the presence of sacred artists had drawn beasts, so at any moment there could be sacred artists conjuring massive ghostly swords against monkeys, silver crocodiles snapping jaws down on flashing cages of lightning, or flocks of razor-taloned birds clashing against Forged techniques of crimson light.

Lindon and the others skirted the bounds of the fight. The first of their pursuers crashed through the woods behind them—one a half-human red dragon, another a female figure in a brown hood and a stone mask.

They couldn't ignore the battle and keep pursuing the Akura teams. Unfortunately, Lindon couldn't avoid it either. He evaded an emerald lance and a conjured spirit that raked claws in his direction, narrowly missing his chin.

*Dross,* Lindon thought, *how many people are here?*

[Seventeen, counting you. You can count yourself, can't you? Of course you can. Sixteen. No, wait, that's confusing. Seventeen. Wait, do I count?]

A quarter of the people who had started out on the island were left. The rest were either waiting their hour to return, going for one of the other two crowns, or waiting to see how the fight shook out.

Lindon stopped behind a tree, waiting for the others to push through the stray attacks as well. *We're the largest group here, and we can't keep waiting for our other teams to join us. We should regroup and push for the crown. Let them know.*

Dross relayed the message, and in a few seconds they had all gathered. Mercy hung from the top of a tree, watching the fight with excitement in her eyes. Yerin stood closer to the battle than anyone, white sword in her hand and hair blowing in the breeze, occasionally deflecting a Striker technique headed their way.

Naru Saeya crouched behind a tree, the peacock feathers in her hair somewhat wilted, tending to her wounds. Eithan ran a comb through his long, blond hair as though he were in his own home. He snatched a flying knife from the air and used it as a mirror.

"Where's Pride?" Lindon asked.

[I told him!] Dross said. [You can't blame me!]

Mercy sighed and pointed.

Lindon found him between a richly dressed woman with flying swords hovering around her head and a young man in blue robes with rings of lightning crackling around his arms. The three of them exchanged attacks in a rapid sequence of blows that would have been hard for him to follow before he advanced to Underlord.

[Stormcaller,] Dross said, indicating the man in blue. [Cult of the Weeping Dragon. The woman is probably from Moonwater, the nation next door to Ninecloud.]

The Stormcaller shot a blast of blue-and-yellow lightning madra at the woman, who caught it on a globe of green madra in her left hand as she used her right to direct the swords against Pride. Pride leaped over one sword, back-fisted a Striker technique from an unrelated fight and kicked another sword aside. He had closed the distance with the lightning artist, but a floating metal shield appeared from the lightning artist's soulspace and deflected Pride's punch.

"Sword girl," Mercy shouted, and everyone attacked her at once.

Dragon's breath, the Rippling Sword, an arrow of shadow, a green pulse of wind, and a mundane knife flew at the woman at the same time. She defended herself well, taking only a cut to her leg from the knife, but their second volley finished her.

Which left Pride to pour madra and soulfire into one huge blow against the Stormcaller. The lightning artist managed to get his shield in front of him in time, so the strike launched him into the jungle. At which point he must have fled, because he didn't show up again.

Pride did not acknowledge them. He dove deeper into the fight.

"He has the right idea." Naru Saeya pushed up to her feet. "Eliminate as many as we can."

As she said it, a further light streaked down from heaven. Now that the battle had destroyed many of the trees in the area, the sky was clear, and Lindon could see the golden column stretching between the sky and the earth. It wasn't close; it seemed to be falling at a distant end of the island.

*Dross, how long has it been since the first crowns appeared?*

[Six minutes exactly,] Dross said. [Well, not *exactly*. As closely as I can estimate. Is the error in the timing of the crowns, or in my calculations, or in your fleshy human brain?]

"Well, that's a wonderful chance," Eithan noted.

Now that there was another crown, the competitors who were interested in an easier battle had started to slink away. Even those who wouldn't have a chance to reach this distant crown would leave, because now it was clear that more crowns would appear every few minutes. Only those close to actually seizing this prize stayed behind.

The fight closest to the crown was a three-way battle between two blood artists in black leather and misty red veils that looked like Goldsigns and a woman who was clearly a member of the main House Arelius. Her long, yellow hair was tied back into a braid, her blue eyes were bright, and she wore tailored green pants, a ruffled pink shirt, and a short green jacket. The Arelius crest was sewn in white on the back of her jacket.

Bright sparks crackled on each of her knuckles, and Lindon thought they must be the beginnings of a two-handed Striker technique until they never went away. Her Goldsigns, then.

[House Arelius, though even you could tell that. The others are disciples of Blood-Chorus; he's one of the warlords controlled by the Eight-Man Empire.]

A Forged red wolf leaped from one of the blood artists. The Arelius woman pierced it with a lance of crackling light, but a gust of bloody rain landed against her and started to burn through her skin. She screamed, stumbling back, but still put up a shield to defend herself.

When she saw Eithan, she brightened and shouted something. Once again, Lindon felt as though he *almost* understood, unsure whether it was another language or a thick accent.

[She wants him to help,] Dross explained.

That had been obvious, but Lindon was still curious. *Can you understand what she says?*

[Of course I can. I was originally the guide construct to an international facility.]

*Can you translate?*

[Sure, yeah, no problem. Ahem: she says something along the lines of, 'I want you to help.']

Lindon's hopes were dashed.

Pride landed among the Blood-Chorus artists before Eithan reacted. He landed a black-rippling punch on one and shrugged off an attack from the other with the gray haze of his defensive Enforcer technique. One of the blood artists made a grasping motion, and Lindon could feel the power of blood aura spike as Pride staggered. A Ruler technique.

Before Pride could counter it, silver sword madra crashed into one enemy and black arrows ravaged the other.

Eithan helped the Arelius woman to her feet. She asked him a question and he responded in the same language.

While the rest of the team cleaned up the two from Blood-

Chorus, the Arelius woman said her farewells to Eithan, cast a last regretful glance at the gold column of light, and then ran off into the trees.

"Pardon if you don't want to answer," Lindon said, "but what did you say to her?"

Eithan waved a hand as though to say it was nothing. "Oh, certainly. She asked me if I would help her seize the crown, because the further House Arelius makes it, the better chance we have to rebuild. I said something about me being a core descendant of House Arelius who fled after the death of our Monarch, and she said that she understood and would leave this crown to me. Then she ran off to wait for the rest of her team to return."

Eithan's smile was unshakeable, and Lindon couldn't read anything in it. The rest of the team had eliminated the Blood-Chorus pair and was defending the crown's beam of light.

Lindon stared at Eithan, waiting for him to elaborate.

[...I think he's telling the truth,] Dross said.

"Do you ever intend to tell us where you came from?" Lindon asked, a little irritation leaking into his voice.

Eithan's eyebrows rose. "Did you want to know? You've never asked me."

Lindon stopped. Surely that couldn't be true.

"I have certainly withheld *other* information from you, but you've never once asked me where I came from."

"Oh. Apologies. So...where did you come from?"

Yerin shouted as Pride's hand closed around the crown, and both Eithan and Lindon turned.

Yerin had a hand on the hilt of her sword, and Pride's body

swirled with Enforcer techniques as he kept his eye on her and held the crown in one hand. Gold light still streamed from the ground into the sky, passing through his arm.

"I'll be dead and buried before I let you wear that," Yerin said.

Pride stood about two inches shorter even than Yerin, but he still looked down his nose at her. "You have quite an attitude for a servant."

Her Goldsigns flexed, silver madra gathering on their points, and Eithan stepped out with his hands raised.

"Hold on, everyone, hold on! It's times like these that we should remember that we are on opposing teams and should therefore fight to the death."

Saeya held her sword defensively between her and Mercy. Mercy looked frustrated, but still conjured an arrow to defend herself.

Lindon felt as though they were all rushing to conclusions. "Pride," he called, "who should get the crown?"

Pride continued his staring match with Yerin for a long moment before he looked over to Lindon. "The one who has the best chance of making it to the end of the competition. My sister."

Yerin and Mercy looked equally surprised.

"Agreed," Lindon said. "But there are supposed to be twenty-eight more crowns. We should carry this one with us until we have at least two more."

"So that *your* team can use them all?" Eithan squinted suspiciously. He raised his fist to the sky. "The Akura family keeps their boot-heel on the common man once again! Down with the oppressors!"

[Ah, there's...one more thing you should perhaps consider,] Dross said, but Lindon continued the conversation.

"Apologies, five more," Lindon corrected, keeping his frustration under control. "If they keep to the pattern, another one will appear in six minutes. Ten an hour, at which point the first round of people eliminated will return. If we're the largest group here, that's plenty of time for us to get enough for everyone and wear them all at the same time."

Dross tugged at his attention. [That's a great plan, I really admire that plan, but there's some information you might not have.]

Yerin and Pride nodded to one another, withdrawing their spirits. Saeya sheathed her sword, and Mercy had already happily banished her technique.

Eithan held up a finger. "Ah, but what if more crowns stop appearing after a certain number are held in place? Also..." He lowered his finger to point off to the east.

[Oh, *now* you pay attention! I grab your brain, and nothing, but as soon as he twitches a finger...]

Two golden lights, clustered together, were moving closer.

A trio of dragons flew over the trees, their screams echoing through the jungle. Lindon extended his perception.

"How many are there?" he asked Eithan.

"Seven. Three golds, two reds, a green, and a black. It's nice that they're colored for easy recognition."

"Change of plans," Lindon said to Pride, but the Akura was already ahead of him.

He tossed the crown beneath some of the intact trees, the golden beam of light following it. The crown itself couldn't be seen from the air through the thick canopy, only the beam of light. Then he veiled himself, slipping behind a bush.

"Back to the plan," Yerin said.

Lindon's intention had been to gather up all the remaining Akura faction competitors and ambush Sophara together. While she would certainly have gathered allies of her own, he was confident that with at least ten people, they could overwhelm her and retreat.

It almost didn't matter if some of them were lost. The farther back they could push Sophara, the better their chances of eliminating her.

Lindon switched to his pure core, tightly restraining his madra into a veil. He crept closer to the dragons, tucking himself beneath a thick leaf so he could still see a hint of golden light in the distance. Naru Saeya and Yerin moved nearby, with Mercy and Pride behind the crown. He had lost track of Eithan almost immediately.

The dragons would be suspicious if they saw the crown and no fight around it, but they would have to get close enough to see it. They could burn through the trees and descend from the air, but they probably wouldn't; flying so high toward one of the gold beams of light would make them easy targets for Striker techniques.

And if any did dive straight for the crown, Mercy and Pride were there to hit them as they landed. Everyone else was arranged to attack if they approached on the ground.

It wasn't anything like a perfect plan, but it was a quick strategy that would serve them better than a stand-up fight. Not only did the dragons have seven to their six, but Sophara frightened Lindon. Based on his practice against Dross' model of her, he wouldn't be surprised if she could eliminate him and Yerin together.

Unless Dross could get some more first-hand observation of her and build a combat solution against her. Or if Yerin's Blood Shadow ended up being more of a factor than he hoped. He hadn't seen the gold Underlady fight against any real sacred artists yet—only trials and projections.

He crouched in the damp soil and the humid heat, occasionally flicking away insects the size of his thumb. Veiling himself restricted his spiritual perception, making him feel blind, as though the dragons could be sneaking up behind him at any second.

He would've felt much better with Blackflame running through him—not only would the madra itself give him some much-needed emotional support, but then he'd have a Striker technique ready. But veiling pure madra was much more effective than veiling the Path of Black Flame.

His tension reached its peak when two streaks of golden light loomed closer, moving through the jungle. Bushes rustled, as though something large were pushing its way through the leaves, and then trees began to crack.

Two trunks split in either direction as huge, bestial red dragons shoved their way through. Sparks flew from their nostrils, smoke from their crimson scales, and burning ember eyes flared as they twisted serpentine necks from side to side. They scanned the jungle, their perceptions passing over him...without reacting.

Lindon let go of some tension. Shadow madra and pure madra were difficult to detect when veiled, but that only accounted for four members of the group. Yerin and Naru Saeya would have a harder time veiling themselves, but obviously it had worked.

He could almost see the fire aura around the red dragons even without opening his Copper sight, and just their presence ignited some of the sticks and dry leaves beneath their feet. Flames licked their claws, smoke drifting up into the sky.

The others followed next.

The green dragon was a young man who appeared mostly human. His human skin was a brown almost as dark as the pair from Dreadnought City, and green scales ran down his ears and the sides of his neck.

A pair of wooden horns twisted up from his forehead. He wore emerald robes and carried a twisted driftwood staff that matched his horns. His hair flowed like moss down his back.

Two gold dragons came next, and like him, they looked more human than dragon. From their heads hung strings of scales that imitated hair, and the scales that ran down their throats only accented their pale skin. One was a man, the other a woman, but not Sophara.

They carried themselves with no weapons and visible arrogance, thin tails whipping at the underbrush as they walked. They were dressed in rich robes and jewelry, as though to cover themselves in gold to compensate for the scales they'd lost.

The columns of light from their two crowns hung back.

There were five people here. Eithan had said seven. Sophara and her black dragon must've hung back, holding on to their two crowns, sending the rest of the team forward to pick up the third.

Lindon tensed. He had no way to signal the others. The first person to move would commit them all to an attack. Should he wait? He was almost as afraid of the black dragon as he was of Sophara—he would be able to withstand Blackflame far more easily than Lindon could, which meant that Lindon had virtually no way to hurt him.

He hadn't been able to do much research into the black dragon team; there were too many contestants remaining, and some of them were less well-known than others. One of their contestants was listed as 'Black Dragon Prisoner,' so he wondered if the black dragons might be forced to fight by the gold dragons. That might be a weakness they could exploit...but it might not. He would still prefer not to fight a black dragon.

Attacking now meant they could weaken the enemy party while the two most frightening members were gone, but Sophara would only have to flee for an hour. Then she could have her revenge on anyone left.

While Lindon debated, the gold dragons passed him, and the choice was taken out of his hands.

A green blast of wind madra caught one of the reds in the body at the same time as a wave of silver sword-madra. Pride was there so quickly it looked like Yerin's Striker technique had carried him, and he slammed a foot down onto the other red's skull.

Neither dragon died. They roared, sending fire madra flooding around them, but a wave of pure madra almost instantly wiped it away.

The attack had taken only an instant, but the other dragons weren't waiting around. Golden streams of Flowing Flame madra spewed into the woods, washing over the human attackers, just as the green dragon released a pulse of life madra. It felt more like a perception technique than an attack; he was looking to pinpoint them amidst the jungle.

So he was the one who shouted and turned when he felt Lindon behind them.

With the speed and grace of the Soul Cloak, Lindon had dashed behind the two gold dragons. Focused on their Striker techniques, neither reacted quickly enough to stop him.

He used an Empty Palm in each hand. Just for good measure, he added a wisp of soulfire to both techniques.

His hands struck them both in the lower back, and huge blue-white handprints flared at the hit. Pure madra flooded them, disrupting their madra channels, and they staggered forward. The woman whipped her tail at him, but without madra Enforcing it, it didn't have enough force behind it.

She was still an Underlady and a dragon, so she hit like a kicking horse. But Lindon had the Soul Cloak moving through him, and he snatched the tail from the air with his right hand. He hauled on it, pulling her off her feet.

In the meantime, both red dragons flowed away in pulses of white light.

For a few seconds, Lindon was engaged in hand-to-hand combat with both gold dragons. Without his training at the Akura family, he would have had to disengage and run. This time, he held his own, matching their blows without giving ground.

Even without Enforcer techniques, they were almost as strong and fast as he was. But the Soul Cloak made the difference, so he was able to move around them, keeping them in each other's way, preventing them from using their number to their advantage.

Lindon had been most concerned about the green dragon interfering, but he was filled with black arrows. His scales glowed emerald as he focused his life madra on himself, trying to purge himself of Mercy's shadow-venom.

It did no good when Naru Saeya's rainbow sword slashed through his neck.

Eithan strolled up to Lindon's fight, casually slapping the Underlady in the face as he tripped the Underlord. They rolled to the ground, and Mercy had them bound in Strings of Shadow before they could react.

Even so, they began to tear through the madra. Their spirits were coming back under their control...slowly but surely, they would regain their powers from the effect of the Empty Palm.

But Lindon was no longer concerned about them. He stared through the trees at the two retreating pillars of golden light. Sophara was running.

And something else was barreling through the trees at them.

The black dragon obliterated the two trees that the reds had knocked over. Lindon couldn't tell if it was a male or a female; it had a long, snake-like black body, with two huge wings and a pair of massive claws in front. Its eyes were like Orthos'—solid darkness with two fiery rings where its irises should be.

It blew dragon's breath down the forest.

Rather than black-and-red, like Lindon's, this was a solid bar of darkness with a few red sparks here and there. It radiated the power of destruction so strongly that the smaller pieces of debris nearby crumbled to dust and burned away in its passing.

Eithan, of course, reacted first. He held both hands out, and pure madra spun around him, catching the Striker technique as though in a whirlpool. It twisted, spinning back at the dragon.

But the black serpent took his own attack on his scales, ignoring it, and swept its breath from side to side.

This time, it was Lindon's turn.

He dropped his pure core and drew on Blackflame, his eyes heating up as they matched the black dragon's own. The Burning Cloak ignited around him and he leaped forward, driving his white fingertips into dark scales.

His hunger arm began to feed.

Before reinforcing his arm with the Archstone, it had been difficult to draw madra into his cores. The Ancestor's Spear had used scripts to guide madra in that way, and though the binding was capable of the same thing, it had to be carefully controlled.

Since then, Lindon had grown much more familiar with the technique, and it had grown stronger. But he rarely encountered madra that he *wanted* in his core.

This time, he feasted.

The dragon's madra flowed through his arm and into his channels, surging into his Blackflame core. The energy was wilder than his Path of Black Flame, more primitive and savage, with a heavier emphasis on destruction. It was as though his human madra had diluted it, and this was the primal source. But it was compatible, so he drew as much as he could.

In only a second, the dragon noticed what was happening. It cut off its breath, convulsing wildly, trying to shake Lindon off. Lindon held on with the strength of the burning cloak and the power of his Remnant hand. The hunger madra even helped, latched on to the serpent like a leech.

Finally, the dragon twisted around and breathed a Striker technique into Lindon's face. Lindon raised his left hand and met the dragon's breath with the same technique.

From inches away, Blackflame met Blackflame.

Dark fire exploded, incinerating leaves and consuming the edges of Lindon's Akura sacred artist's robes. He stumbled back, the force of the dragon's spirit pushing him away, losing his contact with its scales.

For a moment, they glared at each other with identical eyes, neither backing down.

Then the dragon was *riddled* with Striker techniques.

The rest of Lindon's team tore it to shreds, and the sacred beast shrieked and twisted. He was astonished that it didn't die immediately.

It tried to get off another dragon's breath, but finally it dissolved into white light.

Lindon caught his breath, trying to still the fiery storm in his core. His channels ached, and he would need Little Blue's help when he returned, but they were victorious. Their ambush had worked flawlessly.

An enraged scream shook the forest ahead of them.

"BLACKFLAME!" Sophara's voice echoed.

And the two crowns moved back toward them.

Lindon hurried over to Eithan. "We have to stick together. There are six of us. We can hold her off."

Eithan looked into the distance. "Can we?"

Lindon thought he understood the implication and cast out his perception. They had not been quiet, and Eithan must have sensed enemies closing in.

But Lindon didn't feel any. Even the few native creatures of the island he sensed were fleeing, as though they had been frightened off. It was only Sophara.

Pride stood at the front of the group, black lines on his skin whirling, chin tilted up. Shadow madra shrouded his arms.

Mercy crouched in a tree, arrow held in each hand. Eithan stood off to one side, and his smile looked more like a grimace of anticipated pain.

Saeya cradled one arm and spread her wings, forcing her sword up. Yerin stood shoulder-to-shoulder with Pride, blade clutched in both hands.

Lindon's spirit and body ached, but whatever burst through the underbrush, they could handle it. He coaxed some soulfire out of his spirit and fed it into a dragon's breath.

[We certainly *look* prepared,] Dross said. [I have a good feeling about this.]

As the two columns of light from the crowns approached, Lindon and his allies all unleashed Striker techniques. Even Pride hurled a stick like a spear.

Flames of liquid gold crashed through them like a tidal wave. Lindon couldn't imagine releasing such a large technique so quickly; one second, there was nothing, and the next second the trees had been swallowed by gold dragon's fire.

His bar of Blackflame punched through, as did Eithan's pure madra, but before he could sense if they'd done anything, Sophara was among them.

Eithan and Pride reacted first as the dragon-girl landed, tail lashing, golden scales falling around her face likc hair. Pride's strike was like a crack of black lightning, and Eithan came down on her with a spear of blue-white light.

A golden disc, etched with script, was Forged in the air above her head. It intercepted Eithan's attack, and she ignored him, instead wrapping her tail around Pride's wrist and wrenching his attack off-course.

But she didn't follow up with an attack. Instead, she rushed forward, fueling her jump with a soulfire-assisted Enforcer technique. She was dashing to the back...where Mercy, Saeya, and Lindon waited.

*Dross,* Lindon demanded. He had already called up the Burning Cloak, and black-and-red light played around him. The explosive strength of Blackflame filled him.

[I can give you an edge, but the rest is up to you,] Dross said. The world didn't stop, like it had against Harmony or Seishen Kiro, but Lindon could suddenly follow Sophara's movements much easier than before. She was going for Saeya.

He kicked ahead of her, drawing dragon's breath into his hand. Thanks to Dross, he *knew* where she would go. He could see his Striker technique burning through her.

So he and Dross were equally astonished when her golden eyes flashed with a pale light and she slipped to the side. Black dragon's breath drilled a hole in the ground. A silver wave passed over her; she had somehow managed to avoid Yerin's Striker technique at the same time.

[That's...ghostwater,] Dross said.

There was a sound like a splitting melon, Saeya's voice coughed, and Lindon turned to the side to see her dissolve into white light.

*You didn't know?*

[My records are incomplete! *Incomplete!* How many more times do I have to—]

The golden disc floating over Sophara shifted position to catch three black arrows, but she was already whipping her tail into Lindon. He blocked with his left hand, Enforced by the Burning Cloak, while gathering more dragon's fire in his right.

The bones in his forearm cracked.

He flew back, tumbling, losing his grip on the Burning Cloak. Thanks to Dross and the grace of his Underlord body, Lindon managed to control himself enough to land on his feet.

His arm hung limp and useless, the pain virtually paralyzing him. It wasn't only broken; her tail had torn skin and muscle, ripping him open from elbow to wrist. The others had engaged Sophara in combat, which was the only thing that had stopped her from finishing him off in midair.

*Backup plan,* Lindon said to Dross.

[Fifteen feet behind you and to your left,] Dross responded.

If they failed to eliminate Sophara in an ambush, then odds were good they wouldn't be able to prevent her from passing the second round. The next-best thing would be to keep her away from the crowns, but she was much more of a monster than anyone could have expected.

So if they couldn't prevent her from reaching the third round, they had to at least stop her from eliminating them all.

Lindon followed Dross' directions, reaching down with his Remnant arm.

From beneath a bush, he grabbed the crown.

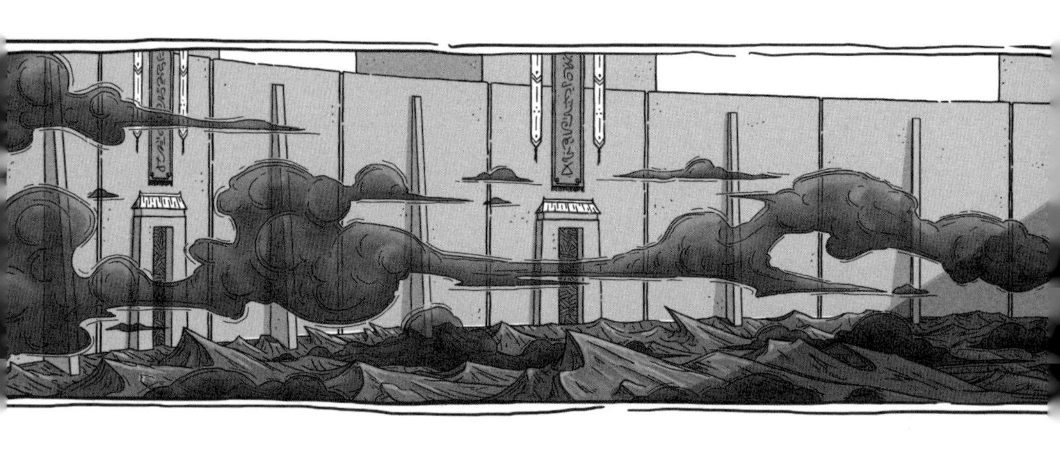

THE DISC FLOATING AROUND SOPHARA MADE HER ALL BUT IMMUNE to Striker techniques, she was physically stronger than any of them but Yerin, and the ghostwater meant that even Eithan couldn't keep up with her. She kept dashing and running, engaging them one at a time, and every exchange ended with one of the Akura faction injured.

By the time her movement slowed, indicating that her single drop of ghostwater had run out, she was still in better condition than the rest of them. Either they would outlast her madra...or she would destroy them all.

Guided by Dross, Lindon pushed his Soul Cloak to the limit. Sophara hammered at Yerin's sword, tearing the blade apart with her claws, then dashed to the side to avoid the counter-attack. She was too fast and precise to be caught, and when she saw Lindon standing in her way clutching a crown, she didn't avoid him. She dove right into him, eyes blazing.

As she did, Lindon placed the crown on her head.

Heat stabbed through Lindon's ribs as Flowing Flame madra drove through his chest. His spiritual defenses fought against it, but his own madra weakened as breathing became much harder.

His vision fuzzed. He was an inch from death.

But the light around Sophara turned white.

She faltered as she realized what had happened, and then her fury redoubled. Once again, her spirit surged to the skies, and she unleashed a tide of golden flame.

There was no stopping it. Lindon braced himself behind his white arm, straining the hunger binding to its limits, weakening the attack as much as he could.

No matter how much he siphoned its power, he was still swallowed by fire.

He gritted his teeth instead of screaming as fire madra covered him from head to toe. It was like trying to clutch a live coal in his bare fist.

But as quickly as it had begun, it was over, and he hurriedly vented burning madra from his arm. Smoke rose from his charred robes, and he was sure he was missing some hair, but all told he had emerged unscathed.

Yerin had ended up far away, but she was still alive. Mercy had hidden in her tree. Pride was on one knee, bracing himself with a hand, but he had weathered the tide of fire. Eithan...

Eithan was dissolving into white light.

He faded away before Lindon could catch a glimpse of him, but Lindon was shocked. Eithan was the *most* suited to survive a massive Striker technique. Had he let himself be burned away? Why?

The aura of ghostwater had faded from Sophara, but she still did not waste time. Her golden eyes touched on Lindon, but then they moved to the weakest enemy remaining. The one crouched and panting on the ground.

Pride.

[Shame,] Dross said. [I was hoping he could eat more attacks for us.]

It wasn't the end for someone "killed" in this round, Lindon knew. They would be re-formed in an hour, unharmed. But the competition would get fiercer as the round progressed as fewer crowns appeared.

If Pride was eliminated now, he wouldn't make it.

Lindon leaped forward, gathering pure madra into his Remnant hand. It didn't conduct the Empty Palm as well as his flesh hand, but it was good enough. The newly enhanced version of the technique didn't have to hit Sophara's core dead-on. If he could only slow her down, he and Pride could both survive...

[This is why I should be in charge of your body,] Dross said.

Lindon landed between Sophara and Pride, driving his Empty Palm at her midsection.

She didn't even slow down as her claws tore off Lindon's head.

Ziel sat against a tree and waited, hood shading his eyes and hammer leaning against him. He had brought it in his soulspace, but keeping any item inside his fractured spirit was agony, so he let it sit by him.

He knew the Stormcallers were here, and the champion of the Dawnwing Sect would have hunted them down one by one with righteous fury in his heart. It wouldn't matter if he made it to the next round or not, so long as none of them did.

But Ziel wasn't that man any longer. The memory of the Weeping Dragon taking up the sky, its living lightning decimating his students and friends, had played in his mind so many times that it had scraped him raw. Dreadgods couldn't be blamed for the destruction they caused; he might as well shout at a hurricane for daring to flood his house.

It was the Dreadgod cultists that had stoked his rage, as they looted and pillaged in their master's wake.

They had chased down the fleeing Dawnwing sect as rain and thunder poured from the sky. Ziel had stayed behind to hold them off as his junior disciples and students escaped.

It hadn't worked. As it turned out, one of the Weeping Dragon's lightning strikes had caused a landslide that wiped them all out.

So Ziel's duel with the Sage of Calling Storms had been for nothing.

He had lost, of course. Even at the height of his power, he was no Sage. And instead of killing him, the leader of the Stormcaller cult had mutilated him. Cutting apart his spirit and stitching it together...wrong.

Afterward, he had been allowed to live. *Forced* to live, almost.

He was no threat to the Storm Sage, no threat to the Stormcallers without a sect behind him, and certainly no threat to the Weeping Dragon.

He had drifted along like a dead leaf on the wind, formerly one of the proud geniuses of the Iceflower continent. He had fought as a champion of the Eight-Man Empire as an Underlord in the last Uncrowned King tournament. Then, as now, he'd made it to the second round.

This year, he was exactly thirty-five. That was a cruel twist of fate. A few months older, and he wouldn't have been allowed to participate.

He felt twice his age.

Ziel let the first two hours of the round pass him by, his emerald horns resting against the bark of the tree behind him. Crowns fell and moved, some turned white, and no doubt many battles were won and lost.

He watched through half-lidded eyes, staring through the leaves at the sky.

Northstrider had heard of him through the Beast King and had come for him. One of the youngest Archlords ever, an elite among elites, fortuitously reduced to the level of a mere Underlord. The Monarch had declared that Ziel would certainly be allowed to enter.

One of the other factions was bending the rules in a similar fashion, it seemed, and it wasn't as though Ziel could exert any more power than a real Underlord. Far from it. Ziel could pass most spiritual power detectors as a Truegold.

The poison that ravaged his body had undone most of the enhancement soulfire had given him, and holding anything—even soulfire—in his soulspace was like trying to hold a mouthful of needles. He might as well not be an Underlord.

Years of treatment at the hands of the Beast King had countered much of the poison, but he could still only barely be considered an Underlord. If not for his skill and experience, he would never have passed the first round.

Without Northstrider's personal request, he wouldn't have participated in the tournament. Not even when the Monarch revealed that the Ninecloud Court had methods of restoring his soul. Their royal madra could do miraculous things to spirits. He only had to make it far enough in the tournament to earn a prize from them... and, not coincidentally, to improve Northstrider's reputation.

Ziel still hadn't wanted to do it. What if the Court *could* restore him to his former power? He had no sect left. There was nothing to fight for. Revenge did not return the dead.

Another golden light descended from the sky over the island. This would be the twenty-fourth, give or take. And it was fairly close.

Ziel groaned like an old man as he pushed himself up on his hammer. He had the body of an eighteen-year-old, but he didn't feel like it.

Slowly, he dragged his weapon through the jungle toward the crown. He had come this far, and it wasn't every day that you received a personal request from a Monarch. He had to at least give it a token effort.

Though he was the only one of the Wastelands team who had made it past the first round. If Northstrider really expected a victory out of them, he should have trained up some better candidates.

The beasts of the jungle moved through the trees around him, but he ignored them, marching onward. He wasn't afraid of them, and even if they somehow did make it past his hammer and tear out his throat, he didn't care.

Evidently they could sense total apathy, because they let him pass.

Ahead of him, the column turned white. He couldn't see much through the thick trees, only the light filtering through the leaves, but he sensed a battle fading away.

He pushed his way past a leaf bigger than his head to see who was wearing the crown. If there were too many people, he would turn around and leave. There were still at least eight crowns left. He hoped he had waited out the most intense fighting, and maybe he could scoop one up unclaimed.

The boy wearing the shining white crown wore a pair of blue armbands Forged from vivid yellow-and-blue lightning.

Stormcaller madra.

Ziel and the boy stared at each other for a long moment. Ziel saw the shining dragon that flew on unnatural stormclouds of madra. Bolts like the ones wrapped around this man's arms had slithered through doors, hunting victims. Lightning from the Sage's fingertips had wrapped around him, searing his spirit...

Ziel shook himself as something stirred in the ashes of his heart. This didn't matter. The fight wasn't worth it. If he won, this one Stormcaller wouldn't really die. Even if his death *was* permanent, what of it? It would change nothing.

Ziel turned, his gray cloak fluttering behind him. He could find another crown.

"Dawnwing!" the Stormcaller exclaimed.

The man recognized the symbol of Ziel's sect. He had been there that night.

He should have kept his mouth shut.

The next thing Ziel knew, his hammer was covered in blood that slowly dissolved into light.

It felt like no time at all when Lindon reappeared on the beach. The first thing he saw was a panting, bleeding Pride crouched on the sand next to him.

Golden light streamed into the sky behind him.

Lindon's head jerked up, scanning the treeline. He knew an hour had passed, but the thrill of battle and the shock of death still flowed through him. "Where's Sophara?" he asked.

"Passed," Pride said, struggling to his feet. He was broken, battered, and almost two feet shorter than Lindon, but he still held his head high. "It worked."

He held a crown, and Lindon looked to it. "What happened to the other crown?" Sophara had been carrying two.

"My sister took one, and Yerin Arelius the other," Pride said. "She actually refused to take it. Mercy had to force it onto her head just like you did to Sophara."

"What about that one?" Lindon asked.

Pride held it out. "This is for you." He glanced to one side. "I suggest you take it quickly. It hasn't been long since I won it."

Lindon stood still, watching him.

[It's an imposter!] Dross said.

"Gratitude, but why would you..."

Pride made an irritated noise and shoved the crown onto Lindon's head. Instantly, Lindon was bathed in a pillar of white light.

"I owe you nothing," he said, turning his back to Lindon and limping toward the trees. "Defend it on your own."

[That was nice,] Dross said. [I still don't like him.]

Naru Saeya flew low, dodging branches, as she circled a tower of gold light in the distance. She couldn't know what had happened since she was killed, so she had to assume that she was the last remaining member of her team.

*Her* victory wasn't important. It was the team that mattered.

As she kept her spiritual sense extended, hunting for danger, she felt something behind her and slowed down. After making sure there was no one else close to her, she flew backward.

Eithan had emerged at the edge of the jungle, just where they had arrived at the beginning. He brushed his robes off, giving an annoyed huff when he found a spot of mud around his knee.

"You didn't last any longer than I did," she said, and in truth it soothed her pride. She had thought that if anyone survived, it would be Eithan.

He gave her a beaming grin. "I thought you could use the company. No telling how many crowns are left, but we should be able to grab a pair."

"On one condition," Saeya said. "You take the first."

He paused. "I have to admit, I was expecting a different condition."

She folded her wings and began walking, perception extended. "I'm not a fool. I know you didn't have to take that hit."

Eithan glanced up at the sky, perhaps looking to the invisible constructs that allowed the participants to watch them. "What? How dare you. Perish the thought."

"I don't want my name to spread, but the name of the Blackflame Empire. I need you to make that happen."

It hadn't been an easy journey for her, but Saeya had eventually admitted the truth: she wasn't cut out for this. The more she trained against Yerin, the more she saw the girl's unlimited potential. Potential Saeya didn't have.

Besides, her true passion wasn't advancement. She just wanted her home to prosper.

Eithan stretched one arm, then the other, the thread-of-gold on his ornamented robes flashing in the sun. "Bargain struck," he said. "Let's go give them a reason to remember us."

⬡

The second round worked as intended, dividing the number of participants in half, but it also split the Akura faction.

Only one of the Frozen Blade competitors made it out, and none of the Akura backup team. Akura Grace told them how the team of dragons found them before they made it to Lindon, and she had been eliminated. When she returned, she hadn't been able to claim a crown in time.

He was greatly relieved when he saw that Eithan and Yerin had both passed, though neither Pride nor Naru Saeya had managed to secure a crown before time ran out. He had mixed feelings. True, the fighters most likely to win had passed, but Pride and Saeya had given up their personal chances for the team. That only increased the weight on him.

When they returned to their rooms, Mercy and Lindon were gathered together and visited by the Ninecloud Soul.

"Congratulations on passing the second round!" The warm voice said from within the rainbow light. "In the morning, you will be led to the Archlord prize vaults, from which you will select one sacred instrument of your choosing. In future rounds, you will be permitted to use weaponry up to Archlord in your matches...although allow me to caution you that an Underlord weapon suited for you will produce far better results than an unsuitable Archlord weapon."

"Understood!" Mercy said brightly.

Lindon's imagination was already running away from him.

The Archlord vaults of the Ninecloud Court? What would they be like? Why did he have to wait all that time until morning?

"One week after you claim your prizes, you will fight in the third round. These will be one-on-one matches to the death, although of course the protection of the honored Northstrider is still in effect. However, unlike later rounds, you are not competing as an individual, but as a team. Only when the last member of your opposing team loses will you be considered victorious."

Mercy stepped closer to the rainbow, hands clasped behind her back. "Question! Can the same person fight each time?"

"Full rules will be provided to you tomorrow, but yes, of course.

As long as you win. Someone who loses this fight is eliminated from this round...but not from the competition. Either your whole team will survive, or none of you will."

[Ah, so last round was intended to reduce half the remaining individuals, and this is designed to get rid of half of the remaining teams. It's like some kind of human-eliminating system.]

"Who is our opponent?" Lindon asked.

The light flashed, acknowledging him, and the image of a human bound in chains appeared in its center. Lindon had noticed the man around the tournament, but hadn't spent any time investigating him. He looked older than thirty-five, haggard and worn and no more than skin and bones, but maybe captivity could do that to someone.

"You face the one remaining member of the black dragon team. He was registered in the tournament as the Black Dragon Prisoner."

[You know, I saw his name on the lists, and I assumed I was reading it wrong. Or there was something wrong with your eyes.]

"During the second round, he was unchained and left to his own devices," the Ninecloud Soul went on. "He ran around the island eliminating everyone and everything he encountered. Our records do not make it clear whether he sought out the crown or whether he accidentally ended up with it after killing everyone else."

The image of the man started wildly thrashing, tearing at his restraints, snapping his teeth and lashing a long black tail behind him.

"Now that the rest of his team has been eliminated, we have decided to list him under his real name: Naian Blackflame."

Dross gasped. Mercy covered her mouth with a hand and looked to Lindon.

Lindon watched the broken man strain against his chains.

For almost two years, Lindon had heard about how the Path of Black Flame would erode the mind, body, and soul. He had seen Orthos' transformation after the damage was reversed by the wells of Ghostwater.

But he had never seen what happened to a human.

After a few more pleasantries, the Ninecloud Soul vanished, leaving Lindon in a quiet room with Mercy. Birds chirped from the rafters, and clear water babbled as it ran in a creek throughout the room.

When Mercy finally spoke, her voice dragged out as though each word pained her. "I'm sorry to do this to you, but it gets worse."

[Doesn't seem too bad so far!] Dross said to both of them. [It's all of us against a mad, injured prisoner. I feel like we can handle it.]

Mercy searched Lindon's eyes as though checking to see if he was ready for bad news before she continued. "We didn't do well enough last round."

That was no surprise, though it hurt to hear.

"Monarch Shen's Dreadgod teams still have eight people left," Lindon said. He'd seen the lists. "Sophara is still ranked first, and most of the other top ten ranks are taken by the Ninecloud Court. We do not have the strongest individual, nor the most participants, nor the best team."

As he spoke, his feelings firmed: he was still confident.

"And what does it matter?" he went on. "The only thing anyone will remember is who is still standing at the end."

Mercy's look was full of compassion, but she and Lindon were drawn to the door at the same time as they sensed a powerful presence approaching.

"Not the *only* thing," Mercy said.

Fury burst through the door a moment later, hair scraping the doorframe and chest bare from within his outer robe. Knocking must have been a courtesy he left behind in his advancement.

Lindon bowed over a salute, but Fury waved that aside. "Monarch meeting is finally over," he announced, throwing himself down on the couch. "We're losing."

"What was on the table?" Mercy asked quietly.

Her uncle—who, now that Lindon thought about it, was technically her older brother—raised his head to peek over a cushion. "You should come to these things, you know. If you keep it up with your advancement, you'll lead the family someday." He let his head drop back down. "And then I wouldn't have to go."

"I know the Dragon King must be gaining influence..." she prodded him.

"Yeah, his little snake is making the rest of us look bad. Charity thinks the dragon girl might end up a Sage, and if she makes it to the top eight, I won't be able to deal with her myself." He let out the longest, most drawn-out sigh that Lindon had ever heard. "The cat and the snake are speaking with one voice, and thanks to little Sophara and those cults, the rest of them are listening."

[I can guess what he means,] Dross said, [but I'm a little afraid he is actually talking about cats and snakes.]

*Reigan Shen and the Dragon King are working together,* Lindon explained, though in truth he didn't understand much of the situation.

Mercy looked like she did, from the way she frowned and chewed on her lip. "So it is about the Dreadgods?"

"Of course it is. You saw the teams that Shen brought, and did the other Monarchs band together and kick him out? Didn't say a word. Any more than we did when the Nineclouds put Miara as their team captain. Maybe I should slap on a wig and a veil and push around some Underlords."

Lindon wanted to ask more questions about that, but Fury didn't slow down. "More Monarchs have died trying to kill the Dreadgods than any other way, but Reigan has the others convinced that he's found a way."

"How?" Lindon asked. The question came out of him so quickly that he forgot to be polite.

Fury pointed to him from the couch. "The cat has a key to crack open the western labyrinth. He claims he'll use it as bait, drag the Dreadgods in, and the security measures on the maze will weaken them enough for us to kill them and craft their corpses into the most powerful Divine Treasures the world has ever seen. The cults, of course, think he's just waking them up."

The Herald sat straight up. The wind stirred, gathering him until he sat on air and drifted to face Lindon and Mercy. "Problem is, the first thing the Dreadgods will do is run straight through Akura territory to get what they're after. *We* take on all the risk."

The western labyrinth.

Lindon's throat tightened. He knew where that was. His right hand curled into a fist.

It wasn't the Akura clan who would be taking on the risk, but the people in their territory. The people of Sacred Valley.

"Mother won't let them," Mercy said confidently.

"No, she never has. But half the Monarchs feel like cities and towns are only holding us back, and most of the other half are listening because there's nothing at stake for them. If it weren't for Northstrider, we'd have been run over already."

Lindon's spirit shivered as a massive spiritual scan passed through the whole building.

Fury tilted his face up. "Yeah, I'm talking about you. No need to show off."

The scan passed.

"How can we help?" Mercy asked.

"Don't just win. Send a message." He held out a fist, and red eyes blazed. "Crush Naian in two seconds, Mercy, and show them why they should be afraid of us."

Lindon thought of the man straining against the restraints, a prisoner of the dragons and a victim of Blackflame madra. He could spend the week looking up records of Naian's techniques from the second round and training against Dross' model, but Naian Blackflame wasn't the goal. He would spend more time training against Sophara.

"Pardon," he said, "but I have a suggestion."

Both Akura turned to him. Mercy looked surprised, and Fury curious.

"We have two people against his one," Lindon said. "Everyone expects us to win. And they expect Mercy to be stronger than he is. I think, with your permission, that we can send a stronger message." For effect, Lindon let the Path of Black Flame bleed into his eyes. "Let me defeat him, Blackflame to Blackflame. We can show them that even when we play by their rules, using their Paths, we are still stronger."

Fury's eyebrows raised, and he turned to Mercy. "Can he do it?"

Mercy responded with instant confidence. "Yes."

The Herald shrugged. "All right, Lindon. What do you need?"

"Your guidance in picking a weapon tomorrow," he said. "And, if it wouldn't be too much trouble, I'd like access to a Soulsmith foundry. I have a plan."

**Information requested: Reigan Shen, Monarch of the House Shen**

**Beginning report...**

**Path: King's Key.** Reigan Shen is its creator and sole practitioner. A force Path touched by the authority of space. As a Jade cub, he was lucky enough to bond with a Sage's Remnant that had some command over space. His Path involves control over an extra-spatial vault in which he stores weapons, techniques, and even enemies.

Reigan Shen is a creature of ambition.

He was born to a pride of regal white lions on the western plains of the Rosegold continent, a prince of this line of sacred beasts. His diplomatic victories were matched only by his impressive record in combat, and before he turned twenty years old, he had united the plains under his family name and reached Underlord on a Path of his own design. If he had been allowed to continue his life uninterrupted, he would have led his tribe to unprecedented prosperity and ushered in a new treaty between the local human cities and sacred beasts.

The Dread War disrupted his fate. When the twelve Monarchs attacked the Wandering Titan in an attempt to destroy the Dreadgods once and for all, Reigan Shen distantly sensed the battle. And when the other three Dreadgods woke to defend their brother, beginning the greatest slaughter of Monarchs since the creation of Cradle, he saw the start of that fight as well.

It was his first glimpse of true power, as such things are measured in his Iteration, and it filled him with awe. The conflict broke most of his home plains, and many of his pride lost their lives, but he led an expedition to a nearby human city. His goal: to find out the identity of these godlike beings whose battle had broken the earth and spread across the sky.

That same year he began his search, the Dread War concluded. The two surviving Monarchs convened the handful of Heralds and great families remaining in the world. Together, they organized the Uncrowned King tournament in an effort to pool their resources and raise up a new generation of Monarchs.

Reigan Shen reached these families just as they had begun their search for powerful Underlords. He was the victor of the first Uncrowned King tournament, and that fortune became the foundation for decades of conquest.

Now, the Monarch of the King's Key Path has a reputation as a conqueror and a glory-seeker, an imperialist and a daring innovator. He is known to be generous to his people, but ruthless and cruel to all others. He is always looking for the next legendary deed that will spread his own myth.

So when he approached the four Dreadgod cults, promising them each that he intended to awaken their masters for good, they had no reason to doubt him.

**SUGGESTED TOPIC: THE LIFE AND DEATH OF TIBERIAN ARELIUS. CONTINUE?**

**DENIED, REPORT COMPLETE.**

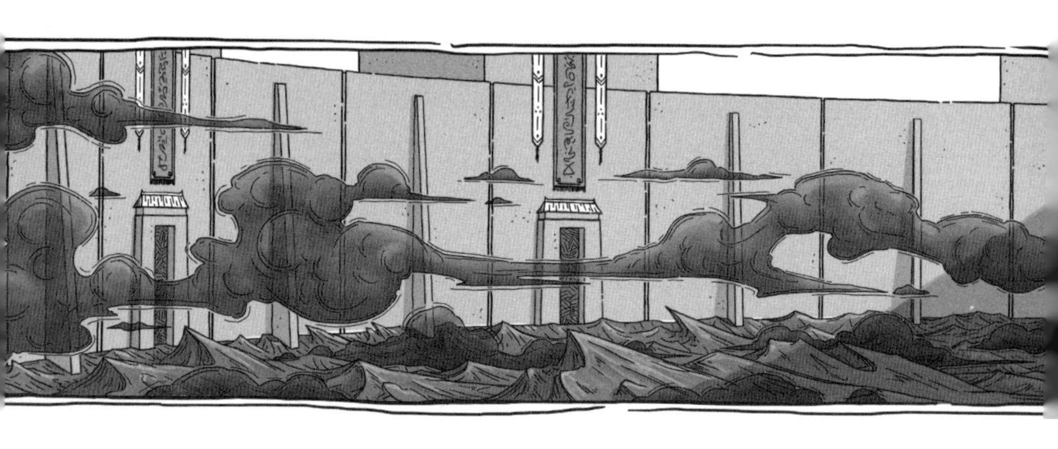

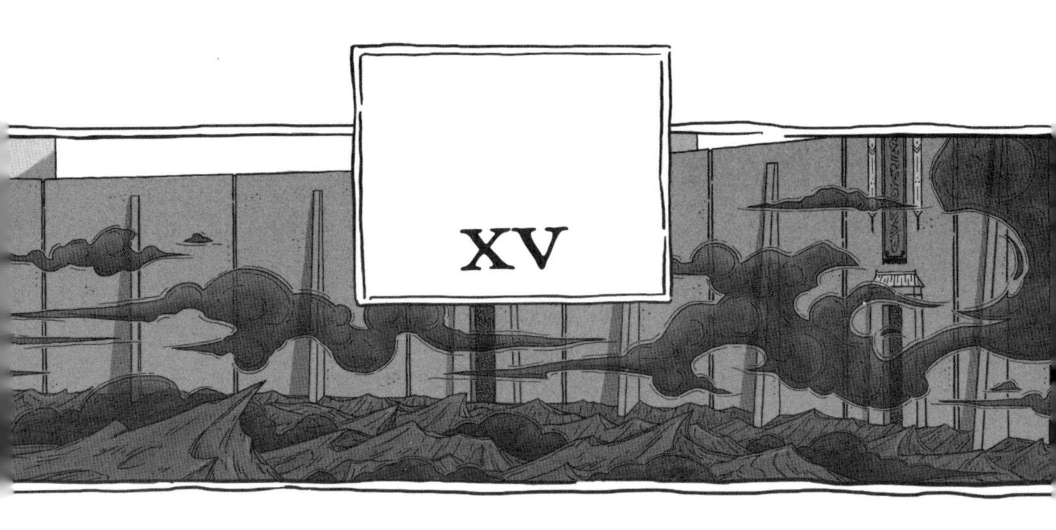

# XV

The competitors were kept in a waiting room before the main event. It was a small, gray room with only a pair of benches against the wall, a low table, and a cabinet.

Mercy engaged in a series of stretches on the opposite side of the room, but Lindon sat on the bench, cupping Little Blue in his hands.

The spirit stared up at him, her chimes full of confidence.

"It's okay if you're scared," Lindon told her. "This will be dangerous. I'm not sure it's worth the risk."

Little Blue stuck two fists in the air and whistled.

Dross didn't manifest because of all the foreign gazes around—Northstrider could probably see them from the other side of the world if he wanted to, so there was no guarantee he wouldn't glance into the waiting room with his spiritual perception.

But Dross still spoke into the Riverseed's mind. [We're attached to a big human Underlord, aren't we? Let *him* do all the fighting. That's his job!]

Blue gave out a burbling sigh.

[What! I'll have you know that I have as much courage as any dozen memory constructs! Which is...hm, that would be none. Twelve times zero is zero. Well, I have more than that!]

Lindon leaned closer, looking into the Sylvan's ocean-blue eyes. "If you're scared, we can call this off. There are things I can try on my own."

She gave him an unusually serious look and a single, resolved nod.

Without further hesitation, Lindon drew Little Blue into his soulspace. He could feel her revolving there, between his cores, curled up as though asleep.

[I am being serious now, though: don't let her get hurt, okay? Or me, if that were to come up for some reason.]

Lindon snatched up his shield and slipped it over his left hand. He'd created it himself, with Dross' help, from scrap materials and dead matter that the Ninecloud Soulsmiths had allowed him to use. It was made primarily from force madra, with an Underlord-level defensive binding and a few protective scripts here and there. It wasn't compatible with his Blackflame madra or his hunger madra, so he couldn't use it on his right hand, but he still found himself attached to it.

He had taken the bulk of the shield from a turtle-Remnant. It was a broad, stone-gray shell.

Orthos would have been proud.

The madra felt a little unstable, but it shouldn't cause any problems for him. If the shield was destroyed in this fight, but he managed to save Naian, it would be worthwhile.

At the touch of his madra, a sword hovered above him and behind his shoulder. It was a *real* sacred instrument, a masterfully crafted weapon covered in elegant script.

The double-edged blade was wide and tinged with just a hint of blue, its runes stylized to look like crashing waves. The hilt and guard were a pale green that reminded him of wind aura and carved with the image of powerful gusts.

Wavedancer was the weapon's name, and it was a masterpiece. Its Archlord spirit was as graceful as its physical form, and it had no binding, so he could use it even as an Underlord. According to the description from its creator, it was meant to "Bend the swiftness and power of an ocean storm to the protection of its owner."

It was a comforting presence behind him, using his madra as fuel to hover, but he didn't feel the same connection to it that he did to the shield. Maybe it was because of its aspects of water and wind, or maybe it was that he'd made the shield himself. Regardless, he needed an Archlord weapon, and this had been the most suitable for him.

Dross took over controlling it immediately, so he didn't have to waste his concentration.

"Apologies," Lindon said aloud, "but I can't control what happens to Little Blue. I think it's worth the risk. So does she."

Dross grumbled. [Is this Blackflame your long-lost brother and you just never told me? Wait, now that I've thought of it, I actually do want to know the answer. He's not. I know he's not. Is he?]

In the ravaged twenty-five-year-old Blackflame, Lindon saw

Orthos. Between what Orthos had been before meeting Little Blue and what he had become after Ghostwater, there was a world of difference.

Orthos had gotten his life back. Maybe Naian Blackflame could too.

Mercy pulled her hair back, tying it into a tail with a string of sticky black madra. Suu rested against her shoulder, her new lens hanging on her forehead over her left eye. The lens was her Archlord prize from the last round: a circle of scripted purple glass that enhanced her vision in half a dozen different ways. She wore a newly tailored version of the Akura team uniform, the high collar framing her face in bright violet and the cape sweeping out behind her.

He wore the same, his outfit broader and bulkier than hers. His halfsilver badge hung over his chest, though he'd been forced to leave his void key behind again. With the turtle shield on his left hand, Wavedancer hovering over his right shoulder, and Dross and Little Blue in his spirit...he was ready.

Lindon stepped forward into a script. Colors swirled in the runes for a while, scanning his weapons and soulspace for anything beyond his station, until it finally flashed white. He was approved.

He stepped aside while Mercy walked into the scanning circle, her purple eyes concerned.

"I can still fight him, if you'd prefer," she offered.

He took a deep breath, working the fingers on his Remnant hand. "Gratitude, but I need to try. Besides, it's better if we have you in reserve in case I mess up."

She laughed, but he hadn't been joking.

Once the script lit up for her, she moved past to join him. Distantly, he could hear the noise of the crowd and the voice of the Ninecloud Soul as she introduced the two factions.

He could do nothing else to prepare. He was as ready as he would ever be.

After a minute of silence, the heavy stone wall began to grind upward.

Instantly, a gust of wind and a rush of noise blew in. The dry air smelled of ash, and Lindon wondered why. The arena hadn't smelled like that the last time he'd been there.

When the wall finished opening, he saw what had changed: the arena was covered in dead trees.

The sandy stone that had been the arena floor before was now covered in a thick layer of white-and-gray ash. Dozens of brown, leafless trees rose from the ashes, dry and ready to burn.

The Ninecloud Court had prepared a battlefield suitable for two Blackflames.

"...led by the daughter of Monarch Malice herself, the Akura family!" the Soul announced, and the crowd roared in response. The colorful Monarch towers around the arena were once again packed with people, though the Akura crowd closest to him was muted. The shadowy veil around their tower deadened even sound.

Lindon and Mercy strode out in their plum-and-violet uniforms, with Lindon one respectful step behind the Akura heiress.

The rainbow light of the Ninecloud Soul spoke from above the arena, flashing with every word. Northstrider still stood in the middle, black-scaled muscular arms folded across his chest. His eyes were closed as he waited.

Only a few seconds after Lindon stepped out on the ash, another section of wall on the opposite side of the arena began to rise.

"Naian Blackflame, fighting for the black dragons!"

The skeletal young Underlord rushed out, flecks of spittle flying from his unrestrained snarl. His eyes blazed with hunger, and he rushed through the layer of ashes on bare feet. Lindon was somehow disconcerted to see that Naian didn't share the Blackflame eyes that he and Orthos did. The Goldsign of the main Path of Black Flame was their tail.

Compared to the visions Lindon had seen in the dream tablets, Naian looked even worse. His tail whipped behind him in a frenzy, dirt and grime smeared his matted, unshaven face, and wild, stringy hair hung from his head.

Worse, he was still shackled; a scripted collar around his neck shone red, and Lindon could tell that he was attempting to force madra through it. His hands were tied behind his back with a series of scripted chains.

There was no reason in him. He rushed at Northstrider like a mad dog unleashed.

And slammed into an invisible wall only inches from the Monarch. He fell backward, howling with pain, twisting and writhing to get back to his feet with his hands tied behind him.

A few scattered laughs sounded from the audience, but Lindon saw nothing funny.

Northstrider finally opened his golden eyes, looking first to the Akura team, ignoring the Blackflame artist who was trying to break an invisible wall with his teeth.

"Which of you fights first?" he asked.

Lindon stepped forward. "This one will, if it pleases the Monarch."

"It does."

Lindon turned at the sound of stone grating on stone. A booth had risen from the arena floor, surrounded by scripts.

"Akura Mercy. You will watch from inside this room unless and until your turn comes. The battle will not touch you."

Mercy bowed and returned, patting Lindon on his arm before she left.

Leaving Lindon to face his opponent with Northstrider standing between them.

Overhead, the rainbow voice played up the match. "A fighter from the Blackflame Empire versus the last descendant of their original royal family!"

Aside from wondering if Naian really was the last descendant, Lindon gave her words no thought. He focused on the man lashing his tail at the transparent barrier in front of him. He could hear the passage of the tail through the air—that was not a weak blow, but against the will of the Monarch, it might as well have been breeze from a sparrow's wing.

"He will be unbound, won't he?" Lindon asked quietly.

"As much as he can be," Northstrider answered. The Monarch's attention turned to Lindon, and Lindon's spirit shook. He felt a spike of worry for Dross, but the mind-spirit was stunned into a sort of awed silence by the Monarch's sheer presence.

"Do not let compassion disarm you," Northstrider said. "He is no less deadly for his condition."

Fireworks sounded overhead, and Naian snarled at the sky.

Northstrider unfolded his arms, and Lindon cycled the Path of the Black Flame. Naian noticed, turning to glare at Lindon with dark human eyes. Lindon met them with the eyes of a dragon.

With a hiss, the metal collar around his neck split apart. It fell to the ash, and the belts around his arms whipped through the air as they unraveled. He looked down at himself with surprise, stretching his arms, staring at his own fingers.

Then a Burning Cloak sprang up around him, thicker and wilder than Lindon's, like an unrestrained forest fire. He howled.

"Begin!" Northstrider commanded. He, and all barriers restricting the fighters, vanished.

Lindon used a Burning Cloak of his own, closing the distance between him and Naian. He knew from the dream tablets that reason would not work on the Blackflame. Certainly not while black dragon madra still poisoned his mind. Lindon needed to weaken the man first.

He kicked up ash with every step, landing beside Naian, reaching out with his hunger arm. The more Blackflame madra he could drain away, the more lucid his opponent would become.

Naian didn't react the way Lindon had expected he would. For the first instant, he didn't react at all. He stood, staring at his own hands, a furious Burning Cloak blazing around him.

As though it had a mind of its own, his tail struck with blinding speed.

It slapped Lindon's Remnant arm so hard that a crack appeared on the back of the white hand, and a lance of pain shot through Lindon's spirit. In the same instant, it struck again, stabbing at Lindon's face.

He got his shield up in time, taking the blow on the metallic surface, but it hit like a hammer. Lindon was thrown backward, skidding to a halt in the ash.

He twisted his shield in an instant, readying dragon's breath, but Naian was gone.

Lindon felt burning heat in his spirit from behind and threw himself aside as a bar of dragon's breath slashed from left to right at neck height. Naian followed it up, using the red-and-black madra like a furious sword.

An actual sword would be faster; every stroke of dragon's breath took a little time to gather. But the Blackflame made sure that Lindon had no time to recover, dashing at him with the Burning Cloak in between Striker techniques. He fought like a furious beast, mixing the Cloak and the dragon's breath into an unrelenting assault. Only by blocking with his shield and his flying sword could Lindon keep up.

*Dross!* Lindon called desperately.

[Done,] the spirit replied, and suddenly Lindon could see a ghost of his opponent overlapping his actual movement. A ghostly echo that preceded his action instead of coming after.

Dross moved the flying Wavedancer to block a punch while Lindon sheltered from the Striker technique behind his shield. He pushed the dragon's breath back, stepping forward. And now, in the prescient shadow of Naian's movements, he could see an opening.

In a burst of the Burning Cloak, he leapt forward. His right hand landed on the Blackflame's thigh, and he triggered his hunger binding.

It felt chaotic but powerful, far denser and more potent than his own. The main Path of the Black Flame used a Jade cycling technique that focused on power, not on expanding the core like his Heaven and Earth Purification Wheel did.

This original Blackflame madra reminded him more of the black dragon's power, but more tempered and controlled. No less potent or explosive. The original Blackflame madra mixed into his core, blending into his spirit just as the dragon's had.

Naian didn't like having his soul drained.

He lashed out with a kick that Lindon anticipated, breaking off the hunger technique after only a second. The shadow that Dross provided rushed at Lindon, who raised a shield to block the attack... which didn't come.

Instead, Naian used a technique that Lindon had never seen before.

He gripped his right arm in his left hand, the fingers on his right hand forming a claw and trembling as though under a great weight. Madra pooled there, and aura gathered, as though he was focusing his Burning Cloak into a single punch while also using a localized Void Dragon's Dance.

[We should stop that,] Dross suggested, and Lindon could only agree.

His flying sword swept in, striking at Naian from the right, and the Blackflame heir fought it off with lightning-quick flicks of his tail. At the same time, Lindon swept in a dragon's breath from the left, and Naian dashed away.

Each step was a burst of speed, powered by the full-body Enforcer technique, but there was a moment in between each leap where he had to come to a stop. Lindon aimed for those moments, following him with both a sword and a beam of madra.

That exchange only continued for a few seconds, and Naian never dropped his technique. Finally, Forged claws of red-and-black grew from the fingers on his right hand, encrusting from his fingers to his wrist in dark, fiery crystals.

The aura around it stormed with fire and destruction, flashing red and black, and with enough madra condensed into the technique to melt through a castle wall. Soulfire rushed through it as well, increasing the pressure until Lindon felt as though he could barely breathe, making the Forged claws vivid and distinct.

*He Forged Blackflame so easily,* Lindon sent to Dross, pulling his flying sword back and raising his shield.

[Most Paths can be Forged. Some sacred artists just have more talent than others.]

Naian roared, mad fury in his eyes, and jumped at Lindon.

Prepared, he lowered Wavedancer in front of him, holding out his shield behind that. Naian didn't bother knocking the Archlord weapon out of the way; instead, he slammed his claws into the flat of its blade.

The technique sent Blackflame madra and waves of flame—conjured by aura—blasting out in a sheet. It engulfed the sword in a cloud of deadly black, red, and orange, and Lindon hurriedly triggered the binding in his shield. The pulse of force pushed some of the fire away, but he was still consumed.

He drained some of the madra from the air with his right arm, pulling it into his Blackflame core, while at the same time contesting the Path of Black Flame with his own spirit.

Even so, he was burned.

The force of the attack shoved him back, and he had to squeeze his eyes shut against the heat, which beat at him like a furnace. While drawing on his fire Path, he had a higher tolerance for heat, but streaks of fire still seared him where the attack pushed through his spiritual protection. His robes caught fire in a dozen places, scorching his skin. Several of the trees around him burst into flame, crackling as they exploded.

Gritting his teeth and cycling Blackflame, Lindon endured. When the cloud of flame from the technique washed away, he was ready to react immediately, though his madra channels already ached. He pushed both hands out in a two-handed blast of dragon's breath.

Naian held up his left hand as though he held a sword...and then he *did*; a sacred instrument manifested itself from his soulspace. A squat, wide orange blade that glowed at its core like a sunset. It had no problem enduring Lindon's dragon's breath.

[Above!] Dross called, dragging his attention higher, but Lindon had already noticed. He opened his Copper sight to see clouds of fire and destruction aura gathering over him in a slowly spinning vortex.

Naian was using the Void Dragon's Dance.

Lindon cut off his dragon's breath immediately, focusing his spirit on controlling the aura released from the burning trees. The rotation of the aura clouds stuttered, turning slower then faster, as he and Naian Blackflame wrestled for control of the technique.

Naian gripped his sword in a trembling hand, snarling at Lindon through gritted teeth, pouring his wild and focused soul into the Ruler technique. He could have attacked, but he couldn't afford the slightest loss in attention. An instant of distraction would yield the Void Dragon's Dance to Lindon.

It was the same for Lindon, but he had joined the technique too late. Naian had control over most of it, and though Lindon poured all of his will into the aura, his grip was slipping. If he took a second to attack, a tornado of fire and destruction would strip the flesh from his bones in an instant.

He couldn't spare the attention...but Dross could.

His flying sword darted over to Naian, slashing at him with wide, elegant sweeping motions. It targeted the side of his neck, forcing the Blackflame to slide away, batting at the weapon with his tail.

Which allowed Lindon to get a firm grip on the Void Dragon's Dance.

Through whatever damage years of captivity and the rigors of his Path had done to him, Naian recognized what was happening. Rather than give into his opponent, he tore at his own technique, trying to disperse it. Lindon firmed his soul, pushing madra out, trying to stabilize the vortex under his control.

Neither got their wish.

Torn between two spirits on the Path of Black Flame, the Ruler technique detonated. In a blinding flash, all the natural fire in the area exploded outward, consuming anything in its path with the speed of destruction aura.

Lindon focused his spirit on defense, which meant that instead of burning through him like a fire through dry tinder, the flame hit an unfocused barrier of Blackflame madra. It slammed into his chest and cracked his ribs, sending him tumbling back.

His eyes and his spiritual senses were stunned, and he lost his breath. He clawed his way back to his feet before he could even feel the world around him again, trying to force his lungs to move. He felt as though he'd been pelted with rocks all over.

Naian had fared no better, a few patches on his skin blackened and cracked, and one of his knees twisted around the wrong way. He limped up, bracing on his tail, and snarled as he drew up dragon's breath.

Lindon wouldn't win a contest of Blackflame. But this had always been about wasting his opponent's madra.

The weaker the Path of Black Flame was in Naian's spirit, the more control his mind would have.

Lindon's channels screamed with pain as pure madra ran through them, but he felt powerful again. Even his Bloodforged Iron body ran better on pure madra, healing his wounds more quickly, fighting the destruction of his flesh that Blackflame caused.

The Soul Cloak sprang up, and he ducked dragon's breath as he ran in, smacking the blade aside with his shield. Naian fought with blinding speed and bestial aggression, but between Dross' anticipation and the control of the Soul Cloak, Lindon reacted better. His shield and his flying sword protected him as they fought at arm's reach.

Fear pestered him—an unwelcome distraction. His shield was breaking under Naian's blade, and his own flying sword was just enough to defend him from the Blackflame's whipping tail. If he took a hit from this close, the fight could be over. He had only his Iron body to rely on.

But he had to create an opening.

*Dross,* he asked, *can you numb my pain?*

[I see what you're thinking, and if you weren't being protected from death by a Monarch, it would be *unspeakably* stupid. But you are, so go crazy.]

Lindon moved aside, and instead of crashing onto Lindon's shield, Naian's orange sword skewered him through the stomach.

The audience erupted into wild cheers, lights flashing from the audience in the dragon tower.

Either Dross really had done something to numb his pain or Northstrider's protection helped, because Lindon's mind should have been erased by agony. Instead, though the three feet of metal scraped his ribs as they pierced him through, he was still able to function.

At least enough to pull Little Blue from his soulspace.

His concentration was shaky. As she emerged, he focused on his blood spraying all over his white arm, leaking through his Akura clothes. Those were expensive...

[Focus!] Dross said, and then Lindon could.

The Sylvan had screamed upon seeing him, scrambling to help, but Lindon pushed her toward Naian. The Blackflame was trying to pull his weapon free, but Lindon's left hand had his arm in a death-grip. At the same time, Dross controlled the flying sword to attack the man's back, engaging his tail.

Little Blue had an opening. And, with a sorrowful note, she took it. Ocean-blue hands landed on Naian Blackflame's wrist.

Cold sparks of her madra passed into his channels, and every muscle in the man's body went stiff. Even his tail froze, and he showed no reaction as a sword plunged into his back.

Despite Dross' stimulation, Lindon's mind was fading. With the last threads of madra he could control, he reached out his right arm and used the hunger binding.

Blackflame madra flowed into him. The less madra Naian had, the better, though it was hard for Lindon to remember why. Some of Little Blue's madra came back to him too, but the spirit was pumping more in, so most of it stayed in Naian's spirit.

The Blackflame swayed on his feet, and Lindon felt the same way. Little Blue was growing pale.

[Pull her back!] Dross called. [Lindon! If you die before she's in your spirit, she'll stay out here! Pull her back!]

It was harder than it should have been, but he managed to follow instructions, drawing Little Blue back through his hand and into the center of his soul. She gave him a sad look as she disappeared, and he wondered if he even saw a tear.

Naian looked stunned, paralyzed, staring into the distance as though watching a horrifying battle. He stayed locked in place, gazing through Lindon.

Lindon tried to ask how he was, but only blood sprayed from his lips.

A harsh, disused voice grated from Naian's throat. "You...pulled me...out. How..."

But Lindon couldn't stay awake anymore. He sensed his spirit one more time, where Little Blue was curled up between his cores. Safe.

He could relax.

Dross called something to him as though from a great distance, and he passed out.

When Lindon came back to himself, he was sitting on a polished stone bench inside a booth that seemed to have grown out of the arena floor. It felt like only an instant had passed.

His body was whole and healthy, his cores full, and his madra channels felt brand-new. Wavedancer sat neatly next to him, sheathed in a thin layer of Forged madra, and his gray turtle shield rested on his knees.

Rather than waking slowly from a deep sleep, he was wide awake. *How long was I gone?* Lindon asked Dross.

[AAAHHH! Where are we? What happened? How long was *I* gone?]

*I hoped you would tell me.*

[We're still sharing senses. If you felt *absolute nothingness* for a moment and now feel like you just skipped ahead a few minutes in time, then we've had the same experience.]

Someone was fighting outside the booth, across a field of ash, but a moment of fear drew his attention inward. He cast his perception through his spirit, finding Little Blue still curled up behind his cores.

She poured into his left hand, waking immediately. When she saw him uninjured, she gave a happy chime, leaping into his chest and trying to throw her arms around him. Soothing madra spread into him, though his spirit was fine. She was whole and healthy, her strength even restored from her efforts healing Naian.

And her actions had worked. Out among the leafless trees, Naian Blackflame was fighting Mercy.

This time, he fought with far more skill than he had shown against Lindon. His sword flashed in complex patterns, striking arrows from the air as he used his free hand to launch dragon's breath that severed a tree in the middle and forced Mercy to jump down.

His expression was serious, his aura restrained. Lindon recognized immediately that he was holding back, trying to avoid overtaxing his spirit and pushing himself over the brink again.

He wasn't healed, just as Orthos had only briefly returned to himself after Little Blue's treatment and the nourishment of Lindon's pure madra. He would need years of rest, and something like the restoration Orthos had received in Ghostwater.

But it was possible now, and that was enough. He had enough control over himself to get help.

[There's every possibility the dragons will seal him again,] Dross warned. [They're not just tying him up for their safety; they're using him as a weapon.]

*I'll get to him,* Lindon said. He had proven that Naian *could* be helped. He would find a way to make the rest work out.

Unfortunately for the black dragon team, Naian could not both hold back *and* fight against Akura Mercy. With Suu in hand and the purple lens over her left eye, Mercy unleashed arrow after arrow at her opponent.

He never managed to close, even with the Burning Cloak; she dodged his every move, tangled him up with Strings of Shadow, and continued shooting. Her arrows seemed to have minds of their own, swerving to hit at the last second, leaving veins of black madra that he had to burn from his spirit.

Finally, he struck her head-on with a bar of dragon's breath...but Mercy strode through it in full amethyst armor, unharmed, walking until his Striker technique ran out. When it did, she already had an arrow nocked and her bow drawn.

She didn't fire it. She waited, the missile seething with shadow madra.

Lindon wasn't the only one who could sense the war inside the Blackflame. He trembled, his head twitching and his tail lashing behind him. His Burning Cloak flickered on and off.

After gathering himself for a long moment, he growled, "I surrender."

Disappointed jeers rose from the crowd as the Ninecloud Soul announced the result. Some of the unruly spectators within the Eight-Man Empire's tower threw food or garbage into the arena, but constructs instantly incinerated it all.

Mercy's armor dissolved, and her bow shifted back into a staff. She wiped sweat from her brow with black-clad fingers and bowed to her opponent.

More elegantly than Lindon would have guessed, Naian returned the bow, pressing fists together in a salute. Then he turned to Lindon's booth and bowed a second time.

Naian did not make eye contact with Lindon, clearly still wrestling with himself. Nonetheless, Lindon nodded in return.

Most of what Lindon did in his pursuit of the sacred arts, he did for his own sake. He hadn't done much that he could be truly proud of.

And he still hadn't, he reminded himself. Not yet. Not until Naian was taken from the gold dragons and restored to control of his own body and spirit.

Northstrider appeared in the center of the arena, and his commanding voice announced the Akura team as the victor. The crowd's cheers drowned out all other sound.

Mercy bowed to Northstrider then hurried back through the ash, beaming at Lindon. Behind her, Naian said something to the Monarch. Northstrider's golden eyes surveyed him, and he responded with one word.

Lindon wished he had been close enough to overhear.

Naian glanced back to the Akura booth one more time and then walked away, picking up his own restraints on the way back to his waiting room.

The back wall of the booth slid up, leading back to the Akura waiting room, and Mercy dashed through the front of the booth only a moment later. "It worked!" she cried. "I knew it was going to work and it did!"

Little Blue jumped up and down on Lindon's hand, chattering away, and Mercy exclaimed, "You were so brave! Were you scared?"

They walked back into the waiting room as the Sylvan began to tell the story with half-understood impressions and hand gestures. Dross interjected here and there, asking a question or clarifying a fact.

As the walls continued to slowly fall, Lindon cast one last look behind him.

Across the ashen arena, Naian Blackflame walked into his waiting room, where Sophara was waiting for him.

The gold dragon did not seem furious, as Lindon had expected. Her arms, with their layers of jeweled bracelets and smattering of gold scales, were folded. She tapped her foot impatiently, staring across the arena herself.

Her eyes locked on Lindon's.

Naian bared his teeth, waving his chains as he shouted something at her.

[I don't have a good feeling about this,] Dross said, and Lindon felt the same way. He looked to Northstrider, who still stood impassively as images from the fight were projected over his head.

As the stone wall lowered past Sophara's face, her golden claws flashed once.

Blood splattered out onto the arena, and Naian's body fell.

Lindon shouted and ran forward, but an invisible force kept him from pushing past the descending door. He was no longer permitted in the arena.

The Ninecloud Soul was already talking about the next fight, the Five Sisters of the Iceflower Continent against the Ironheart Legion of Rosegold. Lindon could see the last Blackflame Prince's body sprawled on the ground, his throat torn out, staring across with blank eyes.

The door closed over Sophara's bloody claws.

"Will he come back to life?" Lindon asked, voice trembling. He already knew the answer, and Dross confirmed it.

[There's never been a delay before,] the spirit said softly. [If he was going to come back, his body would have disappeared.]

Then the wall crashed down, cutting off the sound from the arena. He heard only Mercy and Little Blue excitedly talking to one another, but Mercy trailed off.

"Lindon? What happened?"

He had driven his fist into the stone, leaving a crater. His right hand left no blood behind, though the white madra cracked slightly.

"...just to spite us." He bit off the words, his voice low. Tears stung his eyes, though he couldn't understand why. He hadn't known Naian Blackflame at all.

"What?" Mercy hurried around so she could look into his face. "Did the dragons say something?"

The air flickered, and a massive bulk of a man stepped out, ragged hair falling behind him. His unshaven face showed a hint of anger.

"They always do," Northstrider said. He had appeared in the center of the waiting room as easily as walking out of a door.

The two Underlords both bowed, though Lindon had to force his body to move like a puppet.

"Dragons are beings of destruction," the Monarch went on. "They would rather see a field reduced to ash than see someone else have a bite to eat."

"I'll take care of her," Lindon said. He didn't have a way yet, but he and Dross would figure it out. Blackflame burned through his spirit, and he took deep breaths, cycling the fury throughout his body.

Northstrider's golden eyes flicked between them before settling on Lindon. "Your opponent asked for his last words to be delivered to you."

Lindon felt a pang in his heart. *Last words.* So Naian had expected what happened to him.

"He said, 'The dragon advances.'"

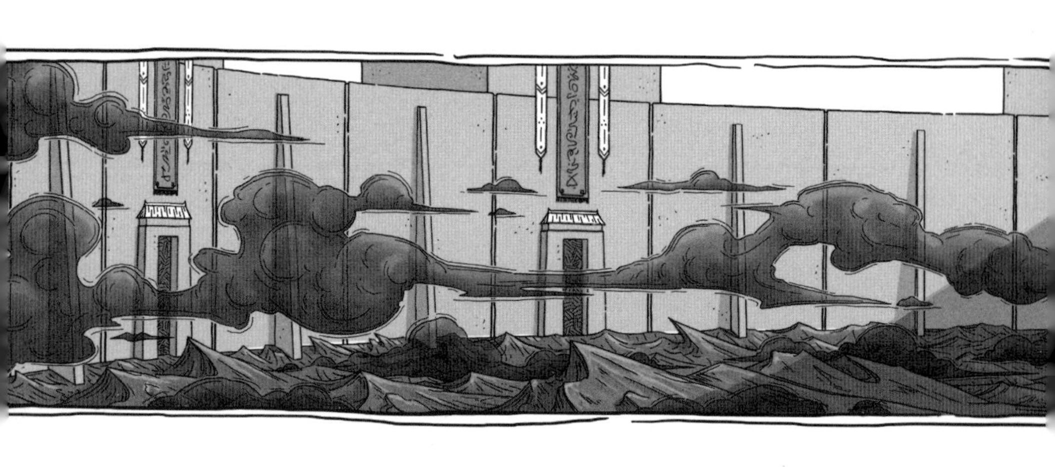

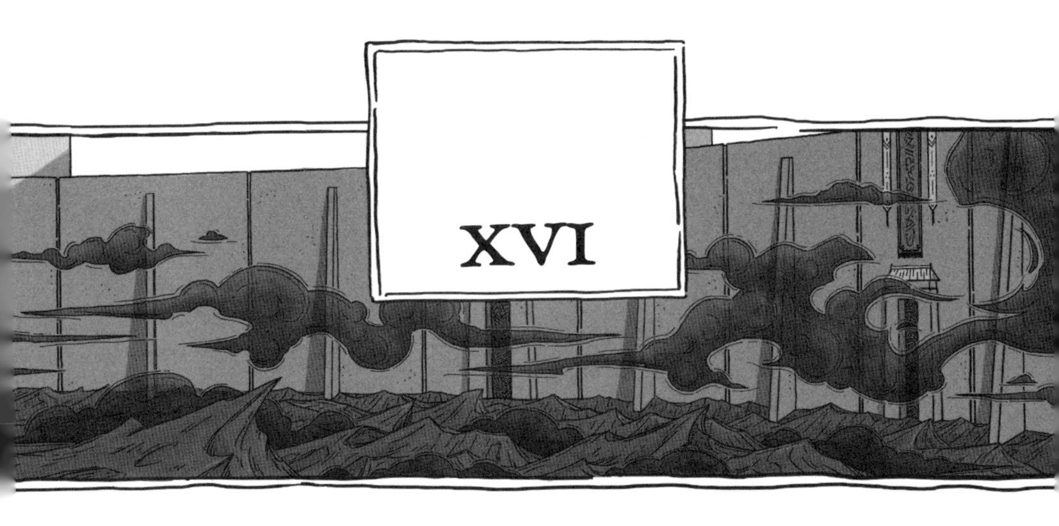

# XVI

In the brightly tiled and decorated hallways leading to their waiting room, Yerin and Eithan ran into the House Arelius team.

If that was a coincidence, Yerin would eat her sword.

Veris Arelius, the remaining Underlady, was the House Arelius woman they had met during the second round. She was tall and long-limbed, with blue eyes that shone like a sharpened blade and yellow hair tied into a braid.

Yerin had never seen Veris' partner in the flesh before, but she'd looked up dream tablets on House Arelius since the last round. Altavian Arelius was in his early thirties, and his blond hair was almost white. He stood as tall as Lindon but not as broad, with legs built for running and arms for reach.

The sword on his back was twice the length of Yerin's, and his Goldsigns were his razor-sharp nails. He was a sword artist who specialized in Enforcer techniques; in her dream tablet, she'd seen him cut through three individual opponents in a row during the second round.

Altavian's blue eyes were as peaceful as a lake on a windless day, and he looked as calm as though he walked around in a meditative trance. He bowed when he saw her, but otherwise said nothing.

Eithan swept up to them both, beaming. "It's a shame that we must meet each other in competition, but at least we will have a chance to learn from the main House."

"If you've made it this far, you don't need any pointers from us," Veris said. Now that she was speaking words Yerin could understand, her accent was clearly similar to Eithan's. The Arelius woman regarded them both with satisfaction. "Five people with the name Arelius passing the second round. I hope that burns *him* to the bone."

"I doubt Reigan Shen is burned at all by our tenacity," Eithan said, and Veris paled. Altavian's eyes widened in shock, and both members of the House Arelius team took a healthy step away.

Eithan flicked a lock of hair behind him. "We're not going to say anything he doesn't already know. I doubt he thinks we have a positive opinion of him after he killed our Monarch and shattered our home."

He may as well have been speaking about ancient history, but Yerin's attention was hooked. She'd gathered that the Arelius homeland had been destroyed, and that Eithan had been there, but now it sounded like a battle between Monarchs.

"I wouldn't hate hearing *that* story," Yerin said pointedly to Eithan.

"Not here," Veris said through her teeth.

Eithan lifted his eyebrows. "You think speaking more quietly is going to prevent a Monarch from hearing us?"

"I *think* a little caution is better than none." She stared him down for a moment before Eithan cleared his throat and dipped his head to her.

"You are quite right. I apologize, I forgot who I was dealing with."

Veris' eyes flicked to the ceiling, but she seemed to relax somewhat. "The point remains that this is a good omen. No matter which of us wins, the Arelius name will echo across the world."

"Mmmm," Eithan said.

That might have been agreement.

The other two bowed and began to leave, but Eithan stopped them with a gesture. He gathered his thoughts before he spoke, which snagged Yerin's curiosity. Since when did he think before speaking?

"The Blackflame portal to the homeland opens in about two years. I would very much like to meet you there when it does. I believe we may be able to help each other."

Veris looked surprised, and exchanged a quick volley of words with Altavian in her language. Finally, she said, "Much of that territory has been lost, but we will find a way."

"Let it be so!" Eithan said triumphantly, and then he strode toward their waiting room. "Come, Yerin! Let's get ready to beat our new friends to death!"

The scripted stone door of their waiting room slowly slid open, revealing an arena that had totally changed once again.

Rather than covered in ash like Lindon's, their battlefield was covered in rectangular pillars. Some of them were only waist-high, while others towered overhead. Narrow alleys wound their way through the dense maze of structures.

Lindon's Blackflame arena had been designed to give them a source of aura, but this seemed to be built to limit their angles and force them into a fight on different levels. Yerin could imagine having to push to a crossroads to get enough space to swing her sword, and leaping up to the top of a pillar to land a Striker technique on someone below.

She wondered why the arena had been customized in this way for *this* particular match—it seemed to be designed to restrict the two sword artists more than anything—but the introduction made the picture clear.

"Arelius versus Arelius!" the Ninecloud Soul announced, to the approving roars of an energetic crowd.

The week since the last match had whipped them into a frenzy, because Yerin couldn't hear herself think.

"House Arelius used to rule over most of the Rosegold continent, before the tragic death of the Monarch Tiberian Arelius only eight years ago. But his descendants are still a force to be reckoned with, leaving branches on every continent! Today, it's a family reunion, as their cousins from the Blackflame Empire have come to test their worth against the heart of House Arelius!"

Arelius versus Arelius...this arena had been designed with their bloodline abilities in mind. The close square pillars would block sight and make hearing unreliable, so spiritual perception and Arelius bloodline senses would be the best way to navigate the fight.

And Eithan had forced her to complete his spiritual perception course. Had he known, even then, that they would be in this situation?

Yerin gave him a wary look from the side. If he had anticipated this far ahead, then she should be a little afraid of him.

He kept looking to the center of the arena, but leaned to the side to speak to her. "Good thing we trained your perception, isn't it? This could have been awkward."

Yerin relaxed. Sometimes she forgot Eithan was only human.

The columns blocked their sight of the other team, but Northstrider appeared in the middle of the arena, standing on the highest rectangular pillar. His wild hair blew in the wind, and he looked down on them with the regal bearing of a king.

"Decide who fights," he said, and Yerin heard stone grating on stone as the booth rose from the floor behind her.

"I'd be more than happy to draw swords on both of them," Yerin said, "but they're your kin. I'll follow your word."

They had discussed their strategy already, but Eithan had directed her to focus on preparing for either fight. She had a plan against Veris and Altavian both, but he had dodged any questions about which of them would fight first. She assumed he wanted to decide at the last moment.

Eithan leaned over so that they were eye-to-eye, looking into her. A moment later, his hand blurred as he slapped her on the side of the head.

It didn't quite *hurt*, but she instantly responded by stabbing at him with one of her Goldsigns. He slid casually to one side.

She scowled at him. "You trying to get me ready to stab an Arelius?"

Eithan straightened up. "Just checking. I don't see *it* in you yet. Why don't you watch me first? It might be good for you."

"I was ready to do that from the beginning! Didn't need a slap!"

"Next time, dodge it."

Yerin grumbled as she walked back to the booth. They were both Underlords now. She didn't have to listen to him anymore.

...though she reminded herself that she still hadn't defeated him in a spar. Once she could beat him, then she could ignore his advice. And slap *him* on the head.

Yerin settled into the booth as the disembodied voice echoed through the arena: "The fighters have been chosen! Veris Arelius of House Arelius fights for the late Tiberian Arelius! And Eithan Arelius of the Blackflame Empire fights for Akura Malice! It's a civil war between these two scions of the same clan!"

Yerin could see the back of Eithan's elaborate lavender-and-gold outer robe fluttering in the wind, his hair blowing alongside it. The image of him projected for spectators overhead looked supremely confident, as always.

She couldn't see his opponent with her own eyes, but Veris' giant illusory image floated in the air opposite Eithan's. The Arelius woman wore loose-fitting pants and a shirt, all in the Arelius colors of dark blue, black, and white. She stood with her hands behind her back, eyes closed, breathing deeply. Lightning crackled in the air around her.

"Begin," Northstrider said, and then vanished.

Veris' eyes snapped open.

A sharpened lance of bright, crackling energy flashed through one of the alleys between the columns. The Striker technique looked like lightning hammered straight, and it pierced the air not where Eithan *was*, but where he was *headed*. He had dashed to the side, but Veris had anticipated that.

Eithan leaped on top of a nearby column as though he had planned to all along, and the Striker technique passed beneath his feet. He cast stars of pure madra to the opposite end of the arena, calling down a blue-white waterfall.

So far, so boring, at least for a fight between Underlords. They were fighting like a pair of archers in an exhibition, like they were trying to show off for the fanciest shot. In Yerin's estimation, Eithan should have closed the distance between them immediately and gone straight for the kill, knowing that his opponent favored Striker techniques.

A moment later, everything changed.

A soaring lightning falcon swooped over Eithan's head, let out a screaming cry, and detonated into a field of storm madra...fifty feet away from Eithan. At the same time, Eithan darted backward, dodging nothing, and let out a burst of pure madra into thin air.

While running, he drew his new scissors—the prize he had chosen from the last round. They were actually an Archlord sacred dagger with the ability to change its physical shape, so he chose the shape of his old weapon: a set of large black fabric scissors.

And *these* carried an Archlord binding. No matter how much madra he had, it would be difficult for Eithan to activate such a weapon at his advancement stage without tearing his madra channels.

He was using them for their other advantage, which he had proudly explained to Lindon and Yerin already. This weapon responded to Enforcement far better than anything else Yerin had ever seen him use.

He flooded the scissors with pure madra, and they burst into a dark ball of gray light. When he stabbed that weapon into Veris' Forged falcon, the lightning technique crackled and burst.

Eithan wasted no time ducking into the pillars, still running.

The images of the two fighters hovered in the air over the columns themselves, and Yerin turned her attention to those when she could no longer see Eithan. They occasionally crossed techniques, with Eithan reflecting a ball of destructive energy or Veris' hair being ruffled by a near-miss from a burst of pure madra, but most of the time it was as though the two of them were fighting against invisible opponents.

The Ninecloud Soul's beautiful voice sounded excited, its rainbow light glimmering from the center of the projected fight. "Our more advanced guests will have already noticed the complex back-and-forth dance between these two combatants. Each is predicting the movements of the other, attempting to corner their opponent by cutting off retreat. Anyone worried that one Arelius might hold back against another can rest easy!"

Yerin couldn't see any of that, and it frustrated her. As far as she could tell, they *were* playing around and taking it easy on one another. Her master had been no Arelius, and she was sure *he* would have followed this fight.

She extended her spiritual perception, trying to sense the interplay between the two, but all she could feel was the flashy back-and-forth of their exchanges.

Breathing deeply, she sunk deep into her spiritual senses. Rather than trying to see the fight, she tried to feel its flow.

For over a minute, she felt nothing. She tried to predict what Eithan would do next, and she got it wrong almost every time. But as she pushed her frustration down and just *felt,* she began to sense something.

It was like the spike of alarm she felt when someone was attacking her from behind, but softer and muted. A feather brushing against the back of her neck rather than a nail through her skull.

*Jump,* she thought, and Eithan leaped away from a crackling claw of madra that erupted from the ground beneath him.

He would loop around the outside of the arena now, trying to push Veris into a bad angle.

And so he did, running from the top of one squared-off column to another, gathering stars of pure madra in the air as he ran.

The fight progressed with both sides trying to pressure the other, but Yerin spent her time trying to memorize the feeling of this elusive state. She wasn't sure if it had to do with the instinctive skill of the Sword Sage's Remnant or her evolving spiritual perception, but she suspected both.

Eithan moved as quickly as he ever had in their sparring matches and used the four techniques she'd seen him use. He slid past every technique Veris sent his way, some of which almost cornered him.

She felt the turn in the fight an instant before it happened.

Veris slipped out from cover to launch a Forged hawk of storm madra at Eithan, and she lingered a beat too long. Yerin felt it.

*That's the game,* she thought.

Eithan's blast of pure madra clipped her shoulder, slowing her next Striker technique for only a second. From there on out, Eithan had the advantage, and she was on the back foot. In seconds, Eithan had her backed into a corner, driving his scissors up under her ribs.

The image faded away, showing golden characters. Though she couldn't read them, she knew what they meant: Blackflame Victory.

Yerin snapped back to reality, and she let out a breath. She felt oddly tired, as though she had been focusing intently for too long and needed a break. She had felt like she was letting her attention drift, and for only a few short minutes at that. Even her spirit felt a little strained.

But she held on to the feeling, committing it to memory. Experimentally, she closed her eyes and tried to bring back that state of heightened awareness, but it was like trying to catch fog between her fingers.

When she opened her eyes, Eithan was standing outside the booth, watching her with a proud smile on his face.

"That's more like it!" he said. "How did it feel?"

"*You* were the one who just won a match. I just sat here."

"And yet your prize is greater than mine, as long as you can seize it." He reached into the pocket of his shimmering gold-and-lavender outer robes, but hesitated. "...one way or the other, we'll be making House Arelius look bad here, but I suppose there's no helping it."

From his pocket he pulled her blindfold.

Yerin looked at him sideways. "I go out there blindfolded, and you'll be carrying me back in a bag. Think I can take their sword artist, but that's if I've got eyes."

The Ninecloud Soul was talking over select scenes from the battle, reproducing them in midair, to the approval of the crowd.

Eithan dangled the blindfold from one finger. "All right. Then what do *you* think you need?"

She needed that sensation of perfect awareness, where she was drifting on the Sage's instincts and her own spiritual perception. She could feel that she was only touching the surface of that state, and she wanted to dive down deep.

But first, she had to figure out how to call it at will. Her master would say that the best way to do that was in the heat of battle.

Yerin snatched the blindfold. "Don't blame me if this gets us a loss."

"If you progress in this way, a loss in this tournament means nothing."

It meant something to *her,* and if their advancement to the next round were on the line, she would never try something like this. In reality, even if she failed, Eithan would have his chance to redeem them.

But when she imagined herself throwing a match by blindfolding herself and then Eithan losing the next fight, she almost gave up.

It was the thought of mastering this mysterious feeling that kept the blindfold in her hand. It was worth a little risk if she could take a step forward. The more pressure she put herself under, the faster she would grow.

She walked up, and Northstrider had returned to his spot atop the maze. He looked from her to her opposite, whom she couldn't see. She guessed they would send out Altavian this time, but she might be fighting Veris instead. Either way, she would have to pray to the heavens that she could sense the future as they sensed her.

"Are you satisfied with your fighters?" Northstrider asked.

Yerin nodded.

"Very well," the Monarch said.

An instant later, the image floating above the match changed. Seeing it from the bottom, it looked like a chaos of color, nothing like a real picture. She didn't know if that was a security measure designed to prevent contestants from looking to see what their opponents were up to or if this was just how illusions of light looked from below.

"Altavian Arelius," the rainbow announced, "versus Yerin Arelius! The bloodline member of the core House against an adopted disciple of a branch family! One born with every advantage, the other fighting for every scrap, but both have made it to the greatest heights!"

Yerin steadied herself. She calmed her breathing. And she wrapped the blindfold around her eyes.

Noise from the crowd surged in response.

"What's this?" the Ninecloud Soul cried excitedly. "Contestant Yerin has—"

"Begin," Northstrider said.

Yerin's spirit cried a warning, and then she was cut.

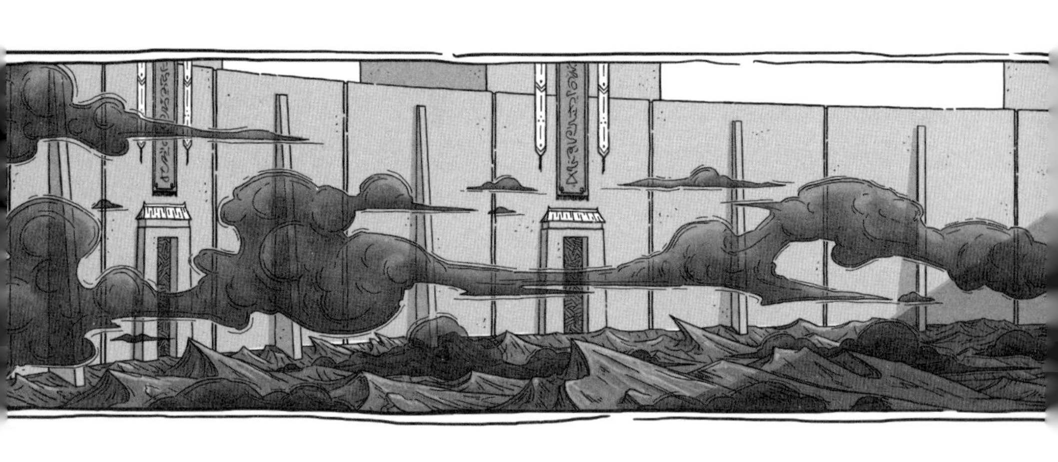

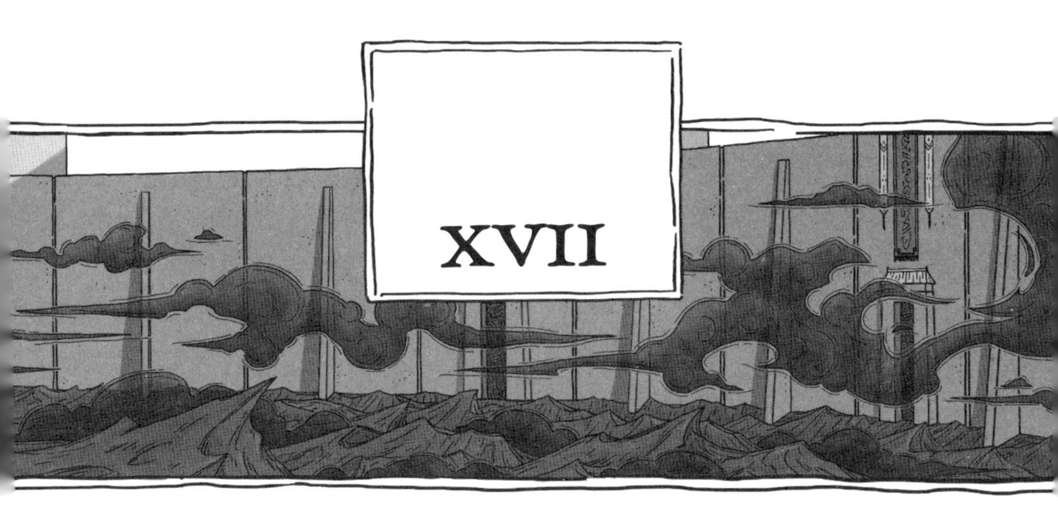


Charity watched as Yerin blindfolded herself and had to push down a surge of anger. Sacred artists, in her opinion, tended to make the same errors when they pushed for advancement. One was to value progress over *every* other objective.

Not only was Yerin risking victory for herself, but the prestige of her entire country. The honor of Charity's family. A failure on her part would have costs Yerin could never measure, and success would mean benefits that Yerin couldn't imagine.

And yet she was hobbling herself, no doubt to train her spiritual perception in some way. She had not known the Sword Sage well, but she *had* known him, and this was absolutely something he would do.

But that didn't make it wise.

The thought was strong in her head as Altavian leaped over the entire maze, touching down only once, and brought his sword down hard on Yerin. He blazed with a silver full-body Enforcement, and the blinded Yerin reacted a second too late to avoid him completely. Altavian's goldsteel blade flashed as it cut her, dragging a slash down the inside of Yerin's left shoulder and gashing her thigh as she backed up.

It was a superficial cut, but it was a harbinger of the rest of the battle. She made a cage out of her Goldsigns, but he cut them from bottom-to-top, breaking the sword-arms open. Thrusting his left palm into the opening, he speared her with five needle-points of sword madra, a Striker technique that dug into her body. If she hadn't been a sword artist, she would have lost right there.

She blocked his next few hits with clumsy movements, bleeding from her pair of wounds, and Charity's irritation grew. Yerin was too slow and imprecise. Almost as though she were relying on her vague spiritual perception as an Underlady instead of her *sight*.

Charity had written this round off as a loss when Yerin slid away from the blade by a hair's breadth, flicking her sword casually against Altavian.

She cut his arm. Blood sprayed.

Then her sword rang like a bell. Instead of an uncontrolled storm, the aura erupting from both their blades struck precisely, knocking Altavian's sword away mid-swing and slicing him across both thighs.

Yerin moved confidently now, fluidly, as though a different person controlled her body.

Charity's annoyance faded, and she leaned slightly closer to her viewing tablet.

It was still somewhat annoying when a sacred artist risked everything for progression...but it was forgivable when it worked.

Min Shuei's heart seized in her chest as she saw Yerin knocking aside a three-part attack from Altavian Arelius with only her sword-aura, following up at the *perfect* moment to push him back and land a cut on his chest.

He leaped away and she followed, a blind hunter.

Emotion choked the Winter Sage, and she gripped her own sword, a twin to the one Yerin was using. The Underlady wasn't moving like herself anymore; her every step, every flick of the wrist, was a mirror of the Sword Sage.

The girl had taken Adama's Remnant. He had given up his life for hers.

Though Min Shuei yearned to hear the full story, she still couldn't forgive the girl for that. He should have had decades yet to live, yet to teach, and instead he had thrown it away on someone who didn't even appreciate his Path.

But here...it was like watching the man she'd loved come back to life.

Yerin drifted through a dream.

The pain of her wounds didn't hinder her in her dream. Even the pain in her spirit, caused by strained madra channels, couldn't touch her.

She moved on pure instinct, without thought, letting her training and experience move her body. It was like letting her Remnant take over, moving her body like a puppet. The sensation might have been uncomfortable if she thought too much about it, but conscious thought would shake her awake.

The dream only faded when her opponent's madra did, as her sword passed through him and he melted into light. Then her peace retreated, and she could do nothing to hold onto it amid the rising tide of cheers from the crowd.

Her injuries slapped her all at once, and she stiffened involuntarily. She gritted her teeth against the agony from the cuts all over her body and the strain in her spirit. It was all she could do to tear off her blindfold.

Long scratches marred the rectangular columns, and she could feel sword aura drifting through the air.

As the Ninecloud Soul announced her victory, she stumbled back toward the booth where Eithan waited.

At a sudden thought, she turned around to look at the visions hanging in the air over the arena.

The model of her was blindfolded, but moved with perfect confidence. She blocked Altavian's sword with her sword-arms, destroyed his half-formed Striker technique with her sword, and took a hand off her hilt to land a punch on his chest. He flew away, and in the instant before Yerin's image followed, a small smile was visible on her face.

Yerin remembered that. She had felt both of his attacks and had known instantly what to do to counter them. It was like she had become water, pouring herself into a vessel, naturally flowing through any crack in his defenses.

From the outside, it looked different. She paused in her step, blood gumming up one eye and flowing from the injuries down her left side, to stare at the moving images. From the steps she took, to the way every blurring movement of her sword moved into the next as though she had planned it all out in advance, she looked just like her master.

She found it hard to breathe for a second, staring at herself. Seeing the reflection of the Sword Sage was a punch to the gut, and she wasn't sure how to unravel it.

Only a moment later, she shook her head and turned, continuing to walk away. She may have inherited the intuition of her master's Remnant, but that wasn't all she was seeing in that projection. There were her own ingrained instincts, which she had honed from years of diligent training and violent competition. And there was something else, that strange feeling that her spiritual perception had brushed across more than once now. Something deeper than the flow of madra.

It was bigger than her. Bigger than the Sword Sage.

And she was sure her master had felt it too. They looked the same because they were dancing to the beat of the same music.

Today, she had learned to hear it a little more clearly.

Her body and spirit jolted, and for a moment she felt her body and spirit *stretch*, and then the pain was gone. So suddenly that it startled her. The Monarch had restored her to pristine condition, as though she'd died and come back.

She covered the rest of the distance to the spectator booth in one leap, landing in front of Eithan.

He greeted her with laughter. "That must have been a wonderful feeling!"

"What is it?" Yerin asked. And, she wondered, how had Eithan been able to teach her about it?

Eithan's blue eyes flashed with joy as he said, "Your ticket to victory."

Sixteen young Underlords gathered in front of Northstrider, and he surveyed them all with features that may as well have been chiseled from stone.

"The nature of the fourth round changes based on how many of you survived round three," he told them, and constructs all over the arena echoed his voice. "The round begins in one week. It is the final elimination round, designed to reveal the eight of you who will be honored as Uncrowned."

The crowd roared, but Northstrider continued speaking without care. "As it happens, there are exactly sixteen of you. I have therefore decided on the best way for you to prove yourselves: single-elimination solo combat."

The crowd rustled, partially cheering, partially muttering.

"I have already chosen your opponents," he went on. "I selected the most appropriate enemy for each of you to demonstrate your skill and resolve."

His invisible will passed over the competitors, sharpening their gazes, drawing their focus completely to him.

"Attend me, for this is the shape of the final selection round. After this, the true Uncrowned Kings will be revealed."

"Ziel of the Wastelands, chosen of mine. You face Therian Nills of the Stormcallers, chosen of Reigan Shen."

Ziel wished he had his hammer next to him. It would have been a comforting weight.

Without it, his hands slowly curled into fists as he stared across at another kneeling youth: a man in his mid-twenties, or so he appeared.

He wasn't the only Stormcaller in the top sixteen. Besides the one he'd eliminated in the second round, the other two cultists had both survived. In fact, six of the sixteen remaining competitors belonged to Reigan Shen.

It was a powerful statement, showing the world how strong the Monarch of the King's Key had made his new allies. The Dreadgod cultists would surely shake the foundations of the earth.

But not this one. This one wouldn't make it any further.

Ziel only regretted that he couldn't kill his opponent for real.

"Sha Miara of the Ninecloud Court, chosen of the Luminous Queen. You face Blacksword of Redmoon Hall, chosen of Reigan Shen."

Sha Miara pointedly refused to look at the young man with the dark sword across his back. Just to rile him up, she pressed her fingers to her lips as though stifling a yawn.

It was all a show. She couldn't *wait* to crush him. It wasn't dignified for a Monarch to compete with her lessers, but she never got to have any fun.

She was glad she wasn't facing the Redmoon girl. Miara would still win, but she wasn't ready for a challenge yet. She wanted to savor one more easy victory.

The challenging fights would come soon enough. Once she was Uncrowned.

"Eithan Arelius of the Blackflame Empire, chosen of Akura Malice. You face Yan Shoumei of Redmoon Hall, chosen of Reigan Shen."

Shoumei stopped glaring at the Blackflame boy she'd met in Ghostwater and turned her attention to the yellow-haired clown who never stopped grinning.

She knew of him. The Blood Sage had spoken of him, after the report of Longhook's death had been confirmed by the sect oracles.

Her Blood Shadow stirred as she stared at Eithan Arelius. It hungered for him. Maybe, if it feasted on enough of his blood, it would inherit the famous Arelius bloodline ability.

Whether it did or did not, Shoumei eagerly looked forward to her match. She would get to prove herself in front of the whole world by destroying the person who killed Longhook.

Eithan gave her a beaming smile.

"Akura Mercy of the Akura clan, chosen of Akura Malice..."

Mercy sat up straighter, eager and just a *tad* worried. She hoped to be matched against one of Reigan's Dreadgod servants, or even Sopharanatoth. The gold dragon would be a difficult fight, but no one left in the competition was weak.

There was a chance that she could eliminate Sophara from competition, which would make the top eight much easier. And it would send a strong message on behalf of her family.

She was worried because there were also two friends remaining in the running as potential opponents. Northstrider hadn't matched anyone against a teammate so far, but he had been clear that he was deciding based on individual suitability. There was no guarantee she wouldn't fight Lindon.

"...you face Yerin Arelius of the Blackflame Empire, chosen of Akura Malice."

Yerin glared at the Monarch.

She would have to fight a friend after all. There was no reason for it that she could tell; there were plenty of fighters left that he didn't have to match up two chosen by the same Monarch faction. Northstrider was doing this just to mess with her head.

Mercy wore her sadness plain upon her face, looking at Yerin with such a devastated expression that it actually lightened Yerin's mood a little.

Yerin was still upset that she had to fight a friend, but if they were going to compete, she intended to do her best. And she wanted no less from her opponent.

She tried to convey all that with nothing more than her eyes, but she must have failed. Mercy teared up.

When the Monarch's gaze turned to Lindon, Dross became excited. If he'd been sitting on Lindon's shoulder, he would've been bouncing up and down.

[He looked at us! Do you think he knows I'm here? Do you think he sees me? He's proud of what we've done, I know it!]

All of Lindon's mind and soul were bent toward Northstrider's next words. None of his friends remained in the matchups, so that took a weight off his shoulders, though he ached for Yerin having to fight Mercy. Now there were seven potential opponents left for him.

And the one he wanted to face the most was also the one he most feared.

"Wei Shi Lindon Arelius of the Akura clan, chosen of Akura

Malice. You face Sopharanatoth of the line of gold dragons, chosen of Seshethkunaaz."

Lindon's heart thrilled with excitement and fear at the same time.

[Well, top sixteen is good,] Dross said. [Nothing to be ashamed of. Stiff competition this year, too, so really you should be proud of making it this far.]

Lindon would have had to crane his neck to look at Sophara, but he imagined he could feel the heat from her spirit in the air.

*We'll get the tablet of her third round right after this,* Lindon sent to Dross. *Then we're spending the whole week training against her model.*

[That seems like a lot of work from me for a guaranteed loss for you.]

Once again, Lindon saw blood dripping from Sophara's claws.

*Even if we lose...we're going to make her work for it.*

**[Target Found: the Angler of the Crystal Halls. Location: Vroshir stronghold Tal'gullour, three months after the theft of the prototype scythes. Synchronize?]**

**[Synchronization set at 99%]**

**[Beginning synchronization...]**

The central world of Tal'gullour was a planet-sized fortress floating in space. When Iri left the Way and entered the reality, the behemoth spacecraft loomed over her.

Hewn from entire moons' worth of stone and metal, the fortress looked like a rocky cliff roughly shaped into a pyramid. It contained a full world of life and power within it—at least twenty billion men and women, with many times their number in plants and animals—but she could feel none of it. She felt only the Mad King.

His aura was a blazing, implacable wave of chaos, like a tide of magma. To most, it would be intimidating, but she had traveled in style.

She had left her ten-by-ten box back in **[ERROR: LOCATION NOT FOUND. RESUMING SYNCHRONIZATION]**...She had left her ten-by-ten box hidden, and had come here in her own stronghold. Iri brought the Crystal Halls with her.

The Abidan considered the Vroshir an enemy organization, but "organization" was too tidy a word for what they were. Vroshir like Iri and the Mad King had no common goals and no love for each other. Iri was fairly sure that the King would devour her whole if he got a chance.

The Vroshir were united only in their methods: they liberated worlds.

When they found a new Iteration, they would scoop up anything they wanted and most of the population and move on. The people would be relocated to one of the massive Vroshir Homeworlds, where their very presence would tether the world even tighter to the Way.

Their old, depopulated home would be consumed by chaos, but who cared? The people were gone.

Iri thought of herself as less of a liberator and more of a collector. The Crystal Halls were both her home and her greatest treasure. The stronghold did not lose out to Tal'gullour in size, easily as large as a planet, and definitely outshone the Mad King's fortress in splendor.

Iri's home was a palace of fluted blue crystal spread like a pair of angel's wings. It had been carved from an astronomically large diamond, and it glittered like a rainbow in the light of the nearby star.

She kept a population of about a billion living in the planet-sized inner workings of the stronghold, both to keep the vessel shielded from chaos and to take care of her collection. For in carefully sculpted displays all throughout the stronghold, she held the universe's most rare, beautiful, unique, and powerful objects.

Which was why the Mad King had agreed to meet her.

She arranged herself on a throne at the end of an audience hall carved from blue crystal. Every inch of the walls, ceiling, and floor was a masterwork sculpture, and she lounged in a throne made of living light, but she had made no effort to dress herself up. *She* wasn't a treasure. Why bother?

She still wore old, frayed pants and an ill-fitting shirt with her own name sewn onto the front. No shoes. Her hair was a long, electric blue mess that she hurriedly tied back before the King arrived.

But her accessories were worth more than most Abidan would see in a lifetime.

Above the crown of her head hovered the Halo of the Deep Earth, a featureless circle of what seemed to be lead. It carried within it the hopes and dreams of a long-dead people, their resolve and their sanity, and it anchored her existence. No Fiend of Chaos could touch her under its protection.

It had a thousand other uses too, but that was the one that concerned her at the moment.

From her back extended a pair of smooth, white-plated titanium arms, which fussed around as she tied her own hair back. They didn't like her doing anything for herself.

These Presence-guided selector arms were one of the earliest parts of her collection; they wouldn't catch her eye now, but she'd made them herself from pieces that had once been difficult for her to acquire. They had a soft spot in her heart. When she lowered her own hands, the selector arms rushed in, smoothing her hair back and adjusting her tie.

Sighing, she left them to it. They fretted like an old nanny.

Her final accessory was Meloch'nillium, a bracelet that appeared to be made of raw starfire but was actually far more valuable. Its sheer radiance would blind any mortal who laid eyes on it.

While she waited, she pinched the bracelet and fiddled with it, trying to get it to sit comfortably on her wrist. It was one of the greatest weapons in her arsenal, capable of striking a blow even against Gadrael, the Titan. She just hated wearing it. It was itchy.

She had authority over all objects crafted by human hands, but she couldn't control comfort.

Chimes sounded throughout the Crystal Halls, a unique symphony that had never been heard before and would never be heard again. That was her intruder alarm.

The Mad King, requesting a meeting.

With a simple effort of will, she disabled her protections, and then the King stood before her.

**[WARNING: SYNCHRONIZATION REDUCED TO 87%]**

He wore a full-faced helm of ancient bone with two horns rising over his head. Bone plates covered his body from shoulders to ankles, armor that he'd carved from the body of a Class One Fiend. At least its physical manifestation.

A mantle of black-furred hide fell from his shoulders and brushed the floor behind him, this from a planet-devouring creature that he had slain.

Within his helm, his eyes burned like red suns.

Her sense of him was of overwhelming significance, an existence of such gravity that it warped reality around him. The crystal floor pushed away as though it melted beneath his feet.

Without her protection, every mortal living in the Crystal Halls would have had their minds shattered by his approach. In Tal'gullour, the King had locked himself in self-sealed chambers. If one day his control slipped, he would kill everyone in the Iteration.

It had never happened. But if he lost control of the Fiend imprisoned in his body, it would.

After millennia of life, Iri knew many unpleasant truths. One in particular haunted her: she knew that the Mad King thought he had his Fiend under control.

There weren't many things that frightened Iri anymore.

The King lifted a jeweled wooden box that he'd brought, head inclined as though to speak...

**[SYNCHRONIZATION INTERRUPTED.]**

The memory blurred, and Makiel felt his awareness returning to his own body. The voice of the Mad King had been enough to disrupt the flow of Fate through which he viewed the past.

The King was one of the most troublesome Vroshir, a man who continued to exist only because the expense of eliminating him was too much for Makiel to justify.

He was a true threat on the level of the Court of Seven, one of the few beings in existence that could match Razael, Ozriel, or Makiel himself in combat.

Makiel's heart hung heavy. He knew what he would see if he continued to watch. But he watched still, with only his eyes, viewing the events through the celestial lens.

The Angler and the Mad King, two of the greatest enemies of the Abidan, exchanged conversation for only two-and-a-half minutes. The Angler acted like a bored child, squirming on her luminous living throne, while the King stood like a regal corpse.

Finally, he offered payment.

When the Mad King cracked open the box, even Makiel leaned forward. Inside was a ball of life and potential, a picture of hope and power, a condensed pearl of raw existence and authority. With the physical eye, it was hard to perceive it as anything other than a ball of light, but Makiel recognized it as one of the most valuable objects to ever exist.

A Worldseed.

Even the Angler scrambled forward to clutch at the box, desperate to put her hands on this jewel of impossible value. With disgust, Makiel realized she probably wouldn't even *use* it, just display it to visitors as another part of her gaudy collection.

The entire Abidan Court only had three Worldseeds to their name, and it was their fate to be used for true emergencies. There was very little a Worldseed could not do.

The Mad King pulled back slightly, and one of the robotic arms on Iri's back reached into empty space and pulled out a black scythe.

Makiel sucked in a breath. He had personally forged the twelve prototype scythes that the Angler had stolen, so he would recognize any of them. This was an artful blend of them all, as though she had taken the best aspect of each of them and fused them together. It was masterful work, he had to admit.

It might not match Ozriel's original scythe...but it would come closer than Makiel had ever thought possible.

Makiel felt his hope die, and he released the celestial lens. He had hoped that the Angler had been the one to eliminate Iteration 943 as a sort of test run. She was entirely self-interested, predictable, and therefore safe. If the Mad King had done it, this was only the beginning.

The King *hated* the Abidan. He would do anything he could to tear them down. With a Scythe in his hands...

Makiel realized his lens hadn't closed. He looked back up into the purple-tinged screen.

He met eyes like two red suns.

The Mad King looked up at him as though he could see across time and space. This was nothing but a memory, a recording, an imprint left on the Way. There was no way to detect such contact before it occurred.

Even so, the Vroshir locked eyes with the Abidan.

Then he slowly reached out and gripped the Scythe.

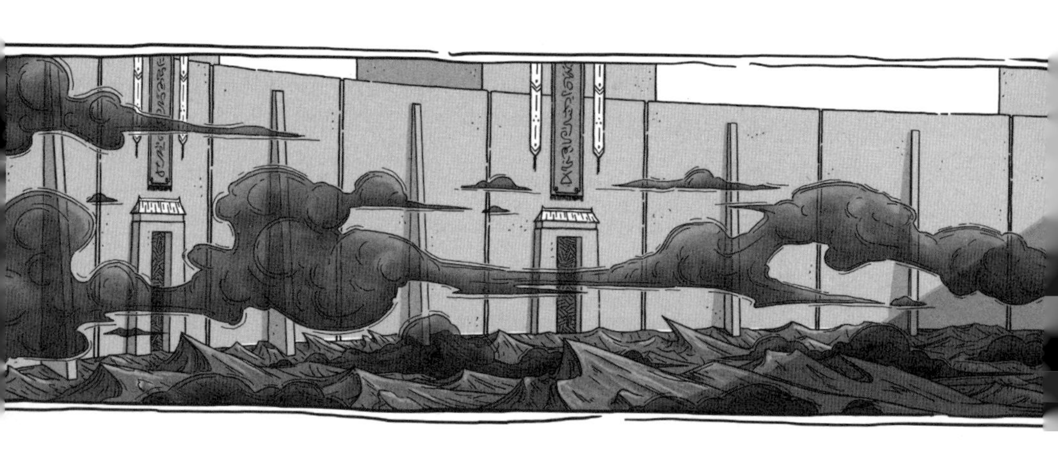

# XVIII

“Sixteen competitors remain,” the Ninecloud Soul announced to a roaring crowd. “Since we have such a wonderful even number, our patron Monarch Northstrider has decided to select this year’s Uncrowned with a round of single-elimination duels.”

The crowd gave a verbal reaction, and the Ninecloud Soul provided a few more details. Once it had finished setting up the fourth round, it returned to the topic that most interested the competitors: the prizes.

“At last, the rewards will begin. Between now and the day of the fourth round, each Monarch will bestow a gift on two participants other than their own. These are truly treasures that would inspire envy in any ordinary sect, and is a chance for the honored Monarchs to demonstrate their legendary generosity.

"As each prize is awarded, we will make an announcement, to express to the world the fortune of our surviving Underlords!"

Eithan popped out from behind a corner to surprise Veris Arelius.

She, of course, was not surprised. She had turned to face him before he emerged, eyebrows raised. "Cousin Eithan, I was just about to sit down to dinner. Would you like to join me?"

Jumping out of nowhere wasn't nearly as satisfying when the other party could feel you coming. "Cousin Veris, a pleasure to see you again. I'm afraid I don't have too much time, I just thought I'd make a request of your House. Could you perhaps consider *not* giving me a prize?"

Her brow furrowed. "You're the best candidate. We don't have so many resources that we can afford to spend them outside the family, and you're our opportunity to stay within the rules."

"Ah," he said, "but not your *only* opportunity. It just so happens that there are two others with the surname Arelius in the top sixteen."

"Not blood members of the family."

"It's not blood relation we need, is it?" he challenged. "It's goodwill...and it's money. This allows me to make sure my students get an excellent gift apiece from someone who appreciates them, while I can take a prize from outsiders."

Veris still looked doubtful, but eventually she cocked her head. "It seems like we were too late. Someone must have very much wanted to reward you."

"Yes," he said, and they both looked in the direction of his room two floors up. "I had noticed that myself."

Within the center of his room, madra from the Path of Celestial Radiance shimmered in a pillar, holding the prize he'd already received.

Veris nodded to him. "We'll speak again before the tournament ends, but until then, don't let me keep you. Go open your gift."

Grateful, Eithan obeyed.

He wasn't altogether excited about his prize. Besides House Arelius and the Akura clan, only one other faction would reward him so quickly. It would be nothing good.

When he opened his room and saw the rainbow column drifting in the center, he sent a flow of madra into it. Instantly, the nine-colored light unfolded, presenting his prize: a majestic golden cloudship the size of his palm, drifting on a cloud of the same size.

Reigan Shen's voice echoed throughout the room.

"Eithan Arelius," the Monarch's recording said. "This is a model of a full-sized cloudship, *The Bounding Gazelle*, among the fastest my Soulsmiths have ever produced. You can use the help, can't you? I know how much you love running away."

The Monarch's self-satisfied voice faded away, leaving the model of the golden cloudship drifting in midair.

Eithan let nothing affect his mind, his expression, or even his spirit. Reigan Shen's spiritual perception could be on him, so he did not allow himself to feel any cold anger, any desire for revenge, and certainly not any flicker of contemptuous amusement. If any emotion showed in his spirit, Shen might annihilate him.

With a smile locked on his face, Eithan thanked the empty air.

A woman's voice lectured Mercy from within the column of rainbow light. "An Archlord's archery is very different from an Iron's. You should be studying deeper principles, or you'll just be propelling sticks with string forever."

A mundane-looking scripted stone, a dream tablet, floated in the air. Mercy might not have been excited except that she recognized the voice in the recording: it was Larian, renowned archer of the Eight-Man Empire.

She had the best archery tutors in Akura territory, but other than Akura Malice herself, none of them could measure up to Larian.

"I'm going to study it right now!" Mercy promised, settling down into a nearby chair and diving into the tablet.

Ziel rolled a smooth, round pill between his fingers. It was an inch across, far too big to swallow, and glossy as though sealed in wax. It was colored cream and pink, and it smelled of a thousand types of flowers.

Emriss Silentborn's voice was rich, motherly, and relaxed. "My Herald Chryleia refined this herself, from fruits and flowers gathered throughout the world as well as a drop of my own sap. It will not restore to you the power you've lost, but with time, it will begin to loosen your knotted madra channels. This will be painful. It will take time, and your soul will need great nourishment. However, with the blessings of heaven, you *may* function as a normal Underlord one day."

Ziel's hands trembled as he held the medicine. Just like that, Northstrider was proven right.

Unraveling his madra channels would not undo the damage done to them or to his body. It wouldn't make him an Archlord again, or put him back on the path that might have made him a Herald one day.

But it would allow him to use his madra without pain and to exert the skill he had earned. When the pill finished its work, he would be a sacred artist again.

He placed the pill in his mouth and sat down to cycle, holding it on his tongue and drawing lines of power away from it and into his core. He had to fight back his hope. Something would stop him. The pill wouldn't work, or the Monarch would take it back, or he would restore his channels only to find that the damage was even more extensive than he'd realized.

Something would go wrong. It always did.

Sure enough, the Monarch's voice continued after a long pause. "...do not push yourself too hard," she said, "but I see only one way for you to become the man you once were. It will take the direct intervention of myself and several other Monarchs. Do you understand?"

He did. There was only one way he would get such attention: if he won the Uncrowned King tournament.

⬡

"It's an elixir," Altavian's voice explained to Yerin. "I know it doesn't look like one."

Yerin looked down at the fist-sized diamond in her hands. She'd grabbed it immediately, thinking it was a construct.

"Put it in a bucket or a bowl and run your madra through it. It will dissolve into a liquid, and then you drink it one spoonful at a time."

Yerin held up the crystallized liquid to the light, wondering if it was worth the trouble, then dug around her rooms for a large bowl. She didn't see why anyone wanted to live with so much space; it became a nightmare finding anything.

"It's called a Diamond Veins elixir," the voice went on. "You have to cycle it a little at a time over the next three days, but it's said to make your madra channels as pure and resilient as a diamond."

She raised her eyebrows as she dug through some cabinets. If the elixir did what it sounded like it would do, she couldn't see why Altavian hadn't taken it himself.

He hadn't finished talking, it turned out. "In our fight, you avoided straining your channels." She had, but only to the degree that any sacred artist did. More durable madra channels would allow her to put more power into her techniques and use them more often.

"Now you won't have to," he said, his voice now tinged with amusement. "You're the one who beat me. You'd better win."

Lindon's prize looked like a heart cast in dark gray metal. It was so detailed that he half-expected it to start pumping blood.

[Do you think it's a threat?] Dross asked.

"Upon examination of your last several rounds," Veris Arelius' disembodied voice said, "we've determined that you rely on your Iron body for healing, but that isn't its primary purpose. It's far better suited to fighting off venom and disease."

[They *have* been watching you, haven't they?]

"House Arelius," Lindon said. "I'm sure they've been watching everyone."

"This Divine Treasure was crafted by our Soulsmiths from the cores and blood essences of a hundred Lord-level Remnants. Take it into your spirit, and it will supplement your Iron body. Every bit of madra you funnel into your Bloodforged Iron body will be a hundred times more efficient, and it should enhance the regenerative effect of your body tenfold. Incidentally, it will strengthen your lifeline as well, though that is more of a byproduct."

With every word, Lindon's expectations grew until they were sky-high.

"This is a reward for your hard work so far," Veris continued, "but we also consider this an investment. House Arelius needs allies now more than ever, and we hope we can count on your loyalty."

Lindon ran his spiritual sense through the Heart, letting Dross get a good feel.

"It looks like our debt to the Arelius family is getting deeper and deeper," Lindon said aloud.

[Absolutely right,] Dross agreed, [except it is *your* debt. I know that's what you meant; I just want to be clear.]

Sophara bowed as she finished listening to Reigan Shen's voice, holding a bottled elixir of her own.

The Monarch of House Shen had made a deal with her divine ancestor. She did not know the details, did not need to question the arrangements of Monarchs, but she knew that she had his support.

Which explained the royal prize he had bestowed upon her.

Advancement elixirs for Truegolds and lower were common sights in powerful families. There were no elixirs that would give enough insight to raise a Truegold to Underlord. There *were,* however, elixirs to help Lords advance. They were obscenely rare, even for Monarchs.

Sophara cradled in both hands a transparent glass vial with a thread of shining, pure silver liquid twisting in the center. It circled in on itself, winding in an endless loop.

The Gate of Heaven elixir was extremely volatile and difficult to refine, even for the world's greatest refiners. The ingredients and conditions for its creation were closely guarded secrets, and Sophara had heard that it even required attention from Sages.

Now she was seeing it with her own eyes: an elixir that smoothed the road from Underlord to Archlord.

She had already been on the verge of becoming an Overlady. Now she could advance whenever she wanted.

Lindon's Void Dragon's Dance fell on Sophara, tearing at her with winds of fire and destruction.

She pushed through the red-and-black cyclone as though through a stiff breeze. He dropped the Ruler technique as quickly as he could—he had practiced for this, trained himself to switch techniques instantly.

He was still a moment too slow. While the dragon's breath formed on his fingers, Sophara had closed the gaps with quick, fluid movements, her feet glowing orange. Golden madra gushed from her hands, flowing into his chest from only a moment away.

He held up his shield and tried to trigger the binding, but her power was too strong. The shield melted, its technique failing. Lindon's flying sword, Wavedancer, was too far away to recall in time.

The fire madra seared him, and her claws were already at his throat.

The vision shimmered and vanished.

Lindon opened his eyes. He sat in a cycling position next to an artificial waterfall in his personal training room, and though he hadn't moved a step, sweat streamed down his face. His breath came in ugly rasps.

The more intense his training with Dross, the more it took from him.

[A new record!] Dross cried. [You lasted twenty-one seconds that time! This is progress!]

Only eighteen tries, and he had exhausted every tactic he knew. He had at least managed to go from dying immediately to holding his own for a few breaths of time, but that wasn't as much progress as Dross pretended.

Birds chirped and flew from a tree planted in one corner of the room toward a bed of flowers all the way at the other. Most of the room was empty space, but evidently the Ninecloud Court believed in decorating everything.

He spoke aloud as he toweled sweat from his head and neck. "Gratitude, but even if I manage to win, I will have only beaten your version of Sophara. The real one will be stronger."

[Yes, she almost certainly has more in reserve than she's shown, just as you do. Yes, she is the strongest competitor in this tournament. Yes, she will have gotten her own prize after the third round that will surely make her even stronger. Yes, she will be preparing for this match against you while you are preparing against her.]

Lindon waited for more, but Dross was quiet.

"But..." Lindon began.

[But what? That was all true.]

Lindon passed his spiritual perception through his body, feeling the glittering motes of ruby sand that now permeated his flesh. The Iron Heart had integrated seamlessly with his Iron body, but he still wasn't sure what that meant.

"I haven't noticed much increased healing in the simulations," Lindon said.

[I've never seen an Iron Heart in action, have I? How am I supposed to know what it can do for you?]

"We should test it."

The door opened just as he spoke, and Yerin strolled into the room. Her long hair streaming behind her like a black banner and the sword at her waist made her look like a warrior from a painting. Her silver sword-arms had been withdrawn, but she still looked ready for battle at any second.

"What are we testing?" she asked, walking up to Lindon. He hurriedly stood to meet her.

"My Iron Heart. It's finished bonding with my Iron body, but Dross can't show me what it can do, because we haven't tested it yet."

[You have perfect timing!] Dross said to Yerin. [You can cut him for me! I only wish I could do it myself.]

"Sure," Yerin said casually, gripping her sword. "A big cut or a bunch of little ones?"

Lindon had to slow this down before it went too far. "Hold on! I'm not the only one with a match coming up. Are you going to be all right against Mercy?"

Yerin frowned, glaring a hole in the wall.

"That...Monarch." She was obviously afraid that saying his name would draw his attention, which Lindon thought was wisely cautious. "He did this to us on purpose. Makes me not want to dance to his song."

Lindon fervently agreed, but he stayed silent to encourage her to keep talking.

"But this is a fresh chance," she continued. "How often do you get to sharpen yourself against a friend without hurting them? My master used to say that you never really knew someone until you crossed swords with them, and I'm starting to take his meaning."

"Apologies; I don't understand. I've never fought *you* outside of training, but that doesn't mean we don't know each other."

Yerin looked up to the ceiling, visibly searching for the right words. "I'd say...I know the you *I* see, but how did that prince Kiro see you? How did Harmony see you in Ghostwater?"

[Last,] Dross said. [Harmony saw him *last*.]

"We have to blunt our swords when we're training. Nothing wrong with that—I'm not trying to take off your ear, and I don't want dragon's breath in my eyes. But it means that we never get to use that last little bit, you know?"

She shrugged. "There's something honest about going all-out. Now that we don't have to worry about killing each other, I get to see everything Mercy's got. And I get to show her everything I can do."

Yerin stood with perfect confidence, her master's sword at her waist, wearing a sacred artist's robe that was the duplicate of the one Lindon had first seen her in. But he saw now how different she had become. These robes were new, not tattered at the edges—her control had grown.

Her skin was smooth, the scars gone. The rope-belt of Forged blood madra she had once worn was missing, integrated into her spirit. Her hair hung past her shoulders, and her face had been sculpted anew during her advancement to Underlord. She looked more mature, a worthy competitor in the Uncrowned King tournament.

She was beautiful.

Her dark eyes turned back to him, and he jerked his gaze away, afraid to be caught staring.

"What about you?" she asked. "What if you had to fight one of us?"

Lindon still shivered when he imagined Naian's razor steel pushing through his guts. It had only been a few days. He saw the hole he'd burned through his opponents on the island. And not just on the island, either. Ekeri the gold dragon had been speared through by his dragon's breath and had eventually died.

Could he picture doing the same to Yerin, even if she would be resurrected by a Monarch immediately? Could he slice her in half with a bar of burning madra? Could he bash her skull in with his shield?

"I'm glad I don't have to," Lindon finally said.

"This isn't the last round. If we all make it, you'll have to fight at least one of us in the top eight."

He shifted uncomfortably. "I *will* do it. But I don't have to be happy about it."

"What's not to be happy about? We could all make it into the *top eight* of the Uncrowned King tournament!" She hesitated. "Uh...three of the four of us."

That left a silence in the room. No matter whether Yerin or Mercy won, one of their journeys would end with the next round.

He didn't want to think about it, so instead he walked up and squared his shoulders against the wall. "Let's test the Iron Heart. Yerin, if you could just give me a little cut on the arm so I can see the difference. It used to take me...what, a minute or two to close up a small cut?"

[Three to four minutes,] Dross responded. [But the circumstances varied. If you intentionally cycled madra to your Iron body, it would be faster, and if you had more injuries it would be slower.]

"Okay, then. Three minutes is the time to beat. Yerin?"

Yerin drew her sword, leaning forward, her madra spinning. "Get ready!"

He held out his left arm and waited.

Yerin's fingers opened and closed on the hilt of her sword. The aura around the weapon stirred...and died again. She clenched her jaw.

"...apologies, is something wrong?"

"No!" She snapped, and her cheeks had begun to color. "I'm just... it feels strange just *cutting* you while you're standing there. Maybe if we were sparring..."

Lindon stared blankly at her. Dross manifested over his shoulder to add his one-eyed stare to Lindon's.

"We train against each other all the time," Lindon said. "You've cut me *many* times."

Although not often, now that Lindon thought about it. It was usually when she used the Endless Sword and it spilled out of her control.

"I know that! But that's a fight, that's different."

"I wouldn't have thought so."

He wanted to be flattered by her concern, but he was only baffled. He had never expected this out of Yerin. What had brought this on?

"Shut up and just...I'll do it, okay? Hold still." She took a deep breath, and then her sword rang like a bell. A small one.

His arm stung, and a razor-thin cut traced a red line about an inch long across his forearm. Blood began to bead at the end, and Lindon could feel his Iron body drawing pure madra from him immediately. He and Dross watched it intently.

After only a second or two, the end of the wound began to close up.

A single drop of blood ran down the side of his arm, and by the time it reached the other side, the injury had already closed.

[Four seconds!] Dross exclaimed. [That's a new record!]

"It took more madra than usual," Lindon noted, but he was as excited as Dross was.

Yerin's ears were still tinged red, but she played it cool, adjusting her grip on the sword. "Another?"

"A few more this time, please," Lindon held out his arm again.

"You don't want to wait for that one to heal first?" It was mostly restored, but the line of skin was still a tender scarlet, like a fresh scrape.

"Oh, that's not worth worrying about. Three would be perfect."

Yerin didn't look happy, but she did as requested. The three cuts healed just as quickly as the first had.

[I'd like to see a deeper cut, but why don't we try out a different kind of injury first?]

"That's what I was thinking," Lindon agreed. He had already cast his mind forward to the fight with Sophara. If he could heal *this* quickly, he might actually be able to take a hit or two from her Flowing Flame madra, which would be invaluable. This could be his chance, and he was eager to discover his limits.

He squared his stance, looking to Yerin. "Punch me as hard as you can, if you don't mind."

Yerin slammed the sword into her sheath. "I need a break," she said shortly.

"Oh, of course. Apologies." She had only used the Endless Sword a few times, but she had her own match to prepare for. He couldn't selfishly monopolize her time.

"What about your Diamond Veins?" Lindon asked. He had been jealous of her elixir—it felt like he was always being held back by his madra channels.

Still facing away from him, she rolled her neck, loosening up. "I can take bigger swings with my techniques than ever before. It's not too soon, either. Now I can work on hitting harder."

"Do you need to? Your Path whittles them down, and then you finish them by hand." No Path could do everything. The Path of Black Flame needed to be able to punch through strong defenses, but the Path of the Endless Sword didn't. At least as far as he could see.

Yerin fished around in her pocket and tossed a dream tablet over her shoulder. Lindon caught it out of the air and activated it immediately.

*The Sword Sage is a wiry man with messy hair, half-lidded eyes that make it look like he's falling asleep, and tattered black robes. Six sword-arms hang limp from his back, and he draws his white sword back. He's about to step forward in a lunge.*

*He faces an animated mountain of steel and stone, a human-shaped armored puppet-construct taller than ten men. The earth aura and force madra radiating from the construct project the idea of invincibility.*

*The tip of the Sage's white blade shines like a silver star as he pulls it back. Lindon has an instant to sense incredibly concentrated aura, madra, and soulfire gathering to a point.*

*In one smooth move, he stabs forward and unleashes his technique.*

*A silver-white Forged sword pierces perfectly through the construct. It is there and gone like a strike of lightning, but it erases a column through the center of the massive puppet.*

*The Sage turns, sheathes his sword, and yawns as piles of metal and stone crash to the ground behind him.*

Lindon pulled himself out of the dream, breathing deeply. Yerin noticed.

"You see me doing that?" she asked.

"I can't imagine how *anyone* does that." It was beautiful, the synchronized blend of spiritual movements. No waste at all. And the Forged sword was so perfect that it was more beautiful than his Archlord Wavedancer; it was as though he had created the ideal sword from madra and aura.

Yerin extended all six sword-arms, flexing them in the air. "Well, that's the target I have to hit."

Lindon hefted the tablet. "He was higher than an Underlord when he did this. You have time."

"Tell me the last time you listened to someone who told you to take your time."

That struck home. It was disturbing to look at himself from the outside. From his perspective, Yerin *did* have time, and rushing things could hurt her. He wanted her to take it one step at a time.

But he could relate to the urgency she felt, and it would be hypocritical to suggest someone else slow down.

Instead, he manifested Dross.

The one-eyed purple spirit appeared above his palm, blinking in the light. [Hey! I was watching your embarrassing memories!]

"Can you simulate something for Yerin?" Lindon would have to ask about the embarrassing memories later.

Dross stretched his mouth into an expression of extreme discomfort. [Eeeehhh...thanks to Charity's madra, I probably *could,* but you can't imagine the headache. And it won't last very long. Also, I don't want to.]

"Gratitude," Lindon said. "Can you model the Sword Sage's technique we just watched?"

Yerin straightened up, eyes wide, and scurried closer. She looked to Dross with expectation.

[I speak straight into your mind and still you won't listen to me.]

"Please, Dross," Yerin said earnestly. "This could give me new wings."

Dross hissed through his teeth, glaring at her and then at Lindon. A moment later, their surroundings vanished.

It was as though Lindon, Yerin, and Dross stood on darkness and were surrounded by endless black. The Sword Sage appeared a moment later, lifelike, holding his sword back.

Yerin reached out. "Seeing him with my own eyes again..." Before she touched him, she lowered her hand. Her lips twisted. "That's a knife to the gut."

Power gathered on the tip of the Sage's blade, then he stepped forward to drive the light forward.

"Hold," Lindon commanded, and Dross froze the scene. He groaned as he did so, as though to emphasize how much effort it had taken.

Yerin and Lindon examined his stance, his spirit, and the light beginning to stretch from the end of his weapon. It was a bare ghost of a sword, not the full, vivid technique they had witnessed in the dream tablet.

"Soulfire, madra, aura," Lindon said. "All woven together so I can't tell where one begins and the other ends."

Yerin leaned closer until her chin almost touched the technique. "Something's tickling the back of my mind. I had a better sense from the dream tablet, but I think there's something else about this technique. It's itching at me, but I can't track it down."

Something else beyond the madra, aura, and soulfire...

"Do you think it could be a Sage's power?" Lindon asked quietly.

"That's a hair off the target. I wouldn't contend it's another power...but I'm not stone certain it isn't."

[Uggggh aaaaaannnnd that's all you get.]

Abruptly, the vision snapped off. Lindon and Yerin stumbled back into reality, standing in the middle of the training room.

Dross panted heavily, heaving exaggerated breaths, and even swept one of his stubby pseudo-arms across his forehead as though to wipe away sweat.

[I told you it wouldn't last long. And if there's something you couldn't sense in my simulation, it's because *this* one—] He stabbed an arm at Lindon. [—didn't pick up on it. Or the dream tablet didn't. Or I didn't. But I'd put my bets on this one.]

Dross slipped back into Lindon's spirit, but Lindon was already thinking along lines that he had tested in his own Paths.

"You'll need to layer techniques," he said. "It's like using a Ruler technique, Striker technique, and Forger technique at the same time. It might take soulfire to hold it all together."

Yerin's sword was out of its sheath, and she swung it to limber up. "You've tried this before, have you?"

Lindon coughed into his Remnant arm. "It was harder than I thought."

"I'd rather swallow my sword than try this without the Diamond Veins," Yerin said, settling into a stance like the one her master had taken. "Likely to shred my channels to pieces. Even if we do get it right, the rocky part will be using this in battle. Haven't practiced enough to form a binding, so I'll have to practice until it's carved into my spirit."

"We'll be with you," Lindon said.

Dross groaned.

Yerin flashed him a smile as aura began gathering around her sword. The weapon started to hum. "Say we do get this right. We ought to think of a name for it."

Lindon started making a list.

When he wasn't needed for the tournament, Northstrider vanished back to the ball of dark, floating water that served as his Monarch viewing platform. Or so most people believed.

Eithan found the Monarch sitting on the ground of an alley in Ninecloud City, eating grilled vegetables wrapped in a layer of soft bread. He could not have looked less like he belonged. His massive, muscular frame made him look like he'd squeezed in between the two buildings, and his ragged hair and mismatched clothes belonged in a much dingier alley.

This alleyway was paved with smooth quartz and it had been cleaned with admirable zeal, even in the places most couldn't see. Mentally, Eithan saluted the Ninecloud cleaning crew.

Golden eyes fixed Eithan, and he had to close down his spiritual senses in order to keep breathing. If he sensed the full attention of Northstrider upon him, he would lose control of his madra.

The Monarch's eyes returned to the floor, and he took another bite of his vegetable wrap. A floating barge passed overhead, music and laughter and flashing lights drifting over them.

Eithan gave a beaming smile. "What a lovely evening we're having, wouldn't you say?"

Northstrider chewed.

"You know, I was reading up on your Path, which is of course quite famous. A fascinating study. There are scholars who have made their entire careers of unraveling your secrets."

The Monarch reached into a tear in space, pulling out a clay jug. He washed down the vegetables.

"As I'm sure you know, I have some students in this tournament. One of them has a very interesting arm."

Northstrider produced a second vegetable wrap.

"Not a *unique* arm, certainly. In many parts of the world, hunger bindings are not at all rare. But I'm sure it didn't escape your attention. I thought you might be intrigued to know that the arm isn't his only aspect that might interest you."

Eithan's view was replaced by a brief flash of blue light, and then he *appeared* in the center of a crowd. It was a party, from the looks of it, with colored lanterns floating overhead and hundreds of people dressed in their finest. A few of the closest staggered away at his sudden appearance, but by then he was already moving.

Northstrider had transported him to a completely different section of the city. Someone else would have been lost.

Eithan began navigating back toward where he had just been. *Easy enough. Now, where can I find one of those wraps?*

Lindon sat in the team's waiting room. His Akura robes had been repaired, his spirit was full of madra, and his soulspace brimmed with soulfire. That gray flame played around his shield, which was now in spiritual form, soaking up the fire for nourishment.

In his mind, he and Dross went over the plan.

[I give you a twenty percent chance,] Dross said. [Two out of ten. That's a lot better than nothing!]

For the past week, since the end of the third round, Lindon had done virtually nothing but run mental battles against Sophara. He and Dross had combed the Ninecloud tablet library for all records of her matches, and Dross had even made her faster and smarter to compensate as much as possible for the training she'd be doing on her own.

Over hundreds of fights, they had identified the keys: he had to focus on surviving the first few exchanges, then put enough pressure on her to make her use her drop of ghostwater. That would be the hardest part.

If he survived until it ran out, he could finish her.

If he couldn't, then the Monarchs would get closer to allowing the Dreadgods into Sacred Valley. And a gold dragon who personally hated him would become the most celebrated Underlord in the world.

And he, himself, would miss the fastest path to Overlord. His journey would slow to a crawl.

Mercy dashed into the room in full Akura uniform. She didn't slow down, throwing herself against him and wrapping her arms around his shoulders.

Lindon's thoughts staggered to a halt, though he didn't physically move. Her slight weight crashing into him might as well have been a breath of air.

"You're going to win!" She looked up from his chest and took a step back, but even so, she didn't release him. She grabbed the collar of his outer robe. "You can do this! Don't worry! Do I look worried? No, I don't, because I'm not, and you shouldn't be either!"

She was practically screaming at him, and Lindon felt flash-blinded.

"Forgiveness, but what is happening?" he asked.

She took a deep breath. "Yerin couldn't be here. They called her away."

"Who did?" Lindon asked. She couldn't be preparing for her match—her fight was against Mercy.

"The Ninecloud Soul. So I'm going to say what Yerin would say!" She slapped him hard enough that it echoed throughout the room, though he barely felt it. Yerin would have broken his jaw. "You have a sword! Stab the enemy!"

[That *does* sound like Yerin,] Dross observed.

The circle on the door had begun to glow dimly, and Lindon's nerves returned. He gently extracted himself from Mercy, stepping up to the stone slab as the script-circle glowed brighter and brighter.

"Thank you, Mercy." Lindon drew just enough Blackflame to set a torch of anger to his spirit. "I'll see you in the next round."

The door began to slide up, showing the dark floor and letting in a flood of screams and cries. He cycled his madra as memories spun in his mind.

Suriel showing him the death of Sacred Valley.

The Bleeding Phoenix covering the sky from horizon to horizon.

Ekeri's gold-scaled chest burned through by dragon's breath.

The gold dragon Herald, clutching a piece of the Temple of Rising Earth in its talons.

Sophara tearing off Lindon's head with one swipe of her claws.

Naian Blackflame in chains, then collapsing bleeding to the floor.

On the other side of the door, she was waiting for him.

No...she was standing in his way.

The door slid slowly open, revealing the floor and letting in... silence and darkness. No screaming crowd. The shadow aura was thick, shrouding much of the arena, forming a barrier to keep him and his opponent isolated. The ground was slick, black, and irregular, like the stone had melted and then been frozen into place. His footing would be uncertain.

When the door lifted fully, the shadow aura didn't stop him from seeing all the way across the arena, where his opponent saw him at the same time.

Not Sophara.

Yerin.

Her hand was frozen on the hilt of her sword, her dark eyes quivering in shock. Lindon stood rooted in place as Dross babbled in his head, insisting that there must be a mistake.

Northstrider stood between the two of them, black-scaled arms folded.

Rainbow light shimmered overhead, and the Ninecloud Soul cried, "Now, the first two fighters in the fourth round of the Uncrowned King tournament face their true opponents! Sacred artists, welcome Wei Shi Lindon Arelius, chosen of Akura Malice and representative of the prime Akura team...and Yerin Arelius, chosen of Akura Malice and representative of the Blackflame Empire!"

He could hear the Soul perfectly, but nothing from the crowd. Or perhaps Lindon had gone partially deaf.

Northstrider flicked his fingers, and suddenly the air carried both competitors forward. Yerin was visibly furious, and she focused her anger on the Monarch. Her six sword-arms burst out of her back, but he did not acknowledge her.

"This is not a punishment," Northstrider said quietly. "Nor is it a plot. The measure of a sacred artist is how they respond to unexpected challenges, so I arranged this round to provide such challenges."

Yerin glared at him. "You ready to swear that to the heavens?"

"The heavens do not constrain me," Northstrider said, unaffected. "You should worry only about the opponent in front of you."

Every breath rasped in Lindon's lungs. He couldn't take his eyes from Yerin's face.

"I surrender."

"No," Yerin and the Monarch said at the same time.

Now Yerin had turned her anger to him. "This is a sour turn, but it won't beat us. You bring everything you have...and so will I."

The bonds of air released her, and she drew her master's sword.

The audience cheered.

*We were so close,* Lindon thought. They had almost made it. One final round before the eight Uncrowned were chosen. He and Yerin could have both won.

Now he either had to give up his prizes or he had to take them from Yerin. It was as though he'd lost already.

"Begin," Northstrider said, and vanished.

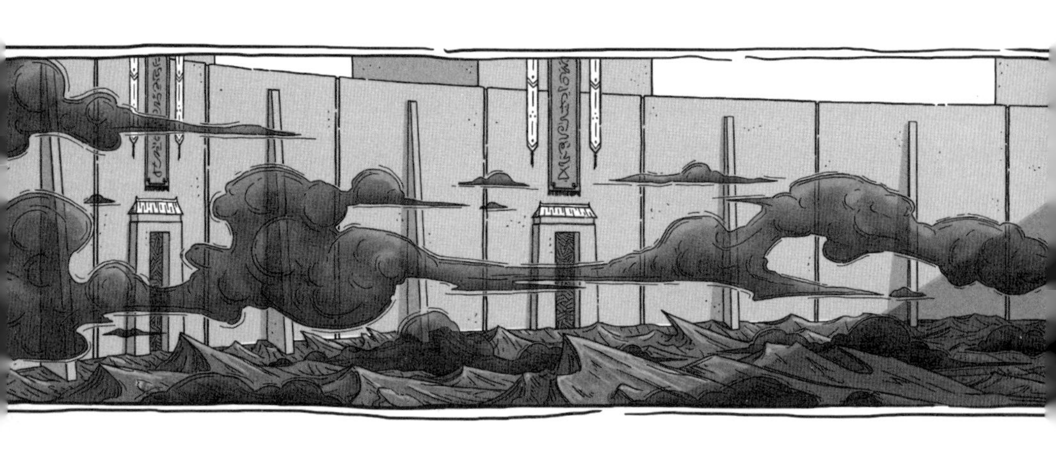

# XIX

YERIN CLOSED THE DISTANCE FAST.

It was only thanks to Dross' enhancement of his reactions that Lindon managed to pull the shield from his soulspace and block the swing of Yerin's blade.

It felt like getting hit by a cloudship at full speed. The blow launched him backward over the warped obsidian surface of the stage, pain stabbing through his left arm as he fought to right himself in the air.

The Soul Cloak rippled into existence, surrounding him with a smooth blue-white corona. His newly enhanced Bloodforged Iron body drew madra to heal his left arm, which—he only now realized—had broken.

The strength and control the Soul Cloak gave him allowed him to land, skidding on the surface, shield raised.

Yerin was already bringing her white sword down on him. Her eyes were fixed and determined, her hair blowing behind her, her black robes rippling with the force of her spirit.

The Sage's blade crashed down on his shield, blasting air away from him in a ring. The Soul Cloak trembled; thanks to its strength, his arm didn't break again, but the Enforcer technique was reaching its limit. Even the shield's material was strained, its outer layer beginning to stress and deform.

Lindon's legs buckled, and he fell to his knees.

He'd known she was strong. Her Steelborn Iron body had started to show its real potential once she'd advanced to Underlord, and he'd seen how she had handled her opponents up to this point.

But he'd never *felt* how strong she was.

[What are you doing?] Dross asked. [Fight back!]

Lindon had been sure he could. In the top eight, he could fight. Once they had both obtained their goals.

Now, fighting back meant pitting his ambition against hers. He would be cutting down her chance of living up to her master.

And, though they were protected by a Monarch, though he had prepared himself for it, though there would be no lasting damage... he still didn't want to hurt Yerin.

Six sword-arms emerged from Yerin's back, and suddenly the air had claws. The Endless Sword technique tore at him, and though he pushed back with the power of his soulfire, Yerin was far better at controlling sword-aura. Slices appeared on his skin, cutting through his sacred artist's robes.

His Iron body repaired the cuts almost as they were made, but blood still streamed from him in ribbons, and he was losing madra.

Yerin lifted her blade, and it ignited silver in a complex dance of both madra and aura. The Flowing Sword, her weapon Enforcement technique.

She set her jaw and her dark eyes met his. There was a strange depth to them, as though she were pleading with him.

"You're holding more than this," she said. "Pull it all out! Let me see it!"

Lindon didn't know how to respond, but she wasn't waiting on him. The shining sword came in high, and he blocked with his flying sword, but the force knocked him back. The second strike came low, while he was still trying to recover his stance, and the Soul Cloak let him slip aside before he lost a leg.

An aura blade from the Endless Sword kicked his shield to one side, and the point of her sword came straight for his throat.

He poured soulfire into the Soul Cloak.

Immediately, the nimbus around him raged like whitewater. He moved without thought, slipping her stab, ducking the follow-up attack from her sword-arms, anticipating and blocking her counter-strokes with his shield and Wavedancer.

Wind whipped around them as they traded dozens of blows in a breath, Yerin looking for an opening, Lindon closing off every angle. He ran, and she followed, and they clashed again, sending peals of thunder throughout the arena.

It couldn't last.

He was running low on soulfire, letting it flow into the Soul Cloak. His pure madra was being drained by the Cloak and by his Iron body, which had to constantly heal him. Her every blow cost him another chunk of power just to endure, and if he blocked or dodged any attack less than perfectly, he would be chopped in half.

The Flowing Sword technique on her sword grew stronger and stronger with every exchange, shining more brightly silver as it wrapped more strands of madra and sword-aura around itself. Soon it would slice straight through his shield.

And Yerin's spirit was growing more and more chaotic.

She was angry.

"Fight me!" she shouted.

It was all Lindon could do to hold on. He jabbed his shield at her in a half-hearted swipe, but she brushed it aside with a look of disgust.

Before he could fully recover, she kicked him in the chest.

He managed to get his shield between them, but the impact still sent him flying backward. Once again, he had to scramble to land on his feet, shield forward. He was out of breath, straining to keep his madra under control.

[...I'm not some sort of human behavior expert, but I think she wants you to fight her,] Dross said.

Lindon couldn't muster up the energy for a response. He resented Northstrider, who had put him in this situation. Why did he have to fight Yerin at all? They had almost been selected as Uncrowned together.

Yerin hadn't followed him. Face twisted in anger, she drew her weapon back with both hands.

Here it came. The technique they had developed together and named together. Their adaptation of the Sword Sage's strike, which they had designed to be her decisive ending strike.

The Final Sword.

To his Copper sight, she was a metallic sun. Sword-aura gathered in a storm around her, whipping her hair and robes. The Enforcer technique on her sword expanded until she held a silver torch, and she glared at him as she braced her stance.

Lindon released the soulfire of the Soul Cloak, sending it into the shield instead. The protective Forger binding in the weapon activated, creating a transparent barrier between them. Fueled by his pure madra and his soulfire, it might be able to take the Final Sword...but the shield would break, and he wouldn't be able to recover quickly. Yerin still had her Blood Shadow, too.

He had already lost.

Yerin would be mad at him for a while, but this wasn't his fault.

Instead of driving her blade forward and sending the Final Sword flashing at him, Yerin leaped. She carried her heavenly silver blade with both hands, raising it overhead to smash it down on him.

He kept his eyes open, bracing himself for the brief flash of pain before defeat.

"DROSS!" Yerin roared.

Time came to a halt.

**INFORMATION REQUESTED: HOW TO DRAG LINDON OUT OF SELF-PITY.**

**BEGINNING REPORT...**

Yerin hangs in the air above Lindon, expression furious, Final Sword cocked behind her head. She's beginning to Forge its power into the shape of a massive blade, and her six sword-arms are poised like stingers.

Lindon sees himself, crouched there, hiding behind his layered stone-colored turtle shell. A blue-and-green scripted sword hovers nearby, ready to dart in and protect him. A transparent dome covers him, but it looks fragile. He doesn't see determination in his own eyes, he sees...doubt. Hesitation.

Weakness.

*How do I fix a broken Lindon? I think mine needs replaced.*

"Fighting her will hurt us both, Dross," Lindon says. He cannot speak in his own voice, but Dross understands him. "It will be better if she wins."

*Yes, is this the Soulsmith? Can you transplant a Remnant spine into my sacred artist?*

"I'm not going to hurt her. It isn't worth it."

*You're hurting her* now!

Lindon hesitates, bringing his attention back to Yerin's expression. Anger was her response to pain.

"I'm giving her what *she* wants."

*She wants you to listen to her,* Dross says. His mental voice is quiet.

Lindon has no response.

*She wants you to see her full power, and she wants you to trust her to handle yours. She wants to see the* real *Lindon, not...is it too much to call you a cringing wreck? That sounds like too much.*

Lindon watches her face. Yerin has been angry with him before, but never so disappointed.

He wants her to be happy with him. Proud of him.

He wants to show her how far he's come.

*Now, are you going to show her?*

Lindon lets out a mental sigh. "I thought you didn't understand humans."

*I don't understand any of this. But I do listen.*

Lindon steels himself. For the first time, he turns his mind to the problem in front of him. To defeating his rival.

"If we're going to do this," Lindon says, "then we're going to win."

**REPORT COMPLETE.**

"DROSS!" Yerin roared, the Final Sword taking shape around her blade. It looked like a massive madra replica of her weapon, complete with hilt and guard. It was hazy at the edges and translucent, not as smooth or complete as her master's, but she could sense its power even so. And now she was turning it against Lindon.

She was furious. Furious with Northstrider, first off, because pitting them against each other had been a sneaky trick. That was the move of a coward and a thief, not a Monarch.

And every second the fight crawled on, she grew angrier with Lindon. In his other fights, he had been amazing. She wanted to fight *that* Lindon. She wanted to test herself, to see if she could measure up, and to show him what she could do. In a fair world, they would have only faced each other after they were both Uncrowned, but who lived in a fair world?

When she had seen Lindon against her in this arena, she had been bitterly disappointed, but also excited. Where else except this tournament could they fight without holding back?

She had hoped he would feel the same way.

Yerin fell, plunging her massive technique down on Lindon's shield. The bright silver-and-white light of her technique Forged into a heavenly sword that crashed into him like a deadly wave. Madra screamed as the two powers clashed, sending off blinding sparks, and the ground rumbled with the force.

The Final Sword chewed through his barrier in seconds, and her heart dropped. Dross hadn't been able to persuade him either.

This was not how she wanted to win her crown.

The last of the barrier shattered, but as soon as she was through, her blade clanged against something solid. And stopped.

The sword Wavedancer. Its broad blue-tinged bulk hovered over Lindon like a second shield.

But it could only block so much. A waterfall of silver power still thundered down onto Lindon, washing over the flying sword.

Her feet only touched the ground as her technique began to fade, and she pulled her master's blade away. The sword-light died. For an instant, she expected to be jerked away from the arena instantly, her anger still unsatisfied.

Then she realized Lindon's presence hadn't disappeared.

A solid turtle's shell rushed at her chin. Yerin caught it on one of her sword-arms, but Lindon had anticipated that. He pivoted into her, plunging his white fist into her gut.

Breath rushed from her lungs and she flew back, head ringing. Her spiritual perception caught the madra lingering around his skin, and she realized what he'd done. He had blasted pure madra from all over his body, covering him in an inch of spiritual armor. Eithan's technique.

The sword-aura had still passed through, which he must have weakened with soulfire control. But he couldn't have stopped everything that way.

Sure enough, she caught a glimpse of him as he followed her. He was covered in blood...but his eyes had life in them. He loomed over her, blood matting down his black hair, shield braced in his left hand and his Remnant hand still tightened into a fist. Wavedancer hovered over his shoulder.

Though his clothes were torn and madra essence streamed from cracks in his shield, his spiritual pressure pushed against her like she was facing a deadly enemy.

Finally, Lindon had shown up to the fight.

Before even landing, she spun in the air, sweeping her master's sword at him. She had dropped her Flowing Sword technique already, so this was a raw hit with no Enforcer technique, but her strength was enough that it would send him flying and create some space.

The Burning Cloak sprung up around him, outlining him in black and red. Her sword passed over his head as he ducked low.

And she lost him as he vanished.

Her spiritual sense followed him as his burst of speed carried him behind her. She landed while striking out behind her with her Goldsigns.

Lindon didn't step into their reach. Instead, three feet from her back, he shoved both of his hands forward.

Two bars of dragon's breath shot toward her.

She almost wasn't fast enough to react. Her six sword-arms closed into a cage behind her, flowing with her madra and with quick flames of soulfire.

The Blackflame madra hit, the heat searing her back and her spirit, but her madra held it off. Still, she wasn't on the Path of the Endless Shield. If she let him land hits, he'd roast her alive.

Reaching her perception inside her spirit, Yerin called for help.

The Blood Shadow peeled away from her front, a spiritual copy of Yerin in shades of crimson. As it materialized, it drew the black sword from Yerin's second sheath.

Ruby lips twisted into a smile as Yerin's red copy saw the opponent.

"Lindon," the Shadow whispered, drawing out his name. The parasite laughed as it leaped over Yerin, swinging its blade down at Lindon's head. Scarlet hair trailed behind it, and its laughter was like a bubbling swamp.

Yerin would have preferred not to call the Shadow against Lindon. It had some strange fascination with him. But if she wanted Lindon to let loose, she had to do the same.

The stream of dragon's breath cut off as Lindon defended himself, his shield knocking the black sword aside. Without pressure on her, Yerin turned and joined the fight.

Now they were back to where the fight had started: Yerin on the offensive and Lindon scrambling to save himself with his shield.

But there was a world of difference this time.

Soul Cloak flowing around him, Lindon moved like a new person. His shield stopped her blade, its binding activated for a fraction of a second to block the aura of her Endless Sword, while with the other hand he drove a massive Empty Palm at the Blood Shadow.

The huge blue-white palm print crippled the Shadow for a moment, but he had already begun a new attack. His eyes became red circles on darkness, and his calm blue-white nimbus turned to furious black-and-red. Powered by the Burning Cloak, he dashed back from Yerin's Striker technique, struck the paralyzed Blood Shadow with a backhand blow of his shield, and swept a finger-wide dragon's breath at Yerin.

He wasn't as strong as she was, so he never met her blows strength-for-strength. He deflected at just the right angle, slipped aside by inches, dodging and counterattacking in the same fluid motions.

He fought Yerin and her Blood Shadow, directly, without backing down. Guided by Dross and his new combat training, he moved as though he could see her every motion a second in advance.

Together, in that empty world, they danced.

Yerin's anger had blown away. She exulted in the fight, and whenever she had to abandon an attack to stop a stream of deadly madra aimed at her face, joy built in her heart.

This was it. This was what she wanted.

Lindon saw her at her best, and he moved up to meet her. She didn't need to hold back for him...and he pushed her forward too.

To match each other, they needed to be at their peak.

Her spirit shouted a warning, and she cast her perception upward. A broad, swirling bank of black and red aura hung over their heads like stormclouds. Every time Lindon switched to Blackflame madra, he molded the aura a little more, gathering it, setting it spinning. Preparing his Ruler technique.

While fighting, he was building a Void Dragon's Dance.

Yerin laughed out loud. She and her Blood Shadow leaped away from Lindon without a signal, creating distance. She reversed her grip on her master's sword, holding it point-down.

Lindon didn't wait for her to use the technique. He reached up with his left hand, extending Blackflame madra, pulling a cyclone of fire and destruction from the sky. In an instant, it would consume the entire stage. She had nowhere to hide.

"Surprise," Yerin said.

She activated her master's sword.

It had taken Lindon and Dross both to the point of exhaustion to keep up with Yerin and her Shadow. His madra channels and body throbbed with the effort of switching cores so many times so quickly while fighting. They had pushed his body, mind, and spirit to the limit.

It had been exhilarating, but he couldn't enjoy it yet. He had to win. For that, he had prepared his Void Dragon's Dance.

Weaving the Ruler technique while keeping Yerin's attention all on him had been nothing short of a miracle, but he'd done it. He felt when her perception rose to the sky and she and her Shadow leaped away, preparing their defenses. He had caught her.

But when he pulled spinning fire from the sky, certain in his victory, Yerin's sword burst into icy white light.

It glowed, sharp and cold, for just an instant. Yerin had carried that sword for three years, since the day after they'd met. He had never seen her activate the binding, never heard her talk about it.

He'd forgotten it.

[I, uh, I did not model that.]

White Archlord madra swallowed up the stage.

Frigid cold pierced Lindon to the bone as ice madra saturated the air. White haze swallowed the entire arena-world, now a domain of wintry fog. He could still see clearly, but the cold seeped through his muscles, stinging his spirit.

Sharp white stars hung in the air, like snowflakes frozen mid-fall. They resonated with sword aura, like the points of ten thousand knives.

On top of all that, there was something...strange about this world of frozen blades. He was finding it hard to move. Either this madra had aspects he couldn't sense that were holding him in place, or there was another property to this technique. Even his madra seemed half-frozen, his cycling as sluggish as honey in winter.

Yerin sagged onto the ground, holding herself up by her master's sword. Sweat ran down her face, and she heaved deep breaths, her spirit weak. She had strained herself to activate an Archlord binding. Lindon couldn't believe she'd done it at all. She met his eyes, glowing with satisfaction.

[You know what's amazing? Those Diamond Veins,] Dross said. [One big technique after another, and she hasn't even torn her madra channels apart. She really got the best of you in the prize department, didn't she?]

Yerin may have had to recover from the sword's technique, but her Blood Shadow didn't. The spirit moved easily through the frozen space, smiling, holding a black sword in her pink-tinged hand. She swept a Striker technique at him, winking as she did.

In an instant, Lindon and Dross ran through his options. He had several. All of them required a sacrifice, so he chose the one he preferred.

While the silver-and-red wave of madra rushed at him, Lindon poured madra and soulfire into his right hand.

Back when he'd advanced to Underlord, he had absorbed the power of the Archstone. It hadn't *replaced* the binding in his arm, it had only altered his original technique...and made it stronger.

Now, he pushed that binding beyond its limits. Hunger madra rushed out, drawing in everything, as though his hand had become a hungry void.

The Blood Shadow skidded to a halt on the ground, fighting the pull, clawing her way backward. Yerin rose to her feet, gathering her power and preparing to attack.

Lindon's entire mind and soul were caught up in guiding the

technique. The arm was already beginning to splinter; if he lost control for one second, the limb would explode with the technique incomplete, and he would be at the center of a massive detonation of unstable madra.

The arm, set free, howled with gluttony. It greedily consumed all the spiritual energy in the space. The Striker technique swirled into him, along with the pale strands of icy madra from the Sage's sword. The freezing white mist flowed like a river into his arm...and almost burst it. The Archlord madra was far beyond anything the arm—or Lindon—could contain.

When the wintry world started to crumble, Lindon's spirit reached its end.

*Dross, help!* Lindon begged.

[Uh, listen, I *will*. I'm not saying I won't. But that's going to be it from me, do you hear me? It's going to take everything I have.]

*Just do it!*

Without another word, the spirit added his will to Lindon's.

The Remnant arm had begun to burst at the seams, leaking madra, but together the two managed to wrench the spiritual power around. He used his pure madra to push it, direct it, keep it from consuming his spirit from the inside. His hand had devoured some of the essence, but there was far more than it could contain.

It was all too powerful for Lindon to contain, but he could push it in a certain direction. Guide it.

He vented it toward Yerin.

A river of pale madra far bigger than Lindon's body *thundered* out of him, deafening as it tore the air. It was a rush of white and silver light, with streaks of red and even black. The unstable, imbalanced rush of power sprayed over Yerin's entire half of the stage, engulfing her and her Blood Shadow.

Focused, it would have easily destroyed them both. But Lindon couldn't focus it—he could only channel it.

When the deluge ended, he staggered, his arm hanging limp at his side and hissing out madra. His vision doubled, and his spirit screamed in pain. His pure core was tapped out, and Dross was exhausted.

But he had decided to win. Yerin wanted him to give this his very best, and he wasn't done yet.

Before the massive cloud of madra had settled, Lindon readied his one good arm and tapped his Blackflame core.

Working together, Yerin and her Blood Shadow managed to turn the tide of overwhelming madra that Lindon had managed to send their direction.

It had been close.

They had stood shoulder-to-shoulder, swords out and shining with madra, fighting the river of power with everything they had. Her Shadow laughed the entire time, even as the mix of spiritual energy screamed around them, and for once Yerin agreed.

*This* was what it meant to go all-out.

Her Blood Shadow lost power, bleeding ribbons of madra. Yerin's whole body trembled with effort, her madra pouring out of her like water from a leaky bucket. A little more control, and the attack would have wiped them both out.

But Lindon couldn't direct an Archlord's madra any more than she could. Together, she and the Shadow hung on until the flow tapered off.

When it did, she wobbled on her feet, her own breath harsh in her ears. The unfocused power still hung in the air like a white cloud flashing with dozens of other colors. The chaotic madra blocked out her spiritual perception and all her mundane senses.

Sweaty hair stuck to her forehead. Her core was dim, almost empty. She could sense the Blood Shadow's weakness as well, but Lindon couldn't be in much better shape. Hurling an attack like that had to be almost the same as taking it head-on. He had to be done.

A spear of dragon's breath broke the cloud.

The Blood Shadow took the black-and-red bar of madra on its blade. The spirit stumbled back, falling and catching itself with its sword-arms.

Yerin slashed a Rippling Sword horizontally through the cloud. She was shooting blind, but maybe she'd get lucky.

A shield shoved through the white madra, three feet from her face. It shattered her Striker technique, and then turned sideways as Lindon straightened his arm.

In that moment, she saw him as their enemies always had. He towered over her, built like a guard tower, his eyes burning circles of red on darkness. His clothes were shredded and burned. Drying blood streaked his skin. His right arm hung mangled and useless against his side.

Her heart swelled with pride.

Dark fire kindling in his palm reminded her the fight wasn't over. On instinct, she brought up her sword against his budding Striker technique. Though little energy remained in her limbs, her Steelborn Iron body made sure her swing was a vertical blur. She cut through the Blackflame fireball, breaking it, and before Lindon could conjure another, a red Rippling Sword flew at him from the side.

He turned to face it, and Yerin created space between them.

This was her last chance. He would outlast her in a prolonged fight; of course he would. He was a madra monster. Even his wounds would heal in time, though she wasn't sure if his Remnant arm would come back. Knowing him, he probably had a way to repair it.

She had to finish it now. She drew her blade back, pouring all her madra into one last technique. A second Final Sword.

A blink later, the Blood Shadow kicked Lindon away and began echoing Yerin. The crackling storm of energy was a blend of red and silver, but Yerin's was a silver so bright it was almost white.

Deep in her mind, it alarmed her that the parasite had a version of the Final Sword. Yerin had never shared that with the Shadow, and she herself had only learned it recently. The Blood Shadow had never practiced.

Those were thoughts from a nightmare, but they belonged later. She had a fight to win.

She was prepared for Lindon to sweep dragon's breath at them, but if he did, she could use the excess energy of the rising Final Sword to protect herself while the Blood Shadow finished him.

In that razor's edge of time, she found her consciousness sinking into the elusive state she'd touched throughout the tournament. She could feel an extra force in her technique, one she had never felt from herself before. It felt like her master.

She had proven herself. She was going to win.

Then Lindon lowered his hand into a claw.

If Lindon strained his shield any further, it would break, and the detonation from its destruction would end him.

If he used Striker techniques to strike at one of them while they prepared their techniques, the other would move on him. So he released his shield and took the best option left to him.

The only secret he had kept from Yerin.

He lowered his left hand, and claws of Forged Blackflame madra formed on each of his fingers, until it looked like he was wearing a dragon's claw like a glove. A miniature Void Dragon's Dance swirled around it, dragon's breath filled it like blood, and a focused Burning Cloak surrounded it all.

With the full power of his spirit and all his remaining soulfire, he forced all those techniques together.

Months ago, Akura Fury had shown him how to layer techniques. He had used that advice to improve the Empty Palm...and to work on one original technique of his own. He and Dross had spent *too* much time, far more than Dross wanted to, theorizing and simulating and practicing. It had taken him months to be able to Forge Blackflame madra at all, and even now he could only hold it together for seconds.

When he had taken in raw draconic madra from the black dragon, he had refined the technique again. And once more after absorbing the original Path of Black Flame from Naian.

The technique coalesced into a massive dragon's claw that streamed black-and-red power. He lifted his hand, Forged claws battering him with heat and destruction, and looked across to Yerin.

She was laughing.

Yerin dashed forward, her Shadow following her a second later. Both of them dragged their devastating techniques with them.

As Lindon ran in to meet her, a serpentine stream of dark fire flowing behind him, he realized he was smiling too.

Two Final Swords struck his technique: The Dragon Descends.

Lindon's full power met Yerin's, and the stage ripped apart.

Akura Fury laughed and clapped as the wall-sized view fuzzed.

All the Akura Underlords were silent.

Charity herself was astonished. She glanced at her father, who was applauding so furiously that some of the Truegolds in the back of the room had to run from the sound.

She leaned closer to Fury, speaking lower so that the young generation couldn't hear her. "If I'm not mistaken, that was a touch of the Sword Icon. How is this the work of twenty-year-olds?"

Fury threw an arm around her neck, hooking her tightly, still laughing. "These kids are amazing, aren't they? I can't wait!"

She slipped away from him to preserve her dignity, but he didn't seem to care. Fury bellowed laughter, delighted at the prospect of new opponents.

More Truegolds ran from the room, hands covering their ears.

The view of the stage was obscured, and the projection for the audience disrupted by wild madra, but a Monarch's perception could not be blinded.

...and Sha Miara wasn't a Monarch at the moment.

She shook the Herald, Sha Relliar, by his outer robe. "What is happening? Show me!"

"You will see very soon," her caretaker responded. He glanced down at her. "It looks like you face more competition than you expected."

She pulled up her viewing slate so that her nose almost touched the image of Lindon and Yerin. "I'm sure I can beat them. But...do *you* think I can?"

"Of course, Your Highness."

Mercy pointed from the blurred view to Pride, who sat sullenly, arms crossed.

"You see? You *see?*"

"...I didn't say they were weak."

"Could *you* do that?"

"Enforcer techniques aren't that flashy. It's wasteful."

"You couldn't," Mercy said confidently, turning back to wait for the image.

Pride's jaw tightened, but after a moment he let out a breath. "Fine. Maybe he *is* good enough for you."

"I told you!" she said excitedly. "I said they were...wait, what did you say?"

The Winter Sage chewed on a fingernail, her heart torn. Yerin was directly responsible for Adama's death, but at the same time, she hadn't abandoned his legacy after all. In fact, there had been just a hint of the Sword Icon in that last attack.

She *had* inherited Adama's Remnant. Maybe that was all it was, in which case it wouldn't happen again. But if not...

Min Shuei turned abruptly, interrupting her students, who had been hotly debating Yerin's techniques. With no explanation, she left.

As soon as this round ended, she would see the Monarch Northstrider. She had to demand the right to tutor Yerin herself.

Before one of the other Sages did.

Northstrider watched the final clash of techniques one frozen instant at a time.

Of course, Yerin Arelius had achieved a reflection of the Sword Icon. Anyone with any authority of their own would take notice, but it was most likely an anomaly. Underlords could not sense the Way clearly enough to manifest an Icon. It was a demonstration of the sacred artist she might one day become, nothing more.

He was far more intrigued by Lindon.

This was the Truegold who had gone to Ghostwater and made it out with a mental construct. Northstrider had taken note of him already and found nothing extraordinary.

He was beginning to reevaluate that.

Lindon had grown too quickly. Each round he fought, he moved like a different person. Every time Northstrider thought the boy's mind-construct would reach the end of its capabilities, he was proven wrong. In this battle alone, Lindon had managed to compete with the Sword Sage's disciple by showing reaction and processing speeds that should have been impossible for an Underlord.

Yerin had called out the word 'Dross' just before Lindon's performance spiked. He had thought it was an insult...

...but what if it was a name?

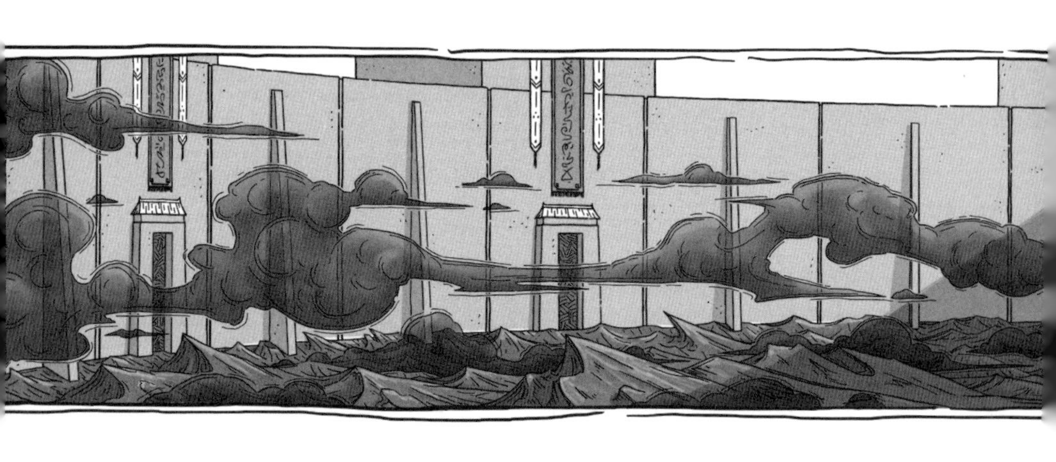

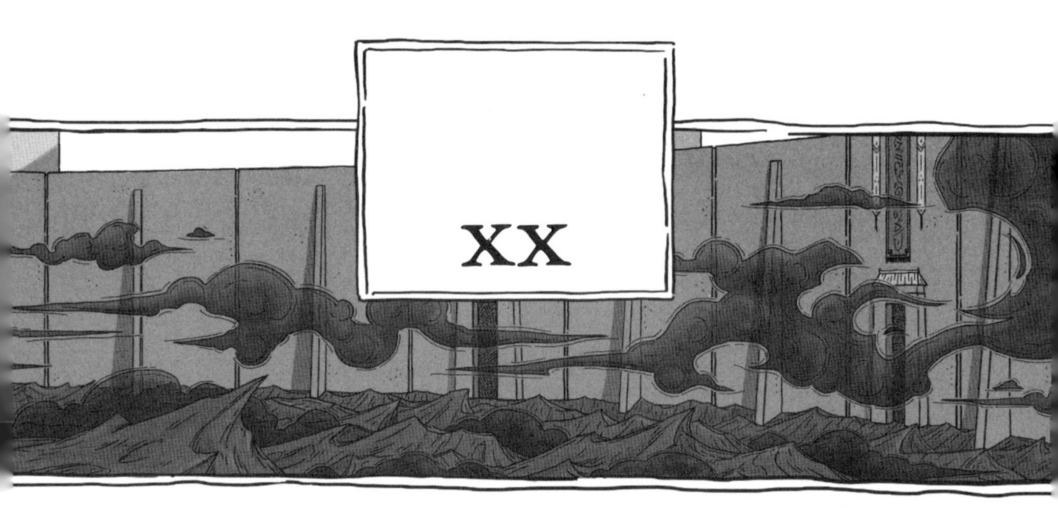

# XX

**Information requested: Northstrider, wandering Monarch of the Trackless Sea.**

**Beginning report...**

Northstrider was born with a connection to blood.

His parents died shortly after his birth, never knowing that they had each carried a dormant bloodline legacy. These traits mixed in their son, producing an unmatched connection to blood aura.

As an orphan, he was taken in by a local warlord, who collected pods of one hundred abandoned children at a time to defend him from the attacks of his enemies. He raised and trained them by teaching them to hunt water-drakes, lesser dragons that skim the surface of the ocean to the north.

All one hundred children were raised on the meat of these drakes, but Northstrider's innate abilities allowed him to absorb more of the remaining blood essence in the flesh than anyone else.

At every opportunity, he would return to the ocean to seek out stronger prey, and it became known that you could almost always find him walking north.

Thus did he earn his name.

He grew strong quickly, beyond his age, always hunting more powerful quarry and moving deeper and deeper into the ancient places of the ocean.

He discovered that the sea floor was a trove of treasures both natural and otherwise, and eventually found himself at the entrance to a vast labyrinth. Therein, he found madra that intrigued him.

At that point in his life, he had never been formally instructed in a Path. The children of his pod were taught rudimentary techniques but were left to adapt them to whatever aspects of madra suited them best.

When Northstrider integrated the bindings he found in the labyrinth into his blood madra, the Path of the Hungry Deep was born.

**Path: Hungry Deep.** A Path focused on devouring the physical and spiritual strength of dragons, as well as their latent authority, using them to empower the user. Most techniques are rudimentary, but become complex in execution when brought to life with the touch of the Dragon Icon.

The Path of the Hungry Deep is the most powerful hunger madra Path still in modern use.

**SUGGESTED TOPIC: TECHNIQUES ON THE PATH OF THE HUNGRY DEEP. CONTINUE?**

**DENIED, REPORT COMPLETE.**

Lindon woke knowing that he'd lost.

At the last second, it was as though Yerin had changed, though he'd sensed no extra power from her. Her technique had landed just that much sooner than his.

And that was enough.

He had re-formed inside the gray waiting room, sitting on a bench. His body and spirit were in perfect condition. The room was silent, empty. It was as though the fight hadn't happened.

"I lost," Lindon said, and his voice echoed hollow in the quiet room.

Dross slipped out of his spirit, turning to look at him with his wide purple eye. [But what a *fight!* You know what they say: it doesn't matter how you play the game, only whether you win or lose. Wait, no, the other one.]

"...I thought I was going to win."

He'd been more than willing to surrender when he first saw Yerin. He didn't want to hurt her physically, and he didn't want to hurt her emotionally by taking away her chance to become Uncrowned. For the same reasons, he had been willing to hold back and let her beat him.

Because deep down, he *knew* he'd win.

Since getting Dross, he'd never faced an opponent that he truly couldn't defeat. As soon as he'd chosen to give it his all, he had resigned himself to beating Yerin. But he'd been fooling himself. He wasn't good enough.

Behind him, the door hissed open. He turned away, unwilling to look Mercy in the eye. Worse if it was Charity or Pride.

"I've never been good at consolations," Eithan said.

Lindon let his eyes close. It was hard to imagine anyone he wanted to see less right now. Maybe Sophara.

He heard Eithan walking up and sitting down on the bench across the room. "Mercy was coming in to cheer you up, but she allowed me the honor instead."

Lindon would have much rather seen Mercy.

"I don't need consolation," Lindon said, forcing his eyes to open and look at Eithan. "I'm happy for Yerin."

His smile was gentle. "You know, people can feel two things at once. Even when it seems like they should be opposites."

On Lindon's shoulder, Dross gasped. [You can feel two things? That explains so much!]

"Gratitude, but I'm fine. I tried and I lost. There's nothing more to be said."

Eithan scratched at his chin. "Hm. As long as I've known you, you've been willing to do whatever it takes if it accomplished your goal. That's one of the things I admire about you. But I've always wondered one thing: what will he do when he pours his heart and soul into something and still fails?"

Lindon's vision blurred and his throat tightened. "I don't know what you want me to say. It's too late to do anything. I failed."

"I want you to tell me," Eithan said, "what you're going to do next."

Next. What did he want to do next?

"Yerin won." He straightened himself, organizing his breathing, pushing his pain and disappointment down. "I'm going to go see her."

Eithan eyed him. "Congratulations from you will mean a great deal to her, but are you in shape for that?"

"I don't know," he said honestly. The last thing he wanted to do was to dampen her excitement after winning the round and earning the right to become one of the Uncrowned, but he had to be with her. If she had fought someone else, he would have wanted to be the first to see her after her victory.

Without waiting for another word from Eithan, Lindon left the room.

### Outpost 01: Oversight

Makiel projected a map of Abidan territory in front of him. The nest of flowing blue light representing the Way spread into a roughly spherical shape, each branch dotted with points of light like berries on branches. Iterations.

On the outer layer, too many of them were tinged with gray, illustrating the corruption of the Void.

And now, four of them were black.

After removing the first world, the Mad King had struck three more times. Testing Abidan response time. Makiel's foresight. His weapon's capabilities.

Soon he would have all the information he needed. The testing would end, and he would strike.

Who knew how far he could make it before the Judges could counter him? They were spread too thin as it was, fighting the incursions of chaos at their borders. Would he make it as far in as Sector Fifty-one? Would he make it to Asylum, to break out the other Class One Fiends? To Cradle, the birthplace of the Abidan? To Sanctum itself?

He cast his sight forward, into the future.

The Court of Seven had already given a united ruling, despite Suriel's misgivings: they would salvage as many lives from the outer sectors as they could, retreating deep into their territory. Far deeper than Makiel had ever planned.

There had been ten thousand worlds under their protection, a thousand fully integrated into their system. They would now protect only the core twenty sectors. Two hundred Iterations.

The rest...left to fend for themselves. Now he followed the ripples of that decision out to the future.

It wouldn't be enough.

He saw it as though his map of the Way sped through time. Gray corruption claimed light after light, Iteration after Iteration, until it eventually came to an equilibrium and stopped. Some worlds shattered to fragments while others struck an uneasy balance with chaos and survived, though tainted. Still others were eliminated or stolen by the Vroshir.

But the Mad King wasn't satisfied with more territory. He wanted to destroy them.

With his false Scythe, he led the charge. The Judges would survive, the Abidan would survive, but it would cost them. Core worlds would be lost.

He could see no further, but from such a position, there could be no doubt that the Mad King would rule.

So he reversed his sight, bringing it back to the present. He spun it out again, reading Fate.

Before long, his course was clear. They needed to recruit.

Usually, the Abidan only allowed recruitment of those who had ascended beyond their Iterations of their own power. Every deviation from that was a slight violation of Fate, which could tip the world that much closer to chaos. The Abidan interfered in mortal affairs only in dire need. And often not even then.

Now, risking a bit of causal instability was by far the lesser evil. It was that or eradication.

Makiel willed it, and his Presence stirred to action, appearing in Sector Control headquarters for Sectors One through Twenty-one as a purple eye the size of a head. It delivered his orders.

An action of this scale would often require the permission of the entire Court, but in this case, it was an order to bend Fate to preserve Fate. Well within the remit of Makiel.

In world after world, the order went out and was obeyed: encourage recruitment.

In Sanctum, this would take the form of open screenings and recruitment drives for the Abidan. In Jubilee, the Court would offer wishes in exchange for service. In Solitude, they would contact the

Wise Serpents that ringed the world and ask for a gift of talented recruits. In Obelisk, they would wait at the top of the Tower, surpassing Threshold and taking in people directly.

Their efforts would be tailored to each of the hundreds of worlds, but it would result in thousands of new Abidan over the coming years. Their ranks would swell to more than the Court had seen in centuries.

They would lose some Iterations, and such deviation from Fate would create an unprecedented surge in corruption. But the new Court would handle it.

Then the Mad King could not destroy them. They would survive.

With a heavy heart, he finished delivering the message.

He concentrated special attention on Sector Eleven. Not only did they protect Asylum, which would surely be a top-priority target for the King, they defended Cradle. And Cradle would be among the most delicate of worlds to recruit.

Of all the Monarchs in Cradle, every one had already refused recruitment by the Abidan. They would no doubt encourage others to do so as well. The Abidan would have to descend personally, representing the heavens, and appeal to the Monarchs' successors. The next generation. They would have to offer a prize of great value, and the result might be only one or two new Abidan.

But it would be worth it.

Now, more than ever before, the Court needed soldiers.

Even as Lindon dashed through the heavily decorated tunnels beneath the arena, the whole building shook with cheers. The Ninecloud Soul would be replaying highlights from the fight, instructing the crowd and following the match with hours of feasting and entertainment for the rest of the day. The next match wouldn't be for a week, but the Court turned the time between rounds into a festival.

Yerin would be mobbed by strangers. Enough people had tried to talk to Lindon already, mostly from the Akura family, that he could only imagine how many wanted a moment with Yerin. He needed to get back to her side as soon as he could.

Suddenly the building went silent. He slowed his steps, looking around, but the others in the hallway looked as confused as he did.

A moment later, a sound like birds screaming tore through the Ninecloud arena. Lights flashed from the walls in all colors, and the Ninecloud Soul's voice resonated out of nowhere, sounding panicked: "All guests, prepare for imminent spatial transfer—"

Lindon dashed backward, trying to get away from whatever was about to happen, but a blue light consumed him.

Just like when he met Suriel, the world was replaced by a river of textured blue that pressed against him in all directions. He couldn't breathe, and Suriel's marble in his pocket suddenly grew painfully hot, but in less than a second it was all over.

He stood around the edge of the arena beneath the Akura viewing tower, sunlight beating down. The arena was quiet, the towers completely empty. Whoever had transported him here, they had removed the spectators at the same time.

He saw the other eliminated contestants against the wall close to their original towers; Pride and Naru Saeya stood next to him, Grace and her team nearby, the Frozen Blade students drawing blades. Everyone looked wildly around for an explanation.

Fifteen young Underlords stood in the center of the arena. The remaining participants in round four. Lindon was the only one to have been eliminated so far, and whatever was happening, it pained him that Yerin and Mercy were facing it while he was looking in from the outside.

Fourteen of them looked ready for battle, but Sha Miara was the lone exception. She stood staring at the sky, wearing a grave expression.

One by one, everyone followed her lead. The viewing-towers that held spectators during each round were quiet and empty, but the Monarch platforms floating overhead were still active.

Figures hovered in the air above the platforms. Over the Eight-Man Empire's plain tower, a circle of eight gold-armored men and women hovered. Akura Malice stood in midair over her mountain, shrouded in shadow. The Dragon King's cloak rippled in the wind as he flew over his throne, Reigan Shen lounged on the roof of his palace with a goblet of wine in hand, and even Northstrider stood with his hands behind his back above his dark globe of water.

The Arelius tower seemed doubly empty by contrast, its storm flashing blue but no one hovering above it.

The very presence of so many Monarchs made the air feel thick. Every second pressed against Lindon like a knife against his throat, and Dross' silence felt heavy, as though the spirit was afraid even to think.

Moment by moment, the Monarchs stayed motionless. Quiet. Waiting.

Lindon couldn't imagine what was happening. Was this a plot by one of the Monarchs? If so, how had they trapped the others in it?

Then, for the second time in his life, Lindon saw a blue light descending from the sky like a sapphire dawn.

He fell to his knees a step sooner than everyone else in the arena below Monarch. It was the only proper thing to do; Lindon felt the awe in his soul. Even Sophara fell to her knees, groveling with head bowed. Sha Miara went to one knee, but she turned and looked to the Ninecloud's rainbow tower—the feminine figure hovering over it was hidden by nine-colored light.

Seconds later, the heavenly messenger emerged. He was so far up that a Gold would barely be able to see him as a distant figure, but Lindon's Underlord eyes could make out his features.

He felt almost blasphemous for the thought, but compared to Suriel, this man was a disappointment. He had the features of an ordinary human, a pinched face with a thin beard, and dark hair cropped close to his head. His eyes were the beady black of a rat's.

But he wore the same eggshell-smooth white armor that Suriel had, and over his shoulder drifted an eye with a purple iris. It looked like an Akura eyeball the size of the man's whole head.

The eyeball turned in a circle, looking at the Monarchs, but the man didn't. He looked down to the gathered Underlords.

"Children." He sounded as though he stood right next to them. "I am Kiuran of the Hounds. Do not be bound by this world. The most talented of you will one day be offered the choice to leave, to emerge from this cradle and truly live. Do not take the example of your elders. When the invitation comes, accept it, and let your eyes be opened to the real world."

Northstrider's spirit stirred, and his gold dragon eyes glared. His muscles strained against each other, as though he was fighting not to speak. But he said nothing, and the messenger did not address him. Reigan Shen gave a smile, baring a fang or two, and took a long draught from his goblet.

"The Court of Seven occasionally sponsors this tournament," the messenger went on, "to give promising young recruits a taste of the world beyond. You are blessed, for now more than ever, we wish to nurture your talents."

He extended his hand, palm-up. "I give you the new grand prize of the tournament: a weapon of the gods."

A silver-edged black arrowhead appeared hovering over his palm. It looked fairly ordinary to Lindon, but the aura of the entire world twisted and fluctuated as all seven Monarchs reacted.

Rather than watching them, Lindon looked to the center of the arena. Eithan, on his knees, stared at the arrowhead with an intensity Lindon had never seen. His smile was long gone.

The messenger smiled at their reaction. "Long ago, the founder of House Arelius created this weapon which he called Penance. It is a penance for its target and, unbeknownst to most, its creation was an act of penance by its creator."

The House Arelius crowd gave a shout, but Eithan's gaze was glued to the arrowhead.

"He made the right choice, ascending to the heavens, and he brought this weapon with him. Now we return it to the place of its birth."

The arrowhead drifted up, flashing black and silver. "Penance was made with a singular purpose: to kill. That is what it does, and nothing less. It can be used to kill one being in this world without error. This, children, is the power of life and death."

For the first time, he looked to the Monarchs, and he didn't bother to look respectful. His sneer covered his face and infected his voice. "No doubt you will squabble for this, but the results of this tournament are now guaranteed by my master: Makiel, the Hound. No competitors can be added or withdrawn, the rules must be upheld as before, and Penance will not function for anyone other than the rightful champion. If you break the rules, you will be judged. If you kill or punish the champion for possession of this weapon, you will be judged. Tread carefully, for the eyes of heaven see all things."

The eyeball on his shoulder shone brightly, spinning to pierce each Monarch.

None of the kings and queens spoke a word. Not even to agree. Now none of them looked so self-assured anymore. Even Reigan Shen scowled through his white mane, goblet forgotten.

The heavenly messenger looked down on the competitors, and his smile was gentle again. "Fight hard, children, and do not let fear hold you back. Instead, let desire drive you to even greater heights. You are the future, and the Hound values the future above all else."

Lindon stared at the arrowhead. The messenger held a life in his hand. Anyone's life—a Sage's, a Monarch's.

Even a Dreadgod's.

[Whoever gets that won't have an arrow,] Dross whispered. [They'll have a target. Everyone in the world will be after them.]

*Even if the heavens protect them from reprisal?* Lindon asked.

[Heaven is a long way away. Humans are right here.]

When the world began to glow blue again, Lindon lunged for Yerin, but he was swallowed up. Only a breath later, he stood in the center of a bright-tiled hallway, exactly where he had been taken. A nearby Truegold woman in Akura colors fell to her knees and started muttering.

The Spirit Cloak sprang up around Lindon, and he started to run.

Yerin was now in danger. Whatever the heavens said, the Monarchs and their champions would do anything for a weapon like the arrowhead. He had to gather everyone they could trust and stick together; keeping Eithan and Mercy and Yerin in the same place would be the best way to keep them safe.

And he had to tell them they couldn't win.

Out of fear of a Monarch's reprisal, he hadn't even told his friends Sha Miara's true identity. The time for that was past; they had to know they were competing against a Monarch.

He had almost reached the end of the hallway when a black-scaled hand shot out from nowhere, grasping at his throat. With the impossible grace of the Spirit Cloak, Lindon dodged.

The hand landed anyway.

It was like a hammer slamming into his neck. He crashed to a halt, choking and gagging past the sudden pain in his throat, his technique dispersing. He sagged to the floor, looking up through watery eyes.

A huge man, at least Lindon's size, now loomed overhead. His clothes were mismatched and ragged, open at the neck to reveal the rock-hard muscles of his chest. Wild hair spilled down his back, and his face was unshaven, but his vertically slitted golden eyes glared down on Lindon like a king passing judgment.

[Master...] Dross whispered.

Northstrider spoke only two words.

"Who's Dross?"

**THE END**

*of Cradle: Volume Seven*

*Uncrowned*

LINDON'S STORY CONTINUES IN

# WINTERSTEEL

CRADLE : VOLUME EIGHT

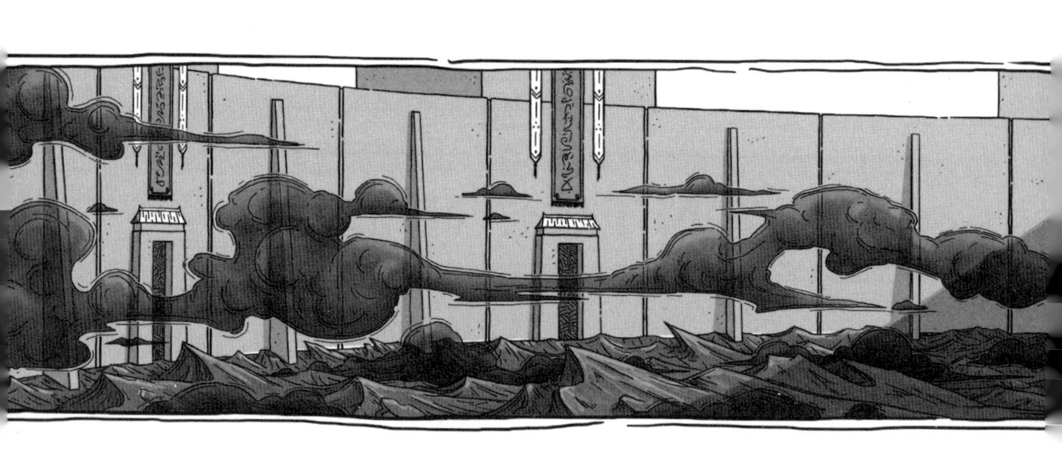

# BLOOPERS

Makiel's viewing lens flickered to life, a purple-edged rectangular screen that could show him anything in existence.

**[Target found: the Soft-Serve Sorcerer, a wizard whose ice cream will make you scream! Beginning synchronization...]**

Grumbling, Makiel lifted his remote control. He pressed a button and his Presence blinked. The view on the lens changed.

**[Target found: Wedding Wars, wherein fifteen newlyweds charge at each other with maces and shields. Beginning synchronization...]**

Makiel pulled out a second remote. "The Vroshir! I'm trying to watch the Vroshir!"

The view in the lens fuzzed to static.

**[Target not found. Have you tried changing the input?]**

Makiel threw his remotes to the ground.

The door slid slowly open, revealing the floor and letting in... silence and darkness. No screaming crowd. The shadow aura was thick, shrouding much of the arena, forming a barrier to keep him and his opponent isolated.

When the door lifted fully, the shadow aura didn't stop him from seeing all the way across the arena, where his opponent saw him at the same time.

Not Sophara.

Little Blue.

Lindon looked in confusion as the six-inch Riverseed charged him on her tiny legs. "What's going on?"

Little Blue pulled out a knife.

Something the Winter Sage said caught Yerin's interest. Was it Sacred Valley itself that had opened the Sword Sage to the attacks of mere Jades? Yerin had always assumed it was the poison. But if there was something about the place...

"Hang on," Yerin said, "how could a bunch of Jades kill the Sword Sage?"

Nearby, Eithan frowned. "That's a good question. I wonder why no one has ever asked that before."

Pride held out the crown. "This is for you." He glanced to one side. "I suggest you take it quickly. It hasn't been long since I won it."

Lindon stood still, watching him.

[It's an imposter!] Dross said. [Get him!]

Lindon's dragon breath burned off Pride's head.

"Oh, you wiped out the Rising Earth sect?" Fury's tone was light, even conversational. "I see, I see."

Fury dropped the boulder and pulled his hands back behind him, gathering energy between his palms.

"KAAAAAAAAA..." he shouted. Blue light grew brighter and brighter between his hands.

"MEEEEEEEEE..." The light was blinding, and Lindon could

sense the spiritual pressure. Whatever Striker technique he was about to release, it could obliterate the whole city.

"HAAAAAAAA..."

A Forged box of rainbow light dropped around Fury, so dense that Lindon couldn't see through it.

"Enough of that!" the Ninecloud Soul said nervously. "You want us to get sued?"

A pillar of rainbow light beamed down from the ceiling, Lindon's prize suspended in the center: a string of letters and numbers.

"...what is it?" he asked.

The Ninecloud Soul sounded shocked. "I...I can't believe what I'm seeing. This is a gift fit for a Monarch: a code for Rebel Galaxy Outlaw by Double Damage Games, available now on the Epic Games Store!"

Dross gasped. [You mean the greatest game ever made? I never thought I'd see it with your own eyes...]

Lindon was no fool. He seized the code.

**WILL WIGHT** is the *New York Times* and #1 Kindle best-selling author of the *Cradle* series, a new space-fantasy series entitled *The Last Horizon,* and a handful of other books that he regularly forgets to mention. His true power is only unleashed during a full moon, when he transforms into a monstrous mongoose.

Will lives in Florida, lurking beneath the swamps to ambush prey. He graduated from the University of Central Florida, where he received a Master of Fine Arts in Creative Writing and a cursed coin of Spanish gold.

Visit his website at *WillWight.com* for eldritch incantations, book news, and a blessing of prosperity for your crops. If you believe you have experienced a sighting of Will Wight, please report it to the agents listening from your attic.